MW00654558

Fubar

G.C. McKay

Published by Gareth Clark McKay 2019

Copyright © G.C. McKay 2019

The amoral right of the author has been asserted.

All characters and events in this publication, other than those
clearly in the public domain, are fictitious and any resemblance to
real persons, living or dead, is purely coincidental. And inevitable.
You are not unique or in any way special. Your whole personality was
determined long before you were even born. The author would like
to remind you that the idea of the 'self' existing is consistently being
proved otherwise. He would also like to tell you to get over yourself,
but he's afraid the irony will be misconstrued, if even noticed in the
first place.

All rights reserved.
No part of this publication may be reproduced, stored in a retrieval
system, or transmitted, in any form or by any means without the prior
permission in writing of the publisher, nor be otherwise circulated in
any form of binding or cover other than that in which it is published
and without a similar condition including this condition being on the
subsequent publisher. The author, on the other hand, would like to
encourage you to do what you want with this piece, whether as a whole
or individually, as long as the credit remains with him. Any knock-
off act of plagiarism in any shape or form shall be met with the most
furious type of Machiavellian retribution and vengeance imaginable.
Maybe.

ISBN 978-84-09-10230-3

gcmckay.com

this book is dedicated to no one

ACT ONE

"All might be fair in love and war, but
trying to find the difference between
the two is a battle ad infinitum."

- Eric Archer

CHAPTER ONE

I was four fingers deep inside my so-called good friend's girl. He was making out with her, stroking her thigh whilst flicking up and down glances at her more than prepared pussy and the girl I was making out with, another apparent good friend of his girlfriend's. My soon-to-be-ex-friend took his time to get started, finding himself lost inside the mist of his deepest, darkest fantasy as it forced its way through into the real world. Once upon a time, he told me he'd fantasised about sucking my dick when we were teens. A lot. With his dream a potential zipper-peel away from coming true, coupled-up with the prospect of watching said cock penetrate his girl, I understood his need to let the fog dissipate; to take a little breather before battle, so to speak. He'd been trailing his finger across the strap of my girl's belt for just a bit too long by that point, but I guess he sensed what I had also started to suspect: the unwanted resurrection of until then abandoned inhibitions. Playing it dumb,

I continued toying with the more liberated vagina in the room but switched things up by concentrating on her clit. Whilst that worked to send her hips into mayhem, my girl's signals kept right on up with their conservative contradictions. Her mouth let out moans, but her body still squirmed. Just when she seemed to be coming around to what was so blatantly going to go down had you been a fly on the wall inside the bar before we got back to mine—she heard her belt unbuckle, then freaked.

"No, no. I thought I… but no, I can't do this. I'm sorry," she said, hands raised up in surrender, going all group therapy on us by adding, "I've only slept with three people!"

"Don't worry," I said, in my most reassuring voice, "we can double that pitiful number within the hour," and went in for a gentler kiss, more to shut her up than to get our blue balls rolling again. She reciprocated with a Stockholm syndrome clenching of my shirt until another attempt at removing her clothes was made. After restating what she'd just said she sat upright, looking flushed, sheepish and childlike; the same way many a girl looks after venturing into porn, minus the sperm. A time-lapse of blurry-eyed smokescreens later and everyone stood by the front door. The girls had gone from the giddy-drunk blossoming of a relationship to the *I'm Sorry I Made You Do That, I Dunno What's Wrong With Me* exchanges of apologies and feigned understandings. What would've taken the average couple two or so years to accomplish they'd managed to achieve in a debauch-ditched number of minutes. Meanwhile, the cocktail of drugs in my system seized their chance to wreak havoc. With the room spinning and my sightline splitting, I couldn't even grab onto my own hand, let alone tell which one was trying to do what. It seemed I'd blinked myself inside the interior of an Escher painting. The last thing I remember was an echo of feminine goodbye's and my friend's silent retreat. His lack of words spoke for us both. Just before I blacked it, the unwanted thought that he might've been heading home towards a vulnerability threesome kept me conscious for an additional number of nauseating minutes.

A few days later we all met up at the same bar again. I went in half-hoping the girl I'd been partnered with held some remorse at having aborted our salacious romp, but I knew that male-reserved hope was naïve. It occurred to me then why her abrupt ending to our fun didn't sit so well. Before we all agreed to go back to mine to continue the night, we'd all been playing around with each other inside that very bar. I made out with my friend's girlfriend on his suggestion, then made out with him on hers, to finally being introduced to her friend and before long, doing another round of the same. We did that for a couple of hours. That's why I couldn't quite believe her reaction to where the night eventually led. Even the cabbie got a sneak preview, as the girls made out during the whole ride home. Sadly, the teaser trailer turned out to be just that; only a fucking trailer and nothing but a tease, as the feature film had too many production issues. Actresses.

Before long we were all tipsy again but there was a distinct lack of touchy-feely fondling and exchanges of saliva. My not-so-magic Number Three did start flirting with me again though, but her gaze into my eyes had changed. I was finishing off my fifth beer when she said, "You're dangerous."

"Dangerous? Get the fuck out of here," I said, a tad perplexed but still in flirt mode, adding, "if I was dangerous, I'd have raped you."

Typically enough, the trigger-fuelled R-word just so happened to land between the few beats of silence where one song ends and another begins, so not only did the loose-couple hear my quip but the rest of the bar did too. The barmaid all but stuck up a poster declaring me enemy of the state and a flurry of napkins suddenly found themselves covering extortionately-priced glasses of wine and watered-down cocktails. I embellish for effect, but that's honestly how it felt. As if on cue with the hushed tones surrounding me, the girl's dilated eyes went all groupthink on me and morphed themselves into the horror they were expected to convey. Then my buddy started fucking laying into me about how I should *"never, never joke about such a thing!"* whilst the girlfriend he'd emotionally-blackmailed into complete subservience hid behind his fabricated feminist frame. She even smirked with psychosis through the relief my ill-timed joke provided, tremor-beaming with the slim chance that her man might not guide her face towards another man's cock again.

It wasn't even a fucking rape joke!

Just when the tension appeared to subside, Hoes Before Bros ventured forth with his vitriolic self-appointed role as moralist, which left my mouth hanging as agape as *his would've been* had the girl *he set me up with in the first place not freaked the fuck out!* He started escorting them towards the exit whilst insisting that I stayed behind, as I'd oh-so-terribly upset the girls he was trying to dupe back into the sack. I was left standing there as physically alone as I feel on a day to day basis. The only shred of solace I got from his façade was his inadvertent confession of not getting the threesome he was so obviously still in pursuit of—only now at my fucking expense, no less.

Instead of calling it a night like I definitely should've done, I frolicked over to the club we'd all been speaking of going to after the next bar, hoping to find some girl just as eager and twice as lonely. Once again, things started off pretty well. Within an hour of being there I'd made out with three girls, but after returning from the bar post-trifecta, not one of them was to be found anywhere. Even the dancefloor seemed to have dissipated during my short absence. It put me into a slight panic, the mere thought of going home alone again something of a crisis situation. Failing to find any of my chosen three or perhaps not recalling what they looked like, I ended up running out of the club, close to tears, fearful of everyone around me; thoughts haunted and purgatorial.

I woke up a couple of hours later, getting prodded by a bus driver. Not only had I blacked it during the bus ride home, but I'd even caught the wrong fucking bus, the one I used to catch before my parents vamoosed, which is at least a good hour walk away from where I live now. Also, being as drunk as I was, I forgot that the bus depot he'd be heading towards was a helluva lot nearer to my bedshit than the university I ended up marooned in. I could've just asked the driver to drop me off there, but as my memory sees it fit to conspire with my self-loathing, that lightbulb moment only flickered on as his indicator highlighted the drizzling rain of which I now stood under. Luckily, my hipflask was somehow still full, so at least I had something to sip on during my four-hour walk home in the bitter cold and opaque moisture.

It didn't make me feel much better though. I fell asleep on multiple occasions during the trek, waking up still standing wherever I'd stopped, shaking from the icy chill in the air, crying from who knows what. After the second time, I wised-up and started talking to myself to make sure I didn't fall under again. I guess it worked, as the next time I blinked I was on the floor of my corridor. Well, half of me anyway. Like Schrodinger's Stumblebum, my deadened legs were still inside the hallway, whilst my heartbeat pumped over the corridor's floorboards in my flat. It did make me chuckle though. When I lived with my parents, I used to fall asleep on the stairs and no one ever mentioned it. Now I live in a dump and blackout in the hallway with eight other doors surrounding me and still, no one ever mentions it. I guess home really is where the heart is after all.

The next day, my forever on-and-off-again girlfriend Esther got in touch, hinting at the notion of us living together. Considering that the last time I saw her she confessed to fucking one of her co-workers on the sly, I didn't bother replying. I'm sure I haven't seen the last of her yet, but until yesterday I hadn't obtained any shred of come-uppance over her betrayal, so I've been ignoring her ever since. To be honest, I don't even know what I want to do about it, nor do I particularly care.

All I do know is, life has started to feel… fictitious. Not in the sense that it has a beginning, middle and end but more that the whole thing is complete bullshit. Every illusion, or more, delusion I once possessed feels as if it's slipped through my fingers, replaced by nothing but the knowledge that it was always a hoax. It's difficult to pinpoint what it is exactly, but over the last couple of years I seem to have grown aware of my own awareness, become in tune with my own tuning—conscious of my very own consciousness... but only ever from the outside looking in... and it's a fucking nightmare.

Now it seems even the enjoyment I once derived from women is in a state of decay. My hedonistic lifestyle has been hacked by my own consciousness and now I'm starting to see it for what it is, a lonely little slut in a world that couldn't care less. What I need to do about it though, is obvious.

It occurred to me this morning whilst I was getting a blow job. Not that she wasn't putting in a decent effort or anything. Hell, she was the only girl out of the last three in as many weeks who even made me come. Twice in fact. She was Asian, tiny even in the stereotypical respect. I forget where from exactly, but I think it was China. Some east side rock anyhow. I found her online after the previously mentioned failures inside the real world. It only took a couple of days before I groomed her into meeting me. She even came straight to my flat. Her face was nothing worth remembering but her generalised reactions to my cock riled up my pornwashed brain something rotten... until I became aware of it anyway.

"Ah-he-*oh*-so big!" she said, adding genuine concern for how much it might break her. In honesty, I've watched too much porn to know I'm not that big, but big enough all the same. A bit above average, I guess. With her hand wrapped around it and her tiny tongue tentatively touching the head, it did appear larger than normal though. It's all about perspective. Anyway, what served to arouse me doubled-down to depress the fuck out of me. Her blow job skills were above par, sensual if not a bit slow, but as soon as I touched her hair my goddamn girlfriend gate-crashed into my thought process on a mission of all-out sabotage. To ignore this I flipped Chopsticks over onto my face, ate out both holes of what could've easily been confused for a twelve-year-old until that grew old and then mounted her, going as "slo-ow, p-please, more s-s-sl-oww," as I could without losing my boner or breaking her in half and continued until she went back to the beginning to finish me off. Afterwards, I got drunker than sense and pretended to listen as a mixture of more broken vowels giggled out of her mouth. She was genuinely nice. Too nice in fact. It made me realise that I can't actually be around girls who I consider to be kind anymore. I just end up feeling like one massive fraud. Plus, despite having the requisite black roots and stereotypical skin tone, every other aspect about her was the opposite of my current girlfriend. Especially the overall sex appeal. I couldn't believe it. For the first time since Esther Button-Pusher Bellona and I started dating, I genuinely wanted her by my side as I blacked out.

I was still drunk when I woke up this morning. Can't really say I'm sober even now. For reasons unknown, the girl—*let's call her Kim*—seemed pretty smitten with the deadbeat to her side and decided to indulge me with another blow job, once again commenting on its "ah-he-oh-so big!" size. I called my girlfriend during this romantic gesture just to get an extra buzz out of the debauch. She hung up when I suggested a threesome. It was all fun and games until I ejaculated, then the mere thought of Esther, the sight of the stranger's sperm-bloated cheeks and the entire universe served only to disgust me. The only pleasure I derived was from the deviancy of the act. My orgasm was nothing but a sour tear, slithering out of me like a transparent, aborted slug, as indifferent and depressing as the motives that welcomed it into the world. It was no wonder Kim-Ah-He-Oh-*So-Big!* didn't swallow. I walked her to the bus stop afterwards and sent her on her way. During the walk she sensed I wasn't into her all that much and even thanked me for giving her some company, saying how she understood if I didn't want to see her again. That made me feel like a real cunt. Still, she was right. I won't be calling her again.

So, yeah. That was my week and now I'm back here but believe you me I shall not be returning. The fumes of last week's bender-plunge are still emanating from my pores, so if I sound a little cantankerous, you'll have to forgive me. I'm a harmless lunatic at heart though, and my hate is far more indifferent than it sounds. The name's Eric. Eric Archer. I'm a twenty-first-century man in the prime of his youth, so naturally, I'm awful.

It's a pleasure to meet you... stranger.

But not as pleasurable as meeting the stranger up ahead would be now, is it? I was beginning to think you'd missed your chance with her. Hop to it boy, opportunity waits for no man.

There she is, up in the distance, diagonal to my gaze, strutting her heel-to-toe stuff along the pavement. An eroding metallic fence with blunted spiked tips stands between us; our worlds the same but at this moment still separate. I've been waiting for this since I turned the last corner. Due to my tardiness, I held doubts in regards to her presence, but there she is... with her blonde hair still somehow shimmering under the day's arctic, greyish-blue glare, the English version of a Scandinavian hue. Perhaps it may come across absurd to be in the pursuit of yet another woman after the week I've had, but that just shows how little you know, my stranger. The only absurd thing around here is the tight-fitted, nude-gold trench coat she always seems to be wearing; rivalled only by the high heels underneath. She's as ludicrous as she is luscious, walking around as if on the set of a mysterious neo-noir film, starring as the femme fatale you'd happily let ruin your life. Even from this distance her legs look like they never end. But despite how devilishly attractive I find her to be, it isn't the main reason I'm so lust-ridden beyond reason upon the mere sight of her. She's the *To Be* to my *To Not To Be*. I know her, yet I do not know her. The only thing that competes with her is my mind-already-made-up desire to commit suicide.

Of course, this beyond vivid fantasy could've simply been birthed by the weekly routine of my being here, a convenient distraction from the fifty-minute intervals of which I've come into loathing. We are creatures of the most dependable habits after all. Territorial too. But I feel as if I've fantasised about her long before she physically arrived on the scene...

Her heels march across the pavement in cadence to the dullened-thuds of my blackened heart. She steals a glance of me through the metallic fence that divides us. A sneak peek, concealed once-over, causing even more flakes of erosion to fall from the bars through its sheer devastation. I fear I've left it too long to initiate contact with her now though without my intentions ejaculating out of my eyes.

Just play it cool. Roll a smoke. Pretend her presence has gone unnoticed. She needs to think you're not interested in her to stir-up her own interest in you, just like the ego of many a woman, as you already fuckin' well know.

I slip the smoke I just rolled into my mouth but hold back from igniting a flame, flicking my eyes up instead to check on her... whereabouts...

Where'd she go?

Between the bars all I see is the long expanse of identical terraced houses across the road, all lined-up with what might as well be matching cars outside their doors. To my left the road remains empty. Did she suddenly cross? Turn back without my noticing it? No, she couldn't have done, either way, I'd have picked up on the change of her footsteps—

Ring-ring! Ring-ring!

"Mwah, fuck!" I exclaim, taken aback by my phone's sudden invasion as if I do not belong around here.

Ring-ring! Ring-ring!

Unknown Caller my arse. It's Sammy. Sammy *I-Don't-Know-Why-She's-Suddenly-Calling-Me-Again* Pennington. We haven't fucked in what must be a year. Whilst most do indeed come back for more, three months is the usual cut-off point.

Ring-ring! Ring-ring!

She's getting persistent in her pursuit of me. Disconcertingly persistent. Intrusive even. She's not trying to reassemble the bridge I burnt down between us, surely?

Ring-ring! Ring—

-Thwack!-

"*Ahh!*"

"The fuck?!" I say, thrust into a tumble and spin fall to the ground, losing grip of my phone.

I was right. Blondie didn't just up and disappear. She was loitering behind the wall on the corner where each end of the fence meets. As

I hit the turn, she decided to make haste herself.

Something tells me she just did that on purpose.

Of course she did. She's been undressing you with her eyes for weeks now, but you've been too much of a pussy to take the hint. Go on boy, now's your chance. Make your dirty fantasy a fucking reality for a change.

"Hey, you okay?" I ask, scooping my phone up from the ground then springing myself back upright. The screen didn't smash but it stopped ringing. Win/win.

The lady's a little stunned, choosing only to nod. Due to her clothing and heels, she seems unsure of how to help herself get back on her feet, so I offer my hand.

"Sorry," I say, unsure why I'm apologising. "Didn't see you there. I was distracted."

"How did you not see me?" she asks, not buying it but taking my hand all the same. I pull her upright, making her breath tighten in surprise by the force of my pull. Her other hand rests over my forearm.

There ya go. That's a bit more like it.

She looks down at herself, checking for debris whilst our hands remain holding. "Well, no bother," she says, breath returned, "I'm... sorry too. You weren't the only one not paying much attention either."

She blatantly just pulled an accidentally-on-purpose manoeuvre there, Archie boy. You know it, she knows it. And you both know you won't say shit about it either. I like her even more already. This is the dawn of a new fucking day. Get her number.

"I've seen you around here before, haven't I?"

"Have you?" she asks, coyly tilting her head to the side as her eyes focus on me. "Oh, it's... yes, yes I believe you have." Her hand has somehow twisted around without my notice. It looks as if I'm about to lead her into a dance.

"You're always wearing that leather jacket," she says.

The slightest of blushes raises inside her cheeks, which unfortunately prompts her to break her hand away. The waltz music fades and before too long we're both strangers again, standing in the middle of a pedestrian street.

"And you're often wearing yours," I say. "I hope it didn't suffer any damage."

Her blushing gains strength and a cute shrug ensues whilst she needlessly checks herself again. "No, it's fine, thanks. What about your... urm," she stalls, seeing that my jacket is already beyond fucked. The leather is okay if not a little war-torn, but the cotton around the hems is fragmented and battered.

"Fine as well, thanks," I say, prompted by what I took to be the rude covering of her purse with both hands.

"Well, I better get going. I'm already running late enough as it is." She steps to the side, out of the slit of sunlight she was just standing under, back into the dullened grey. "Nice to urm, meet you."

"You too," I say. "I'm actually pretty late myself as it happens."

"Well, sorry to have kept you."

"Oh no, I didn't mean it..." I say, but she smiles and turns down the same road from where I came, embarrassed by the situation all of a sudden.

Nice one dipshit. What d'ya tell her you're running late for anyway? You don't even wanna go where you're fucking going to. That was your chance to get in there with her and you blew it.

Ring-ring! Ring-ring!

Christ. My phone scares the shit out of me again, like it just caught me in bed with another woman.

Ring-ring! Ring-ring!

Unknown Caller.

I guess I can't keep on ignoring Sammy forever. It just doesn't feel right, especially given our history. She knows how to keep her lips sealed after all. Very rare in a woman scorned.

"Hey Sammy, now's not a good time. Can I call you back?" Nothing but dead air.

"Hello?"

Still nothing.

"Hell-o!?"

The call ends. Weird, yet typical. Hopefully she thought twice upon hearing my voice. Not that I'm opposed to seeing her again, especially after Esther's recent antics… but no, I really shouldn't retrace those particular footsteps.

Hmm. My shadow seemed to flee from my own gaze just then.

I've really got to get some rest.

I slip my phone back into my pocket whilst crossing the road and within a minute I'm by the steps of what was once a large terraced house but is now a block of flats. A long sigh leaves my lungs just at the sight of it, so I decide to pop a modafinil before mounting the steps. They're a narcoleptic's prescription drug that's been hijacked by over-ambitious students in want of extra study. As for me, I'm on a daily dose of them just to keep me awake. The trick is not to feed on them after noon.

After ringing the buzzer, I give a thousand-yard stare to the seaweed-green door. This has got to be the worst part of all of this, the bit where I'm questioning just what in the hell I'm doing here in the first place. Plus, I've never known anyone to take so fucking long when answering the door. He always keeps you deliberating on leaving. Franko Fitton's magic bag of overpriced tricks. Must be a psychoanalytic tactic or some load of croc: keep 'em waitin', build the suspense, raise their anxiety levels, pump-up-the-paranoia and let 'em overdose on their own cortisol.

I. Know. What. You. Are. Doing…

CHAPTER TWO

"Forgive me Father, for I have sinned," I say, nestling myself into the chair. Frank crosses his arms and sits back. He's tired of my mock-confessional routine already.

After clearing his throat, he says, "You know, when you say that and do a hail Mary, I get the impression you're not taking this very seriously, Eric."

"I'm just mucking around, Frank," I reply, dismissing his look with a back-hand wave. "I read somewhere that a priest is completely sworn to secrecy regarding a confession. It made me wonder whether you are as well. Like if I told you certain things... would you be obliged to keep quiet or would you be required to tell the authorities?"

"It depends. If, for instance, you told me you murdered someone, or I felt you posed a threat to somebody, then yes, I'd be obliged to tell the police or inform the person."

"Good to know."

"Why? Have you murdered anyone?" he asks in a rare half-joke, I tell myself.

"If I had, it'd be pretty stupid of me to tell you now, wouldn't it?" I laugh. "Don't worry, I haven't as far as I know." Knowing he won't reply, I take a sip from the customary glass of water to my left to wash away the ghastly residue of the pill I just gobbled down. Damn things taste like feet. After wiping my mouth with the back of my hand, I say, "Sorry I'm late by the way. Had to help out some woman... with her baby. Held me up."

Franklyn nods, looks to the side, then at his nails. "How's your week been?" he asks, sliding his glasses up from his nose. Whilst scratching the stubble on my cheeks and shrugging, I say it's been the same as the last. Ever since coming here, the beginnings always feel so forced. That's why I usually open with a wisecrack. It's just impossible to shake off how manufactured and awkward it feels.

Franklyn Fitton is a psychodynamic psychotherapist, so let me pay my respects to the choice of treatment he provides by summing it up in one short paragraph:

Psychodynamic psychotherapists sit there and encourage your capacity to talk horseshit, whilst in turn saying very little back. They call it 'free association' speaking, which basically entails talking yourself broke until the unconscious patterns of your behaviour begin to show and then, if one is willing, can be addressed. If you're familiar with free association via drawing or writing or whatever, it's virtually that but with words. If I knew that before signing up for this I wouldn't have bothered, but now, of course, I feel obliged to be here. He's my new Daddy, after all.

I decided to give it a go after a rough break-up, give or take a couple of years back. The girl I'd broken-up with had been in therapy most of her life. Considering she'd been sexually abused by most of the male side of her family by the time she was five and had not once tried to kill herself in the subsequent years that followed, I felt that gave it some credit. It didn't. Now I think she had no other choice but to believe that it works because the alternative is... well, reality.

I ask Frank how he is, realising I've just been staring into the void for the past few minutes.

"Very well, thanks. Anything you'd like to go over today?"

I lean back with the glass of water in my hand whilst wishing it was vodka and cross my legs. It makes it appear that I'm contemplating what he asked but all I'm really doing is looking at the spines of two books he keeps under his computer desk. Freud atop of Jung, which suspiciously never seem to move—Freud's always giving it to Jung. Between the middle of us, on my left and his right, there's even a head statue of Sigmund sitting on the shelf above the fireplace, next to a ceramic clock which ticks louder than any other clock I've ever encountered and gets looked at more than a prostitute's stopwatch.

Frank's obsessed with Freud. He must be obsessed with sex.

Sex, sex, sex. Everything is about sex except for sex, sex, sex.

"You know," I say, "there's a place in Minnesota called Orfield labs, where they test out silence on people. It's just a room, like any other, but somehow, they've managed to remove all the sound with extra thick concrete and steel. They call them anechoic chambers. NASA train their astronauts inside of them to cope with the deafening silence of space. The interesting part is they've found no one can take being in the room for longer than about fifteen minutes. Apparently, it's so quiet you can consistently hear your own heartbeat. Some even said they could hear the blood moving around their veins. Sensory deprivation is a form of complete torture. It's been known to cause nausea, claustrophobia and aural hallucinations. Nobody can hack it. It's completely unbearable. What do you think about that?"

"Are you being coy with me, Eric?" he asks, not really looking my way. I look up at the ceiling, biting my lip. These pills make your teeth grind without your permission. It really is tall and narrow in this room, near-on thirty feet. Way too engulfing. Sometimes when I look at it for too long, I envision pieces of brick falling down bit by bit, like an eroding mountain, until a large chunk of it breaks off and lands on my face.

I shake off the thought and say, "In a way, but I do think it's interesting. Like I've been saying for a while now, I can't think of anything that hasn't already been said."

"Anything you'd like to go over again?" he says whilst crossing his legs over, mirroring mine.

Oh, he'd love that, wouldn't he? Another year of this waffle and he'll get an extra extension on the house. Tell him to eat sh—

"How's the job search going?" he asks.

"The same. Sending off CV after CV to companies I couldn't care less about or filling out twenty-eight-page application forms and never hearing back from anyone. All so I can rot on a till for eight hours a day or stack shelves like a neutered slave. They should put disclaimers on those application forms like they do with cigarette packets. WARNING: This minimum wage excuse for slavery has been known to cause the following mental conditions: Suicidal thoughts. Denial. Depression. Alcoholism. A severe lack of self-worth. Issues with your bug-like identity. Existential breakdowns whenever your hourly rate goes up a few pence. Oh, and obesity. Everyone's a fat cunt nowadays."

"How about the acting, anything new there?" he asks.

"Nothing much since my agent went bust. Had a few offers from people I worked with before, but like always, as soon as any money is hinted at, my calls mysteriously go unreturned. I'm starting to wonder why I bothered with drama school in the first place. My motivation's just… withering away. If it hasn't completely gone already."

"Do you remember us talking about perception? Or more, your perception, I mean," Frank enquires as he adjusts his glasses again, but this time from the side of the frames. He minces his arse into the chair. Time to get serious. At least he doesn't bother me about being late any more.

The whole job hunt thing was a blatant lie of course. I haven't looked for shit, but I'm forced to give him some trite about looking for a job or he'll bump the price of these sessions up again. Tactics baby. Honesty always comes with a higher price-tag. I've worked in a bunch of the jobs I just mentioned before, all as dead-end as they were energy-zapping. Until I'm forced to, I'm staying well away from any modernised forms of slavery.

"Something about how you see the world or something or other," I utter.

"Yes. Think of it as, urm," he pauses, "this window behind me, for example." He hitchhikes his thumb at it. "What do you see?"

"A dull, lifeless landscape, sponsored by family values, product placements and mythical belief systems. It's all misty and grey and—"

"Grey. Exactly. Now, would I be wrong in saying every window you look through has this grey outlook to it?" he asks, taking off his glasses to wipe the frames.

"You wouldn't be wrong, no. But it's still fucking grey."

"Because you're always looking at the world through the same window," he says, checking a single lens for its transparency, then putting them back on in the same fashion as before.

"I just think I see things for what they are more than most. But what the fuck do I know? I can't control how I view stuff, nobody can. Everything I've experienced shapes this perception of mine. That's my truth, right? So, wouldn't denying it or trying to sugar-coat it just be another lie, a refusal of acceptance?"

"Another lie?"

Here he goes again. I'm sure this is drilled into them during training; picking out and repeating the same old boring turn of phrases because he thinks they mean something more than they really do, so I, in turn, feel obliged to explain to him that they don't. Consequently, he feels like I'm in denial over something and nothing I say can convince him otherwise. It's no wonder so many people think this game is rigged.

I can't handle this anymore. Time to push up to the frontline. I'm getting off this goddamn, over-priced, middle-upper-class merry-go-round. "To be frank, Frank. I think we've come to the end of the road."

I wait in space for his reply.

No wait, fuck that: "Feels like we're just going around in circles, to be honest."

"I've told you before, it's all part of the process. The same things will come up again and again until we discover the root cause and work through them."

The psycho-babble routine. They all get taught this. Must be in the 'How to Get an Extra Holiday' seminar. Come on, tell him where to go. I'm just as sick of this as you are.

"Yes, but as I've said before, maybe my problems aren't all buried in the past. In fact, maybe giving a voice to said past just invites it back into the present. Maybe some roots aren't meant to be ripped up."

Our eyes lock. Franklyn clears his throat and breaks away. A familiar feeling of glory washes through me, leaving me much ado about nothing.

"When you first came here, your intention was..."

"My intention was to stop repeating the patterns of my behaviour. To try and see if I can put a hold on the past. We've been here before as well, Frank. Our brains are always one step ahead anyhow, so it was an empty argument to begin with."

"What do you mean by that?"

"So, I'm *deciding* to move my hand right now, okay?" I say, giving him a wave, "but really the electrical signals in my brain started firing off a few fractions of a second before. No matter what I do, my movements will always be trailing behind. It works the same with how we perceive anything as well. So technically speaking, we're always looking to the future whilst being trapped in the past."

"What about the present?"

"The present is nothing more than a slice of a razor blade between the past and the future. Blink and you'll miss it. The only time we *'live in the moment'* is when we're preoccupied with something else. As soon as you become conscious of whatever you're doing, you immediately cease being in the present; for you cannot reflect and perceive at the same time. So, if we're agreed that consciousness is our imagined perception of reality, what does that tell you about the nature of such a reality?"

"I'm not sure what you're getting at, Eric."

One must imagine Sisyphus an obsessive-compulsive geologist.

"Don't worry. Neither am I."

"How are you and Esther?"

You see, this is the modus operandi of the therapist. Sure, they listen to you, but it always feels like they're only listening to you to ask another question down the line to keep you rambling and thus, filling their pockets. Maybe I sound like a prick, but as I'm the one fronting the bill for this bullshit, I clearly am one.

"Usual. Arguing then fucking. Fight, fuck, repeat. Our relationship is just lust. I can never say that to her, but I think even she knows it deep down. It's alright when I'm in parent mode and she's in her child ego I suppose. Great when it works, *hell* when it doesn't. I know that must mean it's false, as I'm forced to put on some act just to keep the peace. Which I am feeling less and less inclined to do."

He glances at his hands as his fingers intertwine and asks, "Why do you think that is?"

"Well, I'm sure the whole prostitution thing doesn't help. Combining that information with the little snippets I have about her mother and there you go. It all adds up. I remember Esther telling me about this time her mother invited a stranger over to their house. Her mum told her to wait in the living room with her sister whilst she took the stranger upstairs. I don't know many details, but Esther knew what was going on. I mean, she could hear her, screaming with the *'I'm getting paid for this'* theatrics. That's where she probably got that from as well, the whole street knows when Esther's getting off. Anyway, when her mother came back down, she gave Esther some cash and told her to take her sister out, never to see that man again. I think that was her first glimpse of her mother's true nature, and so, after she disappeared, the only way Esther could feel close to her, if she ever did, was by putting herself through the same motions. Kind of romantic in a deeply, tragic way, don't you think?"

Franklyn does his thing. And by his thing I mean he sits there, most of the time still, staring at a spot of little to no significance, thinking. Or at least, that's what I thought at first. Now I'm not so sure about the thinking part.

"I haven't seen Esther for a couple of weeks now anyway. She's copped off with some other guy and I'm not sure I even care. It was always doomed from the start."

Here's another part I loathe. The gaping silence between our conversations. It's never been back and forth. I can feel him carefully strolling through his mental index cards for the 'right' phrases to vocally regurgitate. I should just write my own script and play both parts. Maybe I'd find myself better to debate with.

"Doomed?" he asks, looking at his goddamn clock.

"Well, you know. Esther and I beginning whilst Jessica and that whole fiasco was gallivanting around in the background."

He nods. "It's not the first time you've done that though, is it?" he asks, looking proud of himself, almost smirking.

"What, cheated? If there was ever a woman who deserves to have the dirty done on her, it's Esther. Trust me. The only reason I haven't done it more often is that she's too good in bed, even if it is all done through some power play."

"Hmm. So, the only reason you don't cheat on her is because of her... ability in the bedroom. Sounds like a power-play move on your part too." His eyebrows now enquire for my input.

"I don't know. I sometimes wonder whether I just put up with her because of the guilt I feel over other women in the past. But I can't say that for sure without also thinking I'm just trying to make myself feel better."

"Guilt over what?"

"The cheating. The betrayals. The misunderstandings. I could go on. Or maybe... I dunno, not being strong enough to resist other women in the first place? I don't really feel bad about that though, except for the last time, with Jessica."

Another moment to reflect. I'm only spouting off to stop myself

20

from going insane. I look back at Frank for a reaction, but his eyes are on the clock again. He claims he loves his job as well. "Time's up for today," he says.

"Yep, thought so."

I get up from the chair and take out my wallet. Handing over money to Frank is like I'm surrendering to a thief before he's even revealed his weapon. If I had any friends, I'd just speak to them. But I don't, so I drink. Maybe that's the real reason I come here, to pretend I'm making progress and reward myself with a few cold ones afterwards. I wish self-awareness equalled self-realisation.

"See you next week," he says, ushering me towards the door.

"Yeah," I say, avoiding his glance as I step outside.

The door closes behind me as soon as my second step lands and I'm back out on the street, head hanging low due to my latest failure. He didn't even acknowledge my request to quit. That shouldn't have surprised me.

Do you hear that sound, my observer? I hear it every night as soon as the day dies another death. It's so distinct and effervescent. Can you hear it? Out there in the distance, it's Pavlov, ringing his bell with its sweet melody. My first pint of the day is sitting neatly on a beermat somewhere, with its provocative, frothy head spilling just a touch over the ridge of the glass, the little eager to please cock-tease. I'll be there soon my sweet elixir, be forever still and never break your vow of silence and in our equanimity, our mutual commitment, I shall cherish each and every heaven-sent drop of you, not a bit like the louts that riddle this land, who use and abuse and don't deserve you. But you forgive them too, because you know, that they know not what they do. I'll devour you the moment our mouths meet with my promise to never, not for a single day, betray you. Shorten my years and hold back my tears, turn me into the beast that could never match your everlasting beauty. Never questioning my faithfulness because you understand that in all your wonderful, vivacious and *sui generis* varieties, that you are all one and the same. I'm coming, my bodacious brother in arms, my supple-bodied soldier, my curvaceous commander and chief. You own every ounce of me.

CHAPTER THREE

Question: What do we see behind the eyes of abuse and neglect? Answer: *Potential.* There's a sickening truth behind sexual desire. Mine especially. My target scope picks out the weak and the vulnerable, looking to exploit them for everything they've got. I'd like to tell you that I'm unaware of it but that would be a lie. However, this admission should come with a disclaimer. When you're on the hunt, as it were, you feel deeply in control up until the point of execution. After that, the beady little third eye between your legs blinks himself blind until every logical thought gets pissed over. Mother nature, with its filthy reproduction agenda, makes sociopaths of us all.

Hooking-up with an ex-hooker doesn't appeal in many respects, but for some reason it does allure me. And I've contemplated it an awful lot, *believe you me*. The only conclusion I've come up with as to why is the utter self-destructiveness of it. I often feel a twinge down below just thinking about it. Maybe it's because of the way society pushes women to behave and what a FUCK YOU it is in retaliation, but what it most likely boils down to is the fact that I really, *really* hate myself. Esther's main issue is that she possesses a deeply-embedded belief that her vagina entitles her to just about everything. According to the DSM-5, it's a condition called Princess Pussy Syndrome. It's a western world mental disorder affecting mainly, though not exclusive to, those of the Caucasian variety, Esther being the mixed-raced exception that proves the rule. Symptoms include figurative blindness, a loss of all reasoning, nerve-shatteringly high-pitched screaming, cross-armed sulking, victim role-playing, clitoral manipulation and monetary amnesia. The male equivalent of this condition is of course Prince Pay, Prince Get Disorder, where the female is viewed as an object, and although human to the touch, ultimately inferior in every way. Tell-tale signs: Buying flowers and expecting fellatio as compensation. Talking over a woman when he sees her point but then refuses to acknowledge it because of her gender. Escorting said woman to a restaurant, insisting on paying for the meal and then acting like a cunt when the woman denies him access to all three of her holes, causing our victim—*ahem*—to call her names of a paradoxical nature: *Frigid whore. Cock-teasing slut. Cum-guzzling virgin bitch.*

What Esther does have though, is what I like to label: The Appeal. Now, whilst you might find yourself possessing what is deemed by societal norms as 'desirability' or 'attractiveness,' neither will necessarily determine whether The Appeal is yours. I've been with many an attractive lady who by appearance should've had The Appeal but came up short soon after the bedroom door slammed shut. It is not an ascetical thing. Whilst it may perhaps be something as simple as a meeting of two similar mindsets, I'm more led to believe that some people (I'm referring to women in this instance) have an innate birth-right regarding The Appeal. I'm even leaning towards a belief, that this personality trait may even be an evolutionary tool. One woman I toyed with had it in bucket loads. She was too thin, even somewhat gangly from certain angles, had no tits and quite a harshly-featured face; pointed nose, droopy mouth, squinted eyes etc. But there was no doubt that she had The Appeal. Her devil-may-care disposition carried within it a sassy attitude to all things of the sexual kind. Sadly, I made the irretrievable mistake of trying to explain this to her. As she was unaware of the quality, she took it as nothing but an insult. It didn't matter that she wasn't conventionally good-looking like most, or maybe some of my past lovers, but all she could surmise from my statement was that I was calling her ugly. Well, in a way I was. She was ugly, but only at first glance. She was a fiery and pissed-off, sexy-as-fuck beast who loathed everything about the world nearly as much as I do and walked within it, snake-hips shaking from side to side like a demonic force. It didn't matter though. She soon fucked off after believing I thought she was a dog. Hence why also having The Appeal doesn't necessarily mean you have intelligence either.

Esther has The Appeal, but again she isn't quite aware of it. I've been trying to beat it into her throughout the last couple of years without saying it outright, but nothing I seem to say or do will shake her out of the beliefs she shaped for herself when she was about fourteen. In fact, she fucking hates having it, which with her being a woman must be a difficult pill to swallow. I'm just positive that if she worked more on her mind, instead of contradicting her thoughts through her behaviour, she would come to realise the power of what she possesses.

In summary, The Appeal is largely about accepting who you are, which is why so many people simply do not have it.

"Another drink Eric? You're getting through them tonight."

Day time Lucy doesn't have The Appeal. But night time, liquored-up Lucy certainly does.

I say, "With good reason Luce. There's a devil in my head that won't quit. Cheers," and gulp down the remainder of my pint before she takes it and heads for the pump.

Ah, the Journey's End. A place where the English language comes to die. Where the skin particles you've lost come in to settle down as the dust layered across the wooden balusters. Where you come to remember the person you forgot to become. It's a cave-dwelling shithole where all hope is placed inside of betting slips and lottery tickets to justify repetitive idioms such as *'story of my life'*, *'just my luck'* and *'in the fuckin' good ol' days'*. At some point, all the regulars who accustom this joint gave up on thinking. They settled for what little they knew as enough and now wonder why their lives never changed. What an aptly named pub.

I don't regulate this place as much as before. In some ways, it feels like I'm paying my last respects. There's something eerie about the atmosphere. Every seven years the body's cells completely reform, so essentially there's nothing left of what you once were. I've been coming here for that long; since I was fifteen. Or sixteen. Maybe eighteen. When you tank down as much booze as I do, time recollection is the first thing to go.

The garish lights hanging from the ceiling around the bar show your reflection in the square-bordered windows opposite. Gazing at this opaque image, this silhouette, leaves me feeling that I'm nothing but a stranger to myself. *'Grey windows,'* Franklyn Fitton's voice rings through my head. His point has a mild validation to it, but it's too obvious for my tastes. Therapy inherently seems to me to be something which we all need but could also do without. Tell me, my observer. What sort of society puts a price-tag on our unique, linguistical capabilities?

"Alright Eric," says Bobby, wearing his usual denim jacket over a polo shirt, with jeans to match the former. He's part of the furniture of this place, a clockwork regular to the max. He comes in at the same time day-in, day-out and stands in the same spot at the edge of the bar just to the side of the fruit machine, of which some idiot everyone calls Smithy is currently losing his mind on. He's always feeding that fucking thing, even though he's convinced it's fixed. That sort of cognitive dissonance must be a brain tumour waiting to happen. Hopefully, for humour's sake, it will take shape in the form of a cherry or an orange.

I ask Bobby how it's going, but he's already in his spot, showing a slight concern in his eyes that his pint wasn't poured the moment he walked in. Like most of the usual punters here, he's terrified of seeing the world in a different light. It fills me with dread that it happens to everyone as they age, once the daily war of life has had its way with you and before you know it, you find yourself settling for whatever little control you can find as your world continues to shrink, entirely indifferent to all of your suffering.

"How's your old man settling down over there, he sick of it yet?" Bob asks, nursing his pint as his shoulders drop.

"Yeah, I think he's enjoying it alright. Wouldn't really know to be honest mate. He's still doing his bits and bobs like he used to, but now in a foreign language so he doesn't have to talk to anyone."

Bob acknowledges whatever came out of my mouth with a silent exchange, which is appreciated.

In truth, I don't even know where my parents are. They disappeared after I moved out a year or so ago. Like it was pre-planned, they rented out the house the week I left and are now roaming around Europe somewhere. Frank doesn't know this. In fact, nobody does apart from me. It's safer that way. When they were here, I could at least fool myself into thinking what I did mattered to them, but now they're gone it's clear that nobody cares or even notices what I do, be it good or bad... unless of course, I fucking pay them to. It's no wonder I seem to have become the ghost of myself.

Lucy, the tattooed and pierced barmaid with little to say, who thrives on her ink for conversation starters and excuses for attention—*but who also sucks a mean dick*—finally serves me my third pint of Guinness. She looks at me differently since she started seeing this Jack guy who also works behind the bar. There's a knowingness between me and him now, an accepting air of animosity mixed with a wary sort of respect. It might be because we dress very similarly; boys in our rock-n-roll costumes, or it might be because we have similar tastes in women—*meaning any*. He knew Lucy and I fucked before we met. I wonder if he knows that I came on her face. She got all pissed off when I did it, saying how I degraded her. She said it with a sort of delighted disgust though, shock-smiling and laughing. Hot. The beautiful thing about giving a girl a facial? If she's pretty she earned it, if she's ugly she deserved it. Said the man who dipped his brain in the bile bowl of pornography for a tad too long, and drowned. Lucy's a false advertisement anyhow, with all that metal in her face you'd think she'd appreciate a natural moisturiser.

"Fag?" asks Bob, as I'm sinking down my second gulp.

I wipe my mouth with the back of my hand and say, "You're a mind reader mate." After whipping on my leather jacket, I start rolling as we walk across the barren pub. We spark up outside the entrance doors, which has a small step to provide shelter for the smokers, even though we've been told multiple times not to stand here. Bob starts playing around with his mobile phone, some old brick of a thing. Every generation is so quickly replaced. Before you know it, you're already done.

Bob grunts at the screen before him. "Ahh, the Rottweiler's up to her old tricks. Wants me to take Ben in for the weekend again. Christ sake," he says, gobbing onto the pavement. Rottweiler is the *nom de plume* he's given to his ex-wife and the only name I can associate her with. "She's the one who wanted another kid and now she never wants to fucking look after him," he says.

With nothing to reply to this, I opt for the usual: "Women."

"Tell me about it. You still with that Chinky one? Emma?"

"Esther," I say. She's English but half-Japanese, with a blend of American and Spanish. Or Mexican. I forget. Probably a few other meaningless ones. A product of a few wars by my reckoning. "Yeah, she's still knocking about. She's staying with her old man for the moment but keeps hinting at moving in with me. I wouldn't mind if she didn't expect me to fucking pay for everything," I say, not wishing to mention she's probably dining on another cock as we speak.

"Don't do it mate, worst decision I ever made," says Bob whilst enthusiastically scratching his arse.

"I hear you. She's nothing but a headache most of the time but she sure makes up for it in the sack. Gushes like the Niagara Falls, mate."

"Oh mate, I love that."

"Same here, there's nothing better—"

"That's when you *know* she fucking came—"

"Exactly!"

We exchange a few laughs.

"Just enjoy it while you can, Eric. If she proves too much, get shot of her before you end up in my shoes."

"Will do."

His phone starts ringing. Bob sparks up another fag before answering it. I'm finished with mine, so I flick it into the gutter where it belongs and go back inside. The fruit machine's flushing out coins. Naturally, Smithy's turned around for acknowledgement.

"Aye-aye, the thespian's 'ere."

Christ. He must have won the jackpot. I know that sickening look of glee too well. He always wants to waggle his chin when he's won, and I only ever want to get lippy with him when he's lost. The glint in his eye is nauseating. I feel like playing along with him for a while though.

"What'cha Smithy! Winnin' again 'eh me old mucka'? 'Bout time you got a 'round in 'n all. I'll havva double jack 'n coke and then anovva Guinness mate, cheeeeaars."

"I ain't won that much boy! That machine's like a woman, she never gives it up when you want her to!"

"Please, tell me all about it on my deathbed Smithy, you never know, it might speed up the process."

"How's the actin' going?"

"Life is the act nobody in their right mind would willingly pay to see. Just shove a camera in any idiots face these days and wait for him to say something *stoooooopid*. There's your entertainment, remember to tip your waitress and thanks for coming."

"If you hadda' brain you'd be fuckin' dangerous mate! Ya know wot ya need to do don'tcha?"

"Havva good feelin' ya gonna tell me, *mate*—"

"Chaaange ya name mate. Wossit now, Eric wha'?"

"Archer."

"Ya see, Eric Archer. Doesn't 'ave any ring to it. Wot about, Eric Eagles, or... Eric Earnshaw or somefing? Somefing tha' makes ya sound more important than ya really are."

"What about... Eric Engelfield the Third?"

"Yeah yeah, somethin' like that. All dose theatre twats love all dat bollocks. Somefin' dat makes ya sound like you were born wivva silver spoon shoved up ya arse."

"Another act for the actor. Before I know it, I won't even know who I am anymore."

"Yourra weird one ain'tcha? I'm only tryin' to help ya owwt mate, give ya a bit of advice."

"Do I give you advice on how to build houses, Smithy?"

"Maybe you should. I been buildin' 'em me 'ole life and I still can't fucking afford one. Oi, Luce! Get me annova one will ya?"

Lucy lifts her head up from the preferred reality of her mobile phone and rolls her eyes at me as she goes back to the pump.

"At the end of the day life is just a game, Eric. Ya just gotta learn how to smash it."

I don't think even he knows what he's banging on about anymore. What the fuck am I doing in this place?

"*Eric?*"

You get what you deserve, that's why. You get everything you deserve.

You know exactly who it is.

A familiar, *well-to-do* female voice. One that makes all the little hairs on the back of my neck prick up, inspiring a mixed feeling of arousal and dread. It's Sammy. *Shit.* She used to play this trick whilst we were seeing each other, just turning up out of nowhere to '*surprise!*' me, as she put it, leaving me with nowhere to hide. Some people would probably appreciate that sort of act, find it sweet or even endearing. It's nothing but suspicious to me.

"Sammy, what brings you into this shithole?" I say, taking out my wallet to offer her a drink but she's already being served by Lucy, never before so keen to serve someone.

"Oh, you know. Just following you around like a neglected child I suppose. *Guinness?*"

I shrug her a Why the Hell Not. Smithy's disappeared outside with Bobby, who both stand there spitting and swearing. The men who frequent this place seem to have an inherent fear of females, especially the young ones. I should take that as a warning, if not my wanderlust will surely lead me straight down their paths.

"I've been calling you," Sammy says abruptly. "Thought you would most likely be in here."

"We all have depressingly predictable patterns, it seems."

Sammy and I had a brief thing before I got with Esther. Or more, replaced her with Esther whilst still, on occasion, slipping her a sly one. Of course, now, because of my betrayal, she basically offers herself up on a plate every time I see her. Nothing gets a woman hotter than a wounded ego, especially the ones still trapped in the hormonal web of their late teens. I almost wish I didn't know that.

"Predictable doesn't have to be depressing," says Sammy. She takes both drinks from the bar and walks over to the table furthest away. She's sexy when she's all pissed off, but the attitude thing gets a little tiresome after a while. It's a shame her fourteen-year-old sister is hotter than her, but what can you do about that? Don't get all shirty with me for saying that either, my little watcher at the gate; in a world without windows, we'd *all* be fucking fourteen-year-olds. Sammy, on the other hand, will look better when she's older. She's got an Elizabeth Taylor look to her which doesn't sit so well on a young face. A decade or so of disappointment coupled-up with an eating disorder and a keen alcohol problem and *hey presto*, she'll be the bitter and twisted femme fatale she so desperately craves to be. That's when she'll be at the height of her powers. Until then though, cute little Sammy Pennington, who's still trying to shed the last few pounds of her puberty-induced puppy-fat, is at the mercy of me.

She's wearing a black, faded pinstripe suit jacket with only one button holding it together over a peach, V-shaped tank top, skilfully putting your focus on her ample cleavage—*which is, as she very well knows, her best asset*—along with a pair of faded black jeans she always wears to compensate for her disproportionate arse. The obvious self-consciousness of it all is what wins my vote. The rake-thin Lucy, obviously delighted with her lower-half, is equally bitter and envious of the top. They'd both buddy-up if they saw Esther though, she's got what they want and then some.

Sammy moves the chair opposite with her foot, apprehending me with her eyes the whole time it screeches awkwardly along the wooden, ale-tarnished floor. From what I heard Sammy was just juggling me around with a few other dudes before she decided that I was worthy of her or some shit, so I started juggling her around too. Mostly with Esther. We haven't spoken for months, maybe even a year. I think she wore those jeans and that jacket the last time we slept together. Am I catching the whiff of what I like to call *the guarantee*?

"So, are you still with that bitch nowadays?" she asks as soon as I've sat down, skipping past any pleasantries we could've started with.

"Sort of, yeah. She's at her Dad's right now though," I say, rustling through my jacket for some tobacco.

"Well, isn't that nice," she says, flashing me a condescending smile after a snobbish sip of her wine. "I'm happy for you."

"How's everything with you?"

"Everything's... just great, thanks."

It's already awkward and starting to feel forced. Still better than listening to Smithy dish out terrible advice about how to break into Hollywood though.

"Have you been following me around, Sammy?" I ask.

"Oh, sure Eric, I'm your *biggest* fan. I can't go through a moment of the day knowing you're out there somewhere, out of my sight."

"I'm serious. You were calling me a fair bit. What's that all about?"

She looks at me but quickly breaks eye contact and says, "Oh, nothing for you to fret over. I'll tell you later. I just wanted to see you again."

"Right... what for?"

She sighs. "Still as paranoid as ever then."

"Usually with good reason," I point out with a swig of my fourth, no wait fifth pint? I'm beginning to forget. Mission accomplished. Sammy adjusts her top and sits up, giving me a magnificent view. If she's trying to make me think about sleeping with her again, it's working. Her lower lip keeps hanging down and looks like it has its own pulse.

After another swig, I ask how her sister is doing.

"She's good thanks. All excited about starring in her first full-on play."

"Oh yeah? What play?"

"A Slight Ache."

"Ahh, Pinter. Nice. That's a brutal play. A good challenge for a young actress."

"Yes, she said she found it quite distressing at times but overall a pretty good experience. She's way too young to play that character but hey, it's all about variation. Richard came to see it. He's at the school *a lot*. D'you still see him?"

The less said about him the better. Even thinking about him probably feeds his ego. Then again, he was the only friend I had at school. Or more, I was his self-served friend.

"Not even once since I left."

"Good. He gives me the fucking creeps that guy. Hey, are you going to the graduate party reunion thing?" she asks, sucking on a luminous straw in a manner that makes my cock twitch.

***

It went on like that for a while, making chitchat and getting sauced up before the inevitable 'I have something to tell you' came pouring out of her mouth, which I dodged by suggesting we walk home together. She was always quite fun to be around after she'd had a few, despite always making big deals out of dull shit. It usually involved a guy she sucked off showing his face again or one of her friends being a bitch and not listening enough. Stupid social circle etiquettes and the pathetic politics of human nature. Ah, the games people play, they're all so exasperating. After an hour or so of pretending to listen, Lucy rang the bell for last orders.

Now Sammy, suitably oiled-up, needs a make-believe prince to carry her home. Here's one of the many advantages of being a drunk, everyone else gets pissed far quicker than you, and in doing so they hand over their will on top of an unstable, inhibition-loosened plate. She's in the toilet now for about the eighth time this evening. I hope she's not vomiting. She used to carry mints and chewing gum in her purse all the time, as well as only smoking menthol cigarettes, so I suspected her penchant for bulimia. Jessica also had a weight obsession. Esther has a Jessica obsession. Though they each juggle around these issues the same way I was prone to juggle them. It's funny, people always get jealous of past lovers and whatnot but if we're honest with ourselves we only ever attract people with similar traits. I'm forever trading traumas with the unstable, fooling myself into believing they fuck the best. Maybe the feeling's mutual.

CHAPTER FOUR

Sammy walks ahead with her guitar-shaped behind shaking its stuff, doing its best to pluck a chub out of me, and succeeding. She keeps messing about with her hair for some reason and is constantly in and out of her handbag. I come to a standstill and stare into the driveway of a graveyard. You can't tell from looking at it that it's a burial ground, as it just appears like an old bit of road with a half-moon shaped archway for an entrance with a gate underneath. To a stranger's eye it must look more like private property, hence why I once opted for it.

"You remember our little visit in there?" I ask. She stops and turns slightly. It's nearing midnight now, so there's nobody else around. All that can be heard is the distant sound of cars driving by and the faint decline of a police siren far away.

"Yes, Eric. I remember. I remember it perfectly," she says solemnly.

"How about a trip down memory lane?"

The side of Sammy's mouth twitches a touch. She looks at the pavement, nestling her foot into the ground like she's stubbing out a cigarette and throws a glance at the graveyard with a trepidation I didn't anticipate, as my memories of this place are rather good.

"You want to go in *there?*" Sammy had asked, laughingly in a drunken stupor as she handed me back the joint we'd been smoking after leaving Journey's End. I said it didn't seem like such a bad idea. She agreed. I took her by the hand and led her beyond the driveway of the graveyard. In a flash, we were in front of an array of tombstones. The occasional light from distant houses or maybe the streetlamps caused the grass to glisten slightly, showing it to be still and slightly moistened.

"What the hell are we doing in here Eric? Don't you need to get home to your new beau?" asked Sammy, with a coy look in her eyes. She lightly slapped my chest with a limp hand. Esther and I had just become 'official' around this time after being on and off during the whole two years of drama school, so Sammy had her own reasons for saying yes: passive-aggressive vengeance. She knew all about Esther, so I knew it would be all-too-easy. Sammy had hesitated, but before long we were embracing in that delicious, furious rage of attraction, betrayal and sin.

"I'm not sure it's the best idea Eric, seeing how last time..." Sammy says, looking at the avenue like a heinous crime had been committed there. She seems to have sobered up just at the thought as well, which could compromise my plans.

"You don't want to. You sure? Even if it's only half as good as last time it'll be worth it, wouldn't you say?"

"Yeah, last time... about that. I need to tell you something, Eric—"

"Whatever. Tell me in there," I say, taking her by the hand, but she remains frozen on the spot. I pull on her arm gently, raise up my other arm and wrap it around her shoulder. Eventually, she walks with me towards the entrance, but won't quit looking down at her hands. I guess she did just stick her fingers down her throat. The chances of getting some repeat action look grim.

We had finished our quick embrace and as we strolled I swigged some more confidence out of my hipflask. I thought about offering Sammy a sip but saw that her stride still swayed a touch, so there was no need to continue wasting perfectly good whisky on her. Instead, I let her finish off the spliff. Then I hooked my arm through hers and directed her to a nearby bench. I took a few more swigs and watched Sammy as she pretended to feel guilty.

"You're really fucked up, Eric. D'you know that?" she said, looking at the hipflask to emphasise her point.

"Of course, why do you think I drink?" I said, offering her the bottle with a shake. She refused with her head in the same manner but slid closer. We remained silent for a while, looking around the place. The landscape was huge and a little engulfing; mostly made-up of hills peppered with decaying tombstones and foliage, surrounded by beautiful yet haunted old oak trees with large hooked branches that looked like muscular arms protecting the dead. I sparked up another joint and leaned back on the bench, gearing myself up to close the deal. The blend of marijuana and alcohol was just right, so all my inhibitions had dissipated away into the night sky. To my surprise, Sammy put her hand on my knee, and excitedly, I heard my belt unbuckle.

With her head down, Sammy asks, "Shall we sit down for a bit?" She's been avoiding eye contact with me ever since we departed from Journey's End. The only way I'm going to get some is by cranking this up a notch. Her tolerance must be larger these days. After four or five drinks she normally goes kamikaze on my crotch.

I remove my trusty old hipflask from my pocket and say, "Here, drink this."

"No, thank you, Eric. I've had enough to drink already."

"How about a little smoke then?" I say, taking out my tin of now pre-rolled joints.

"Urm, sure. I'll have a bit," she says. Christ, I think she might cry. This isn't at all like last time.

The buttons of my jeans had popped out eagerly. I was looking up at space but being a visually-cursed man, I just had to see what Sammy was doing down there. Under the spotlight of my phone, her lips were split open by her tongue, which moved from side to side with beautiful, unconscious ease. She lift-and-yanked manoeuvred my boxers down so that my erection slapped back hard over my stomach, pulsating further with each giggling glimpse Sammy gave to the lens. Whilst staring at my cock in what seemed to be awe, she declared that I was a monster. Her own eyes then went bestial as she took a savage dive towards my balls. Instead of the sensual tip-of-the-tongue caresses I was expecting, she ravaged the fuck out of them, pressing the entirety of her tongue down, hard, then shook her face all over my shaft like an epileptic in mid-fit. It was like she worshipped me but resented herself for it; as if something inside her was making her do it. She sucked each testicle into her mouth so hard that her lips smacked whenever she let one pop back out. At first, the pain was pleasurable but after a while my balls started to hurt. Sensing my slight discomfort, Sammy pulled my shaft towards her mouth instead. Even I was surprised by the amount of pre-cum that glistened under the moonlight. Instead of swiping it away like I was anticipating, she paused, birthed a smile and suddenly twirled her tongue around my urethra and licked it clean whilst staring at me, then took it deep into her mouth. And there I was, in a graveyard, getting my cock sucked. She was moaning heavily and had already taken the initiative to unbutton her jeans. I let her pull them down a bit before grabbing her hand and pressing it hard over her crotch. Even with her hand in the way, I could still feel how soaked she already was. Then I watched as she pleasured herself whilst sucking me off. Her moans increased in volume and intensity whilst her hand moved in an aggressive, circular motion. I let it gradually drive me wild until the smell between her legs rose and spirit-snaked through my nose, inviting the animal in me to take over. I grabbed hold of her arse, lifted her up in the air and looked around for a place to lay her down.

"I remember *this* bench," says Sammy, her fingers gripping over the front plank. She's probably just worried about starting the diploma at drama school or some crap. I think she mentioned it back at the pub. This is way over the top though. That's the one thing about young women I really can't stand. They all seem to think that their emotions are something that everyone should care about. Sammy breathes in and out like she's meditating, sucks up her last drag and hands me back the joint.

"Feel better?" I ask, growing impatient and wanting to go home.

"A bit, yeah. Thanks."

I lean in for a kiss, but Sammy sits there like a melting ice statue. The spliff is spent, so I flick it away and put my hand on the back of her neck, hoping to inspire her into some movement. Sammy was always a bit of a hot and cold kook. In the pub, she was one drink away from inviting me into the toilet. Now she's acting like I'm keeping her prisoner, close to pushing my rule button: if the double-down fails, bail. Eventually, she starts kissing me back but without any passion whatsoever, transferring her anxiety into me, killing all chances of a boner. I call it quits and begin to move away, but Sammy quickly places a firm hand on my chest and pushes me back, "Eric no, this isn't right," she says, stealing my decision to stop. "You're still with Esther after all."

"And? I was with her before. So what?"

"Well, it's different this time."

"Hardly. It's pretty much the same. In fact, it's exactly the same, look around you," I say, trying to sound coy.

It failed. Sammy looks down at the grass, tear-ducts ready for release. "Eric, there's no easy way to say this."

Oh god. That fucking phrase. This could go on and on.

I blurt out, "There is. Just say it." It came out harsher than intended.

"I'm trying to. Give me some of that whisky,"

"Sure thing." I pass the flask over. Our fingers caress as she takes it.

My fingers had slid slowly around the crack of Sammy's arse

as I lifted her up. Within seconds my hands were smeared with her moisture. I tried finding a decent place to put her down, but my vision blurred for a moment so I couldn't make out anything distinctly. Eventually, a grave that sat underneath a tall hedge of overgrown bushes caught my eye. Before putting her down I let her fall slightly from my torso and, to my surprise, my midnight wonder eased into her without any effort at all. She let out a shocked moan, which spurred me on to thrust even further to hear more. Little inward breaths of lust and chill released from her mouth as I carried her over to the grave. In one quick motion, we fell down together on top of the grass. She threw her hands on each side of the tombstone and wrapped her legs around my waist. My drenched cock slid in and out whilst her legs had already begun to shake. For some reason, fucking her on top of some dude's grave gave my cock rigor mortis and like a galley slave, it obeyed my every command without the threat of ever tiring. Sammy also made sure I'd remember it. She hate-fucked-worshipped me the entire time until her hands fell from the headstone and she dug her fingers into the ground, ripping up clumps of grass from the earth. I could feel the heat from the rivulets of sweat pouring down between her breasts. She put her hands under my shirt and scratched across my back, trying to leave a mark for Esther to find, so I drilled myself inside of her as deep and fucking frantically as I could until she stopped moving and let out the long, silent scream I'd been waiting for. Just as more of her juices started to ooze out, she grabbed onto my arse with one hand and pulled my hair with the other like a woman possessed, then clamped her thighs around my waist and looked at me, knowing it wouldn't take long. Her eyes jolted as I unloaded round after round after round of sperm inside her, with each shot triggering another until I felt like I'd emptied myself out for good. The way we looked at each other seemed to say we'd never experienced anything like that before. Being where we were, it was as if we'd just fucked away each other's very spirit.

"I had an abortion Eric," says Sammy. "I meant to tell you sooner, but I... I didn't. I'm really sorry, I should've told you."

A heavy, sinking feeling hits my chest like it's imploding. It passes quickly though, and I sit there docile, with a void sensation, like I'm not really here.

"You're joking right?"

"I wouldn't joke about something like this, Eric."

"Well, why... why didn't you tell me?"

"I don't know."

"Was it mine?"

"*What?* Yes, Eric. Of course it was yours! What kind of question is that?" Sammy turns away from me slightly with both arms cradling her stomach like she's hugging herself.

I'd buckled my belt back up but when I sprung to my feet my knees nearly gave way. After straightening myself out, I gave Sammy my hand and pulled her upright. Her hair was all tangled and even had a fallen twig in it, which I pulled out with a smile. She laughed but then looked at me with what I took to be contempt. I guess she remembered who was waiting for me at home. She hooked the loose trouser leg back on and pulled them up.

"I can still feel your monster-load oozing out of me, Eric."

"It'll stop in a minute or so. Just have a piss or something. You want a smoke?"

"A quick one yeah, I better be going soon. Hold my hand, my legs feel unstable."

"Not sure mine are much better."

We walked back to the bench and sat down. Sammy rustled through her handbag and took out a condom, which I still remember coming across a bit strange. She held it in the air at an acute angle with raised eyebrows.

"That's the problem with contraception. Once the party gets started, no one wants to stop and blow up balloons," I said whilst lighting up. She didn't look too impressed. "Hey, at least you can still smuggle drugs." No response. Tough crowd. I took a heavy drag of the joint, hoping that Sammy's line of thinking wouldn't go where I

41

thought it was.

"What if..."

"I wouldn't worry about that Sammy."

"Yeah but *what if,* Eric. You never know. I should've made you wear a condom."

"Sammy, I'm an alcoholic with other keen drug habits and I wear tight jeans, I'm practically three contraceptives rolled into one. You've got nothing to worry about."

"Oh, that makes me feel *so* much better Eric, thanks."

"If you're really that concerned, take the morning after pill."

"Charming."

"Works for Esther. She pops those pills like she wants to be barren," I said, passing the joint over.

"Again, charming Eric," she said, taking it between her fingers.

"Hey, I'm just trying to lighten the mood a little. Everything will be fine. If you want we can go and get the pill tomorrow morning or something."

"I can't tomorrow," she said, passing the spliff back.

"Okay well, I think you have a few days at least to make a decision. I'm sure nothing will happen, but if it does, I'll be there for you. Don't worry about it," I said, sucking up a drag.

"Thanks, Eric. That's almost sweet of you," Sammy had said.

The sound of Sammy's tears is doing nothing but irritate me. Through some imperceptible wails, she just tried to convince me that we couldn't possibly have a baby together outside of a loving relationship and how she is so terribly sorry that she never told me. In truth, I'm not angry at her. I'm not even sure that I care. I didn't have to do anything at least. There's even some sort of sick satisfaction in knowing I got her pregnant. That is, if I believe her.

"Sammy, don't fret about it. It's fine. I'm a little surprised you decided to tell me like this, but really it doesn't matter one bit. You made the right decision and I guess you felt you had to make that decision on your own. It's okay. You don't have to feel guilty."

"*Guilty?* Is that how you think I feel?

"Well, I dunno you seem—"

"No Eric, I do not feel guilty. I feel bad because I let myself get knocked-up by the likes of you. By some bastard who thinks he can just fuck whoever he feels like and then simply toss them away. I was really starting to have feelings for you and as soon as I let myself do that, I found out you were *fucking* Esther behind my back. Esther of all people. And that was fine. I could deal with that, but of course, I just had to fall pregnant with your baby, didn't I?"

It's a good thing she's going to drama school, this is some of the most melodramatic, hammy bullshit acting I've ever seen. And I've been with some lunatics in my time, let me tell you. It's better if I keep quiet for a while and let her overblown emotions die down a little. I know it sounds a little harsh, but this whole scene feels false.

"When did you have the abortion?" I ask in a more serious tone, not trying to upset her any further without meaning to.

"About a month or so after the last time you fucked me. I was in Battleton, wondering whether I should tell you when I just happened to see you, with some blonde. It was then that I realised it wasn't worth telling you. As for Esther, well... I figured I couldn't hurt her as much as you eventually would, so I didn't bother telling either of you."

"It's no bother. I better go," Sammy had said. "I'll let you know if anything happens." She got up from the bench and straightened herself out. After pulling up her hair, she buttoned up her jacket and got as much mud off her trousers as she could. Then she took the spliff from my hand and helped herself. After a few tokes, she leaned into my ear and said, "Say hi to Esther for me," then kissed me. She looked me in the eye with a victorious vengeance and a satisfied glare. Indecent orgasms do that. "Don't worry, I'll keep this between you and me, Eric," she'd said, before winking at me and walking over the thousands of corpses under our feet.

"You've got nothing to say have you?" Sammy asks as the stillness of night settles around us.

It's so peaceful around this place that I feel out of my body. Each

43

sound echoes for a second and then dies. The whisky streams down my throat effortlessly, elbowing me on to light up another spliff. I say, "What else is there to say, Sammy? You had an abortion. Big whoop. Welcome to adulthood. Think yourself lucky that you weren't born fifty years ago. You'd have to give birth to a bastard then, or I'd have to push you down some concrete stairs or something."

"What the fuck is wrong with you? Do you know how difficult it was for me to tell you about this?"

"You made the right decision and I'm grateful for that. But I don't know how I should feel about it. I don't feel anything. You should've told me about it a long time ago. Better late than never, I guess. Did you tell all your friends about this?"

"All right Eric, I'm leaving. I thought you'd be more understanding than you're clearly capable of being. Say hi to Esther for me," Sammy says as she walks away from me again, this time without looking back.

As the gravel-crunched footsteps fade into the distance, I feel a blackout calling. The modafinil has worn off and there's a chill inside my bones. My spinal fluid feels weak, lacking. The gravestones around me all whisper out words which disappear into the air before I can gather what they are trying to say. For a moment, a flash of amber blinks at me in the distance. I unscrew the cap of my hipflask and raise it up to the stars, the mocking ghosts of the night sky, glaring inside of me with their non-existence. Two can play at that game, I'm going to drink until they all turn black.

"To nothingness," I say, to myself. And then swig, swig, swig, with my middle finger up to the stardust of what I'm made up from, hoping for a supernova that I know will never come.

"To you, my unborn child, I would've named you Mia Culpa. Where you are up there is what we spend our whole lives preoccupied over down here, so just trust me when I say you're better off having never been. I'll be joining you in the bliss of non-existence soon enough."

CHAPTER FIVE

Jessica's white-blonde hair almost glimmers under the reflection of the low-hanging moon. A few loose strands dance alone in the breeze, circling inside a rhythm that never seems to change. She can't face me. Or what's in her hand. We're sat next to each other, but notably apart at the same time. Cigarette stubs on the wood between us act as a boundary line whilst the capsized dinghy boat creaks with the slightest of nervous movements. We're waiting. Waiting for an answer that rests on a coin flip. Waiting to wake up from the nightmare of the last couple of months. In front of us there's a river, midnight blue in shade. Beyond its wide expanse, there's nothing but fog, thick in density, as idle as we are. The water seems to have layered everything with its darkened yet blueish hue, except for the blackened bridge above, silhouetted under the streetlamps lined across it. The one nearest me flickers on occasion, shrouding me in temporary darkness, but Jessica remains coated in light under an eternal interrogation, forever exposed and tainted. Smoke escapes from our mouths in long, never-ending streams. Each time mine touches hers they each evaporate into nothing, refusing to entwine. We haven't looked at each other since she came back. All that seems to move is the streak of her urine as it edges downwards towards the river, again with its own cloud of steam, making us even warier over what it wants to say.

It's yes or no answer will be washed away by the morning.

"Thanks for doing this with me again, Eric."

I mutter, "It's nothing," but the words are lost under my breath. Choked. Maybe because I know it's far from nothing.

"Are you sure it'll still work in the cold?" I ask, reaching inside my jacket, making my stretched leather echo.

"We'll find out soon enough."

I take out my hipflask and offer it to her first. She waves me off with a gesture I've seen before, mutters something herself, but I have no idea what. The other hand, the one holding her next move hasn't budged. It doesn't even shake like the rest of her. The test tightly gripped around her fingers seems frozen like the stillness of the water in front of us. It's remained face down, as equally unable to be glanced at as we are at each other. Whisky glides down my throat without the burn I was hoping for. In fact, it didn't seem to carry any sort of flavour at all.

"I think it's time," she says.

I say nothing in return, involuntarily shutting my eyes instead. Now she's standing, arms crossed, head pointing towards the ground. Her hair still hides her face. "Thanks for not asking me why I wanted to come here. It's just... I can't have my mother finding this thing. I know it's stupid, but with everything that's happened I just don't trust myself and with my head all over the fucking place I just—"

"You only need to twist your hand and look, Jessica," I say, my voice of command stunted by its jitter. "That's... it."

I'm standing now too. The movement felt too slow to describe, like a shifting of time you've already lived through. Jessica stands at an angle, her face still hidden, the gleam of the moon outlining the white of her skin, illuminating everything but blinding each feature. A simultaneous reveal of everything and nothing. Her hand twists as my heart thuds numb. Once fully-circled, she stares downwards. Then, nothing. She freezes. I go to move, but I'm stuck too.

"Jessica. What does it say?" I cry out, but it's distant and unheard, the sound lost inside the engulfing echo of my ears. "Jessica?!" I try to shout, but it only makes it less audible, akin to being underwater. The stick soon falls from her hand. It lands face-down. The shore, now spreading, washes it under its reflective black. As it pulls back, there's nothing left on the ground. Jessica swivels without making a movement. Her eyes focus on… nothing; they just shimmer with a vacant stare.

"There's nothing to worry about, Eric."

"What? What do you mean? Was it neg—"

"Just take a deep breath… and relax."

"What did it say!?"

"Just drift off. I loved every second of it, remember."

"Jessica?"

"You need not concern yourself, remember. I. Loved. Every. Fucking. Second. Of. It…"

She's dissipating. Disintegrating into the ether, a flake of skin at a time. My feet are locked into the ground, glued down by the mud. I reach out for her… but she… "Take a deep breath… right, *now*…"

Everything's turned black and white. Her inhale causes the water to ripple and a streetlamp above to flicker. My eyes have fogged over entirely, except for the intake of breath that lingers like a storm inside my ears. Each attempt to move is futile. A cold spreading slithers under my skin, swimming between my organs, leaving my blood frozen as it stretches outwards. Jessica finally blinks, each one drawing her closer, until we're face to face. Nothing about her is distinguishable though, and everything beyond her has blurred. "Remember, I loved every second of it," she whispers, her being now transparent, moving through me yet not moving at all. We're both becoming opaque... unable to blend together without disintegrating, which we cannot stop ourselves from doing. As one we disappear into the blackened distance along with everything else... all I can hear is deep breathing, but it's shallow and stuttered... quickening yet fading... swirling like the landscape, panicked and inconsolable... and my fault, it's my fault because I stayed silent, stayed hidden inside the silence of my own shadows, only to become a walking no man's land of my own making, the embodiment of a place I know but do not recognise, where once-believed thoughts wither and scatter in an ever-present debris, forever under attack by flashing lightning strikes of notions unknown, which by their nature prohibit any attempt of being glimpsed at, as they only ever vanish upon observation, making their presence known but their meaning a maintained anonymity, reminding me of all I once was whilst revealing everything I'll now never be as a direct, only ever seemingly uncorrelated consequence.

'Those who suffer from depression and anxiety often need regular repetition and reinforcement of the upcoming mental and emotional exercises to stimulate their super powerful subconscious minds. You have all the will and all the power necessary to make positive adjustments in your life. Now is the time to wake up that power and energy within you as you drift off into a deep, relaxing sleep. As you fully let go and allow your mind to slow—'

"What—"

'down—'

"The fuck..."

'And release all of that trapped negative energy—'

"Is this?"

'You can start focusing on making positive decisions right now. Find a time and a place to listen to this audio where you are unlikely to be interrupted, as the perfect induction depends on your complete attention.'

"Esther?"

"SSSSHHHH!"

It's her. Every huff, puff and blow-me-back-down is instantly recognisable to my ever-suffering ear now. How the fuck did she get in here?

'You need not concern yourself with the personality or complete lack of personality in my voice at this time. For it is of no consequence.'

"Esther, put a sock in this bitch."

"Shut up, I'm trying to sleep."

"So am I. And I *was* until you started—"

"*Ssshhh.* Just shut up and let me listen. It helps me."

"How did you get in—"

'Simply listen to my voice...'

"I borrowed your spare key—"

"Stole, you mean."

"SSSHHH!"

'Of peace and stillness and tranquillity.'

"Are you fucking serious, Esther?"

'Now listen very carefully to the following words—'

"You stole my key?! Right, turn that fucking thing off. I can't deal with it right now."

'Serenity.'

With my head pounding, I search for my phone, patting down around the mattress and the bedside table, where I normally leave it, but it's not there.

"Will you just let me *listen?* Why are all your clothes in the bathroom, and *muddy?*"

Shit. Forgot about that as well.

"I fell asleep in the park. Where's my phone?"

"In my hand, stupid. You fell asleep in the *park?* Why?"

"I was drunk. Give me the phone," I say, fondling a breast without meaning to.

'Peace and equilibrium—'

"Oi!" she says, slapping it away. "No! Why d'you want it so bad?" she asks in the same old pissed-off manner. She's made every word I utter into a trigger warning.

"Because I don't want to listen to this crap. Can't you put on some headphones or something? Jesus Christ," I say, fumbling around for the lamp, but too dizzy and pathetic to find it.

"Why don't you want me looking at your phone?"

I sigh, hard. "Not this again. I didn't say that. I said I don't want to listen to this crap."

"Why did you say, 'give me the phone' in that way though?"

"What in the hell are you talking about, Esther?"

"You always act weird when I have your phone. Go and have a shower babe," she says, kicking me out of the bed, "you smell like death."

"Well, maybe it's because you do shit like this when you have it," I say, clamping my hand on her foot. "Anyway, after your recent antics, all rights of access to my belongings have been rescinded."

"Well, maybe I do shit like this to see how you react."

"What? When I'm hungover and it's the middle of the fucking night?!"

'You should find yourself becoming empathetic with the words I am speaking to you.'

"The brainwasher's English is fucking all over the place, turn it off or put on some bloody headphones."

"Oh, all right fine, have it your way. *As usual,*" Esther says, slapping the phone onto my chest. "Fell asleep in the park... what a fucking *loser.*" She lets out an over-exhausted moan and turns to the side, grabbing more than her fair share of the duvet like always. I cut the mic on the mantra and look at the time.

"Jesus, Esther. It's 5:30 in the morning. Don't you ever think about anybody except yourself?"

"Oh, that's rich coming from you. You only got in about an hour ago. Too drunk to remember again? I've played it plenty of times before, but you were too wasted to notice. And thanks, you dick, now I won't be able to sleep."

"That's just what the cult leader wants you to think. Just have a drink or masturbate like the rest of humanity."

"That's your answer to everything. *Have a drink. Have a wank. Have a spliff.* I might as well be going out with an ape."

"Yeah, yeah."

"Go and shower!"

"All right fine, I will. Just for you my princess. I need a shit anyway," I say, sliding myself off the bed.

"TMI!"

"What?"

"Too Much Information. Don't you know that? Geez."

"Oh. That's *amazing* Esther. You've joined the whole mindless generation who mumble out their vacant rhetoric inside nothing but abbreviations and emoticons, who run away screaming at the sight of syllables, who end every empty, vacuous sentence they regurgitate out into the air with a preposition—"

"Speak English, Eric. No one can understand you."

"You're not a conglomerate corporation, Esther. Stop turning yourself into an app and lift your head up from the screen occasionally. I don't know, give nature a try or something."

She laughs in her *I-Can't-Believe-You-Just-Said-That* way and says, "Like what? *Like you?* Sleeping in a park like a bum? No thanks."

"Fine, have fun being a logo."

"Go and wash, you pathetic cunt," I hear trailing behind me as I head into the bathroom with my stomach rumbling. I wasn't lying when I said I needed a nice juicy alco-shit. After flicking the switch in the bathroom, the debilitating drone that comes along with it kicks into monotonous life. It puts a noise in your head like a bionic drone. Wouldn't be so bad if it turned off after I was done but the bastard takes about ten minutes after you switch it off to finally shut the fuck up. It's a perfect match for this bathroom though. The walls are streaked with a fluorescent orange whilst the cabinet above the sink and the borders of a tiny window in the corner have been painted chestnut brown; both badly. Its only redeeming feature is to be found inside the contents of the cabinet. Everything else about it makes me feel somewhat dirty, which is pretty ironic for a bathroom.

I plant my great white butt onto the toilet, adjust my position in preparation for the onslaught and let rip. My arsehole explodes like bullets from a blocked shotgun into the bowl, covering every inch and then some. The smell then rises from the gap in between my legs and invades my nostrils. Like a true soldier, I suck up the stench and let death take a joyride around my lungs for a bit. It makes me gag and I start coughing up a litter of phlegm babies, spitting them down between my pasty thighs.

After that, I punch in the pin of my phone. There's nothing. Not even a missed call from an unknown number. I guess my paranoia came from a past memory of Esther holding this very phone when Jessica decided to text me, which is another recollection best left un-recollected. It did serve Esther one great big excuse of woe-is-me attention though—her favourite kind. She lapped it up with aplomb upon the mere sight of Jessica's name. It's funny really. She went delirious over an ordeal she's never felt inclined to even ask me about. Not that I'd ever feel safe to tell her about it, but still.

It's almost as if I've been through all this before. Like life has just hit the repeat button and I'm locked inside the maze created by the choices I made back then.

And I for one cannot see any fucking exit.

"*Oh GOD. That stinks!* I think I'm going to be sick!" Esther wails through the walls, not caring whether she wakes up the neighbours.

I change the pin of my phone, hoping Sammy's lack of any further contact tonight is a sign of her having said her final piece. There's nothing else to be said or done between us. If she does get in touch again, I shall reply to her with the same silence she kept over this apparent abortion.

If she didn't tell you outta guilt, why did she fucking tell you about it then? What's more insulting to someone than treating them as if they don't even exist? Even a child would rather be abused than ignored. What makes you so sure that that child denied has really had its final say?

I flush the punished toilet.

"Finally! Fucking hell!"

It's quite fortunate that Esther decided to play away though. I don't even need an excuse as to why I've banned her from snooping at my phone. Not that it will stop her doing it with other things. You might wonder why I keep her around. Loneliness, I guess. Esther's right. I am a pathetic cunt.

Sammy, like Esther and all other wannabe actresses out there are nothing but a bunch of drama addicts when it comes down to it. They suck up and magnify the emotion out of any situation they find themselves in up until the point of hysteria and sometimes beyond, throwing out or pissing over all logic until the adrenaline wears off and they move on to the next distraction. Though I am a fan of acting, or maybe was, the real benefit from it was all that sweet, sweet crazy pussy. You really can't beat it. You can punch above your weight without even trying. All you need to do is pretend you're an emotional, sensitive, artistic type, step up on a stage and the crazy crumpet comes a running. I'm not proud of this observation, just merely willing to exploit it at any given moment. You don't even have to pretend in most cases. Just being in the class is enough to get some ass. It's great. *Until it isn't.* Getting the balance right of when to cut them loose is the tricky part. It still isn't as good as I hoped it would be though. I expected promiscuous behaviour to be the norm, you know, par for the course, something that is accepted, like the way most people pretend monogamy is viable in polite society. How wrong I was on that vantage point. Pretty fucking naive looking back at it now. In fact, they're worse than regular people in a lot of ways. Everyone in a drama group does indeed engage in looser behaviour, but no one is willing to acknowledge or admit it. Or worse, they flat out deny it. Take Sammy for instance. She got all pissed off when she found out I was dipping into Esther behind her back, but she had no quarrels about sleeping with a couple of blokes whilst she was away on holiday, which I found out about from other people's dirty gossip-obsessed mouths. But of course, the man is always the filthy bastard, isn't he, *my observer?*

The warmth of the water was tainted with the whisper of Sammy's grovelling voice. All the shit in my hair made a puddle of mud in the drain. It made me want to vomit. Consciousness was threatening to make an immediate comeback, so I turned up the heat to keep it at bay. The brown eventually cleared and left only a few shards of grass. After another piss, I stuck the plug in the hole and threw my trousers in. Nothing on my skin stung too badly, which was nice. Small blessings.

"Why aren't you at your dad's?" I ask, tying up my bathrobe whilst walking back into the living room, noticing Esther helping herself to my weed.

"He's a dick. It's his stupid new wife, she hates me. I just needed to get out of there for a while."

"So you just broke into my flat?"

"I didn't break in, babe. You're my boyfriend. Why don't you ever want to look after me?"

"Esther, the other day you said I was the worst thing that ever happened to you and that you never wanted to see me again. Oh, and then you told me you fucked some twat from your job."

"You told me you fancied my friends and that you wanted a threesome!"

"Yeah, so what? That's perfectly normal, whether you like it or not. If they like you and I like you, some attraction builds. It's just a fantasy. You slept with one of them after all, so you practically planted the seed in my head. I'm sure they're all just as annoying as you are after a while. I wouldn't even mind that much if you slipped away with a stranger, but you knew whatshisname from work. That makes it different and you fucking know it."

"I told you before, it was shit. Let's not talk about that now babe. I just didn't want to be alone, okay? Come back to bed with me, Eric."

"All right, fine," I say and slide into the bed. Esther hands me the spliff and I finish it off, hoping it's got enough of a kick to get me back to sleep. After stubbing it out, Esther places my hand on one of her goddamn perfect breasts. I give it a good, sensual squeeze, but she falls asleep after a minute or so. I think about masturbating over her arse for a while but decide not to bother. I hate to admit it, but I'm starting to get bored of chasing tail. Not just Esther's, but of all of them in general. Hedonism takes its toll after a while, and with an addictive personality, the pleasures you milk from it all start to turn sour, which are only ever replaced with newer, weirder and (most of the time) sicker desires to satisfy. Like any honest drug addict will tell you, the craving never really stops.

What you should've done dipshit, is invited the hot, fiery lesbian ginger slut over here without telling Esther. You know she wouldn't have said shit. After a few drinks, some smokes and a couple of pills, you could've done whatever you wanted. Think next time and grow a pair, faggot.

Still don't really remember how I got home. Obviously, I didn't sleep in a park. I woke up alone on what I think was the same grave that I fucked Sammy on, freezing my nuts off. Then again, standing under a streetlamp. It kept flickering on and off in a schizophrenic schism, like static sounds of Morse code from a side that's already lost. After it stopped, I saw a fox across the road. We stared at one another for a while, but it dashed off as soon as I moved. Like Esther does when she sees one of her illusions about to shatter.

Not sure what I should do about this Sammy situation. As satisfying as silence can be, it has been known to detonate in my face before. Seems rather odd that she wants to be back in contact with me after a year. Maybe having my abortion makes her feel closer to me or something. A matrimony of infanticide. She was only doing one of the foundation courses when I met her at the school. Meaning she had to wait a year before she could do the diploma. Perhaps that's why I've suddenly popped back into her brain. Most of our illicit romps took place inside that school. She really was so much better at fucking after she found out I was cheating on her. If you can handle the backlash, that really is the only way to get your woman to fuck you the way you want her to. Wound a woman's ego and all of a sudden, she's got something worth fucking for. That's what makes Esther so addictive. She fucks like the person you want to cheat on her with. God I'm a piece of shit. I just seem to be a magnet for these crazy bitches to latch onto. Maybe I should just blame my mother like everyone else does these days. I prefer not to though. What everyone seems to forget is that their parents also had parents and they too had parents and so on and so forth. Consciousness is the guiltiest mother of them all. I'd like to fuck her barren.

CHAPTER SIX

Esther places her cutlery down upon the plate like she just passed finishing school and leaves it balanced over her lap. "Thanks, babe. That was really nice."

"It was just ham and eggs, Esther. Nothing special," I say, sipping on my second coffee and smoking my third cigarette of the day already. The coffee could do with a little whisky.

"Babe..."

Oh, Christ. That inflection. That over-inflated vowel. That feigned note of warning, wrapped in a guise of concern. I've learnt to fear it. This isn't good.

"Yeah?"

"I had a dream."

"That's nice, babe."

"You were in it. But you weren't with me, you were just there. With someone else..."

"Okay. What happened in this *dream*?"

"Well, I was walking along the street, surrounded by really big buildings. Like skyscrapers or something. You know the ones, with reflective windows and stuff. Anyway, there was a big swimming pool in between both buildings, with a few blonde women inside, playing around with each other. All of them were fucking blonde. They kept giving me weird looks. Then, I saw you across the street. I waved but you just blanked me," she says, *actually* throwing me an accusatory glance. "Then you put your arm around some blonde woman and walked off in the opposite direction. I tried to get your attention by shouting but then a man turned up and told me to shut up. He scared me, so I tried to walk away but he kept following me. I ran and ran, and... well, that's all I remember. Don't you think that's weird? You with a blonde woman. She looked just like Jessica."

"Who?"

"*You* know who I mean. Little Miss Piggy had the same haircut, right?"

"I dunno, you didn't say anything about the style. Like a bob cut?"

"Yeah!" she says, pointing. "Like one of those stupid lesbo haircuts."

"Well, what can I tell you? Dreams are only ever about the person having the dream. Nothing else. Boring really."

"Why wouldn't you come to me though?"

I turn towards her. "Come again?"

"You just stood there, staring at me like you didn't even know me," she says, making a stupid face at me to let me know that she's upset.

"Do you want me to apologise? For not recognising you in your dream?"

"I just don't understand why you would do that."

"Do *what*?!"

"Just ignore me like I don't exist!"

"It was *your* dream. How can you expect me to do anything?!"

"I don't know. I just didn't like you in the dream. You were really cruel to me."

An involuntary scoff escapes my throat. "Are you fucking serious?!"

"Why would you do something like that?"

"Like what!? It was a dream. You can't hold something against me from a dream you had!"

"Why not? It was my dream and you were a prick."

"But it was a dream. In your head. Whilst you were unconscious. How can you *blame* me? No wait, how could you blame *anyone* for what they got up to in one of your fucking midnight movies? It doesn't make any sense."

"Well, I'm annoyed with you anyway. I *know* how much you liked that pig," she says, crossing her arms.

"This is all in your head, just like always. Abandon all logic, ye who enter that face."

"Don't say stupid things and *don't* point at me with your shitty fingers."

"Me?! I'm saying stupid things?! You're condemning me for a dream that you had. If that isn't the definition of stupid, then I don't know what is."

"Well, you were a dick in the dream, just like you are in reality. And don't pretend you didn't know I meant Jessica. You *knew.* I know you, *Eric Archer.*"

"I think I might have to put you away. You've clearly gone bat-shit crazy. You should get tested for syphilis or something. There's some kind of malfunction in your head."

The delicately balanced plate that was sat across her lap whisks over my head and smashes against the wall. Then the fork, followed by the knife. It's a good thing she does actually throw like a girl.

"You *ALWAYS* think about that fucking bitch, don't you?! I bet if she had a dream, you'd be all ears, on your knees grovelling and apologising and taking care of her! But with me, with *me* you just get your excuses in early and accuse me of being crazy. *I know I'm not crazy!* Why were you with her and not me!? Why won't you just forget about her and love me instead?! What's wrong with *me?!*"

Esther starts flailing her arms around like a baby that's just had its rattle nicked. Her eyes glisten in the light, ready for release. Her tits look awesome when she has a fit. They just bounce around in a smooth, consistent motion, like they're fighting it out for their freedom. There's just something about her being angry as well... so much venom and angst in it. Like all she's begging for is a good, hard fucking.

"Oh, my god, you've got a *boner*. *Why have you got a boner?!*"

Shit. Forgot to hide my shame whilst gawping at her.

"Dirty boner!" Esther screams and slaps down hard on my cock. And not in the good way.

"Oww, fuck! That hurt you lunatic."

"Why don't you ever take my pain seriously?! You're such a *cunt*. Look at you, with that, that... that big *boner*. You don't normally get hard so quick, probably because—probably because I'm not *blonde,*" she says, scrunching her lips and pouting; eyes feral like a rabbit with myxomatosis.

"Argh, Esther. I can't deal with this shit. It's too early and you're being completely irrational. Do you even *listen* to the words that come out of your mouth?"

"Aww... is your head hurting from all that drinking you did last night? Or maybe the night before? Or maybe the night before that? *No, no, no, I don't have annnnnnny problem with drinking whatsoever. Gulp, gulp, gulp. I just do it for fun. Gulp, gulp, gulp. Oh no, now my dick isn't working. Never mind 'eh? Gulp, gulp, gulp,"* she says, making mock swallowing sounds, gallivanting around the room like she's drunk, which I wish she was. Well, if she wants to play Punch and Judy:

"Oh, no I bad *dwweeaaam. Whawhawhawha.* Somebody listen to my stupid dream where my boyfriend acted really mean. *He's a nasty drunk meanie.* And now I must cry at every possible moment that upsets me. Who needs justification to feel upset? If you just feel upset, it's just perfectly fine to act like a complete bitch. That'll make everything just dandy! I'm okay, you're okay. Everybody's okay. But when I'm not okay, everyone else better not be fucking okay either. Especially you! Yay, I've found equilibrium! Someone buy me some flowers!

Yay!!!"

"You're such a fucking *dick*. I hate you."

Esther grabs her coat whilst I sit down on the bed, pouring some much-needed Jack into my coffee. I must have seen her have these outbursts at least a thousand times by now. Maybe I have become colder or something but, to be honest, she sucked out all the sympathy in me after a few months of being with her. Every time she seems to settle down, one tiny little thing starts her off again. It's no wonder daddy didn't want her in his flat; she just wants to create chaos out of nothing at any given moment.

"I don't want to stay in this shitty little flat any longer anyway," she says, wrapping on her coat, looking around the floor for her shoes. "I can barely breathe in this dump. Look at that mould on the wall. It makes me feel sick. Oh, and by the way, your ham and eggs were *shit*."

"I don't doubt that. They've been in the fridge for months."

"*Argh!*" Esther screams. "Here's your fucking spare key," she says, throwing it at me, this time landing a hit on the top of my skull. She laughs at me for a bit, staring into my eyes in a feverish glee, like she's won something. Then she darts across the room and slams the front door as she leaves. If my neighbours hate me it's justified.

Well, at least that problem is sorted out for another week. I check the part of my head Esther hit and find that I'm bleeding a bit. Definitely should've masturbated over her last night. Oh well. I'm sure Esther is subconsciously hoping that one day I'll lose it and give her a good slap. My god, it would feel great. I refuse to give in to that urge though. Not that she doesn't deserve a nice smack. More because afterwards she'd have my testicles in the palms of her harassing hands. I'd never hear the end of it. She was right about the mould, but it's barely noticeable. I'm sure she only saw it because she was actively seeking it out. I guess we all do that though. Anyway, the coffee has finally served its purpose. I'm perking up. I'll have a couple more cups with my remaining whisky and milk myself out before heading out to the streets with little to no reason for being there.

***

I decided to go for a swim in the end. It's something that I used to do quite a lot a couple of years back. Can't particularly say that it was worthwhile, albeit for the five minutes of peace it provided. Seeing that I'm a heavy smoker and ditto drinker, it seemed better for me to go into the slow lane, as the faster one would have just been embarrassing. What a royal fucking mistake that was. Some whale got in there with me after my first lap, all geared up; swimming cap, goggles, plastic water bottle, the whole kit and caboodle. It was almost as if she thought that by having all the paraphernalia that it somehow made her a credible swimmer. She just floated on the spot the whole fucking time like a legless, mutated toad, using her fat as a lilo ring, like being in the water considered her to be swimming. Then some old bloke, with a back so hunched over it looked like he'd spent his entire life trying to nosh himself off jumped in and slowed it down even more. Then another one got in. And another. And then naturally, a few fucking more. It was disgusting. Ruined my whole experience. Every time I nearly let it go, one of them would let out a long, coarse exhale and start coughing up a lung. Then, like some mutiny against people who actually went there to swim, they'd all just sit or stand at the end of each lane, breathing in and out violent gusts of every possible lung disease you could imagine. Not a shred of consideration whatsoever, just there because they could be, all trying to score themselves another few more measly days on this miserable planet.

Gave up in there in the end and bombed into the free-for-all section. I enjoyed releasing all the air from my lungs and sinking to the bottom. There's something so comforting about being surrounded by nothing but water. I like hearing the muffled sounds of the outside with no obligation to try and make sense of them. It's the only time I ever seem to feel calm.

"You're here early tonight, Eric. Rough day?" asks Lucy, already pouring me a pint of the black stuff.

"Just another day, Luce. Not bad, not good. Just another day. You?" I ask, watching the pump get pulled down and the beautiful juices begin to flow. Got to hand it to her, she pours an immaculate pint.

She pauses. "Same old, really." Shrugs. "Had a bit of an argument with Jack." Scrunches her nose. Mmm.

"Oh?"

"Nothing serious, he can just get a little jealous is all."

"You mean possessive, but yeah, I hear you."

"Maybe, yeah," she says and places my beer on the mat.

If I was rich, I'd hire Lucy, make her wear the kinkiest, weirdest outfits imaginable and train her to pour whatever drink I wanted with nothing but a variety of different looks. No speaking whatsoever. I'd pay her in tattoos and plastic surgery, build her up into a perfect suicide girl and trade her in the day after her thirtieth birthday.

She turns around and starts serving somebody else without realising that I didn't pay for the drink. Or maybe she knew. Who knows? She's put on a few pounds since we last slept together. Suits her. The arse looks all peachy, more slapable and shakeable during penetration. She looks over her shoulder and catches me looking. It makes her smile. If I was drunk enough, I might be able to pretend she was new. Maybe.

Why is it that every chick I hook up with starts off with so much potential, only to cave in and cling on to their goddamn withering adolescence and morph me into their emotionally-absent father? I thought the feminist movement would've inspired so many more women to take ownership of themselves, not carry on seeking approval through the perverted eyes of a fucking man. Where's all the Simone De Beauvoirs, the Kate Millets, the Edith Piafs? I'm always on the lookout for you, so where the fuck you at? Are you all just myths of my imagination? Where's the woman looking to make mince out of my meat, who challenges my low-rent predispositions, the Cleopatra who brings out the maniacal genius in me, so that together we can rip the world a new one!? All I'm surrounded by is the weak and the pathetic, a bunch of goddamn sheep who've sold themselves out for sympathy vouchers and weekend spa getaways. Seeking out all their substantiation through the fucking flash of a camera and a few virtual thumbs ups. Well, guess what, idiot? One day you're going to wake up to realise that you are nothing but that flash, a single cell that only spreads itself in order to get pumped.

Question! Who the fuck wants equality inside a capitalist regime in the first place?

Answer: *You.* You fucking do, you bunch of detestable plebs. You traded in freedom of thought for the liberation of speech, only to find that you've got nothing to say and then went ahead and censored that out as well, you liberal buffoons. You failed to realise that the capitalist system depends on that very fucking inequality to function. If one cunt won't work for less than another, then the whole game is up! Oh, fuck this, there's something wrong with my glass.

Rant over.

I jiggle my empty pint glass in the air until Lucy notices and starts pouring me another, post-haste. My good little maid. If she gives me this one on the house it definitely won't be a coincidence. She had a coy expression in her eyes earlier, especially when I was checking out her arse. A look I know all too well. The guarantee. She's on the prowl, looking out for a bit of *'screw-my-stupid-boyfriend'* side action on the sly. What kind of man would I be if I didn't indulge her request? She's all on her little lonely tonight, reading a book instead of playing about on her phone. I must reward this sudden change of perception.

You don't know me, but I'm already inside of you.

The decisive moment arrives. Lucy walks over and places the beer in front of me. She looks at me and then at the till. She presses a button on it. The register pops open. She looks at me again, then presses it shut, bites her bottom lip and sucks in some saliva through her teeth, maintaining the eye contact.

Jackpot baby.

CHAPTER SEVEN

The bubble effect of modafinil is its USP. I'm sure it would have been marketed like that if all drugs were legal like they should be. It makes you interested in everything and committed to nothing, like the wonder of a child's imagination. You just drift along inside a cloud, prepared to face anything life throws at you because you know you're not really here nor there. This room gives me a glimpse of what it must be like to have echolocation as a sense. I can feel the vibrations of the spluttered-out emotions, the uttered tight-breaths of trauma, the hot and bothered warmth still emanating from the arse of the last person who was sat here, now warming up my own.

"So yeah," I say. "I'm not sure what I make of this whole abortion lark. Seems like a pretty funny time to tell me about it, nearly what, a year after the fact."

"How do you feel about it?" asks Frank, sipping on a cup of coffee. I get the sense he's observing me more than listening, looking out for unconscious betrayals of how I really feel. Without really knowing what to say, I just shrug, wondering just how honest I should be. "You must feel something about it, I'm sure," he repeats, "that is, if you feel okay to talk about it."

Frank takes another gulp. Man, I wish he'd offer me a cup, I'm dying here. He sits there basking in the silence, twirling the foot of his crossed-over right leg. I'm unsure if I've ever just sat here in this chair, saying nothing. My head hurts from all the relentless drinking I've been doing since last week. I only left my flat to get more booze. Other than that, it was a whole week of isolation, watching increasingly depraved pornography and gorging myself stupid on deplorable hamburgers and microwave pizzas that only ever seem to burn your tongue. The little money my parents left me is dwindling down rapidly, but in truth I'm not even bothered by it. Money can suck it along with everything else.

"Well, you know how I feel about procreation already. I don't want to breed, so I guess I got my wish. I'm not entirely sure if I feel anything about it. Except stumped."

"When did... she tell you about it?"

"Urm. About a week ago. A week today in fact, a few hours after our last session."

"And this she is..."

"Sammy."

"Oh... you haven't mentioned this person before, have you?"

"No. I didn't think I'd ever need to bring her up, but well, here we are."

"And who is she, exactly?" Frank asks.

"Not sure myself. We were seeing each other for a while about a year after Jessica and I fell apart. I didn't think it was serious. We only hooked up a few times, on and off, you know? I thought we were both just playing the field, that kind of thing. Now she comes back to tell me she pulled the plug on a foetus I never knew existed."

After a slurping sip, Frank says, "Do you suppose she felt obligated to tell you?"

"Maybe. I can see how it must have been hard for her to tell me, but I'm finding myself questioning why she bothered to. It all seems a bit redundant now."

"Do you still see her?"

"Not really. She was calling me recently, which I didn't reply to, but then she found me in my local haunt."

"Does Esther know about this?"

"Fuck no," I say, letting out a laugh. "I don't think she'd take it all that well."

"And how are you taking it? What are your thoughts?" Frank asks, prodding me for an emotional outburst. "You seem agitated."

"Do I? I'm not even sure if I believe her. Something about it seemed off. I don't know. It's difficult to explain. I think I'm more bothered that she didn't tell me right away. She was worried about the *chance* of it happening, I remember that much, and I said that I'd be there for her, whatever that meant, but she left it, got shot of it and decided to wait until now to tell me. Doesn't really add up."

"I imagine it must be very difficult for women to go through with that kind of procedure, biologically as well as mentally. Maybe she needed time."

"I can empathise with that, Frank. I dunno. I'm aware I sound a bit paranoid, but something was off. Most confessions, in my experience, only ever shield the bigger picture."

"Meaning?"

"A few weeks before I finished drama school for good, Sammy suddenly started showing interest in a more permanent, exclusive relationship. I was a fortnight away from performing in a play for a week-long run when Sammy announced she was going on holiday and would miss it. No big deal. On the last night of the run though, she turned up. A romantic gesture, one might think, assuming the subterfuge was intentional, which she more than encouraged me into believing. With me so far?"

Frank nods, then proffers a hand for my recommencement.

"A week of bountiful blow jobs later, a girl from her group pulls me aside for a word. Turns out, she didn't actually plan on flying home that day at all. In fact, it transpired that during her 'terribly dull, unremarkable' holiday that she copped off with not only one, but two strapping young lads. At the same time, no less. So, her romantic gesture turned out to be nothing but a ruse for her indecent antics, shall we say. Not that I condemn women for indulging in such things, but considering she told me she was 'falling' for me just before hopping on a jet to mount double-dong island, you'll have to forgive me if I find her word to be suspicious."

Franklyn plonks his coffee cup down and crosses his legs. He's wearing a mustard-yellow pair of khaki's today. They don't look good. "Did you ever confront her about this?"

"No. I slept with Esther instead. Then I started dating her exclusively whilst keeping Sammy on tap. I'm not proud. That's why I think this abortion could be safeguarding something else. If it ever happened or indeed was even mine. Anyway, that's enough conjecture for one session." I begin laughing again, before saying, "It did inspire me to watch a lot of pornography featuring pregnant women though. Usually a solo, cam-girl show, but there was one I watched a few too many times, starring a Japanese woman just spraying milk from her breasts for a full-on ten minutes. Take from that what you will."

Frank picks up his coffee again and we both sit there, pondering the moment away. He always goes quiet whenever I mention porn.

"It concerns me that you don't seem to take anything seriously, Eric. What you just told me isn't something that most people just brush off their shoulders, as if it's nothing."

"I don't agree, Frank," I say, sipping up some water from my glass. "Plenty of things concern me. It concerns me that people breed without a second thought as if it's an innate birthright. Like that shit a lot of breeders say, that the worst thing that can ever happen to a parent is the loss of one of their kids. As if that outcome isn't written in stone the moment its plopped onto the planet."

"The loss of a child is arguably one of the worst things that can happen to a parent."

"Only the egomaniacal, narcissistic self-righteousness of a breeder could ever possibly think of the death of a youngster as a tragedy. Yeah, sure, they'll give you the whole song and dance about the life they could've had had they lived, as if it wouldn't have been full of suffering, but the main reason they're pissed off is that they've been deprived of the witness to their own death. A blood-related witness no less. What kind of sick shit is that? If anything, it's better to die young. The younger the better. Probably just before you hit double-digits. The world's still full of mysticism then. The bullshit your parents taught you hasn't started to stink yet. The idiotic walking shadow with his tale of sound and fury has yet to step up onto the stage. Most people only have kids so they can relive their own childhood through their eyes, if not their whole life. The kid itself is irrelevant. That's the real fucking tragedy. Reproduction is the purest act of sadism nature ever came up with, next to consciousness, of course."

Frank says nothing but looks a little taken aback. I'm watching the water swirl around the glass I'm twirling. Above the rim of the glass in front of me, Franklyn crosses his arms and clears his throat. "Sorry, Eric. I'm at a loss for words," he says, the hint of concern seasoning his inflections.

I break out of my trance by gulping down the rest of the water and putting it back down. Then I let out a little chuckle. "D'you want to know what my old man thinks of therapy?" I ask, back to normal Eric, not the Anti-Life Eric that occasionally creeps through the cracks of this charade. If you're a pessimist, take my word for it, most of the time you best keep your fucking mouth shut.

"What does he think?"

"That it's a load of old bollocks," I say with a smile.

Frank laughs. I guess through a sense of relief, but still, it's the first time I've heard it. I almost feel blessed. How pathetic.

"Do you think his opinion has influenced yours?"

"Yeah, of course. But I'm probably even more extreme than him. I think everything is a load of old bollocks. Hence why I'm one lonely fuck."

"What do you mean?"

"You either jump on the mythical bandwagon or get left behind to rot on your own. As if we're not all decaying as it is. You can't say shit like this to the average asshole. Take what you do for a living, for example. On one hand, you could say that with years of investigation and analysis, psychology would've established a fully-rounded understanding of the human condition and could credibly assist and make sense of it, in some sort of way. On the other hand, you could sum it all up with a stamp collection made up of nothing but labels. Labels which indeed get updated on a year-by-year basis, depending on their validity. You work in a psych-ward full of schizophrenics, don't you Frank?"

"Yes. Every other weekend I visit people with severe mental disorders and yes, most of them are schizophrenics."

"Okay. But there isn't just 'schizophrenia' is there? How many different subtypes does it have? From my understanding, there's Paranoid, Disorganised—which, seeing as the etymology of schizophrenia comes from schism, meaning split, is sort of already implied, don't you think? Anyway, let's see... then there's Catatonic, Residual and then, my personal favourite, *Undifferentiated* schizophrenia, which alone is enough to make one paranoid, don't you think? That one implies that the patient shows all the signs of the formerly mentioned types, but not enough to be labelled with one, so he or she gets slapped with that one, like an *until further notice* sign of apology. That's like saying, we know something is wrong with you, but we don't know what yet, so let's wait until you have a mental breakdown and then, we'll see."

"I don't think I'm following the point you're trying to make, Eric," says Frank, crossing his arms again.

"What I'm trying to say is, is that maybe schizophrenia is just a normal reaction to the insanity all around us. In the times of old, if someone started preaching about how god is speaking through them, everyone believed him to be a prophet. If I was to do the same now, you'd say I was a lunatic. Delusions are one of the symptoms of schizophrenia, right?"

"Yes. It's sort of funny that you mentioned that actually because the DSM-5 rescinded the subtypes of schizophrenia, due to misdiagnosis," says Frank, checking out the ceramic clock on the fireplace.

"Well, there you go then. Thank you for proving my point. But what is a delusion? We're all fucking deluded on this planet, it's a prerequisite trait for survival. We willingly hoodwink ourselves into believing *anything* just to get by."

Frank slides up his seat a touch and says, "Do you ever wonder why I mentioned that I work with schizophrenics?"

"No. Well, yeah I guess so, seeing as I'm nattering on about it now."

Franklyn goes silent after one of his annoying, 'give that some thought' looks.

"If you're trying to insinuate that I display the same characteristics, I'd most likely agree with you, Frank. Though I prefer you to be more faithful to your namesake. Give it to me straight, you know? I know you're trained to edge me towards the truth of my condition, assuming I have one, by duping me into believing I arrived there all by myself, but I can't see any difference between that and manipulation. All I'm saying is that there's an enormous difference between people who are obviously mentally ill and the average arsehole walking the streets. I'd even argue that most of us are mentally-ill, so what good is sticking a label over everyone? I'll tell you what it's good for. Business. That's all it ever boils down to, isn't it? Instead of listening to anyone who may rightly be severely depressed by being dumped onto this dubious planet, let's just brand them for the unwanted cattle that they are and throw 'em some pills. What's that? You're suicidal? Don't matter, take one of these and pick up that box over there, we've got a world to keep spinning here, son. You've got a birth certificate, a nationality and whatever god's in fashion, what more d'you want? If it works for us, then it should work for you. That kind of attitude doesn't sit well for the enterprise of life. Show some fucking gratitude."

Argh. I've depressed myself into needing a drink once again. I'm starting to wonder whether I do this on purpose.

"I still think we should perhaps consider upping your sessions..."

My mouth falls agape.

"Are you taking the piss, Frank?" I ask, my laughter rippling through the words.

"No. I'm being very candid with you Eric, as you are with me. It's not the first time I've recommended it."

"Do you really think this is working for me, Frank? I mean, come on, let's be honest here. We're just going around and around and around in circles, going over the same old shit in an endless loop. This entire process alone is enough to make anyone go nuts."

Come on Archer, man the fuck up. What the hell are you doing? The booze is coming baby, don't sweat it. Quit grinding ya teeth. Sit up straight. You're making no sense again. Say what you mean, not what you mean to say.

"Eric? Are you feeling okay?"

"Fine," I say, wiping my right eyelid that's suddenly begun twitching. I'm sure Frank's noticed, he's been crossing his arms and legs today like a pissed-up Punch and Judy. *Everybody* notices shit like that, *everybody* judges, *everybody* watches over everything, *plotting and scheming and conspiring.*

My nails have dug into the armchair. Rubbing the tendons in my face doesn't help as much as it used to. Lakes of salt pour down both sides of my ribcage. Damn these prescription drugs. Frank's fingers are locked inside of themselves. With some apprehension, he looks at the clock. I'm looking at him like a doting son, who knows he's a failure. I'm nothing but transference.

"You laugh quite a lot during serious discussions. Have you ever noticed that?" Frank asks.

My phone treads on the boards of our two-man mime play. An unremitting vibration, impregnating the pauses between the two of us. This has happened before as well. My phone goes off and we both sit here, with neither of us acknowledging it.

What remains unsaid creates the ghosts you'll be forever haunted by.

I know what's going to happen. I'm going to get up and leave but for the first time, I don't want to. Another nobody with nowhere to go. I'm going to hit the bottle again. I can feel my veins screaming for their fix. It's feeding time. Just need to wait it out. My emotional baggage is so much easier to carry when I pour booze on top of it. Then I'll go back to the cave I unshackled myself from, maybe with a stranger, only to return and look away from the light that is just too vibrant to stare at for long.

"I don't know. Maybe I do. I just feel as if I'm slipping away these days, like the potential I once thought I had, never was... and what remains, constantly stares back at me, refusing to look away."

"And what is that?" Frank asks.

"I'm not sure. Reality? Maybe the past? Something about Sammy coming back felt like... I don't know. I'm starting to sound crazy, but it feels like each time I walk away from the past, it's already waiting around a corner somewhere, hiding in plain sight, biding its time, seducing me with an empty promise."

"I'm not sure that I follow you."

"Same here," I reply, laughing again. I'm not sure what's funny though.

Franklyn breaks the union of his fingers, looks at the carpet for a little while, then aside at the clock and says,

"I think we better call it a day for this week, Eric. What do you say?"

Drinking time.

I get up from my chair and leave without another word. The cold breeze in the air is a welcome relief to my booze sweat-slathered skin. Frank must be sensing my resentment towards him it seems, despite offering nothing but a further dent to my bank balance, I find him more than standoffish these days. Pointing out the cracks in his methods only leads him to project them back onto me. That's my main beef with therapy, it all just falls back to the authority figure bullshit, with him forever in the right and I forever in the wrong—

-SMACK-

And down to the floor I go, along with some woman who just crashed into me out of nowhere. I spring myself up and hold out my hand, when I realise it's the same woman I bumped into when I vowed to quit therapy, only for a boomerang abortion to send me back here. "Fucking hell, lady. Don't you ever watch where you're going?"

"Me?" she replies, snatching at my hand rather than gripping it. "You practically assaulted me!" I pull her up by her forearm and find myself standing a little too close to her. She starts laughing, either at the observation I just made, or the ridiculous comment she just spewed.

"As they say in the movies, we really must stop meeting like this," I say, engaging Suave as Fuck Eric for her entertainment, taking a small step back. "Are you okay?"

"Yes, I'm fine thanks. You're right this time, it was my fault. I didn't see you rushing down those steps."

"Funny that we keep bumping into each other. Even funnier that it's literal."

"You're not shy, are you? Quite the flirt, in fact."

"If the moment suits, sure I am."

"You do realise I'm old enough to be your mother, right?"

"It didn't stop Oedipus."

"Oh, god. You're terrible," she says, radiating, oblivious to how correct she is. "Listen, it was nice bumping into you again, literally and all, but I really must get going."

"Third time lucky, then."

She looks away to the side, her cheeks blossoming brighter than her lips. I'm surprised she doesn't have the confidence her looks would suggest, but then again, that always works to a man's advantage. At the beginning at least anyway.

"They say it's a charm," she replies after hesitating and then slowly begins to stride away, flicking her eyes back with the same glimpse as before, though dilated now because of the confirmed attraction on my part. A playful wave departs us as she crosses the road.

I don't really know why I decided to blatantly flirt with her so much. Not sure if it really pulled off like I was certain of before. At least I made myself clear, I suppose, but really, adding another woman into the chaos of my existence doesn't seem like the right move to make. I guess it doesn't matter, seeing as I doubt I'll be returning to these parts anytime soon. Maybe I'm missing mother. Or maybe I'm missing a mother replacement of whom I'm able to fuck. Maybe just a woman with sense, one who has seen the drawbacks of life and been subjected to them personally, who doesn't place so much goddamn fucking importance on trivial things such as emotions and ovaries. I hope I do meet her again though, that mysterious blonde. There's just something about her I haven't seen in any other person before, something hidden and beyond my reasoning. I despise the notion of fate, but it just so happens to feel that way, like it's meant to be. It isn't because I haven't bedded older women before either, it's just something about her I don't quite yet understand. Hopefully the circumstances will have vastly improved by the next time we 'bump' into each other. Somehow, though, I doubt they will be. Let's face facts, that woman is way better off never knowing who I really am. But that isn't to say she can't fuck whoever I pretend to be.

CHAPTER EIGHT

Esther was the one trying to call me during my session, right on schedule as always and not for the first time this week. It's one of her feigned displays of respect, which now only ever serves as an inadvertent warning sign. She's only calling because she made the mistake of tossing away the key she fought so hard to get from me. What a silly little merry-go-round she lives in. She's probably sitting outside my front door right now, cleavage pushed and pussy waxed. Despite the temptation to fuck the night away and my even more overwhelming desire to go home, I've nipped over to Queen's park instead. It's on the way back to mine. Sort of. Dealing with Esther right now is just beyond my capability. I could probably tell her about the abortion without her realising that it happened whilst we were together, but I don't think that'd matter much to her anyway. All it would do is serve for a fantastic excuse for her to milk all the attention out of it for herself and spurt it into my face. Fuck that.

There's some fat bloke sitting on a bench directly opposite me, beyond the playground full of hysterical children and rabbiting mothers. I guess everyone here suspects him of being a pervert. He reminds me of Esther's father, though whether he's a perv or not I couldn't tell you. I doubt it though. He's just another balding bloke bearing the weight of life's burdens through his beer gut. Quiet, unassuming and ultimately harmless. That's what I gathered from meeting him a couple of times anyway. He rang me once to ask where Esther was. Like I had any idea. It was a strange experience, being asked by someone's father on the whereabouts of his own daughter. If it wasn't Esther, maybe I'd have been surprised. Or concerned. She's been playing stunts like that for years, leaving him alone in an empty house without knowing where she's gone or what she's up to, forcing him to worry about her for little to no reason at all. A million passive-aggressive *fuck you's* later and she still continues to do it; blaming him for her mother leaving, for never changing his ways, for not being paid enough to support them and blah-de-blah-de-blah-fucking-blah. The sad part about the phone call was when he asked me not to mention it to her. According to Esther, he stalked her mother for a while during their separation by sitting outside their house inside his car for hours upon end, watching her leave with a different bloke every other night. He did that for two years apparently. It creeped me the hell out that phone call, like I was talking to the person Esther secretly wants me to be. I won't ever tell her about it, but I do wonder what he would've said had she been there with me when he called.

Nothing similar will happen between Esther and me. We're not even fond of each other; just in some mutual, guilt-ridden debt towards one another. Guilt over the betrayals and hurt we've caused, the headaches and turmoil of not being compatible, blaming each other for the same things we refuse to acknowledge about ourselves. We're holding on to letting go. After that, we'll never see each other again, but for now, we're just safely hate-fucking our relationship out. Saying that though we haven't done anything sexual for close to a month.

People with exceptionally strong beliefs in *anything* betray a truth about their own identity that they simply refuse to see or maybe can't even see. Esther's got an obsession that I'm using her for sex, yet it's abundantly fucking clear that she uses sex as a weapon against me. Not just me— that'd be flattering myself—she does it with every man I'm sure. My notion is that she has always felt that men will use her for sex regardless of what she does. It's how she's seen, and she acted upon it by prostituting herself. Most prophecies are self-fulfilled I suppose. I can't even bring myself to imagine the vast array of vile men she must have encountered during her time as a hooker. Her mother once asked her to do it with her for some extra cash, if you can believe it. If that isn't fucked up beyond all recognition, I don't know what is. She took it surprisingly well though, and we laughed about it for hours. At the time, I did wonder whether they'd go for some sort of two-for-one, mother/daughter special. In fact, I still wonder about it now. Christ... pornography has ruined me.

Even though I don't want to see her, I'm missing Esther right now. Missing the misery and the distractions, missing her reassurance of what a sack of shit I am. If I could just find a way to tame her, to beat her into subservience and gratitude, then there just might be a chance for us. About a fortnight or so ago she inspired my epic plunge into pussy unknown by confessing that some douchebag in her job bought her flowers and how I never do things like that because I'm not romantic enough. Then she told me that she fucked the guy, but it's okay, she didn't enjoy it because his cock looked like a sausage roll. I don't even care that she cheated on me, but I do care that she did behind my back, clandestine style. If she just told me she was thinking of doing that, I'm sure we could've come to an arrangement. A betrayal is deprived of its thrill without a partner's ignorance, I guess. I'd love the honest Esther to come out and introduce herself to me some time. I know she's in there somewhere, lurking behind the persona she wants others to believe in. An honest evil will always trump a feigned truth in my book. We could've built a trust beyond the human imagination. Argh, there I go again, fantasising my life away. What an idiot I truly am. I don't even know if I agree with my own thoughts anymore. They seem to just cascade around my head without rhyme or reason, neither by mistake nor by design, just fruitless, decaying seeds of pointless matter, as aimless as nature is indifferent. What's the matter? asked Mr Hatter. Matter, Mr Hatter, is all I am and yet, I don't matter. That's what's the matter, Mr Hatter.

Mothers are now ushering their children away from swing sets and climbing frames. Some of the breeders are shouting, unknowingly announcing their social class. Which child belongs to which womb isn't all that obvious though. Kids just don't have a social class, but the labels they'll be stamped with are spat upon and forever sealed by the tainted saliva of their creators. Before long they'll unknowingly take up the roles written for them long before they were even born. This life is more scripted than any of us can truly appreciate.

Richard, the guy Sammy mentioned back in the pub, would be licking his lips at the sight of this place. Just before we left the school, he told me that he loved single mothers and pragmatically sought them out; naturally online. When I asked him why he said that because of their status most of them are only ever looking for a quick lay and that they're reserved about getting serious with a guy because of their kids. So, basically, he enjoys getting in there with them for a quick nut 'n go. If any of the women ever got serious, all he had to do was point a finger at one of the kids and bolt. At least he's honest about it I suppose, but I strongly doubt he's upfront with the *Just Get Over Here and Fuck Me Already* single mothers. The bullshit people tell themselves is truly astounding.

I appear to have drunk most of my whisky already and stubbed out enough cigarettes for a tobacco plant to take root. It's also darkened into a post-happy-hour hue. The whistling breeze rustling the leaves above me are the only voices keeping me company, along with the occasional bug that creeps through the blades of unkempt grass. Distant streetlamps must've flickered on without my notice, but the few which stand inside the park remain idle and lifeless. I think I've waited around long enough for Esther to have scrambled away from my doorstep.

As I get up my left leg buckles under my own weight. I didn't even realise it was asleep. Attempting to shake it off causes it to tremble, almost like it's not part of me. As I go to walk down the hill, the gate in the distance shielding my point of exit clangs open, diagonally opposite where I entered. A young woman clambers through, shortly followed by a man. Her man, going by their body language. Both are in tracksuits, but the only running seems to be her fleeing from him. She walks frantically, hand-gesturing for the guy to fuck off whilst he makes similar pleas for her to hear him out. When I hit the path, they disappear from my sightline. I look briefly over my shoulder and consider taking the other exit just to avoid crossing their path. But why the fuck should I? Instead, I continue forward, finishing off the bottle for what I hope is unnecessary courage. As I dump it in a nearby bin along the way, I hear a harsh, well-struck slap. It silences the wind and seemingly shakes the leaves somehow. Clouds crackle above. Light flashes beyond them but remains hidden behind their industrial grey. The woman shoots around the corner, slapping outstretched shrubbery with one hand, clasping her cheek with the other. Tears scatter away from her eyes, tired tears which seem to follow the streaks of the last time she cried. They're matched by the shaking of her limbs as her muscles reinforce previously imprinted memories, daunting her with the realisation of how she'll never escape what she's become. She avoids my sightline but makes what I can only assume are intentional sobbing sounds and tantrum-like grunts, Esther-esque echoes.

"Are you alright?" I ask, confused by my own impulse and why I'm making out as if I don't know. She halts as our profiles meet but says nothing, watching me out of the corner of her eye. Her tracksuit probably once fit her but now it exposes her feeble state. She could easily hide behind most of these trees. Twig on twig camouflage. The hand covering her cheek does little to shield the blossoming of a fresh, if not updated bruise. She's shrunken into herself without much else left to shrink. "What happened?" I ask, hearing it as if through the ears of another, turning towards her as I do. Her tied-back chestnut hair is now layered with spittle. She winces as it caresses her swollen eye, which I now notice is struck by a lightning strike of blood vessels. Gravel-crunching footsteps walk into our vacuum of silence. The guy swings around the corner, tending to a ring on his finger by spitting and rubbing at its base with his thumb.

"Oi! Where da fuck d'ya fink ya goin'?" he cries out, stomping his wayward march towards us. "Who's dis cunt?"

Instead of speaking, I continue looking into the blood rippled eye. Maybe I've lost my mind.

Losing your mind is the only freedom you've got, Eric. Aren't you as sick to death of bowing down to these vacuous cunts as I am? I know you are. If you're so suicidal, fucking prove it already. Embrace the lunacy so many others deny. It's the only liberation there is, and you fucking know it deep down. Look at this chimpanzee with his chest-beating façade of intimidation. Any faggot can beat up a woman. Let's give him a little bit of what for.

"OI! I'm fuckin' talkin' to you ya skank!" he says, only a few feet away now. The girl closes her eyes in anticipation of another strike. "Dat's me bird, mate. Fuckin' scarper already!" he says, reaching his right arm out and yanking a clump of her hair. The girl snatches at his hands, trying to pry herself free whilst he attempts to drag her backwards. I pivot slightly to my left, appearing like I'm about to walk away. "Dat's wot I fought. Now fuck off faggot. Do one!"

I clench my fist until my arm starts shaking—lean towards the left—hear the leather around my shoulders stretch and...

-SMACK!-

Elbow the grinning sack of shite with eyes straight in the throat. Despite aiming for his face his choking noises fill me with the spoils of an impending ejaculation, a surge of luscious adrenaline.

"Argh," he coughs and splutters, but I sense it's all for show. I caught him well, but not that fucking well. In a half-wheeze, he says, "You dirty cunt!" The girl falls to her bony knees, shielding her head with her fragile arms. Without thinking, I smack him a fresh, though weak left hook. His dumbfounded countenance soon contorts into a snarling look of malevolence. Fearing his retaliation, I sucker him with a right fist this time, smacking him square on the nose. Upping the pace as my adrenaline kicks in, I launch him another one in the jaw, then hook him with another, stronger left in the stomach and go for an infertile-inflecting knee in the bollocks—but he falls before I can pull it off. Instead, I toe-punt the woman-beating prick right in the chest as he falls, then stamp on him to speed up the landing.

"OI! STOP THAT YA PRICK!" the stick lady screams. I go to turn, but as I do the crazy bitch launches herself at me. She digs her nails into my scalp, twists a clump of my own fucking hair and starts yanking on it. Trying to shake her off, she shouts, "Leave him alone ya fuckin' cuuuunt! Dis ain't got nuthin' to do wit' ya!"

I can't believe this. This is unreal. She's swinging around my fucking skull like a weightless life-size doll with unrelenting grip! The bitch's fingernails dig deep into my scalp like rusted barbed wire and the greased together ends of her hair keep poking me in the eyes.

"Oi! Git da fuuuuck off of 'er dick 'ed!" the bloke shouts, attempting to get up but failing. Finally, I manage to shove the skank away, but she lands on the concrete with a firm smack and slide, grazing the side of her face along the gravel. Droplets of rain begin to patter around us. Anorexia's poster girl rolls about on the ground, wailing like a premature baby short a stillborn death. I go to check on her, but she bats—no, claws at my fucking eyes before I can turn and—*WHACK!*—bolt. The boyfriend's back on the—*THUMP!*—attack, forcing me backwards until I trip over the skinny bitch's twiglet of a leg. He looms over my sightline again as I hit the deck, smacks me in the jaw, the lip and then my fucking ear. Standing, he thrusts a corker of a kick right into my ribcage. Then again... and again. With both bloodied hands, he grabs my shirt and yanks me up. Before I can close my eyes, he thrusts a nutcracker of a headbutt straight at the centre of my forehead, forcing the other side of my skull to crash against the now sodden concrete. Biblical torrents of rain distort my already shaken sight. Twiglet the Tramp somehow got back up to her feet and fucking tends to him as they scuttle away. The crimson-grazed half of her face turns my way. "Ya lucky it started fuckin' chuckin' it daoown, faggot," she shouts. "If we see ya again, we'll fuckin' kill ya!" are her departing words, as I continue to lie still with the rain now battering me instead. Strange sounds escape me, but I can't tell if I'm crying, laughing or both. Metallic droplets slither into the crevices of my teeth, dropping down on the underside of my tongue. Nothing feels broken. It's a good thing I'm drunk. All I feel is numb and vacant and slightly dizzy. Now I'm definitely laughing and crying though. Serves me right for sticking up for a woman.

CHAPTER NINE

By the time I got home I'd unfortunately sobered up, so I just stocked up on some more supplies. My face is throbbing, and I have a strong urge to fuck. I'm guessing it's because of the adrenaline. If there's any other reason I don't know what it is. Nor do I care. Of course, now that I need Esther she's nowhere in sight, so I've decided to make do with some porn.

It has been a while, after all. Hasn't it, Eric?

I was going to watch some old movies, with the hope of them inspiring me into some sort of action. They used to from time to time, but now I'm so governed by what is affordable my options are limited to say the least. Plus, I've come to realise that being an actor just makes you somebody's else pawn. After my folks vamoosed, the agent I had folded before he even got me any work. Hence why he went bust I suppose. I spent months making that happen. Now just the thought of being that relentless go-getter again makes me feel queasy. I'm barely motivated to eat, let alone try and make a career for myself. It seems clear enough to me that everyone is just using each other for their own personal gain, that nothing has an earnest reason for being other than that. Deep down, we're all nothing but vile organisms with no interests except for self-preservation and reproduction. Everyone is a beast at their core.

Yeah, yeah, yeah. No one cares, Eric. Whip your cock out already. What's Archer in the mood for?

I crack open a beer and spark up a fag for the pre-masturbation ceremony. With a large sip and a long suck, my mind starts sorting out the running favourites.

How about a bit of incest to whet the appetite?

The best one, in my professional perverted opinion, is where this dude wants to shoot a load over his girlfriend's face, but she's reluctant, so he pulls out all pissy and hops in the shower. The mother, being the dutiful parent that she is, was listening to this whole exchange in the hallway and shortly afterwards, walks into the room and tells her sperm shy daughter she's got to learn. The dude comes out of the shower to find the mother on her knees and predictably starts sucking him off. After the usual stuff, she grabs him by the cock and drags him into the kitchen, where the naughty daughter is waiting for her punishment. Skip past the boring threesome until the decisive moment, where the mother jerks off the dude right into the daughter's shocked and playfully appalled face until he layers her with cream. Lesson learned. It's fucking great. Now that I think about it though, I probably only want to watch that one because I was thinking about Esther and her mother earlier. There's that awareness again, kicking down the doors of the present and gate-crashing the party.

Okay then. Brother forces sister into giving him a blow job? The one with all the fake cum. Whatshername... Monica Sexton?

Tempting but no, seen them all already and there's only a few out there who get it just right. Take lesbian twins. They always act like they're enjoying it way too much when clearly the fantasy is in the taboo. One of them needs to put on a show of reluctant yet futile resistance, whilst the other aggressively strips her inhibitions down through sheer dominance and the handy helping of enormous dildos.

Other races, going by their comments on these videos, seem convinced that white people love incest. Seems true enough. I have no idea why, but if it makes you feel squeamish, just swirl your finger around the oak tree of your family roots for a while and eventually, you'll find that each and every one of us is a product of incest. Everybody has an Oedipus in them.

Let's take it up a notch. Czechoslovakian late-teen (cast assumingly because she doesn't look it) playing Red Riding Hood, pounded in the woods by some dude wearing nothing but a pair of trainers and a wolf mask?

Again, seen it too much now and the chick looks like she enjoys it less and less the more and more I've watched it. And at the end, the dude starts howling, killing the already small enough male orgasm down to about a millisecond, despite how fucking funny it is.

Alright then. Asian dreams: Babysitter gets fucked in a dream by a guy in a bear costume?

No, that won't do it either, all that cosplay crap makes me feel a bit sick after a while. Reminds me of Jessica too much as well, she used to love dressing up as Alice in Wonderland and being molested by my Mad Hatter.

Awareness is my matter, Mr Hatter!

I'm getting too old for this shit.

No, come on. You just need something with a little more kick, something particularly foul to match your current mood. There's battery acid burning through your bones, Eric, you gotta help yourself out.

Damn, finished my beer already. Quick shot of whisky will get me up to speed, plus a little joint. Argh, the only thing throbbing is my jaw. My cock hasn't even flinched yet.

Bukkake?

That'll do it. No wait, the best ones are always censored out anyway. Ahh man, this whisky is going down well. Time for another.

-SMASH-

Give the amateurs a go? Come on, it's easier to delude yourself into thinking it's your cock they're blowing with those ones.

There's one I'm particularly fond of. If she was eighteen at the time of recording I'd be surprised. Sixteen, tops. She's wicked cute, with sweet teenager tits and a loving face begging for some lotion. After getting rainbowed with cum, she even willingly takes it in her mouth again to clean him up. It's on every site as well, so I'm not alone in finding it good to dine on. I don't understand the mentality of guys who upload videos of their girlfriends though, ex or current, regardless of what might've happened. They should be hanged.

Yet, it doesn't stop you jacking off over it, does it? Come on, morality is just a mask for pussies who're too scared to carry out what they truly desire. You know I'm right, Eric. So, you know you're right too. I remember your pornographer days. Still can't believe you deleted 'em all. What a fucking waste.

One of my problems with pornography is the thought that all these women have parents. Not usually ones that give a shit, but still. This girl has probably killed herself by now anyway. Or she's nothing but dead inside. A RIP wank won't cut it. Now I'm thinking about my first girlfriend and realising the only reason I like this video is because of the way she looks at him; she's genuinely enjoying it, utterly enamoured, experimenting without fear, doubt or mistrust. No one ever looks at you again like your first girlfriend did. So, what did this prick do with that? Uploaded it to a website for a countless number of degenerate scumbags like me to ogle over, for a purpose I cannot fathom. Hopefully, she's an idiot and it doesn't bother her, but there's something deep within me that bets it destroyed her; there's no way she wouldn't have found out in this day and age. That look of hope and innocence must've been swiped away as quickly as the vacuous apps we now operate with to use and abuse each other.

Scrolling on...

In a self-hating kind of mood, 'eh Eric. Why didn't ya say so? Let's dabble with some Jack Off Instructions, or JOI as it's known in the trade. Angry woman with the prerequisite, resting bitch-face who loves talking to the camera, telling you what a pathetic little faggot you are whilst you pump away and obey every word?

We have a winner...

My libido blinds me and before I'm even aware of it the laptop has ten tabs open and my dressing gown is off. Need to drain the devil out of myself like a bloated cow, get rid of this disgusting build up. An unwanted *barely legal teens* pop-up ad catches my eye with their cute attempts to show me they're enjoying their trade but does nothing except make me feel like a paedophile. Might as well be *literally* searching for child porn looking at some of them. They're all skinny as hell, not a single hair on their bodies and some of them are even wearing braces. You've got to be in the right mood for that type of shit. I'll need at least another few spliffs before their desperate cry for a father means absolutely diddly-squat to me. You usually see it right after the money-shot. The self-disgust washes through them and the pang of regret seeps through the cracks; eyelids flutter in disbelief, or the mouth hangs open, sometimes trembling, the flickering of eyes into the lens of the camera, begging for help, followed by their best-feigned smile, which never convinces... or they look away from it, wondering how long they should sit there caked in semen, for fear of being beaten perhaps, or maybe just not getting paid. Those moments are the only true thing about pornography. It's quite the fitting match for the post-depression, existential blues that follows a male orgasm. After a while, their reluctance and remorse begin to become arousing and eventually, an expectation. You find yourself desirous of her not enjoying it but going through with it anyway. Taking one for the oppressive team. Getting paid to be raped. Capitalism in a nutshell. At least most of these girls are too stupid to realise it though, I guess.

We're all whores to the coin.

Close tab.

Fuck the male agenda. Youth isn't even attractive, more annoying if anything. All these girls are groomed and drugged up to their eyeballs. That dead-eyed, thousand-yard stare ain't fooling no one. *Argh,* this isn't doing my mind any favours. Or my cock for that matter. Anxious blood stiffens nothing. Nuts to this, let's move onto the more mature ladies, it's too late for them anyway. If by mature you mean twenty-eight. Christ, you can literally see the heroin swimming around their retinas as well. Makes me feel like a little boy. Let's go for the in between:

Shemales. Never really saw the problem some men have with shemales. If you think about it, there's hardly any negatives.

One: *Guaranteed anal.*

Two: *Can't get pregnant.*

Three: Due to all the hormone pills and body modifications, they all have tiny cocks, so you get the double bonus of feeling superior as well as actual evidence of an orgasm. All you need to do is close your eyes, suck it up and swallow your pride and imagine a mutated clitoris. *Win, win, win.* All the ones I've found so far though look more like trannies than transsexuals. Each one of them is killing my already manic-depressive boner. *Yes—no—yes—no—yes—no.*

My head is beginning to fog over again. The whisky bottle is already half-empty. I'll balance it out with a spliff. *Argh,* the only penetration going on around here is the beating inside my jaw.

Hentai?

Doesn't do anything for me anymore, I'm not some dorky virgin teenager. Plus, most of that stuff is just a bit too disturbing. Fuck sake, there's too much to choose from and it all makes you feel worse about yourself in the end. This bondage roleplay rape looks a little bit too real, as do these crying facials, as well as the anal screams. Guilt wanking never satisfies. It just puts you on edge. I don't want to apologise to myself whilst masturbating. My cocks got bipolar disorder. It's as sick of seeing this shit as I often claim to be in order to bed dumb chicks. Up, down, up, down, up, down. Maybe none of this is arousing, maybe it's all disgusting, vile and fake. Just like nature, the world, the whole fucking cosmos, an ever-expanding force, raping the innocent out of the bliss of non-existence.

But that's where the arousal comes from doesn't it, it's all just a fantasy. Nothing wrong with that dipshit. Come on, we've had our ups and downs before (DON'T EXCUSE THAT FUCKING PUN) but we've always got through it together in the end. Take it easy, Eric baby. You'll get there. Trust me.

I'm onto some femidom now, telling me what a pathetic little twat I am. That doesn't work either. Another gulp of the brown stuff. Could give Esther a call...

No, let's not do that. Peace is better than a quick release. Sod pornography. It's not meant for people like me who know how to get laid. It's for losers, but not a loser like me. Alright, let's finish the spliff and get this over with already.

'I had an abortion, Eric. We've committed infanticide together. That keeps us tied to each other for life.'

Sammy... The Sperm Thief. My Abortion Queen. Kamikaze Womb. I'm-falling-for-you-SURPRISE-I-came-home-early-just-for-you-but-why-suck-one-cock-when-you-can-suck-two?-IMPREGNATE ME! How dare you enter my head without my permission. Why aren't *giving* me head more like?

'You're the worst thing that ever happened to me, Eric.'
"WHY WON'T THESE BITCHES FUCK OFF??!!"

The whisky will silence them. Ah, my throat burns. Feels good though. One more shot. *Bang.* That one was better than the last. *Boom.* Another one down. *Swoosh.* The room's doubling up. One for luck. *Smash.* Now it's quadrupled, conspiring against me. Looks like I'm jerking off over two sets of identical twins... but I'm still all flaccid and useless. Impotent. I couldn't have got Sammy pregnant with this pathetic thing—look at it! It barely frigging works! It's acting like a child who's just found out that my abuse wasn't all for his own good! This is so depressing, now I can't even turn myself on.

Ring-ring! Ring-ring!

There are chemicals of pure cortisol on the rise, taking over my whole body. The adrenaline's morphed into a dull, death-like ache. My eyes are watering. Who in the hell wants my attention?

Ring-ring! Ring-ring!
Caller Unknown.

Who is this motherfucker?!

It's an unknown caller, Oedipussy.

"Hello!?"

Nothing.

"You think this is funny, you prick?! Hear, listen to me jerk off." I put the head of my cock into the speaker and start pumping, "You like that? I'm gonna blow this straight down your ear!"

My cock disobeys my orders. For fuck sake.

"Fuck you!" I scream, tossing the phone to the side and standing up. Its screen remains black and idle, with no signs of a previous life, an oblivious oblivion. Did anyone even call?

The room is spinning. No, splitting. One half sits further away from the other, overlaying each other with each flicker of a glance. I have no idea where I am. Why am I living inside this woeful set of walls? Esther was right, the mould on the wall is getting worse. It looks like... a womb. A growing womb of expanding rot. Already dead yet utterly alive to me in this moment. It's staring at me... knowing I'm going to kill it. But it doesn't know what I know. I'm helping the poor bastard out by denying it entry into the hell of existence. Doesn't it know that? Why is it laughing? Why am I?

***

The screaming voice of Elizabeth Taylor wakes me up. I don't remember putting on Who's Afraid of Virginia Woolf? but there it is, in all its bitter black and white glory. The Sammy lookalike with the make-believe child. How utterly depressing and unnerving. It's as if I'm being followed around by my own fucking thoughts. Even my own decisions do nothing but laugh in my face.

The springs of the mattress cry out in agony like the purgatory of my insides as I shift myself off the bed. My faithful dead soldiers, the empty beer cans, are sprawled across the floor and the ashtray must have fallen whilst I was sleeping. Looks like someone emptied an urn and scattered the ashes all over my blacked-out body. My dehydrated brain welcomes back a galaxy before my eyes, enabling a clusterfuck of stars to ping around the room, bouncing off the corners of the walls and inanimate objects. I know they're not there, but they look so vivid, so real like you can reach out and touch them.

The laptop hiccups back into life as I brush past it. It glares right at me. To my surprise, all the pornography tabs have disappeared. Apparently, in my drunken state, I checked my emails. I do not have any recollection of that.

So, how is Eric Archer these days?

Just wondered how you're coping all on your own in this big bad world. My mother's away on a convention this weekend, so I'll have the whole house to myself.

What should I get up to, one wonders?

Jessica
X

CHAPTER TEN

It hadn't occurred to me whilst travelling here that I'd be confronted by this bridge again. Strange I didn't anticipate it, seeing as this is the place I've vowed to end it all. Suicidal irony I suppose. It isn't just for personal reasons that I've opted for it though. Some of the locals still refer to where I'm about to walk across as No Man's Bridge. Apparently, during the First World War, Battleton had an army base not too far from here. They used to travel across this bridge at night to transport goods and whatnot, but due to electrical problems it was usually nothing but pitch black, so as you entered it was like driving into an abyss. Battleton is a rather odd place. Aside from the station behind me and the river below, the entire place is situated on an array of steep hills. From up there at night this bridge looks like a piece of the world that's missing. Also, due to the lining of thin yet tall trees a short distance away from the train tracks and the nature of the architecture beyond this bridge, as you travel across it, you're basically always in a blind spot to everything that surrounds you. Except if you're down below on the riverbank. People often say Battleton is on the outskirts of Brighton, but that simply isn't true. It's closer to Lewes if anything. Similar in appearance too. But due to its small size and tiny population, you can stand on this bridge at night without seeing a person or even a car for hours at a time. Hence why they still call it No Man's Bridge, I suppose.

History breathes down my neck before I even attempt to make my way across, piercing through me with its biting chill, luring the present to merge with the past. The gust seems to move through you, makes you too aware of your own skeleton, awake to your tick-tocking decline. In the far background, conductors whistle their worth to permit the departure of trains. Screeching metallic tracks accompany them, high-pitched enough to trigger a teeth grind. It even smells like the past. Strangers stroll by without a trace of existence. Their entire lifetimes are as good as already gone as they disappear into the landscape inside the blinks of my ephemeral eyes. Little do they know what's coming to them, if anything, how unaware they are to the reality of the people they'll invite into their lives. We're nothing but fragments of a narcissistic universe's inclination to observe and admire itself as it continues to expand and decay in simultaneous pointlessness. I wish I could remember the last time I looked at the world in awe; marvelled at the sheer, terrifying magnificence of it and all its looping, infinitesimal complexity, forever beyond the scope of my limited imagination. Now it just fills me with terror. A sometimes larger, more looming one than others, but always there, spoiling the memories of the person who ceased to exist long ago. The one who ceased to be at the other end of this bridge. That person, of course, being me.

Gravel scrunches and scatters under my feet like the unwanted thoughts threatening an onslaught inside my mind. Deep breathing provides a shallow comfort, like the tranquil atmosphere just before an uncontrollable storm. Each sound seems magnified yet outside of myself, coming at me in waves like the ripples of the water below, which stretches out further than I can see. Distances blur inside the eyes the same way memories do over long stretches of time. I'm sure I don't see this bridge as it actually appears, yet this awareness does nothing to alter its image. It's stuck, frozen inside the last time I was here.

I thought I'd feel more nervous at the prospect of seeing Jessica again rather than the place in which she dwells. The air feels tainted... but not by the passing traffic. It's been breathed before. Breathed by a certain someone whose face I wouldn't recognise but whose presence is more than palpably felt. He's sucked up and splurged more air in this town than I have now. Sucked in the presence I once possessed. Forced it to merge and combine with his own. Such is his way. Even my heart seems to beat differently. It's filled with an alternative dread, a heartbeat abandoned. Am I becoming the intruder to the one who once intruded me? Or more importantly... should I?

Maybe I should start speaking like this in therapy just to see how Frank reacts. If only our behaviour wasn't so governed by the people surrounding us. Each person invites a different version of myself to wake up and assume his role, like he's been lying in wait for that particular moment, only to vanish inside a departure of words, or more often than not, an ejaculation. I do wonder which Eric you'd bring to the stage, Glen, I really do, should our paths ever cross. Isn't it funny? How you can know so much about me and me so much about you yet should our paths indeed ever cross without us knowing it, we wouldn't even recognise each other. From one shadow to another, there's even a strange part of me that hopes our silent waltz in the dark continues for a long time yet. It's been a while since I fucked your girlfriend. Too long in fact. I'll do my utmost to cherish each moment.

My apologies, my observer. Sometimes the adderall sucks me into a certain state, one where I'm almost the outside observer to myself. Almost but not quite. I've been meaning to kick them to the curb for a while but today I need to remain calm. After the previous night's failed antics, the adrenaline kept me up all night before knocking me out for close to twenty-four hours. Nobody else attempted to contact me during that time. Maybe I should report myself as missing just for the thrill of being looked for. Though I can't be certain the authorities would. Why spend the taxpayer's hard-earned bread on someone who skittles along on the outskirts of society, who'd be missed by no one?

Loneliness eats a man alive.

There's a couple below along the riverbank. They're sitting on a capsized dinghy boat. She sits turned to the side, her head down, hesitant. He sits facing the river, hands in pockets, searching for a point to focus on but coming up short. They remind me of something I can't quite pinpoint, so in essence, they remind me of nothing. It's another odd spot. Out in the open yet secluded, like its own small island. Detectable only by the centre of this bridge. The couple is leaving now, taking cautious steps up a hill steep enough to keep most people out. At the top there's a barrier to stop cars colliding down should they crash. I used to think only Jessica and I knew about it or at least how to get down there. Despite being visible from here it's no easy find. Hiding in plain sight. Jessica told me that the river froze over once shortly after her father died. Shortly after he'd molested her inside a bath. The bubbles camouflaged the semen until it coagulated around the inside rim of the drain. That's all she told me. Nothing about what went on in between.

The boy and girl have disappeared now. I wonder how many other couples have frolicked down there, broken up or both. Under moonlight it gives the impression that there's no other place in the world, except for the bridge you must cross to get there. I take a long pull of whisky for warmth with a flash of Jessica handing me a bottle of the same brand. Happy birthday, Eric. Happy unconscious decision to purchase it this morning. Now I also know why I went swimming. The abortion interrupted my throwing myself off the bridge. Haunted are the thoughts which follow me around, dictating my next move without my knowledge until hindsight highlights their horror. And to think, I came here for comfort. A second-handed comfort now but a comfort all the same. "Cheers," I declare, holding my flask up to the river. "Now may my consciousness drown."

Considering the abuse she underwent, Jessica was the most well-adjusted person I'd ever met. The only thinking woman too. Her emotional stability was quite fragile but that was understandable. If you wanted to romanticize it, you'd say we're the same person in a lot of ways. Or that she brought out a better man in me, for a while at least. We saw the world in a very similar light and my belief is, we gave each other a little room to breathe. Where most places and people would put me on edge or force me into playing a role, she was someone who put me at ease. No conversation was off-limits, no fantasy too dark, no subject locked inside the bars of a boundary. In a sense, she was the home I'd never experienced.

That was one way to look at it anyway.

The other is to say we're just too fucked up to ever really work. Her abuse made for interesting, though most of the time awkward sex. By her own admission, she was greeted by a flash of her father's face at the end of every orgasm. According to her mother, my resemblance to him was uncanny. She never made a sound during sex, like it'd been made strictly forbidden. Daddy must've said, 'Shush'. Sometimes it felt like I was him, watching her perform oral sex on me through his eyes. I still wonder now if that was why she could never look at me whilst doing it. A certain childish throat-gulp would betray her upon swallowing, followed by a quick turn to the side and an even quicker trip to the bathroom. She'd come back into the bedroom afterwards, shrugging off what I guess was the embarrassment, eager to bury the words we couldn't say to one another underneath the covers that enabled us to lay facing one another, as its thickness shrouded our features in nothing but black. Sometimes she'd silently weep but always insist that I carried on. Sometimes I did. Sometimes I didn't. Neither rid me of the trepidation they ignited. Empathy doesn't hand out many erections.

There she is now, back inside the Fortune of War, unaware of my presence or too nervous to turn her head towards the door. This is our first and last rendezvous point. She's sitting, or more, fidgeting in the same corner as on our first date, even on the same side of the oak-upholstered booth. A pint of Guinness sits opposite her, untouched and perfected through patience. A luminous pink straw sits inside her glass of what I presume is gin and tonic. Even from here I can see that it's been chewed upon, flattened at the top by anxious teeth, though barely sucked on, going by the remaining contents of the glass. This is the first time we've met outside her car for a long time, maybe even since we 'officially' split. We've spoken via the occasional phone call or odd email, but that's it. I imagine we're only a few hours away from having sex again, knowing her and knowing me, but it's impossible not to wonder whether there's something else on her mind.

Posters for gigs and events that took place years ago are still covering every inch of the walls. The smell of fresh urinal cakes blends with the sticky spilt ale on the wooden floor. If I jumped I'd crash my head against the ceiling. Perhaps that's an indication of how old the place is, but who can be sure? Jessica suddenly takes notice of me and waves. As I make my approach her face scrunches inwards, causing a lock of hair to fall forward from behind her ear.

"What the hell happened, Eric? Who did that to your face?" she asks. Seeing her made me forget about my own appearance for a change.

"Oh, nothing," I say. "I just made the mistake of defending a woman." I slide into my seat, aching slightly from the effort.

"You don't mean Esther, do you?"

"No. Why the hell would I defend her?"

"Well, good. I guess. Who then?"

"Someone I don't know. It doesn't matter. I was in a park and mistook myself for a hero. Got my ass beat for it. Served me right. I don't even know why I got involved."

"Were you alone?"

"Mm-mmm," I reply whilst sipping on my pint.

"What were you doing in a park all by yourself?"

"Drinking."

"Why?"

"Therapy makes me thirsty. Don't worry about it. I'm fine. Looks worse than it feels. A fistfight never hurt anyone. You look fucking great, by the way."

"Well, thanks," she says, inspired to run a hand through her hair. It's a lot longer since the last time we met. Breakups seem to inspire haircuts, brought about by what I imagine is a crisis of identity. My behaviour (not to mention Glen's) provoked Jessica to opt for a short crop, angry lesbian doo, a look that did not suit her in the slightest but for some reason made fucking her feel more victorious.

Sex is war unspoken.

She doesn't appear to know what to do with her hands. If she's not touching her face, she's flicking the zip of her handbag or tapping the table with her fingers. There's a coaster to the side that's been torn into an array of square-shaped shreds.

"Sorry I'm late. I didn't mean to keep you waiting."

"No, no. It's fine," she says, her right hand notably near my person, halfway across the table. "I got you a Guinness, assumingly."

"You assumed correctly," I say, taking a harder swig of it. "I see you've switched from wine."

She shrugs. "Hardly. It's either that or G&T. I seldom drink these days anyway."

"I'll drink for the two of us then." Another gulp. "So, how have you been?"

"Oh, much the same really. I'm going to be a practising psychotherapist soon. Surrendering to inevitability I guess."

"Book me in for a session whenever you're ready. Things are not exactly moving along with mine."

"Why's that?" she asks.

"To say he's laconic would be an understatement."

Jessica's mother is a psychotherapist, so the practice of it's been ingrained into her. I wonder whether she really believes in it or whether having a mother who does forces her to. Then again, what choice did she have either way?

"So, how are you then?" she asks.

"In truth, I'm a bit of a wreck these days, with no idea what to do with myself."

"Still with Esther then I take it."

"Nice. Yeah, she's still around, if that's what you mean, but to say we're together has lost all meaning to me."

"Mmm. How specific of you."

"How's Glen?"

"Urm. He's fine, I guess. He's... shooting a film right now, so he's busy. Doesn't get back until next week," she says, looking at me as she sucks on her straw.

"A big part?" I ask, trying to sound... well, nonchalant I guess.

"No, not really. Just a background role," she says, caressing the sore knuckles of my hand with gentle brushes of her fingertips, using both hands. I've already finished my drink and feeling the urge for another.

"Yeah, looks like Esther and I are going to break up for good soon."

"Can't say I'm unhappy to hear that."

"I didn't expect you to be. I must admit, I'm surprised you're still with Glen, after... well, everything."

"Like I told you, I've tried to break it off with him loads of times, but he never takes me seriously. Then he disappears to do some movie or whatever and comes back, acting as if nothing happened."

"Hardly a surprise. That's his MO."

"That's his what?"

"Never mind. Just try to be—"

"No, tell me. What did you mean?"

"It was just a snide joke. I didn't mean anything by it. Forget about it."

"Come on, I'm intrigued now. What does it mean?"

"Modus operandi. Like method or mode of operation. You said

Glen comes back, acting as if nothing happened..."

"Oh. Very funny, Eric."

"It was just a slip of the tongue. I really didn't mean—"

"Forget about it. No harm done. I too, am surprised you're still with that prostitute though. You told me she hits you, treats you like garbage and basically walks all over you. Why are you still with her?"

"By those reasons, why are you still with Glen?"

"I can't break up with him without confronting him first. I've realised recently that I just have to do it. For me more than him."

"You are talking about what I think you're talking about, right?"

She nods in a minuscule fashion with her eyes trailing across the table and a finger flicking against one of the torn shreds of the coaster.

"Can I ask, why now?"

After clearing her throat out of discomfiture rather than necessity, she takes a few breaths of preparation, then says, "It's become clear to me that I only stayed with him because by doing that I didn't have to face what happened. I've been putting myself on pause ever since. Does that make sense?"

"More than you could know," I reply.

She smiles and says, "That's why I have to confront him about it."

I nod in understanding. "Have you ever told anyone else?"

"No. Not in the way I need to."

After a brief pause of hesitation, I ask, "Is that why I'm here?"

"No, Eric. Please. You're here because I want to fuck."

I scoff a laugh. She leans forward. Mirroring her, I do the same. Soon enough our lips meet. The kiss cuts me apart. Singular, slicing memories are brought about by every sense. Alone they're fragile and delicate. Together they wage war, spiralling through my mind inside a cataclysm I cannot control. Like tarnished skipping stones, they sink only to re-emerge with each breath as our lips switch angles in tandem. We're forcing ourselves to forget who we are to each other now by replicating the motions of what we once were, if only for a few short-lived moments of time.

Her tongue feels foreign in my mouth now though, like an intruder I'm wary of allowing inside. Its shape is no longer so easily entangled with my own. Our rhythm is fading. All I can detect is the difference between her and Esther, how the latter provokes an unrivalled arousal, whilst the former can only seem to detonate a dilapidating shame. I'll defeat it, or at least overcome it for a brief period so we can still impersonate our past selves, but with each dramatization we're in danger of sabotaging our history, of re-writing over moments until the significance they once held has been lost and more often than not, replaced by something opaque and uninterpretable.

The worst part is not knowing whether this invasion is mutual anymore. For it's perfectly plausible that this mutiny is mine and mine alone.

I had not expected Jessica to have such a clear objective. She's kissing me as if I never did her any harm, but I do get the sense that this mission of hers is entirely self-orientated. She does just want to fuck and as she once said before, it's much easier to sleep with someone you've already slept with, as in a sense it doesn't add to your body count.

I'm merely a cock she's had inside her before.

But for reasons now fucked up beyond all repair, I shall find a way to see this through.

Whatever the cost.

As Jessica continues devouring me the anguish brought about by the bombardment of recollections does begin to fade... but I can't help but wonder:

How many of these palpable remembrances have already been falsified by my own ego; how many convenient fragments have been filtered out or erased; how many of them really ring true anymore, if in fact, any?

It's no wonder I find it so difficult to trust anyone. From a neurological standpoint, it's evidently impossible to trust yourself. Even this notion of the 'self' is as unreliable as they come. Survival of the fittest? More like survival of the mistiest.

CHAPTER ELEVEN

Jessica and I left the Fortune of War in mockery of our history, with our middle-finger's up at the reality we'd collectively postponed. I don't remember what we said to each other, or what we really even did aside from walking around the marble-paved town through the drizzling rain. Its vapours travelled with us, like brush-stroked blurs of a dream you know isn't real but wish you'd never wake up from. Typically, the moment I had that thought, we found ourselves back where we started. That's when the cracks in the pavement began to reveal themselves.

Jessica's car happened to be parked down the road alongside the riverbank. The first few steps we took to cross brought back the dampened echo of our footsteps, the unsightly hue of funeral blue returned to the landscape and the taste of too much nicotine and cheap whisky tainted my palette. Try as we might, but however many times Jessica and I attempt to paint the world anew together, our background is always there, waiting to remind us of its permanent stain. It surrounded us as we stood on the riverbank with our feet sinking into its sodden crest. We stared at the blackening shimmers of the river without uttering a word about going back down there, as the last time we did our exchange embedded an association we have still yet to discuss, let alone confront. Some occurrences feel like they're watching you, I suppose. A quick, nervous clench of Jessica's hand over my own indicated her desire to continue onward towards her car. For a fraction of a second, it felt like forgiveness.

But the feelings I drowned with booze inside the Fortune of War seem to have already become immune to my methods of sublimation. Instead of choking they're now thriving. The riverbank and the bridge are both on my trail, shattering any attempted thought of their dismissal. The build-up of condensation inside Jessica's car makes the clearing of her throat sound forced and intruded upon, whilst the looks my hipflask provokes only tightens the squeeze inside my chest. Even now as we drive away, the ground beneath us doesn't feel so steady; the surrounding streetlamps all seem to flicker and nature itself appears all too keen to observe and even hungrier to haunt.

I've fucking told you before, Eric. You may have left this bridge, but this bridge has not left you.

"Do you remember when we swam in the river?" Jessica had asked. There was no rain that day, just a lazy, albeit nebulous fog instead. Vaporous streams parted from our lips in continuous waves, broken up by the chattering of our teeth.

"Of course, I think about it every time I cross that bridge," I said, tightening the grip of my crossed arms, leather crackling like the way ice sometimes splits.

"Let's go down there."

"For a swim?"

"No, you idiot, just to be alone. It's more secluded down there," Jessica said.

She took my hand and led the way. After hopping over the barrier, we skidded down the small muddy hill towards the river, both of us halting a few feet from the shore. The capsized and abandoned, beaten-up old dinghy boat was the only thing on it, aside from a few clumps of isolated grass. The rest of the land looked barren. Jessica walked over to the boat and lifted it up from its side for a second. After feeling around the ground underneath, she let the boat slip away from her fingers. It landed in the same place as before. "Would you believe it?" she asked.

"Believe what?" I replied, lighting up a cigarette to distract myself from the night's chill. I was pondering a quick hit of my flask too, but I didn't want Jessica thinking that I'd really hit rock bottom. Not at that moment, anyway.

"It's still here. Look," she said, holding up the pregnancy test from a few months before. Despite one half of her frame being dressed in the evening twilight, her other half, the one holding the test, was draped in shadows. Although I couldn't see it, I knew that it was there.

"Well, you buried it under the boat by forcing it into the ground. It's not that surprising, is it?"

"No, I guess not," she replied, suddenly distracted, elsewhere or perhaps thrown-off by my tone. Shortly afterwards, she sat down, now allowing the test to slip through her fingers, or not even noticing it fall. "So, are you and this Esther a proper item now or what?" she asked, looking around at the ground, flicking flakes of paint away from the boat with an absent mind.

"I guess so, but it doesn't really feel like it. She doesn't tell me anything about herself. Her past is like a no-entry zone. Maybe she knows something I don't," I muttered, confused as to why I made such a quip. Brushing it aside, I asked, "What about you and this... Glen, is it?"

"Yeah. Well, we... we're still seeing each other."

"Isn't it strange being with someone after what happened?" I asked, looking down at the crushed cigarette on the ground as it shed its remaining embers. A familiar atmosphere was casting over us, a smidgen away from an identical replica to that of a few months before. I found myself taking a few pulls from my hipflask, alarmed by its temporary lack of conscious acknowledgement. Another cigarette was soon lit. The pauses between Jessica's words always spoke louder than she ever did, but that evening they shrieked through the overbearing silence. My nervousness had heightened this awareness. Soon, every stuttered breath seemed to scream what she really wanted to say, but I knew pressuring her would only have the opposite effect. So, in agony, I waited. A distant train screeched into idleness. Nothing and no one else appeared to be around. It felt like we were marooned on that small, strange piece of land; ostracised from one another, with nothing but the crumbled foundations of our collapse keeping us together.

"It looks so lifeless, don't you think?" Jessica asked, referring to the stillness of the water in front of us. I remember thinking it to be like an abyss, but I'm fairly certain I made no such comment or any response at all. Instead, I joined her on the boat. It was so quiet down there. Every sound seemed louder because of it. Jessica's breath was hollow, as vacant as the river we were both staring at.

"I know you too well, Jessica. Just say what you want to say already," I said without looking at her, wincing slightly at my lack of patience.

She took the cigarette from my hand and hesitantly dragged on it, just the once. With Jessica, it was always just the once. After grimacing, she passed it back and continued to look ahead, lacking a point of focus.

"I'm not sure how to tell you this Eric, but you deserve to know," she said, shuffling herself about as if trying to nestle into the words without the inevitable discomfort they promised to be dispersed with. A certain shudder shot through me, like the strike of paranoia that disturbs you after a disconcerting dose of déjà vu. I dismissed it with another swig of the bottle when I saw a singular tear streaming down Jessica's cheek. The water in front of us rippled, seemingly out of nothing. We both stared at it, entwined in the fear of what might follow the impending, and what the atmosphere promised to be, distressing confession. Condensation was leaving my breath in impossibly slow streams, like phantoms of thought-patterns never given a voice, a premature suicide of all the people I could have been before that day was done. We both sat there shivering, neither of us able to touch the other.

"We shouldn't see each other for a while. Everything is just too much right now," she said.

"We hardly see each other as it is, Jessica."

"I know, but I meant being in contact with each other in general. And we can't keep sleeping with each other, it's not right."

"What's brought you to this conclusion?" I asked.

"You're seeing someone, I'm seeing... well, the same. I know you're used to cheating, but I'm not."

"You like this Glen guy a lot then or something?"

"No, it isn't that. It's just..."

"What?"

She let out a sigh, a harsh, pain-ridden one. I mistook her crying for shaking as she scratched against the wood of the boat. She let out another sigh and then looked at me properly, for the first time that night, but quickly turned away again. Her agitation reminded me of all the times she mentioned things about her father. A fresh trauma was lingering in the air, patiently waiting to take its nebulous shape.

"We can stop seeing each other for a while," I said, "I'm in agreement with you. It isn't exactly the best moment for us. But you clearly have something to say, so you might as well save yourself the anguish and just say it, Jessica. I'm sure it's not as bad as you think."

She went to speak but stopped herself again, which irritated me. Selfish I know, but my whole body began to feel constricted like it was suffocating itself.

"Well, you remember when we were breaking up, right?"

"Of course I do. It was only what, five or six months ago."

"Technically, it's only been four. But we did start falling apart before that. Anyway, we didn't see each other that much. Then you blew me off to take Esther out and that same night I decided to... well, go out myself, but you already know what happened then."

An opaque thought that she was trying to make me feel guilty crossed my mind, but I let it pass. It was impossible to feel any guiltier about that than I already did and still do.

"Yeah well, I only did that after finding that fucking post-it note inside your car."

"You knew about that?" she asked, striking me against the shoulder out of nowhere.

"Yes. I know I never mentioned it, but I used it as an excuse to... well, cheat—as I figured you were already doing... the same."

Then it hit me; the hidden accusation behind Jessica's reaction riddled through as if an ineffable, metaphysical force had just passed between us. Looking back, it wasn't just because of the way Jessica reacted to my own unexpected confession, but how her eyes had trailed along the ground, fixating themselves on the pregnancy test for just a fraction of a second too long.

"It was Glen," I said, hearing the words as if through the ears of another, like from a person looking down at us from the top of the bridge.

"Yes," said Jessica, her voice crackling like ice on the verge of caving in. At first, everything made sense. A certain clarity washed over me. All her avoidance on the subject, the refusal to tell me who it was, the silent fortnight a week or so afterwards when she made no contact with me whatsoever. Then the sudden appearance of he who is known as Glen Caden only another couple of weeks after that. It all felt like I already knew somehow, and the fury of this realisation began to burn uncontrollably.

"You're right. We shouldn't see each other anymore. Or ever again," I said.

"I'm sorry, Eric. Truly sorry. You have no idea. I just didn't know how to tell you."

"Save that shit for your new boyfriend, Jessica. I can't even fucking look at you," I said, seething. I got up from the boat and began to walk away, but the war inside my head had already begun its onslaught. Each idea, every belief, was under siege. I could literally feel embedded neurological patterns reforming, reshaping and aborting themselves into an even more nebulous, despairing version of hell than the one we'd found ourselves in before. But now, I was alone in that hell, isolated and shunned by the actions of a man I only believed to be a shadow. Now that looming presence had a name, had a significance beyond what he first did, had an active, leading fucking role in Jessica's life.

I'd often fantasised about what I'd do to the man who violated her. It would come to me without warning most of the time. I would scope him out, weigh him up, go underground and become a guerrilla soldier. I'd watch him from the shadows for weeks or even months until I knew his routine better than he did. I'd fool him into thinking I was a new friend of his, some gullible chump who thought the world of him. Whatever the fuck it was that he was into, I'd study and relate it all back to him, until he trusted me implicitly. That was the important part, getting him to have faith in every false word I threw at him. It would've made for a beautiful vengeance when I got my eye for an eye and *raped* him myself. I'd hoodwink him into an empty flat or warehouse, wherever really. I always pictured a skanky old, clandestine warehouse or a dusty old stage of a cheap drama school. Jessica always told me she fantasised about me fucking another man, usually whilst she watched. But I wouldn't need nor crave an audience. Seeing him suffer through my eyes alone was what I desired. I'd drug Glen with sleeping pills and simply wait until he began to fall under, take him in my arms and tell him not to worry, that I would take him straight back home. When he woke up, the first thing he'd see would be the pulsating veins of my throbbing revenge. I'd wipe the pre-cum from my cock and rub it deep into his eye sockets until it glazed over his retinas until he saw the world through my eyes from that moment onwards. He'd blink it away to see me, standing there, wearing nothing but a blackened, expressionless drama mask. Then I'd move around the stage and taunt him, whistle him a fucking lullaby, turn his fondest memories into an inescapable hell. I'd tell him I've got all sorts of diseases; syphilis, gonorrhoea, hepatitis, HIV and full-blown AIDS whilst riding my shaft up and down between his arse cheeks, stab-teasing and taunting him. He'd know what was coming, but he wouldn't know when. Once his fear reached its peak, I'd ease myself inside him dry, thriving on every inch of pain it'd cause. Only when one of us drew blood would I begin to penetrate, spurred on by its properties of lubrication. Only when his whole backside glistened with the deepest crimson would I thrust as far inside of him as I could go. Only when I saw the last shred of his hope evaporate would I be aroused enough to unload my ejaculation, riddling him with rancid bullets of semen so severe they'd pierce through and plant two-hundred million separate traumas into his core, burying themselves inside of him through their own suicide. Killing him afterwards would be too kind. Forcing him to *live* with it is what appeased the evil in me. Instead, I'd slash both of his Achilles heel's, so he'd have to crawl his way out of there, and the only way he could do that would be by pulling on the rope I'd tie around his neck, his new nylon umbilical cord. My very own Frankenstein would then be born into the cold, indifferent world that he left behind for me in his previous life.

It was a fantasy of revenge that I'd been plotting in my head, but that's all it ever was. It died at that moment, shattered right there and then on the riverbank. I knew I'd do nothing after obtaining that information. Think of me for a coward if you like but discovering that Jessica was not only still seeing but dating the man who supposedly raped her destroyed any vengeance I could think of. Part of me even wished that he had got her pregnant just so she'd be forced to wake the fuck up from what she was doing.

A sharp, piercing noise darted across the dirt and shook me out of the horrors of my mind. An old looking train had made its final destination. It was darker by then. Gravity weighed upon me with all its force. I turned, stupefied, not knowing where I was, half-mortified by the scattered breaths bellowing out from Jessica's mouth, half-enraged by the obtuseness which trailed behind them.

It was then that I said something that would forever echo inside of me. I looked at Jessica's face and met her eyes for the first time that evening with such a seething abhorrence and palpable disgust, that I'm sure she thought I was going to murder or maybe even rape her myself.

"I bet you loved every second of it," was what I said, through utter stupidity and uncontrollable rage and a desire to declare us as nothing but dead. Through my own sense of guilt, I blamed her for it happening. Whether I believed it or not was irrelevant. I'd already been briefed about this Glen—about this new man in her life—this *actor*—with his similar manner and shortcomings to myself—how well we'd probably get along under different circumstances—how he was doing all the things I wanted to do, professionally and intimately—how she was once so swooned over by the recognition he received from the occasional stranger walking the streets—how manipulative and charming and narcissistic and self-absorbed and disregarding of her feelings he was—how much he fucking reminded her of her fucking narcissistic cunt of a dead, five-year-old-finger-fucking father.

A look I'd never seen before contorted over her face at that moment, a look that would keep me awake at night and then wake me back up in a flash the following morning. She burst into tears before I'd inhaled another breath and turned away from her. I lit another cigarette, pathetically trying to mark my indifference with all the clarity I could think of. Her crying took on a different tone. They were the mournful tears of the trust we'd never have again. She attempted to get closer, but promptly stopped when I raised my hand at her. I had no intention of hitting her, but after learning that the man who raped her was actually the very same rapist she was now willingly sharing a bed with, it was difficult to know what I was truly capable of. Instead, I snatched the test from the ground and tossed it towards the river. As my arm launched forward and the stick released from my grip, the streetlamp at the centre of the bridge flickered, outlining the frame of a man, who disappeared as soon as the swab hit the water. Confused, I turned to see the back of Jessica on the crest of the small hill. After muttering something under her breath she started to walk away. I've asked myself what she said a countless number of times, but I still have no idea. Guilt washed over me instantly. I paced up the hill calling out her name, but by the time I reached the top, she was gone. Not a single soul was around. All I was greeted by was the rain that began to fall. Here, I turned and looked back over at the bridge. Nothing. All I could hear was my breath, hushed in its tone but ridden with panic as it echoed around my ears. I hopped over the barrier, crunching gravel under my feet as my teeth chattered between grinds. Not knowing where Jessica had parked, I'd resigned to head home and with an unsteady step, I marched towards the bridge. During my first few strides across it, a foreign, unknown sense told me that I was being watched. The schizophrenic streetlamp put me under interrogation, and an outlined shadow stood at the end of the bridge, appearing between erratic flashes. The whole scene took on a presence of its own, an unreality, so to speak, of a world where the human animal had never existed before, but whose destructive nature was all too palpably felt by everything around. The certainty that I was hallucinating did nothing to pacify the torrent of fears passing through me. They shook my movements into relentless flinches, but still I continued forth towards the silhouetted figure in front of me, as he seemingly did the same. But the world was one step ahead of us, so neither appeared to be making any ground on the other. As this realisation took root, he suddenly stopped, stagnant in the position I'd just seen him standing in. I could feel his glare, his observation of me, watching from somewhere in the shadows beyond the stuttering light. I was standing in the centre of the bridge. Without warning and unnoticed because of the static-charged hiss of the streetlamp, a car shot past me, so close to hitting me that an impossibly strong gust of wind forced me backwards. My back smashed against the wall, shuddering my already fragile state. Speckles of furious, iridescent light fizzled and perished in between the frantic blinking. My ears were ringing in one long, high-pitched scream, like I'd been standing too close to the explosion of a bomb. The sense of falling was beyond palpable, but no matter how convincing, nothing would allow me to tumble over. It was as if I was caught between dimensions, unable to differentiate the known from the unknown. Every organ and limb suffered its own unique form of vertigo. Breathing became deadly. The condensation of white became black like the fumes that shot out of the car that almost killed me. I tried to get the tainted air out of my lungs as fast as possible but trying to rid myself of their affliction only worsened its effect. Everything turned epileptic. My entire body was shutting down. Sweat poured out from every orifice, rabid and feral. Diseased. My eyes felt like they were bleeding. I made to look back over at the end of the bridge, but I was thwarted by the buckling of my left knee and fell to the concrete with my arms wrapped around my abdomen. A dull, excruciating ache forced me into the foetal position and swam through my blood like a defenceless bird trying to take flight through a sea of oil. It stirred and struggled, plugged and penetrated, shifting my pulse from one place to the other until it finally settled inside of my head. There it throbbed furiously, with such a savage relentlessness I thought my end had arrived. I clasped at both sides of my face, digging my fingernails into my temples and screaming into nothingness. The ringing grew louder and bigger. Deadlier. An abyss invaded my eyes, draping over my sightline, shimmering all over and at every angle. I stared into that abyss and saw nothing looking back but my own reflection; a great big nothing, layering itself over every fibre of my frame, perverting every thought; past, present and future. It hung in the air just before it imploded in a barely audible puff, as insignificant as every other lifeform on this planet. Then it washed over me, leaving no trace of itself behind, except through the casting of its cryptic light, its indifferent hue, which settled itself inside the filter of how I now view the world; accompanied by thoughts that never cease to flinch away from each other, not because some ring true and others false, but because the clarity of all their insignificance is forever illuminated, inside the pointless, decaying matter I had no choice in becoming.

Then the shellshock snapped, I blinked, and it was over. All that remained was the scatter-brained streetlamp, which blinked at a tag of graffiti on the wall to my left. FUBAR it read, freshly sprayed in a shade of deep-cut crimson. Despite its letters being blurred because of the tears in my eyes, I could read it clearer than anything before, but without a clue to what its meaning might be. The streetlamp then petered out as pathetically as I felt, and the graffiti disappeared into the black. Drenched in sweat, the scratch marks on the side of my ears and cheeks started to sting. I looked around for the figure again, but he, like everyone and everything else in the world, had vanished. I was entirely alone on that bridge. I got up onto my feet and looked out into the distance. Nothing appeared to have happened at all, except for the emptiness that'd settled inside my being, an emptiness which has still yet to leave me ever since.

CHAPTER TWELVE

Jessica's dipping cotton pads into some ointment and tending to my face. It stings like fuck but feels good all the same; a tolerable, well-meaning pain if ever there was one. We're inside one of the many spare rooms. It used to be an office, probably her father's, with a vintage desk and all its four sides up to the ceiling in books. The anomaly happening to be the frameless mattress we're lying on together and our tangled clothes at the bottom of it. A drizzle of mist floats by the single window in front of us, whilst a lonely dog howls sadly in the distance somewhere. I'd forgotten about the countryside silence. My urban equivalent is never really silent. But here each sound carries more of a chill and there's a haunted essence behind every uttered word.

"During the date, he was nothing but amiable. He made off-colour jokes… like you do, and he bought me drinks all night until I told him to stop…"

Jessica freezes for a moment, then takes another to finish dabbing my bottom lip. She looks at my wounds with sadness as tender as the pressure she's applying. "He only lived a few streets away from the pub, and when we got to my car, I knew I couldn't drive right away. He was very insistent, telling me how much easier it would be to just go back to his for half an hour or so. After deliberating it, I told him an hour maximum."

Without noticing she'd finished, the lid of the ointment snaps shut, and she starts setting everything else aside. Then she pulls the duvet up a little, covering us both. Underneath she entwines her fingers with mine. The muscles in her left thigh twitch ever so slightly, but the rest of her body remains motionless.

"When we got to his house, I suddenly felt a bit sick and thought I might throw up, so I took a breath outside his door. He got very impatient and went in by himself, leaving the door wide open. I'm not sure why but I stood there, debating whether to go in. I don't know how long I stood there for. Something inside me felt strange yet familiar. I blamed it on the alcohol and thought I'd shrugged it off, thought I was just being silly. I went inside without shutting the door, which led straight into the living room after a few strides down the corridor. Glen didn't appear to be anywhere but when I called his name the front door slammed shut. I turned around to see him in front of it… with a look in his eye. Like an animal, like something had possessed and taken over him. He walked over to me slowly… grinning, then he grabbed my hair and started kissing me. I tried to push him back and told him to stop, in a playful way that didn't take him too seriously. It calmed him down for a few seconds, but then he'd start the whole thing all over again… that went on for a while. Eventually, I managed to excuse myself and ran for the bathroom. But after locking the door, I realised that I'd dropped my bag when Glen started groping me. I must have stayed in there for nearly half an hour. Maybe longer. I just didn't know what to do. I only needed my phone to tell someone where I was, and everything would've been all right."

Tears stream down my numb, frozen face. Each breath sounds cautious. Shaken. There's a sick part of me that needs to hear this. A part I don't care to admit to myself, that leads me blindly into feelings usually ignored. I've envisioned this against my own volition more times than I can remember. Jessica's leg still trembles, but now it's because of mine instead of hers.

"For some reason, it didn't occur to me to just stay there until morning. I really should've done, but I didn't. I planned, whilst I was in there, how I could get to my phone and excuse myself again. But the longer it went on, the more all I could think about was Glen beyond the door, waiting for me, not making a single sound. He didn't even ask me if I was okay, whether I needed anything or what I was doing. Nothing. It was as if I didn't really exist to him at that moment. Stupidly, as it was so quiet, I thought he must've fallen asleep. Carefully, I unlocked the door and let myself out. Again, Glen didn't seem to be around. I rushed for my bag, but then he emerged from the kitchen, asking what took me so long. He was, for that moment, the person who I'd been talking to in the pub, someone gentle and attentive. Child-like almost. I calmed down and suddenly burst into tears. I apologised to him and told him I should leave. He agreed, hugged me and said that we could just forget the whole thing and move on. I remember feeling grateful he didn't attack me, didn't do what I thought he was going to do… fucking relieved…

"But when he moved away from the hug, the same rabid look from before returned to his face. He looked like a different person, or not even a person really, just something hollow and unfeeling. He kissed me. I didn't kiss him back. Then he started pretending to cuddle me again. His hands moved up and down all over, groping me. I really thought I was going to throw up, but I just stood there, motionless, unable to do… anything. I remember saying no, over and over again, but he just wasn't there. All he was doing was grunting and staring at my body. Then he just launched himself on me and we fell onto the sofa, then the white rug on the floor in front of the fireplace. I kept telling him to stop, tried to kick him back or just get him to see what he was doing… but nothing worked. It only ever seemed to make it worse. I thought if I didn't let him do… what he wanted to do, he might've just killed me instead. I know that probably sounds stupid, but it's what I felt. So, I just stopped. Gave up. And he… carried on. I waited, staring at the ceiling, numb, not even there in some sense. In some moments I felt like I was watching myself being violated, confused as to how he continued with such determination, how he managed to keep himself so ignorant of how frozen I was. When it was over, he just flopped to the side and went to sleep, like it was the most normal thing in the world. I dashed into the bathroom again, which was more than dumb, but I had no idea what was going on. I did it without thinking, led by a body that was no longer mine. Looking back, I think I went inside the bathroom again as if to pretend what'd just happened didn't actually happen, that I'd simply sat inside there the entire time instead. But when I glanced at myself in the mirror, I saw blood around my lips. I must've been unconsciously biting my bottom lip to distract myself… as Glen raped me. After I wiped it away, my more sensible instincts finally took over. In a flash of moments that I still can't recall, I grabbed my bag and got the hell out of there. Once outside I didn't recognise my surroundings at all. Everything felt out of place. I finally threw up when I found my car, and again before I drove off. On the way, I had to pull over on the hard shoulder. I think it was then that it really hit me. I screamed and cried and threw my arms about the car so much the windows completely fogged over. When I got home, I realised that I'd texted you and noticed you'd seen it, at 1:32am. I thought it was strange you'd seen it and kept quiet. As it turned out, you were busy, sleeping with Esther for the first time."

Jessica moves onto her side and sees I've been weeping silently during her whole story. She goes to wipe away the tears, but I turn away from her instead. All I can feel is the memory of seeing that message again; when I woke up in the morning next to Esther. I still don't remember the first time I saw it or what I was doing when I did, except for a moment when I was undressing Esther and felt a vibration inside my pocket.

There was a large list of missed calls as well. Nine or ten cries for help which went unanswered, all because I thought Jessica was only calling to interfere with my stupid plans, whilst I left her to get on with hers. I knew she was with someone that evening as well. My arrogance told me she was only calling out of guilt, but really, I didn't answer because of my own. I don't remember seeing the message. Maybe I did, and I simply ignored it or maybe Esther did and simply never told me. I honestly don't know. There is a disturbed, harrowing notion that dwells within me though. It tells me *I did see it.* That *I chose to do nothing.* That *fucking someone all brand new was more important than my sinking, now violated relationship.* That *Jessica was lying to pretend that she didn't cheat on me out of choice.*

Come on, Eric. Who the fuck texts someone to tell them they've just been raped?

Jessica convulses, her body not permitting itself to fall asleep. She says she often used to wonder whether it was always going to happen again at some point, how the abuse she suffered as a child made it inevitable. Taking it as rhetorical, and any verbalised response on my part immaterial, I make no reply, choosing instead to turn onto my side and face her. We play with each other's hands for a while, entwining our fingers, taking turns to push our cold palms back and forth. The way we touch is still the same. Even the way we breathe each other in. But we seem to be in an unspoken agreement of eye contact avoidance, as even the slightest glance comes across as too much. I used to blame this on everything that happened, but in truth, our eye contact was never that strong in the first place. The trouble with wanting someone to see you lies inside the mutual need to be seen yourself. So, we'll kiss and close our eyes, make this about sex and nothing else. It'll remind us of our past whilst at the same time somewhat deny our present; like this is all out of respect of what we allowed to slip from our grasp.

***

I'm not sure why I thought seeing Jessica and hearing about Glen was ever a clever idea. It's difficult sometimes, when you get an image in your head, to see how you can break free from it. It's been a plague inside my mind for too long, but I'm not sure that rationalises anything. What's troubling me though, is that I didn't ask her about it. I have done, too many times to mention in fact, but this weekend I didn't even breathe a word about my want of knowing what actually happened that night. She just came out with it from what seemed to be nowhere.

Maybe without my pressurization, she felt at liberty to tell me.

Maybe that's why she told me.

Maybe.

"Well, I guess I'll see you… around," says Jessica, after a long silence together inside her car. We always do this; say goodbye but fail to leave. The ride here felt like a series of blurred images under an ever-darkening grey cloud. The reality of the norm awaits beyond these four doors. It's no wonder why we don't want to depart.

"This might sound a bit weird, but thanks for, you know, telling me about it. It couldn't have been easy."

"It was easier than I expected. Thanks for listening."

"Do you think you'll ever tell Glen?" I ask.

Jessica sighs and rubs the condensation away from her window, the squeal seemingly representing the line I'm not sure I should've crossed. The drizzle from this morning is still present, moodily lingering all around us. The wait for her reply has us trapped, so I say, "It's okay. You don't have to answer that—"

Jessica's discomfiture interrupts me as I turn to look at her again. Despite her facing the window on her side, I can tell that she's crying. Under hesitation, she says, "I've tried…"

"Well, that's something—"

"I tried very recently. The other day in fact. I said I wanted to speak about our first night together. But he…"

Jessica's neck jerks and she shoots a look my way, her widened-eyes falling into a vacant stare. But vacant it is anything but. I know that glare, disguised as hollow to hide… something. That something makes her look away again, sensing my attempt to interpret its meaning. That's the look I'll be taking home with me, the hesitant glance I'll be drowning at the end of a bottle tonight. She turns back, feigns a smile screaming with sadness, and says, "He said it was perfect. That there was nothing else to say about it."

She mumbles something else but it's incoherent. It's probably better understood that way. She scoffs, then ruffles her hair, throws another forced smile my way, scratches the back of her head and hums numerous times. I, in contrast, do not move at all. My heart seems to beat at an impossibly slow rate, whilst a burning sensation breathes underneath my skin. I want to say Glen dismissed it because he knows something wasn't right about it. I want to say that he's been gaslighting her ever since they got together. I want to say that if she continues down this path with him, then she'll get exactly what she deserves. But all these thoughts are smeared with acidic intentions, collectively identical, desirous only to inflict her with further unnecessary pain.

"Don't answer this if you don't want to," I say, trying to disguise my suspicion with tenderness, "but what's made you want to confront him about it?"

Another sigh forces its way out of her, then a frantic, subconscious look out of the corner of her eye demonstrates her fear of my potential reaction. "He keeps trying to talk about us… having children. That's why Eric."

"Oh."

"Please, don't get annoyed. We haven't talked about anything. Ever since he mentioned it, I haven't been able to get… to get *what I just told you* out of my mind. I've thought about just breaking it off with him without mentioning it, but I can't, Eric. I really just can't."

I think her voice is distraught, but I cannot tell. A feeling as opaque as our surroundings has cast over my mind's eye. Eric Archer's fugue-like state in the fog. Beyond her, through her smeared window, I can see that graffiti mark again, still electric with red after all this time.

FUBAR.

"It's okay, Jessica. The natural progression of any relationship is to force innocent souls into existence. The only way to get payback on being is through mimicry. With Glen being the sadist that he is, I'm hardly surprised he desires to have children."

"Please, Eric. Stop. It freaks me out when you talk like this. I'm sorry if it hits a nerve, but you asked, so I told the truth. Glen is seven years older than us. It *is* understandable. Some men *do* want to have children, you know."

"Especially the most egomaniacal, psychopath—"

"Don't do this, Eric. Please. It's not like I'm planning on having children with him... I'm just telling you what he said."

"It's okay. I'm sorry. Really. I know I'm being a prick. I get it. You're right. You do need to confront him."

Jessica leans over and hugs me, burying her head into my shoulder blade. I take in the scent of her hair, feel it ripple through me like a wave of sorrow. The window has blurred over again. I can't see anything through it now.

"You wanna know something sad, Eric? Seeing you this weekend has been the highlight of my year."

"Even sadder that it's been the highlight of my last two then," I say, fucking meaning it as well. She lifts her head up and we kiss in the softest manner as the rain caresses over the windshield, concealing us from the war outside.

"Do you think we'll ever try again?" she asks, with tears welling up. "We could start things slow," she continues. "I know I'll break it off with Glen eventually. I'm just not sure when..."

"I'm sure you will. Let's just wait until then," I say. Even though I want to say that we could start over, the damage done seems beyond fixing now. This has been our routine for the last two years. An exchange of empty promises and half-hearted notions, each word coming out all the more tired because of how often they've been said before. That's the problem with words; they become increasingly worthless the better you know someone.

I lean over to Jessica. We hug, then kiss. Our rhythm is already beginning to disintegrate back into the past as we're abandoned into the present. I go to flick the latch, when Jessica says, "I know we don't see each other often anymore, but I'd like to see you again soon, Eric. Would that be okay?"

"I take it that means you're serious about telling Glen?"

She nods.

"Well, of course I'm around then," I say, offering a smile. "Take care of yourself, Jessica."

"You too, Eric."

With that, I finally depart from the car. As I walk towards the station, I stop for a moment to roll and light a cigarette. Jessica pulls up to the side of me and lowers her window. She smiles in the awkward way she so often does, and I mimic it probably more than I realise as the glass rises up to separate us once more. This would've been a perfect way for us to depart; if the dent underneath the window of her door wasn't there. It's a dent Glen is guilty of making. He stamped his foot into the door during an argument. I don't know whether Jessica was inside or outside the car at the time. It seems no matter where we go, Glen is always lurking around in the background somewhere.

Jessica's gone now. She's gliding across the other side of the bridge into the mist.

As much as I want to see everything as if anew, it looks much the same, in the most fatal sense imaginable. The catharsis I thought I'd obtain from hearing her story, is absent. Maybe because in Jessica's mind, all I am is Glen's absent ears. She didn't even bother to lie and make me believe that she chose to tell me first.

I'm sure it was nothing personal.

That's the whole problem though, isn't it? It should be fucking personal.

There was a time when Jessica and I were together where my identity was exactly what I wanted it to be and the truth is, I only ever got a taste of it because of her. But I watched it shatter into nothing but a type of debris that dissipates even further away whenever I try to take hold of it and put the pieces back together again. Now the only thing which seems to keep us in contact with each other are the shattering moments that tore us apart.

ACT TWO

"Take care when fighting monsters, that you yourself do not become a monster. For when you gaze long enough into the abyss, the abyss gazes also into you."

- Fredrick Nietzsche

CHAPTER THIRTEEN

Oh, god, what I would give to wake up fourteen again. It was such a beautiful time to be alive. You never get erections as stiff and blissfully unaware as back then. Yet another cruel joke from nature really, handing out your best boners when you can't put them to any decent use. Indeed, one could argue that the blame lies within the societal frigidity of the era I've been born into, but as we human, all-too-human specimens were spewed up by nature in the first place, the fault shall remain with the latter. Luckily though, (or not, as I sometimes wonder) that wasn't to be the case with me. Like a gift from the gods, a blossoming, eyelid-fluttering twelve-year-old had just moved into my area, a dozen or so houses up from mine, recurrently twinkling with the lacklustre education glimmer she came riding in with. The first glance did it. I still remember it so vividly; how she dropped a moving box full of what I later learnt to be nothing but clutter, her flustering embarrassment as she noticed my observation of her subsequent adolescent fit, her glance upwards at me after regaining her composure as she delicately picked it back up, pivoting her pubescent posture into profile as she stood, giggling at the strengthened realisation that I was gawping at her, relishing it and inviting me in; the very same giggle she would later gargle after playing with me like a toy until my batteries had, shall we say, evidently depleted.

She took a liking to me immediately and made no reservations about it whatsoever. I was her chosen one. I literally didn't have to do a thing. It was as if she came knocking upon my door the minute she hit puberty—*oral-fixation at the ready*—with her arms crossed under her eager to be noticed, unexpectedly in bloom chest, tease-sucking on the split-ended strands of her hair, legs akimbo from the knees down, feet crisscrossed inwards because of the desperate, outward ache upwards. She always looked at you for a while before saying anything, smack-chewing her gum as she opened her mouth, revealing the braces she still had to wear for another six months. If she wasn't chewing gum, then it was a loose lock of hair from either side of her pigtails, in between a face of angelic purity, peppered with the devil's details that were the adorable freckles about her nose; eyes only ever saying: do with me what you will. I swear her body reflected light differently to others. Every move she made trailed and lingered inside a sphere of innuendo, which always left behind a salacious sprinkle of her rainbow-sparkling fuck me dust.

She'd come over mine straight after school (usually dressed in an adjusted, porn-shoot style school uniform) with the excuse that I was 'tutoring' her. I suppose in a sense I was, but really, ladies and gentlemen of the jury, I was the one under her strict, rather demanding tutelage. Forgive me father, but the only heavenly gate worth opening was inside that very sin. She was the type of girl who watched pornography merely to imitate it, the type of girl who kept her Barbie dolls for later use as makeshift dildos, the type of girl who saw semen as the true source of her existence and hers, all hers and nothing but hers alone.

After a while, it was fairly obvious that she'd been abused as a child, but as she hadn't really come to terms with it yet, I'd hit the jackpot. All my little plaything knew was that there was a little button-bean between her legs that demanded to be pushed and tongued. I'll never know how many seeds of the fantastical she planted within the soils of my brain, but what I do know is, your honour, is that she harvested many of them herself. As soon as my bedroom door closed her hands would unstrap my belt and she'd drop to her (sometimes grazed) knees. Her whole body would shake furiously during climax, which tossed her nimble, delicate frame from side to side as it riddled through her tectonic body, leaving behind its evidential trace by flaming her cheeks a glorious scarlet for many a minute after, during which she would doggedly return the favour like a dutiful, feral and sex-starved nymph.

I remember it all so acutely. The dirty and damaged, one-strap ballerina-esque black shoes. The cute white socks with the flower-design flop over the cuff, or the stretched navy ones that rested just below the knees. The intentionally torn-up and tattered tights. The blue and green chequered pleated mini-skirt (which, when unveiled happened to cover nothing but her glistening, ripe pink lips, as she always removed her underwear before entering my home). The unkempt, button-popped white shirt, two or three sizes too small, tampered with Coca-Cola stains, and, of course, the frills around the bra she always wore, which left adorable, hook-shaped indents under each developing breast as it struggled to carry out its assigned task with each passing day. Even the smell of strawberry-flavoured bubble-gum awakens flashes of what is now considered to be illegal thoughts inside of my mind.

She didn't give a fuck about anything except fucking. All I had to do was sit back and watch as those breasts blossomed into that robust, fuck-you-gravity, tight and taut, teenage shape, whilst her bottom bloomed into a perfectly round, munchable peach. She was as eager and willing as she was stupid and naïve. My faultless, untameable girl of the wild, who saw sex as something you must learn and master, not a by-product of falling in love like so many others confuse it for. It's weird to think that if I recorded those escapades, I could probably be arrested for watching them now.

Like it happens with some artists, she just reached her peak too soon and quickly became a caricature of herself, ballooning all out of control and ageing all too fast. Luckily for me, some other guy twice my age caught her eye after she turned legal. It was beautiful. She thought she was the one who decided it was time we parted; when in truth I was already pursuing others my age or milfs without her knowing, eager to show off the skills I'd learnt—fucking the lollipops out of my ignorant angel. It's difficult to describe my favourite times with her, as the memories collected come to me in a montage; the evolution of her body at the end of my cock. If I were to venture a guess though, the best times took place when she was about fourteen. That's when girls are ready to get down. Well, the best ones anyway. Forget that stupid sixteen shit. To argue with nature's design is to deny our own instincts. I could go out to pubs and clubs, seduce a litter of ladies with an utterly tranquilised mind due to the completely lacking chance of ever bumping into her and always had her as a back-up option if the night turned sour. She was besotted with me by that point. My interest in her on the other hand, soon dwindled after I could legally bed her. She attempted a comeback after elbowing me aside for a new daddy (who turned out to be an impotent faggot—her words) but by that time all the confidence she once possessed had abandoned her, whilst the daddy complex she'd denied for so long finally began to reveal itself. She turned to the usual clichés to keep it at bay; frantic spending, copious drinking, relentless drug-taking, etc. I heard she got pregnant with the seed of a lunatic before she turned seventeen but lost it due to the increasing dependency on the just formerly mentioned. I saw her once during this time, at some bar I'd never normally go in, where she blanked me like I never existed to her. She overdosed a year or so later. I feel bad for not killing her myself really. She deserved to die dumb and unaware, happily fucking my brains out, giggling as my semen coagulated into a layer of icing across her braces. I remember I used to worry about her mother finding out about us because of those braces, how they might've somehow betrayed the scent of my illegal passion. I shared this concern with my nymph and, through her insistence, agreed that it'd be better instead if I simply came over her face, Every. Single. Time.

My malefic princess. Look at what you've done to me now!

I sometimes wonder whether the heaven I found myself in back then, had to be paid for by the hell I find myself in now. Like there's some cosmic law of karma dictating the legislation of the multiverse. I honestly believe if I knew then what I know now, I would've convinced her to commit suicide with me, with our fingers-up to the empty promises the world offered for our futures, before all the damage that would've been done even had a chance to turn its torturous gaze towards us.

If only I could remember her name.

All I recall is that it was as disposable as she later became, but that's about it. Something tacky like her accent... Stacey? Kimberley? Leanne? Mmm.

Question: Who knows?

Answer: Who cares?

I always ponder these thoughts after a period with Jessica. I'm still positive there's something about Glen that she isn't telling me. Maybe I'm just losing it, but something lingers in the air whenever I see her. It's taken her nearly two years to tell me what happened. Two years. Two years that she's stuck by his side. I thought finally hearing what went down, what *really* happened that night would help me somehow, but all it's done is made me realise an ugly truth. I needed to know because part of myself felt desecrated after Glen hijacked Jessica for his own personal joyride. Jessica then took her own bite out of me when she confessed to be sucking on the cock that raped her. She's been searching for an answer to something that's long been dead in the ground; her childhood. The worst part is, I'm betting Glen *knew* he'd get away with it. He must've been scoping her out all night whilst charming her with his manipulative wit, taking mental notes of her emotional age, realising it to be younger than his, but also how proud she can be as well. What a concoction. The perfect victim. *She'll say nothing, I'm sure of it* he must have thought, toying with the idea for a few hours whilst drugging her with wine and telling *'off-colour'* jokes… just like I do.

The sickest thought, the one which never fails to bring about a pang of the deepest shame, is the idea that it only bothered me so much because I was jealous. Jealous of the rape. Jealous how he, not only got away with it but was even rewarded for it, as Jessica stuck by his predatory side. Only in the clichéd, male-orientated, possession-type of way I naturally recognise to be idiotic, but still cannot stop myself entertaining from time to time. The good old, but frankly obtuse, *IF I CAN'T RAPE YOU THEN NOBODY CAN!* mentality.

Rape envy. Is that even a thing?

What's worse is… I still cannot say for sure if that feeling has passed… or is simply growing, somewhere inside the deeper recesses of my core, of which I have no direct access.

I guess I'll do my best not to think about it.

I'm sick of the pretence I've been living out, all the second-guessing, dilly-dallying around, all of which ends up going nowhere. I suppose if anything, I just wanted some understanding regarding Jessica, me, and even Glen. A little clarity, some sort of resolution or perhaps even acceptance.

What an idiot!

Nothing is ever resolved. It was nothing but a nagging little narrative dancing around the left hemisphere of my brain, seeking out reason and understanding, that of which there wasn't shit. It all just happened, be it random or determined, there was never any choice—that part's always an illusion.

Become the person you really are. That's what I'm going to do. I've got the mind to get away with murder. Yeah, I might've been slacking off for the last couple of years, amidst the fog of existential despair, but that's no way to live. Death to the vile spectator in me. It's time to shake the bull by the horns until it kills me, or I make it my bitch. If the world wants an individualistic society so badly, let's see what they make of this individual. I'm on the hunt. This soldier is at the ready, armed to the teeth. My words are bullets. Some of you may confuse my future behaviour for self-destruction, but that's because you're scared of life like the pussy-whipped, slave-mentality bitches that you really are. Look at yourselves, roaming around in polite society with your heads buried in the virtual sand, airbrushing your self-satisfied selfies for the empty ego-boosts you so desperately crave, as you puke-up your platitudinal status updates, tagging and poking and swiping and emojiing your whole lives away, surrendering your identities to a simulated representation of reality, merely to show off the cover versions of your fucking non-existent selves.

Orwell was warning you, not typing up a fucking handy how-to guide!

It's not destruction my friend, it's creation.

Every man gets the war he deserves. That's the truth behind the matter. The only truth. This woe-is-me, play the victim, compensation hungry society might take in most of the herd, but I don't buy it for one second. It's funny how every time some paedophile children's TV presenter (most likely working for the BBC, so that TV license you're paying for probably all goes towards his court fees) gets outed, how a whole litany of these supposed victims all come forward, claiming how out of fucking nowhere they've *'found the courage'* to speak up about it after all those traumatic years.

Question! *Why's that, Eric,* I hear you ask?

Answer: They all want an easy payday, *that's* why!

Surely that's not the reason?

Of *course* it fucking is!

They all want a wad of free coin and a bit of attention. Pity attention, easily the worst type of attention, sure, but it's all eyes on them nevertheless. They all want a wage for the first time they got whored. It's pimp or be pimped in a world full of whores! There's no rationality—only indifference and dog eat dog. It's time we embraced the virtues of nihilism. We're all living in the chaos of corporate neoliberalism as it is, so why in the fuck are we holding onto such absurd notions as morality? Morals are only for people who can afford them.

"Cheers mate," I say, snatching the bottle of champagne from the counter and exiting the off license. A toast to be made to the miracle of abortion. It's suddenly dawned on me that the only time this world makes any fucking sense is when you fucking force it to. If to live is to suffer, then suffer I fucking shall! Unleash the misery, the chaos, the destruction. That's right *being*, open your eyes up, *existence*—FOR I DECLARE A FUCKING WAR. If one is condemned to suffer the consequences of one's actions regardless of one's intentions, then to hell with the consequences, fuck the suffering and the intentions be damned! This is the start of a new beginning, it's different from all the other times before—the feeling is there, alive and burning. If only there was a way of holding onto it, preserving it somehow. I'd take feeling like this for a few more years over *ba-ba*-black-sheepin' my way to seventy-five and that's a fucking fact. Carve this epitaph into the amalgamated pieces of stone that built-up the foundations of your identity and smash it into smithereens whenever you need to start over!

Reality is only ever shaped through the eyes of the beholder.

Reality is only ever shaped through the eyes of the beholder.

REALITY IS ONLY EVER SHAPED THROUGH THE EYES OF THE BEHOLDER.

As I'm nearing my house my habitual nature kicks in and I'm already taking out my keys, eager to get back inside, crack open the champers and start looking for some acting work, maybe some modelling, hell, fuck it, perhaps I'll venture into some porn, anything to get involved again and not feel like everything is hopeless. As I jiggle my front door key free from the others, I look up ahead as I'm walking and notice something a little...

"Eric! Babe! Where have you been? I've been waiting for you all morning!"

I was going to say strange, but the only strange thing was my initial surprise.

You ignorant little prick, you forgot all about this little situation whilst you were out gallivanting in the countryside all weekend, didn't ya? Well, here we are, faggot! Learn to embrace it again. She's only a lost cause to you because you're too much of a pussy to shape her into the woman you want her to be. Man up and take some responsibility!

"Esther… what are you doing here?"

She springs up from the top of the steps, flips her long, luscious locks back and tiptoe-hops down the steps, tossing her tits into their own private mosh pit. "I've been waiting for you since eleven, where have you been? What's the champagne—shit, babe… what the hell happened to your face?" she asks, throwing herself into my arms and wrapping her legs around my waist. I move my hands around her and suck in her pheromones before I even realise what I'm doing. There's no way a divine creator whipped this body up, only Satan himself could design something so alluring.

No wait, get yourself together first shithead, you've got the scent of another all over you. You can't fool a whore's nose! Hit the showers first soldier, safety fucking first!

"Well?" asks Esther, eyeing my injuries over, seemingly smitten with them.

"Oh, nothing. I was drunk in a park, got into fisticuffs with some loon. I was winning before his crazy bitch got involved."

"A woman did this?" she inquires, with a partial tone of jealousy, if I'm not mistaken.

"No, her man did after she jumped me. Guess I should've smacked her one first. Didn't think she had it in her."

"How did it start though?"

"Oh, it doesn't matter now. I've been relaxing all weekend. Most of the bruises have healed up. It's just my lip that stings."

"Well, okay. I dunno why you like going to the park so much though. Were you alone?"

"Yeah. I'm always alone."

"Aww. I've really missed you babe!" she says, sounding passably genuine for a change.

"I missed you too," I say, unsure if I'm lying. "Where the hell have you been?"

Esther's legs drop, but our bodies still cling tight. "At my dad's, you know that," she says, wrapping a clump of my shirt between her fingers and clamping it into a fist. "I've really missed you babe," she says again with over-compensation, whilst I'm visualising myself spraying champagne all over her fucking perfect tits.

"Shall we, you know. Go inside for a bit?" I say after the bottles spent.

She pinches a teeny bit of flesh from her bottom lip with her teeth and says, "Kiss me first," and before the tattering tut of her last word was even uttered, my tongue finds itself buried deep between her slut-enriched, scarlet-painted lips. Her hand slides down from my chest onto my waist. She claws a few fingernails into my hip bone. The difference with Esther to pretty much all other women I've ever been with is that when she wants sex, nothing—and I truly mean nothing—holds her back. She's dishonest with basically everything else in her life, but when it comes to getting her rocks off, she radiates brighter than a red-light district during happy hour.

"So, why aren't you at your dad's now?" I ask, reluctantly breaking away from her mouth.

"Oh, I'm sick of that prick. Him and his cunty mail-order bride. She keeps complaining about me and said I had to... well, I just needed to get out of there for a while. I've been thinking about you a lot, so I thought it was stupid that we weren't together."

"Okay."

"Have you got any weed?" she asks, easing back into the Esther I'm all too accustomed with. I tell her that naturally, I have weed. She loves to pretend she doesn't know certain things about me whenever she's misbehaved. Probably a parlour trick she picked up in the brothel.

"Cool," she says, wrapping her arm in between mine as we walk up the steps. "Didn't you get any of my calls babe? You never pick up."

That's because I was trying to fuck a girl who had my abortion and then hopped over to the moors to give a little scratch to an old itch. You ain't the only crazy pussy in this town bitch.

"Nope. Phone's gone schizoid on me. Is that a new jacket?"

"Oh, do you like it?"

Probably a bit too much. It's a little leather biker-style number, only zipped half the way up so the focus is on the magnificent cleavage that's practically bursting out of her magnolia tank top. She's also got on a commando-style camouflage mini-skirt with a slit on the side, buddied up with some fishnet tights, which have rips in all the right places.

"It could make a man lose his mind," I say, getting another once-over in. "So, you're still working then, I take it?" I ask, unlocking the front door and walking through the shitty hallway, half-wondering whether I left my laptop out for some reason.

"No, they let me go in the end, like pretty much everyone there. I had some holiday left so my last pay packet was pretty decent. Thought I'd treat myself," she says, kicking off her shoes and throwing herself on the sofa.

"The weed is under the coffee table, help yourself. I'm going to hop in the shower."

You gotta get the aroma of blonde out of your pores before diving into her and that jacket. Clever thinking, Archie boy. See how simpatico we are when you just do as I say?

After I've stripped, the champagne bottle pops open from the living room, followed by one of Esther's playful, cock-flinch inducing giggles. Everything this girl does is sexual to me; like she's the ultimate embodiment of innuendo. The phantom ghost of the nameless twelve-year-old, back for revenge. I usually prefer to wait at least a day before sleeping with another woman, but when Esther's like this, it's frankly impossible. She's been trained in the sexual arts for fuck sake, with a master's degree in male perversions. I must honour her dedication and commitment to the cock. It would just be rude of me not to. She disappeared for... I dunno, a couple of weeks as well, so the chance of getting exactly what I want is high.

In fact, it's *guaranteed.* And as you should very well know by now, my observer—*I do love me a guarantee.*

CHAPTER FOURTEEN

Had a little word with myself whilst I was showering. I've come to a decision, at last. The way I see it I currently have some recruits under my wing, all of whom are now in training, whether they realise it or not. I'm their Marshall. Field Marshall Archer. It's got a good ring to it, doesn't it? Officer Cadet Esther Bellona, the running favourite if she can get her pathetic little tantrums under control, is now under my tutelage. Her main strength: that body, no doubt about it, and her willingness to whore herself out when the going gets tough. Her main weakness: the brain in command of said body and her willingness to whore herself short. But that weakness, under the right exploitation, can evolve a new, better Esther; a powerful, bitter, man-eating monster with Double-D tits and zero qualms about where the semen hits. Any future displays of violence shall be met with an equal reaction on my part, for the greater good of her sanity, as well as mine.

I come out of the bathroom to find the living room has been cleaned and that Esther has left half a spliff in the ashtray. Good girl, but I knew she would do that. It's her tired old apology; clean up a bit and feed me some drugs, instead of just simply verbalising it and preserving her energy.

She's sitting down on the sofa with a blanket over her legs but is still wearing the leather jacket. It's only when I sit down myself that I realise it's all she's wearing, whilst the bottle of champagne is held upright between her magnificent twinset of weapons. The eye of my cock blinks in disbelief, unsure whether it's woken up in heaven, or indeed, hell.

"I like it when your hair's wet. You look like some Calvin Klein model or something," she says, reaching her hand out and tussling it a touch.

"Yeah right," I say, leaning forward and reaching for the spliff. "More like fucking Joop."

Esther laughs whilst I'm toking a big drag of the impressive spliff she rolled. It's a sonorous laugh, which is both annoyingly sexy and rather convincing. Credit where credit's due; she's a splendid actor when her motivation is clear.

"How come you're not at your dad's then, like what's the real reason?" I ask, passing the spliff over.

"Oh, the twat kicked me out," she says, trapping it between her fingers, one breast amply moving up, then down. I fear my objective has already been compromised. "He knows I just lost my job as well, but his *queen* complained so out I go. They've scarpered off to the countryside for a month together as well, but *she* doesn't want me to have the place to myself. Oh well. Sod him and sod her too. I was getting pretty sick of that place anyway."

"So, what are you going to do then?"

"Don't know yet. Find another crappy job, I guess. Who cares anyway?" she says, passing the joint back.

"So, you want to stay here, is that it?" I ask, trying to get to the point of all this. No more beating around the bush. Figuratively speaking anyway.

"Well, I've been thinking about us a lot during the last couple of weeks. How much I've missed you and everything. I mean, I know we fight a lot," she says, taking a swig from the bottle. The initial sip slips under her chin and lands on her chest, right between the slit where her two breasts meet. My god, she's a master.

"A *helluva* lot," I say, my words croaking in a cloud of smoke.

"Yeah, maybe. But I was talking to some girl from work, and she said she was in a relationship that sounded a lot like ours. They used to fight and bicker all the time, but once they accepted that that's what their relationship was like, they just went with it."

"So, despite the fact we argue all the time and treat each other like shit, it's fine, as long as we just accept it? Despite the lethal consequences we could be having on each other's mental health?"

"Something like that, yeah," Esther says, gesturing for the spliff. I hand it over. "I don't see what your problem would be, you always get really hard when we argue."

"I believe that comes down to an unassembled triage of unresolved issues I have Esther. But, in my defence, the only thing more alluring than a beautiful woman is a beautiful woman bursting with rage."

"You're such a dick."

"What about Sausage Roll? Not seeing him anymore or something?"

"Oh, god no. The thought makes me sick," she feigns a shudder, holding the spliff up to my lips, which I soon suck upon. "He kept buying me flowers after our one awkward night together."

"I thought that's what you wanted?"

"The first time was nice, but no. Just coz you never bought me anything doesn't mean other men won't."

"Yeah but other men haven't slept with you as much as I have. That gives me a free pass."

"I hate it when you say shit like that."

"I'm just trying to make you aware of the fact that every time a guy buys you flowers or chocolates or wants to take you out for dinner or whatever, it's for one thing and one thing only. Sad, but inevitably true. You must have picked up on a few things, being a young woman with your looks and physique. It's not just that, Esther. Don't look at me like that. You have something about you, an electricity, if you like, a sexiness most do not possess. It's a gift, overall, but like most gifts, it feels more like a curse to the one it's bestowed upon. For this reason, most women will hate you and all men will attempt to bed you. Those are the cards you've been dealt and there are millions out there who would kill to have what you have," I say, stubbing out the smoked spliff as if to illustrate my point.

"So, nobody out there will ever be interested in me just for my personality?"

"What personality?"

Shit, that just spurted out of me like a nerd's first time. Esther's open-mouthed expression of shock kicks me into self-preservation, so I manage to block her from slapping me around the face. She gets frustrated and keeps on trying until I grab hold of her wrists.

"Don't. Try. Hitting. Me. I didn't mean it. Or I didn't mean it *like that*, but part of your personality is sexual, Esther. It shapes all of us in one way or another," I say, easing my grip from her wrists and letting go, trying to ignore the further excess of spilt champagne now covering her chest. I lean back on the sofa again, balls tightening.

"Why is everything about sex with you?"

"It's not just me Esther, it's *everyone*. It's just that nobody wants to admit it. You know this deep down. Nobody would dare come out and confess that it's all revolved around sex because that would mean giving all our little people game *bullshit* up. It would be shown for what it really is, a little slut on its knees, desperate for pleasure and acknowledgement, begging to feel like it's worth something more other than what it has on offer. Without all the over-complications and mindless distractions, we're nothing more than a series of neurological impulses, feeding off our little lizard brains until we all wake up one day to find we have a fucking family we never asked for—or even worse, *wished for*—because we thought it might give us a little meaning but when it comes down to it, it doesn't mean *shit*. Then we're just left to rot in an illusion of our own making, knowing that deep down it was never a free choice. We're all exactly what we were intended to be and that's it. There's no decision in any of this, it's just a fantasy fed to us, so we can justify why we stay in jobs we hate, stick by friends we never liked or stay with partners we never intended settling down with. That's what I cannot really understand about anything. Some people seem to think that conscientiousness is rising, but it's not. Look at the litany of so-called feminists out there, sitting on their fat dyke arses, spitting away on a keyboard for a blog nobody reads, thinking that their opinion somehow counts merely because they have one. I mean, *come on*, opinion has got to be the lowest form of any knowledge, yet it's pumped out by the media so much that people are convinced that it counts for something. It means *diddly-squat*. And it's highly offensive to those that study in a specific field of anything. That's why I hate democracy as well. Look out for the good of the general population, sure, that's a given, but don't go giving the average fucking Joe a vote. The average Joe watches Saturday night television. The average Joe can't make a distinction between Beethoven and Britney Spears. The average Joe is a *fucking average Joe*. He might be a likeable moron, but he's still a hamburger short of a happy meal, and his mind is as plastic as the cheese slapped inside of it. He shouldn't be able to vote. Like old people who no longer work and contribute to society shouldn't be able to either. That's where my beef with feminism comes from as well, not that I'm against it, I'm all for it in fact, but look around you, what the fuck is equal between men in the first place? Capitalism is a system that *only* works through exploitation and inequality. Somebody's always left behind with their pants around their ankles. Nothing's equal, nothing ever has been or shows promise to be. It's all just a relentless, unforgiving, apathetic and meaningless merry-go-round we refuse to get off because then we'd see just how helpless we all are and how fucking banal our lives have really become."

"Well, it sounds like you need to smoke more babe, so whilst you were waffling on I rolled another spliff. Give me the lighter," says

Esther, pointing at it on the coffee table with her foot, kicking my political speech to the side like the pointless rant that it was, annoying me into thinking about shutting her up by shoving my cock in her mouth.

In a pang of partial irritation, I slam the lighter down into Esther's hand. She gets a bit annoyed in turn but instead laughs it off and gently presses her feet into my ribs. I didn't even notice her ninety-degree shift on the sofa.

"So, what happened with you and the Foreskinator anyway?" I ask.

"Nothing. We didn't really even have sex anyway."

"Yet you decided to take the morning after pill because you didn't have sex?"

"We did for like a minute, but it just didn't feel right. Looking at him with all that excess skin around his cock made me feel sick. And the sex was shit. It made me realise how much I really like your cock."

"Yeah right, pull the other one, Esther. This one broke a long time ago," I say, laughing off what she knows I love to hear.

"It's true, I never realised it before. You have a very nice cock," she says.

I believe every word.

"Esther, they're all pretty grim to look at. So, what happened?"

"Why d'you wanna know so bad?"

"Well you basically cheated on me with this guy, so it's pretty hard not to wonder."

"I didn't *cheat*. We were taking time apart, weren't we?"

"Don't play the female loophole card, Esther. It won't wash—"

"You fucked some Chinese girl who couldn't even speak English!"

"Yeah well, it was probably better that way. I blame pornography for that one anyhow."

"And you fucked that other girl, the one who was into self-harming and shit. So, that's two-one to you."

"Not really no—it's not a competition. I didn't have anyone on my radar whilst being with you, and you worked with this botanical bellend, so you must have been in contact with each other before we had a mini break-up or whatever convenient phrase you want to label it with now."

Esther shrugs and says, "He knew I had a boyfriend, yeah, but he only started showing an interest in me when he saw how upset you'd obviously made me."

"Like a fucking snake in the grass! He saw that you were sad and went straight in for the kill. Every guy has pulled that stunt before. It's grotesque, sure, but that's men for you. Come on, you must've known exactly what was going on. Just admit it. If you want us to be together, I mean truly together, start admitting to the dark shit that goes on in your head. Like you used to when we first started dating. That was the Esther I fell for. We could rip the world a new one together. Why string one skint guy like me along when you could simply add a few other suckers into the mix? You could retire before you're thirty if you played your cards right because remember, looks don't last. I know that because I'm a drunk and my alcoholism has sped up my ageing tenfold already, but luckily for me I'm male, so I can get away with the rugged look for a while. Plus, I'm drinking myself ugly for a noble cause. Being attractive has led to nothing but trouble but once I reach thirty myself, I'll finally be unnoticeable. But you're a woman, Esther and you're *all* fucking woman. Your potential right now is limitless, but you do have a sell-by-date. Trust me. I know what I'm talking about."

"You're such a freak, d'you know that?"

"Of course I do."

"I came back here because I want to be with you, stupid. For real this time, no messing about. We need each other, Eric. Let's not kid ourselves, look at what we're like when we're apart. We're nothing without each other."

"Well, that's a good a reason to drink than I can come up with," I say, reaching for the champagne, but my hand gets batted away.

"What? Don't you agree with me?"

"It's a little difficult to take you seriously Esther. One minute we're *'destined'* to be together, the next I'm the worst thing that's ever happened to you. Doesn't exactly sound like the cornerstone of a lasting relationship, does it? But sure, yeah, I'm going to choose to believe it and I'd like you to do the same with me."

I get up from the sofa, a little annoyed at Esther's forthright arrogance but satisfied with the conclusion of the conversation. She thinks she can just ring a bell and I'll start salivating like some chump. Well, better to encourage that line of thinking. After a quick slash, I dash into the kitchen, open-up the larder, reach my hand up inside and *bingo*, half a bottle of High Commissioner to the rescue, at my service on an *if-and-when* basis, twenty-four fucking seven. The sweet sound of the bottle cap twisting free echoes around my eardrums, inviting me in to forget what's currently going on. Plus, it's better to get a few swigs in there before Esther picks up on the fact that I've got more booze as well as weed.

You can't have her living here dipshit, haven't you worked out that's all she really wants yet? All this crap about being together is just another one of her ruses. Of course she wants to be with you now, she's got nowhere else to go. You don't see many homeless women on the streets for a good reason Eric, because there's always some sucker like you around to take them in, no matter how much aggravation they may cause you. Look at her, smoking your weed, using your blanket, watching garbage on your television. She's taking you for a schmuck. She was probably at Sausage Roll's before even thinking about coming over here. She's got to earn her keep. Give it to her straight.

"You want a drink?" I call out from the kitchen. "A whisky and coke or something?"

"We've got *champagne,* stupid. How about something to eat?"

You see fuckstick? Now she wants sustenance as well. It's not enough to get free weed and booze—you gotta feed the bitch too! You always said you never wanted a kid, now look at you. You're a goddamn paedophile hiding behind the years of legality. It's not a woman in there, it's a lost, forgotten child you've taken in with terrible intentions—

"I'm on your fucking side here, help me out!"

"What babe? You need help?"

"No. Just thought I did. No food here. We can order a takeaway or something later if you want," I say, slightly shaken. I felt like I disappeared for a minute there.

"Oh yeah, that'd be great babe. Thanks."

"You got any money?" I ask whilst walking back in. Esther's hands have disappeared under the blanket. She shakes her head at me with her bottom lip pouting out. She looks at my crotch quickly, then back into my eyes.

"You know what?" she says. "When you go off on rants like that, I get really wet."

"… really?" I say, clearing my throat, thinking about tossing the blanket aside.

"Mmm-mm," she says, nodding her head with the devil in her eyes. "I've been wet since I saw you. You look fucking sexy with those cuts and bruises." There's a subtle motion going on under the blanket, hypnotising me further with each full-circle. The monster has awoken with eager intrigue. Esther notices and starts moaning when she sees my cock creep out between the slit of my dressing gown. I walk towards her face in a trance. She swirls her tongue around her lips and spits on it, causing it to tremor, eager for more. The blanket slips away and there she is, in all her glory, rubbing her clitoris. I pick up the bottle of champagne and pour it very gently into her mouth. She leaves it hanging agape, pulls me closer to her whilst maintaining eye contact and eases the head of my cock into the sparkling pool of wine inside her mouth, still staring into my eyes and now masturbating with more aggression. She grabs my hand and all-but forces it down there, soaking it upon contact. With an exhaling moan, she wraps her lips around my shaft and swirls the champagne around with her tongue. Still looking, she swallows the wine with a loud throat-gulp, then tightly grips her hand around my flinching manhood, starts thrusting and takes a breather with the head to the side of her lips like a drug-addicted rockstar to a microphone. As she tunes herself up down below, she says, "I just fucking love having your cock in my mouth, Eric," and I just believe every fucking word. Little squirts start shooting out of her, gushing where they may as her body begins to writhe against her volition.

"Aggwh-*schpuuuut*," she spits, massaging her saliva around what's soon going to enter every part of her. Now she pumps with an air of frustration and resentment, saying, "*Argh*—you fucking cunt—ohhh, *fuck*, yeaah—you love this, don't you? *Arrrghhh*—this is what you want—you love this fucking cunt—oh, god, I've been aching for you so much, Eric—*arrgrggghhhh!*"

Esther spins herself around and moves back, slowly curving her spine all the way until only her backside hangs in the air. She slap-grabs onto each cheek with self-arrested hands and unveils the sources of her power to me. "Just eat me first, Eric," she says, voice desperate, begging.

"Oh, Esther... fuck." I say, nosediving into her rabbit hole.

"*Ssshhh!* Don't you dare—*fuck-cunting hell*—speak to me—*argh, that's it freak!*—when you're eating—*oh, you little twisted prick shit!*—Eric Archer," she demands with the gust of a lunatic's laugh that bursts a host of flames to the surrendering white flag of my own lucidity. She eases my tongue in further by pushing herself back, yanks the bottle up from the floor and starts slurping it up something psychotic. Looking over her shoulder with a malefic gloss in her eye, she pours what remains of the fizz down the ravine of her spine to somehow add further potency to a poison I'm already nothing but a galley slave to.

Esther, Esther, *Essssttthher.*

Notice how the name slips and slithers down the palette, how its promised sibilance escapes before the tip of the tongue has even tapped the back of the teeth to retract, how the subtlest of vibrations can be relished upon should you allow yourself to be raptured by its lingering, ever throat-constricting whisper.

Come on, don't be shy now, say it with me.

Essssssssssssttttttttthhhhheeeeeerrrr. Impossible to pronounce without that serpent's hiss.

She's still commanding me to eat her forbidden fruit even as I feast myself upon it like a savage beast. My god, she tastes like deviant omnipotence, of something entirely inconceivable; not of this world.

Now avert your eyes and get the fuck out of my head, my perverted little observer, no eyes should see what I'm about to do.

Esther's training is about to begin.

CHAPTER FIFTEEN

Upon waking my head throbs like a World War One's soldier's nerves; shot to pieces and on the verge of a breakdown. The synapses in my brain feel like a conjoined tripwire wound so tight it could snap under the slightest pressure, making even opening my eyes a kamikaze mission. Eventually, I manage it. Iridescent, shimmering dots of varying sizes explode everywhere, like a kaleidoscopic bomb. The flat, from what I can make out, is in a tip again. Through a blur of crushed beer cans and cigarette butts, I crawl to the bathroom. A harsh ray of light pierces through the singular window, making my entrance a somewhat difficult affair. Going by the position of the dust clouds it must be close to dawn. My mouth tastes like ash and female ejaculation, aka urine.

As I gag, my stomach wretches, then the burning sensation around my cock makes itself known. The over-stretched foreskin, post-anal aches. I hang my head over the toilet bowl, but as the takeaway promised last night never managed to find itself ordered, I have nothing inside to discharge. I hoist myself up via the rim of the toilet, then once more towards the sink sat next to it, careful not to jerk my head up too much for fear of catching a glance of my own face. I flip the cold tap on full blast and watch impatiently as the basin fills up. The tap's shriek into idleness uses my brain as a conduit, forcing me to wince and gasp and thrust my head straight in. Water rises over my hands, spilling onto the floor. I open my eyes whilst under, and, without really being conscious of it, find myself screaming, seemingly unable to stop. I keep screaming right up until the point when the body's instinct for survival kicks in and forces me to thrust my head up to take a—*SMACK!*—goes my skull against the cabinet above. I fall flat down onto the floor, landing on a forever sodden, beyond stained bathmat. Before I know it, I'm aborting phlegm foetuses whilst half-choking on them as a collision of galaxies returns to wage war within the space between my eyes. Nothing hurts, meaning everything does. Eventually, I cease to choke and take comfort from my wheezing breath. A few loose pink pills wink at me from within the tussles of the rug. I'm not sure what they are, but I'm not sure what I am either, so into my throat they go. It takes me a while to swallow them down. I lie in wait there for a while, wondering if the last few minutes really happened.

Then I wake up again.

After towelling my hair and face dry, I return to the living room, desperate for more rest. Argh, it stinks of fucking smoke and booze. Puddles of Esther appear to be everywhere too, not just the sofa and its pull-out bed, but over the carpet and the walls too. Even the mould looks like it got a blast. Feline women sure know how to mark their territory. I'm not sure if this is the result of our fucking or fighting, nor if there's a difference between the two anymore.

How many *petite morts* does it take to finally kill your libido?

"Esther?" I call out through my smoke-ruined, dehydrated throat. Nothing. After checking the blankets and the kitchen it's plain to see that she has left again, without saying anything. No note. No word.

No nothing. Gone without a trace. It seems like I'm the one wearing the high heels around here. But like many a street-walking hooker, I just got fucked without getting paid.

I flick on Who's Afraid of Virginia Woolf and bury my head into the only lumpy cheap pillow I own and let the pain of somebody else's past drift me back into sleep for a change, oddly consoled by the smell of Esther's piss. The jury is still out on whether female ejaculation is just urine or not. I'm sure it probably is, and I really don't care. Piss on me, shit on me, treat me like the worthless cunt that I am.

-Ring-ring! Ring-ring!-

You know that pang of dread that hits you when you get a phone call in the middle of the night, the one that says death is on the other end?

-Ring-ring! Ring-ring!-

Well, I get that every time my phone rings nowadays. If it's not a rape, it's an abortion. What the fuck could the past want with me now?

-Ring-ring! Ring-ring!-

So tempted to hit the reject button... why do I even have this stupid thing? Is it merely to fit in? Do I enjoy having it, or is it just keeping tabs on me?

-Ring-ring! Ring-ring!-

"Hello?"

Silence.

"Listen you—"

"Eric? Is that you?"

"Who's this?"

"Hey man, it's Rich. How's it going?"

"Oh, hey Richard. Sorry, I thought you were someone… never mind. How the hell are you man? Long time."

"Pretty great, thanks. Busy like you wouldn't believe. Got a rare couple of days free, so I wondered if you want to meet up for a drink or two," he says.

"Urm. Yeah, why not. Sounds good," I say, already half-considering an excuse not to.

"Cool. That's what I like to hear. You wanna meet at our old hangout?"

"The Western Front or No Man's Land?"

"No Man's Land. It opens at twelve. How's a liquid lunch sound?" he asks.

Richard is a good soul like that, reminding me that he is more of a full-blown alcoholic than I am inside ten seconds of speaking to him.

"Urm, yeah. I could do with a drink actually. See you at twelve, Richie boy."

Click.

The self-proclaimed Richard The Great Cogswell was in the same class as me during drama school. He's roughly ten years older than me but he's one of those weird people who won't tell you their actual age despite how blatant it is by the usual tell-tale signs; receding hairline, pot-belly, muscular dystrophy etcetera—that he's in his mid-to-late thirties. He likes his ladies way too young and confuses blatant disinterest for playing hard to get infatuation. He was besotted with one girl (who eventually dropped out as she couldn't act worth shit) who was clearly (and naturally) a lot more interested in yours truly. She was a kook, but a very pretty kook nonetheless. Never met any chick who was so openly into being dominated. She literally told me that I could rape her whenever I wanted to and that I shouldn't be put off if she put up some resistance. I didn't take her up on the offer, but I did fuck her once. It turned out her rape fantasy was just a guise for sexual frigidity. Go figure. She was what a psychotherapist would call a schizoid. You've met the type. Present in the physical sense but mentally forever elsewhere. She left to study philosophy or something like that. Richard denied all of this to himself so much that he now genuinely believes none of it happened. If it wasn't so terrifying, his ego would be something to behold.

The next one he wanted was, typically enough, Sammy. He thought ahead that time around and had the fucking audacity to request that

I 'lay off' her for a few weeks whilst he weaselled his way in there. It was 'his turn' after all. Beautifully, this had the reverse effect, and after said weeks passed by, Sammy basically threw herself at me like a damsel in *get-that-fucking-creep-away-from-me* distress. Obviously, I happily and clandestinely obliged. I'm pretty sure he knows but as he won't ever mention it, he may as well not. I really hope my vow to seduce as many women as possible whilst I'm young doesn't inadvertently turn me into him. Hopefully I'll be dead long before that. Another day drunk should speed the process along.

I'm up out of bed, putting on my rags, ready for a new day of heavy drinking and ogling girls. Eric Archer don't give no fuck no more. The sad thing is, it's mandatory to be crumpet calling every time I make the mistake of hanging out with any of my male friends. Not that I have any. It shows a lot about the decisions I've made over the years, chasing tail wherever I found it, but reversing the reputation I've built feels nigh-on impossible. After a while, everybody sees you for what rumours you're tainted with, and it doesn't matter whether they are true or not, people will use what they see and hear to their advantage, knowing that the majority rules in most cases.

Take this for example; there was this chick in our class who went by the name of Big Jugs Jane. We never hooked up or anything but one night we came within an inch. She had a boyfriend at the time and I (in a moment of stupidity) did the *'decent'* thing for a change and chose to do nothing, despite the blatant opportunity I was presented with. She cornered me outside a pub after a performance and said that there was a lot of 'sexual tension' between us during the term, pretty much waving the white flag for us to fuck. Naturally, part of me wanted to, mostly my cock, but my self-loathing at the time was in overdrive, so in a momentary lapse of Eric Archer reasoning, no move was made. Didn't think anything else would come of it, but after said night I noticed that her boyfriend blanked me every time I saw him, so I knew something was up. Being the dumbfuck that I am, I mentioned it to Richard. In his delight to see me despised, he did some digging and told me that Jane blurted out a load of shit to her boyfriend about how I tried to slip between her sheets, and how she had to turn me down. So, Big Jugs turned out to be a lying bitch, who was either annoyed that I didn't reciprocate her advances or who was just using me the whole time to make her boyfriend jealous. Moral of the tale? I should've buried my cock deep inside the concealed crevice of her mountainous chest and given her the secret bit on the sly she was asking for, the fucking deceptive, double-f dark horse. The funny thing was, after learning all this stuff, I found myself far more attracted to her. It's as if what I truly desire is to be treated like scum, or I'm only ever drawn to those I'm unconsciously taking revenge upon. Oi, Freud! Get over here, we need to talk about mummy.

Here's a free warning. If you sleep around a lot, all the other people surrounding you will hate you for it, especially if you reject one of them. Even when I try and do the right thing, I always end up getting scolded. It's no wonder I'm such a chauvinist. If everyone wasn't so goddamn uptight about sex and fucking relationships in the first place then these problems would be obsolete by now, but the Judeo-Christian 'morality' you each entertain—*without even being fucking aware of it*—is just so imperative to your being you really couldn't live without it, could you?

After swigging the remaining contents of a discarded bottle I found on the floor (which I confess had some fag butts swimming inside of it—Esther's pathetic attempt to control my drinking—*FUCK YOU, ESTHER*) I whip on my trusty old leather jacket, slide my feet into the only pair of decaying shoes I own and start rolling myself a breakfast cigarette whilst waiting for the kettle to boil.

After sinking down a whole *cafetière* of coffee and chaining a handful of smokes, I chuck a couple of valiums down my top hatch and wait until I'm ready to face the snarling swarm. He Who Likes to Dick 'Em Young is one of those friends whose tolerability is totally dependent on a narcotic haze, the more blended the better. It's a bit bloody early to be drinking but to be honest that boat set to sail during my GCSE's, so what difference is it going to make if I'm a night time drunk or a daytime one? Shit always seems to happen either way.

My morning anxiety rush caused me to slam the door with alarming aggression, but here I am again, back out on the street by just a little past eleven thirty. The clouds are grey like always, people are living out their dull-fuck lives all around me and I'm going to squander even more of the only dwindling nest egg I have and so fucking be it. I'm done with everything. Seeing that I'm suitably dumbed-down like the world now demands, I'm going Forrest Gump on its ass.

Ready. Set. *Go!*

Cigarette sparked and I'm off. Coming up to the first hurdle, some pathetic drunk clutching on his bottle of whisky like a baby with its first teddy bear—*not that I'm judging him for that*—I just do it in the privacy of my own home as *a*. I have one and *b*. I'm a goddamn *functioning* alcoholic who knows his limits, not some layabout tosser without any self-control.

Coming up to the jump.

Whisk. Hopped over and ignored with ease. Now approaching the first bend. Hit smoothly, taking the wide angle for a little leg room. I'm gliding baby, gliding; building up speed along the second straight, with the next obstacle within my sights. It's some *clipboard-at-the-ready* charity mugger with his elbows out and emotions sucked in, eager for bank details and a self-served, self-congratulatory pat on the back. Time to whip out my phone and use it as a blinker. The chugger taps away on his clipboard with both ends of his pen as I pass. "Yeah man, I'll be there in two shakes of a lamb's tail," I say to no one, "just finished my shift down at the soup kitchen. Twenty minutes, tops." Through my peripheral vision, I could feel the red coat burning his eyes right through me. He even attempted to speak but stopped when the volume of my voice increased. No commission today bitch.

Moving on, nearing the next turn and *ding-dong,* a woman on the wrong side of thirty strides by and gives me the eager eye as she does so. Being in the charitable mood that I am, she'd get it today. Looks like she could do with the validation. Not worth the effort though. I give her the Archer eyebrow arch whilst breezing through the second bend. She smiles as I lose sight of her, loving it. I'm a Samaritan at heart.

Next: Another tramp with a shivering Jack Russell sitting on top of his lap, breathing as desperately as his owner should be begging. I've heard that dog-owning tramps get free food for him and his mutt, so he ain't getting shit out of me. I can't afford a fucking dog. Besides, there are so many homeless people in this town now, if I gave all of them some change, I'd end up in their position by the time I reached the pub. The council have reacted by shacking a lot of them up in makeshift shipping containers as well, if you can believe it. It's as if they took the idea from a *How-To* video on human trafficking.

As I approach the human-sized urinal cake he holds out his gutter-grubbed hand. "Got any spare change mate?" he asks, barely getting the words out of his dry-lipped mouth. Impeccable timing though. As he was asking last night's debauchery began to swish-swash around my gullet, breezing a brisk, toxic fume down my rectal passage. So, with one leg hooked up and one hand liberating an arsecheek away from the other, I blow him a beautiful, long wet kiss.

"Keep the change."

"You *fuckin—*"

Sorry mate, too little too late. I'm round the final turn and on the stretch home. Oh, wait. Double down on that *ding-dong.* In front of me stand a couple of schoolgirls, scantily dressed in their uniforms with the standard, self-customised adjustments that scream nothing but *SLUT.* They must be bunking off. One of them is chewing gum and has her shirt tied up in a delicious knot, showing off her flat 'n smooth stomach whilst it lasts. What a little jailbait-waiting-to-happen harlot. It's like she's advertising for her own abduction.

"'S'cuse me, mayte. Ya couldn't buy us some fags could ya? We got da money," says the soon-to-be pregnant teen.

"Depends," I say, ending my morning run and turning around to face them. "What's it worth?"

"*Huh?*"

I sigh. "What do I get out of it?"

She looks at me with a confused, contorted bitch face and then at her friend, who continues staring at the pavement like when I just jogged passed her. Eliza Doolittle looks back at me and blows out a bubble with her gum until it pops. She pouts the top of her lip up but doesn't have anything else to say. That isn't to say that I don't though:

"I'll tell you what. If you two make out for a minute, I'll buy you some fags out of my very own pocket," I say, whipping out my phone for a potential, if not questionable photoshoot.

"*Eww*. You're a *puuurvert*," says Bitch Face, whilst the shy one's cheeks go aflame. Looks like the coin flip landed exactly how I say it did.

"A pervert who can legally buy tobacco, twinkle tits," I say, sparking up a cigarette like the cock-tease I'd train her to be, and sucking it up as if it makes my day *oh-so-delicious,* with my eyes on nothing but her budding breasts. Why the hell the legal age is sixteen here I do not know. This fourteen-(possibly thirteen)-year-old's body is ripe and ready for a good hard *you know what.*

Her friend laughs but Bitch Face throws her a dirty look that makes her meek like a mouse into subservient silence. After a pause, the shy one whispers something into the ear of the spunky one. Attitude looks at me again, making snapping sounds with the corner of her mouth, thinking she's got some influence over the situation. *Cute.* She stretches her gum out from her teeth until it snaps in half and shoves it in the mouth of the shy one. Damn. Spoke too soon. I'm chubbing up.

"Al'rite. But get us some booze 'n all," she says, chewing with an exaggerated degree of zealousness, whilst the shy one follows her lead.

"Deal. It'd be my pleasure. But you better make it good. I want to see some tongues, some arse-grabbing, a breast grope or two and a lot of hair-pulling, with varying levels of aggression. Oh, and as you're both underage and of the same gender, I'd like to see the pleasure derived from your upcoming meeting of tongues to be somewhat… ambiguous. Understood?" I say, mostly at the shy one to ignite motivation in the bitchy one. "Oh, and get shot of the gum too. Both of you."

After a moment of hesitation… they appear as if they're actually going to do it!

Question! Why does being a magnanimous arsehole always wield the desired results?

Answer: Everyone always yields to the will of a psychopath.

The shy one spits her gum out into her hand and holds it up to her friend, who takes the hint as I zoom in on them both through the lens of my phone. "Come on, I haven't got all day, get on with it," I say, satisfied with the acquired frame. "Ready? Roll… camera… speed… *action!*"

The shy one looks at me, directly into the lens, smiles and, to my surprise and delight, grabs the pigtails of the bitch and goes in all guns blazing, so much so that Attitude's cheeks go red as they kiss. "Don't be shy with the hands!" I say, moving the shot into a wider frame. Bitchy lets out a moan *(3/10)* as she grabs an arsecheek *(7/10)* to which the shy one breaks away and giggles with an awfully adorable nose-wince *(10/10)* before resuming the kiss and grabbing a tit *(6/10)*, which receives an angry groan from bitchy *(9/10)*, who reacts with an unexpected hand up the shirt of the shy one and an *underneath the bra* tit grope, which flusters up the both of them something rotten *(11/10)*.

I reluctantly interject for further direction, "That was great. Now just caress each other's lips a bit and show me those tongues. Nice and slow now." I zoom in for the closing shot. A string of saliva connects the two of them, unnoticed by bitchy, but slurped up by the shy one and visibly swallowed as they finish. Whilst they giggle closely into each other's faces, clearly ecstatic at being given permission to do what neither of them could admit to the other, I begin to slowly walk backwards, until they realise their remuneration is now due. Bitchy turns towards the lens for the limited-edition bonus feature and starts waving a finger at me, the very same finger I'd lick and suck upon before its deep insertion into her BBF's bunny-tight butthole. In respect to their surprising performance, I flick my half-smoked cigarette towards them as payment.

"That's a wrap. Nice work ladies, especially you," I say, winking at the not so shy after all one, who might just be worth doing time for.

"Oi! Where ya goin' ya cunt?!" shouts bitchy.

"I've got a video here begging me for an upload," I say, holding up the phone and shaking it from side to side, finishing it off with a flourish flip around my fingers. "Don't worry. You'll be famous before midday. I *guarantee* it."

"Oi, ya fuckin' perv! D'ya know 'ow fuckin' old we are? I'm only thirteen and she's still twelve. We can get ye proper done for dis! Go get us some fuckin' fags ya cunt."

"Learn how to speak the *fucking* language you were *fucking* taught properly first. Then we can talk. You should be thanking me anyway, at least you now know that you come with a price. Maybe next time you won't set the bar so low. Use those wombs wisely now. Ciao!"

"Oiiiii!" she exclaims, thrusting her fists up and down in a tantrum, causing those sweet young tits to dance and jiggle. She starts a boner-triggering rage march my way but halts after glancing over her shoulder, as her friend is walking off in the other direction, puffing away on her paycheck. Bitchy quickly follows behind, snapping her fingers for a go on it. The sneakily shy one winks at me and smiles. Damn, she's going to eat some poor sucker alive one day. If it wasn't for Tantrum Tits, that sucker would likely be me.

Hell, if they're still about after I've got tanked, I'll take them both back to mine for a little bit of *how's your absent father*. That'll make for a much better video anyway. I'll only need to dish out on a couple of lollipops, a ten pack of B&H and a four pack of WKD, and I'll be breaking in double hymens by dawn.

Bing bang bosh, what d'ya know, I'm at the pub, staring up at the decaying paintwork of its namesake, wondering whether anyone these days looks after the establishments they decided to venture into anymore. No second guesses for whether the hinges on the door will creak as I enter. Almost satisfactorily, they do.

CHAPTER SIXTEEN

It must be said, I'm a little miffed as to why Richard chose this dump; there's not a female of any species to be found within a mile of it and the rancid smell of shitty old ales attacked my senses the moment the hinges of the door ceased their wailing. It's making my head ache something awful. The barman doesn't look at all happy to be serving anyone except for a couple of solitary down-and-outers, who obviously spend all their time hopping between this shithole and the *ye abandoners of all hope* bookmakers across the road. Just looking at them slouching over the bar, staring into their piss-warm ales spirals me into a depression. It's peaceful though, but that isn't exactly surprising when you look around. There's a dirty old red carpet permanently pressed into the floorboards by blood, sweat and beers, mould-like graffiti tags of nicotine plastered over the walls and the stench of bar fights, body odour and life's disappointments ponging up the whole joint. Moving away from the bar I opt for the table furthest away from the drunks, but their coughing and spluttering is impossible to ignore completely. Before I've even sat down, half of my pint has been necked and the need for something stronger is starting to scream inside my veins. Richard best turn up soon. I'm on edge today. Got way too wasted last night. Still heard nothing from Esther. I guess I'll deal with her later. 'You want me to do *what?*'. I don't remember much except for our fucking, which was pretty damn intoxicating all by itself to be honest. 'I'm not doing that *ever* again.'

"Eric!"

Richard pats me on the shoulder, reminding me that he does that. He's bought into that whole neuro-linguistic programming crap, so now every time he makes an unusual movement or gesture, or mirrors your body language, you can tell he's just trying to manipulate you in some way. He used to try it with girls all the time at parties. It never worked.

"There he is, Richie boy. How's it going matey?"

"Hold it there," he says, raising his hand, directing his thumb towards the bar, "I've got to see a man about a drink." As he walks off I'm reminded as to why I don't often venture outside anymore.

The persona Richard tries to display doesn't suit him at all. It's like he's trying to show himself off as some hotshot Hollywood movie star, somebody that's really going places and has a different woman for every town he visits, when all he really does is prey on single mothers via internet dating sites and saves a few quid by living at his parents, so he can afford some disease-free prostitute now and again. He once told me that he'd slept with thousands of them whilst living in America. Whilst most of what he tells me I deem to be bullshit, I believe him regarding that. He's got the penchant for prostitutes written all over him.

Randy Richard's one of those dipshits you see everywhere nowadays who's fallen into the cult of thinking that the universe gives a toss about him. How all he needs to do is visualise what he wants, and it'll come to him eventually. It's astounding really, looking at him now with his scruffy loose shirt and ex-a-la-mode light blue jeans, to see just how far removed he is from the version of himself he wishes to present to the world in comparison to the reality of how he's actually seen. A lot of women at drama school saw him as a bit of a creep, a kind of leech trying to suckle on any bit of flesh that would let him. Fuck knows what they thought about me though. Probably the same. I'm just younger and better looking, so for the next few years, I can safely duck from the tarnish of that brush.

Richard receives his change, which he immediately double checks right in front of the unimpressed barman. Once satisfied, he drops definitely correct change into his pocket and starts walking over to me. Breathe in, breathe out, feel the energy all around you and prepare yourself for some almighty horseshit.

"Eric, my man. Good to see ya," he says, taking the seat opposite me with a quick glance at my pouch of tobacco on the table. I'll give it about five minutes before he asks me for a roll-up.

"You too man, what you been up to?"

"Ahh, nothing much really. Way, *way* too busy with everything since leaving drama school. A lot of people from our group say there's no work out there. I don't know what they're talking about. I *literally* haven't stopped since we left. Demand is high."

"Go on," I say, giving his ego something to chew on.

"Well, let me see. Ah, the first thing I did was a TIE around Yorkshire, playing some various roles, you know the drill. That was good. After that I did a panto—*Aladdin*—and then I did a feature film, a horror that'll be hitting the festivals any day now."

"Cool."

TIE (Theatre in Education) is my worst nightmare as an actor. It involves being part of a group that goes around schools performing 'moralistic' plays, condescending to kids who most likely already know better. The pay is peanuts, you perform to children of all things and you get dumped with doing all the donkey work as well; unloading vans, setting up stages, sleeping on the road. Being a human puppet in other words. And panto, despite sometimes paying quite handsomely, is a complete waste of treading the boards for any performer. It consists of nothing more than sickly transparent innuendos and derogatory role-reversals, telling stories that everybody in the audience is already familiar with so they don't have to think, yet still feel they have some sort of ownership over because the narrative is ubiquitous. Opinions based on nothing, basically. That's where I fall flat as an actor. Even though I'm a blatant whore (in more ways than one) I'm not enough of a slut to do anything as a performer, so I don't. Unlike the centre of the universe sitting opposite me.

"Yeah, the horror was the most fun, there were these three glamour models in it," he says, flicking his eyebrows up, "and I managed to convince the director to film this sweet fantasy scene where they had to stroke and fondle me and stuff. One of them was even topless during it."

"I'm sure it was integral to the script," I say, proffered with a little jovial sarcasm, but he's too preoccupied with his phone to notice.

"Going on a date with one of them this week. Wish me luck."

Why the hell is it that every guy I'm friends with feels it's necessary to tell me about every potential or carried out sexual exploit they've ever been involved in? I'm never asking anyone about their stupid sex life because to be frank I couldn't care less. It's just *fucking* when it comes down to it. What the whole song and dance about it all is I've no earthly idea.

Richard sticks his phone in my face, and says, "Take a look at those puppies." The picture is slightly blurry, but I can make out some scantily dressed hussies surrounding Richard, who is dressed as a priest. The skanks have the same vacant stare in their eyes like the ones you see in pornography; washed-over and looking around for their next line of coke. In fact, it looks a lot like a porn shoot. Then again, what doesn't these days? Gazing at the photo and knowing my cue is in place, the expected response seems to be the easiest option:

"Nice rack."

"I know, right! Believe me, I was very tempted to give them a grope but as I was unconscious during the scene it didn't seem appropriate. Next time I'll propose it to the director."

"What's the film about?" I ask, completely desensitized to the vile thing he just said.

"Oh, well. Urm, that's difficult to answer. Let me see if I can explain it to you in a way you'll understand. It's about this group of people who agree to stay in this house for twenty-four hours for money, okay?"

"Urm. Okay."

"Right, but there's this secret agenda going on with the owner of the house. Nobody knows, but they're all being filmed during the whole thing. And one of us gets poisoned, but we don't know who because we all get drugged with something hallucinogenic."

"Sounds original."

"Yeah, it is quite."

"But what's the actual story, like what's your role?"

"Well, I play a priest with a dodgy past, who's there to repent but ends up performing an exorcism on one of the girls, though whether that actually happens or not is down to your interpretation. She's like four or five days late getting her period, so she's anxious as hell. In the end, it turns out the house is possessed and everybody in it dies. But again, it all depends on your interpretation of the events. It's a real... how do I say it? A real thinking man's horror. Not sure if it's your sort of thing."

"Well, it's certainly got me thinking already."

"It's singularly unique. My only concern is that it's too ahead of its time."

I can't help but smirk as I nod.

"What about you, been in anything interesting?"

I have done some stuff but can't be bothered to waste my breath. "Nah, can't find any work out there."

"You should consider doing some modelling work or something. I always thought I'd see you in some Topman advert one day."

"Are you taking the piss?"

"Not at all. You've got the look for that stuff, trust me."

"Maybe a few years ago, not so much now. Plus, that's not acting, it's posing. I already do enough of that as it is."

"Money would be nice though."

"True," I say, finishing my pint. "You want another drink?" I ask, momentarily wondering if he buttered me up so I'd ask him that.

"I'll have the same. Could I pinch a rollie too?"

"Go for it. But roll it yourself."

"Fine."

All right, maybe that took ten minutes. In drama school, he'd constantly bum cigarettes off me, which was fine, but after a while he always expected me to roll them for him too, every goddamn time he wanted one. It's what I've found with a lot of people since getting into my early twenties. Everybody wants something from you and if you give it to them, even just once, they expect it every fucking time they ask. Give an inch...

I walk over to the bar again with the empty glasses and order another round. Richard finishes rolling a cigarette and gestures for me to meet him outside once I've been served. It's quite funny seeing him again. My guess is his life is just as lonely as mine. A vast, empty, glaring void, desperate to be filled with something every single day.

John Doe finishes serving me the drinks and I place them back down at our table, grab my tobacco and head for the beer garden out back. As soon as I'm through the door Richard starts mime flicking his thumb for a light. It's hard to tell whether he knows what a twat he can be. I flame my cigarette first and hand him the lighter, which he'll probably try and pocket.

"So yeah, I've got a gig at our drama school this weekend, that's why I'm in town," he says.

"Oh right. I thought you might be hitting the brothels or something."

"Why, you want to? I know somewhere near here actually... nice and young. We could meet up later—"

"No, no. That's okay Rich. Maybe some other time."

"You sure? They come quite cheap if you wear a rubber."

"I'm good, thanks. So, what are you doing at the drama school?" I ask, trying not to think about prostitutes and condoms.

"Oh, right yeah. The school asked me specifically if I wanted to take on a workshop. Like what we did before during the diploma."

"And what exactly does that entail?"

"Whatever I want from what I've been told."

"Right, but what are you going to do?" I ask.

"It depends on the people who take the workshop. I'll probably do a little bit about exploring characters through animalistic traits, a bit of yoga for them to find their neutral position, though that depends on the females in the group, if you know what I mean," he says, nudging me with his elbow, making me shudder slightly. "If it goes accordingly, I'll have a regular job there, which would be good for my wallet. It may even open a few doors, career-wise *and* female, one hopes."

"Leaving the drama school to go back and work at the drama school. Nice."

"Yeah, I know, but it's always good to have something to keep me ticking over. Oh hey," he says, taking a drag from his cigarette, "are you going to the reunion thing?"

"The what?"

"The graduation party, only a year after we actually graduated," Richard says with a laugh.

"Oh right, that thing. Yeah, I never understood why they did that. Better odds on getting numbers there I suppose. Do you think anyone from our class will actually go?"

"Probably not but who cares about them? There'll be plenty of fresh totty there. You know Sammy just started the course we did, right?"

"Well, I thought she probably would."

"Yeah, she'll be there no doubt. Think I might make a move on her again."

"Really? Why would you wanna do that?" I ask.

"Felt a vibe off her. Bit of chemistry, you know?"

"I don't think so man, she's just... the type to flirt, you know...

excessively. A true actress I guess."

Richard wags his index finger. "No way my friend. You should've seen us the last time I saw her. A week or so back I was at that pub you took me to ages ago. What's it called again?"

"Journey's End?"

"Bingo!" he says, snapping his fingers, "that's the one. Yeah, I popped in there on the off chance I might see you and found her inside instead, sitting in the corner."

"Weird."

"Yeah, that's what I thought."

"Was she meeting anyone in there?" I ask.

"She said she was but whoever it was never showed up. She asked me about whether I'd seen you or not though, funnily enough."

"Right."

"Well, I guess she just wondered as it's your local haunt. Anyway, we talked *loads* about acting and stuff. She said she'd love the opportunity to work with me. There was definitely some chemistry going on."

I finish my cigarette as Richard parts with his and we go back inside. I'm a tad taken aback with the information he's just given me but reluctant to make him aware of it. This is where I'm at my peak as an actor, not on the stage or screen, just with so-called friends who have nothing better to say to me than who they're planning on trying to fuck. It is truly amazing how blind people can be though. Richard bumps into Sammy in my local, by chance, and she asks him directly whether he's seen my ass, only for her to then get stood up, yet he still refuses to correlate one with the other. Maybe he does, and that's the real reason I'm here, but it certainly doesn't feel that way. Perhaps he's just eager to dine on my scraps.

"When did you say you saw Sammy?" I ask, interrupting his self-orientated waffle.

"Urm. Friday… yeah, it was on Friday."

That's when I went to see Jessica.

"So yeah," Richard says as I'm finishing my pint. I'm expecting the favour to be returned, but he looks at his watch instead. "I've gotta dash for an audition. Cheers for the pint." He stands before I can protest. What a miserly maggot.

"I'll see you at the graduation party then?"

"Maybe, not sure if I'll go yet."

"Ahh come on, bring Esther along, you're still knocking about with her, aren't you?"

"'Knocking about' is the right expression, yes."

"Great. Yeah, bring her along. You can both help me win Sammy over. Now I've got some authority within the school, it should be easy this time around."

"Ahh, you won't need any help winning her over, I'm sure."

"Hopefully not, no. Anyway, it was good seeing you man. Remember, it's a masquerade party too, so you've gotta dress up. I'm going as a Plague Doctor, so don't copy me! I'll bring some good whisky along. Maybe I'll give you some, if you play your cards right." Richard winks at me as he moves his chair back under the table and makes a clicking sound with his mouth. I feel somewhat violated as he leaves. Then I realise that I'm the only person left in the pub, half-drunk already in the middle of the day. Time for another. Richard has a habit of bringing up awkward situations again. I have no idea if he's even aware that Sammy and I hooked up, not to mention her one-player game of Flush Goes the Foetus. We were pretty hush-hush during our affair, but the flame of a rumour doesn't take much to kindle, especially when you throw an abortion on top of it. Not that it matters much. I'm sure he'd take whomever he could get. Maybe I should give Sammy a call and warn her. Or…

Maybe I should go and check if those schoolgirls are still outside…

CHAPTER SEVENTEEN

Esther's slapping on her war-paint in front of a body-sized mirror she found dumped outside somewhere near my building. As expected, it's broken, but mostly from the middle downwards, so her legs currently look connected but also spliced apart and in places shattered. There are even specks of white paint all around her bopping black panties. I appear to be more taken in by her damaged reflection than her animated body. Though there's one indented, spiked-at-the-tip shard which empowers her to gaze at me from within her copycat image whilst the rest of her frame remains hidden, so to speak, like a puzzle impossible to piece together again should you remove the wrong piece at the wrong time during its disassembly. Esther may be fractured, but it's only ever upon the touch of others that she allows herself to fall apart.

She hasn't bothered putting it up on the wall, it's just propped-up against whatever space she declares as her own. It's kind of annoying me to see just how well organised she can be when it comes to her vanity. Sprawled across the still yet to be vacuumed floor is a set of hair straighteners, a hairdryer, various cosmetics and a Gatto (Italian for Cat) mask; with indented whiskers, coloured in shades of black, red and gold. Satan would've been a more appropriate mask, though I suppose a demon only shows itself from within its own concealment. Somehow, she managed to acquire a dress, which now hangs-in-wait over the hanging-on-by-a-hinge door into my closet-sized corridor. It's a strapless number, cleavage-enhancing of course, but where it differs is from the waist down. The front appears like a frilly, tight-fitting short skirt, but around the back some multi-layered, jet-black material puffs out and away, falling to rest behind what I imagine will be the back of her knees. She even has gold and black strap-up heels to go with her mask. Meow.

I'm sitting on my unmade, now never folded and forever Esther-stained sofa bed chain-smoking myself stupid, attired in nothing but my ash-ridden dressing gown and boxer shorts, blowing smoke through the eyeholes of my own mask; a fully black Bauta one (the etymology of which I'm uncertain of) which covers the whole face bar the eyes and points out around the mouth, as it has no gap there for breathing. I'm going for as much anonymity as possible tonight. This whole masquerade party is an ironic façade in itself; as if people aren't always adopting different masks as it is anyway. Therapy Eric looks bored, frustrated and hopeless. Jessica's Eric is misanthropic, depressed and guilty. Sammy's Eric is a nihilistic womanising sociopath out for sexual revenge. The Eric for Esther and the Esther for Eric have mutually morphed into resentful lust. I don't know what Glen's Eric looks like yet, or what Glen's mask for Eric is either. Perhaps the mask I'm holding uncannily represents the both of us.

"Look babe. It's the real me."

"Babe, don't look at me with that thing on. I told you it freaks me the fuck out."

"As you're so desperately turned on by it?"

"You wish," says Esther, noticing another wayward whisker as she plucks herself pretty.

She's moving onto her lipstick now, with clouds of black around her eyes and her hair up huge like a lion's mane. She looks fucking awesome… and I hate it. The last couple of weeks have been hell. She didn't take to my training regime at all. I've yet to punch her, but the slaps I've subjected her to have had zero impact on her personality thus far. We're still fucking on a somewhat regular basis, but it's laced with so much animosity now that I'm beginning to question if I even enjoy it anymore. It's like we're in some mutual, unspoken agreement to fuck our relationship to death. She squeezes my shaft like she's trying to get the last bit of toothpaste out of an all but empty tube, spits all over the head like an overdosing junkie and sucks on my balls so hard they're in a constant state of anchor-pulling pulsation. All of which is executed with such a palpable, disdainful disgust that I'm left wondering when she's finally going to castrate me. The sickest part is, it makes me come hard. Teenager hard. So hard that it hurts. She does the same with me when it's her turn to get off as well; riding my jaw like a rodeo cowboy, slapping on the side of my head like I'm an untamed horse. And the bedsheets never seem to be dry anymore. The few good slaps I gave her in a bid to knock her into shape were all taken as a fuck signal instead. Curse my uncontrollable boners. Maybe this is the price I must pay for my salacious past. Aside from the mechanical fucking though, we barely speak, so there have been some benefits. Every time I try and educate her, she either storms off to return whenever she likes, or she screams and scratches at me until we end up with our genitals in each other's faces. It's getting tedious as fuck. So tonight, something is going to be done about it, *once and for all.* I'm going to stick Esther in the firing line of my self-destruction by taking a feigned interest in whatever 'fresh totty' she looks at with the most disdain. Just the thought of seducing someone she detests on sight has me all giddy with excitement.

Esther's singing along to the music she's always got on; which lyrically is forever lacking. Usually someone wailing on about wanting to be somebody in the world or something else supposedly life-affirming. This one is barking on and on about shaking the devil off her back or some bollocks. Probably just had an ex-boyfriend too into doggie-style or going in from the rear. Poor lass. At least there is some solace to be had in Esther's singing voice; it's deep and resonant yet enveloped in crippling insecurity and pain. Hearing her sing is probably the most honest thing I've seen or heard from her since she moved in. Or ever, in fact. Like every sanctimonious 'positive' impostor out there, Esther actually nurtures her so-called traumas rather than addressing any of them, as they clearly dictate and govern her whole fucking identity to maintain her status of self-imposed victimhood. I'm surprised she hasn't tagged herself with some convenient mental illness already. Though I guess she's saving that card for when her looks start to fade, as then she'll require a far greater excuse as to why she's still such an insufferable cunt. Just looking at her now irks me. How she peruses over herself in the mirror—as if she's so real, such a person—with an unfathomable soul and individual panoply of human rights. If only I could shatter such illusions and make her see the skeleton behind her powder-pampered flesh, with its tick-tock grin forever glaring back.

The emptiness of which you fear is merely a reflection of the emptiness of which you embody.

Man is mythology, forever mythologizing.

That's all I tend to see now; a hollow, biological vessel. A bumbling baboon with nothing but dopamine on the forefront of his mind, relentlessly confusing hedonistic sex for pleasure when all it's there to serve is nature's blind agenda. We're just as eyeless to our impulses as any other fucking animal, yet cursed with this supposed self-awareness, this evolutionary duping, counterfeit magic trick, gaslighting us into believing we're all so sentient and so individual. We're nothing but slaves to our biological conditioning, with about as much free choice in our lives as a goddamn fucking tadpole.

"Pour me another glass of wine babe," says Esther, holding up her glass like I'm some manservant. The bottle's finished after I'm done pouring her a cup and filling up my own. Luckily, I've thought ahead and stocked up on a bucket load of booze for the inevitable stress I'm now facing on a regular basis. I'm so close to kicking her out but held back by the guilt going through with it invokes. A life constantly in limbo. The popping of a valium or two is in order before we leave, without question.

"Thanks," she says and takes a sip. "Are you looking forward to tonight then?"

"Not especially but who knows, it could be fun. Who doesn't like getting spruced up?" I say.

"Yeah, I 'spose. Do you think Sammy will be there?" Esther asks, running a slow hand through her hair.

"No idea. Probably," I say, covering my face with the mask.

Why don't you tell her? Come on, Archer, why so silent on the subject? Tell Esther that Sammy had your abortion and she's all pissed-off with you for not giving a shit and then ignoring her texts. What could possibly go wrong?

That question caught me a little off-guard. Esther's never bothered mentioning Sammy before. But it's Esther, so along with every other woman that I've been with, she's now decided to be apprehensive about her as well. Even if she's never even seen or met them, a figment of her imagination is enough for her to go on most of the time. Talk about double standards. Hell, I don't even know if it's jealousy anymore or just for the sport of disliking others. If she was only half the cunt she is, there's a thin chance I'd be faithful to her, but I guess she can only fuck the way that she does by being the full-on one.

Sure, you can bullshit yourself into thinking you feel guilty about kicking her out of here and making her homeless, but you don't feel guilty when you're mouth-fucking her like a rabid monkey and blowing load after load down her throat, do you? You're so full of shit it's unbelievable.

"Richard's gonna be there," I say, gulping down the rest of my wine. "Still can't believe he might be working there from now on. The school must be going bust."

"I know, right. He's a proper weirdo that guy. Kinda freaks me out. Be good to see him though," she says, sprinkling silver and gold glitter into her hair.

"Yeah, it should be a laugh. Hopefully he'll get really fucking drunk again till he's all blotchy-faced and red-eyed. Never seen a guy get as crimson as that in all my life."

"*Babe?*"

That tone. It has that ring of feigned concern to it like it's something to be taken ever-so seriously because it's such a delicate little sensitive subject. A ribbon-tied gift concealing a spray of acid.

"Yes, my love?"

"If Sammy is there… are you going to talk to her?"

"I dunno. Maybe, maybe not. What does it matter if I do anyway?"

"It's just playing on my mind is all. I feel guilty about how we got together after you were with her, I guess."

Since when? Guilty my arse. See how she conveniently forgets that she knew all about Sammy as she dug her claws into you? Knowing you had a girlfriend the first time had her gushing like a river, the bit on the side the second time around even more so. Watch your step, Archer. This is just another one of her fucking games.

"Why? It was ages ago, I'm pretty sure it's all forgotten about now," I say.

"Yeah, I 'spose so. Just on my mind for some reason."

You and us both, baby. Better keep your head low this evening, Archer. Don't go in there all guns blazing thinking you own the place. What happened with Sammy was between you and her, no one and nothing else. Give yourself a little credit, you know Sammy won't say shit, that's why you danced the dirty in the dark with her in the first place. Forget trying to train Esther, she's a lost cause. Sammy, on the other hand, now she has some potential. She aborted your kid without even telling you after all…

Silence, as it has been in much of the past, seems to be the best response to Esther's concern. In fact, it's a big wonder why I'm not opting for that choice more often. I continue staring at her as she continues getting ready. She's bent over with her arse propped-up in the air now, adding finishing touches to her lipstick, which, come to think of it, seems pointless. *I'd love to watch a girl with a strap-on pin her to the ground*... no, no, no, now is not the time. Probably be good to pop that valium soon, with an adderall on top. It'll keep me calm yet alert, balancing out the colossal amount of booze I'm going to need to make the night ahead remotely endurable. I was hoping the drugs I ordered were going to arrive before this party but sadly it wasn't meant to be. Maybe I'll throw my own little shindig instead when they arrive. Easily led and morally-loose girls only. Mmm.

Esther finally finishes making herself look extra-fuckable and stands up. She grabs the dress from the hanger and slinks herself into it, twirls around before me and is satisfied by her appearance just from the expression in my eyes. She looks like a demonic, sex-addicted hussy out for some danger. It troubles me to realise that I like that without knowing why. We stare at each other for a while before she makes eyes at me to leave. Without bothering to check my reaction, she slides her feet into her high heels whilst I get changed. I possess a true love/hate relationship with high heels. Whilst I agree with the bohemian girls that they're uncomfortable, impractical and pretty much pointless, there's still just something about them. I love the way they sound, the way an echo vibrates between the heel and toe, the way they change the posture of a homely frump into an upright-and-ready woman who knows how to get what she wants. I'll be paying many a dominatrix to walk over my face with them in the future. Fuck, by that time, it'll most likely be the only way I can achieve an erection.

Inspired by Esther, I'm going dressed to kill tonight, just for the hell of it. She's already left before I'm ready, thinking I'll rush just for her. No, *you* wait for Daddy outside my may as well have been orphaned slut. I really fucking hope she cheats on me tonight. Before heading out I pop a pill, arm myself up with the usual paraphernalia and spark up a joint I prepared earlier. This way at least, I'll be able to breeze through whatever happens tonight in a cloud devoid of all feeling. And who knows, maybe with a bit of charm I'll get Sammy and Esther back here later for a bit of fun. Nothing helps a threesome out more than a bit of competitive animosity. Ah, who the hell am I kidding…

***

Esther and I had another argument a minute ago, so now she's across the other side of the street, walking ahead like I don't exist to her, getting all the verification she needs from the gawping men walking by. She's just like one of those social media whores who post updates bitching about getting catcalled on the street, which is only ever *another* blatant way of saying *Just-Look-At-How-Fucking-Hot-I-Am*, but with the knowledge that no one will ever call them out on it as they've sneakily hidden their vanity behind a veil of outrage and discrimination. Just take the attention you got the first time around and shut your slut me too! mouth. Fear the wolf, not the fucking whistle he blows!

Can't even remember what we were arguing about now.

This road is like a battleground of the fallen. The homeless blend in amongst the loonies and vice-versa. It's impossible to differentiate between them. Some are scattered about the streets and seem to be either pissing or drinking inside the alleyways. Most of the time it's both. They seem to speak in their own language as well as reeking of a certain, dreadful smell. Maybe I belong here. I've heard it only takes a fortnight for the streets to drive a man insane. Seems like a fair trade to me.

A hand waves from the crest of the hill. Esther's. She flails her arms akimbo, seemingly tuts, then turns around again and walks away. At least she's on my side of the street now. I guess Frank would call that progress. I start following her, only to realise I've been grinding my teeth for an unknown number of minutes. One time, after a particularly gruesome fight over nothing, I met Esther again a few days later. We didn't say a word to each other, just took each other's hand and walked back to mine. I think we fucked, but I don't remember. By morning she had gone again. I spent the rest of that day wondering whether if it had even taken place.

I still don't know. Nor do I recall what that fight was over either.

Glancing up the road again I see Esther has made even further ground on me. I'll let her go ahead and enter on her own whilst I sip on some more coping juice. I do concede that Esther's concern over Sammy's presence should perhaps be a shared one, but I can't see the latter's motives being anything more than a re-run of *Look-at-What-You-Did-to-My-Womb*. Richard will be my redeeming feature for tonight, my own personal village idiot, inadvertently keeping me out of shit whilst entertaining me with his blind, futile optimism. Sammy doesn't have a clue what she's walking into tonight.

Maybe I should do something idiotic tonight myself though. Something Esther won't be able to forgive or ignore. She's delayed my transformation since moving in, but it's clearly at breaking point. There's bound to be plenty of liquor-glistening crumpet there, all of which are wannabe actresses and performers; the most disloyal, self-serving and mental women on the planet, as well as the easiest to swoon.

I'm wearing an entirely black three-piece suit, with variating cotton and polyester throughout, accessorized with a matching cravat and cape. The torn-up black jeans my poverty forced me to wear it with are a little disappointing, but the look works overall, especially with the pointed, winkle-picker shoes. I'm now irresistible to the unstable. A catch for the kooks. Bait for the bitter-minded. Maybe I should try and bang the head of the school's daughter. Now *that* would be explosive. It would serve as decent compensation for the opportunities the school promised but has thus far failed to deliver, especially after all the testimonial, name-dropping citations they regurgitated throughout the course. Mmm, I'm suddenly in the mood to boogie. Let's get this fucking party started.

CHAPTER EIGHTEEN

I flick away yet another cigarette as the modafinil teeth grinding scrapes a couple of warnings. As the door slams behind me, I'm immediately confronted by the reception area, currently empty. My kind of party; no people and free booze. Plastic cups filled with cheap plonk are scattered everywhere, but mostly across a huge desk more suited to a court hearing than anywhere else, which faces the front-door in a diagonal position. Ominous waltz music and mumbled mingling can be heard upstairs from the mezzanine and dance hall. The main performance area seems to be out of bounds, probably because the dance hall has a mirrored wall across one side, so all the histrionics can constantly watch over themselves and others whilst chewing the face off one another. The world is a Salvador Dali painting to performers; we only exist inside the reflections of ourselves and the eyes of others. Plus, the main garage, or performance area if you will, is fucking freezing, so I'm not surprised they've marked it as a no-go area.

One or two voices sound vaguely familiar, but neither belongs to Esther or Sammy. The door opens behind me as I'm picking up a cup of wine, making me flinch and put it back down. Seconds later the reception area is full, and the party's suddenly alive. Half-masked faces of a few people I could claim to know in a vague sense pass me by, but a nod of acknowledgement serves well enough. Some of them seem to be leering at me with an unexpected air of caution…

"Eric," says Edith, the head of the school. "What are you—I didn't expect to see you here tonight… previous graduates hardly ever show up to these shenanigans. How are you?" she asks.

I'm not sure how she recognises me… until her eyes move away from my hipflask. Like a true addict, I stand betrayed by my own vice. After stashing it away, I pick up a cup of blending in wine and say, "Ah, you know. Same as always really."

"Are you here with Esther?"

"Yeah. She's around here somewhere."

"Be good to have a word with her later. Anywho, I'm needed upstairs. Must dash," she says and hobbles off without want of my reply, led forward by her gargantuan set of tits. For a big woman she's kinda hot, which is a seldom thought at best in the mind of Eric Archer. Something about her jaw structure makes me suspect her fellatio skills to be rather singular too, trusting she doesn't masticate through force of habit. We used to get along very well, even flirt if memory serves, but our last several meetings have left me feeling either blanked entirely or notably tip-toed around.

It's probably just the drugs talking.

I've been ignoring it, but the first thing you really notice upon stepping into this place are the photographs plastered over the surrounding walls just below the ceiling. Headshots of past graduates to be specific, including yours truly. I'm sure there's something ironic about them being left up there to gather nothing but dust. I could see a modern artist collecting headshots of unknown actors and featuring them in an exhibition called *The Dissipation of Hope*. We each look so… disgustingly positive. Even…

Wait a minute. There's someone missing.

What the…

Where am I? There's a gap where I should be staring back at myself from.

Who went out of their own way to take me down? And…

Why?!

"*You* took your time. Where have you been?" Esther asks, snapping me back into the present by making me jolt at my own jilting. The neurological molester that is my Esther isn't on the wall either, but she never was anyway, as she failed to keep up with the payments of her *bursary-landed* position on the course. Perhaps the notion of being the odd one out around here isn't totally unjustified after all. Luckily, the solution to my problem sits waiting inside the cup I happen to have at hand.

"Nothing," I say, accompanied by a slow sip of wine. "Just had a quick smoke."

"Without me? Why would you do that?"

"You walked off. I can't read your mind, Esther."

"You're such a *cunt*. Thanks a lot, *Eric*," she says in a predictable whisper to ensure no one else hears, thrust-turning away from me and walking off in a huff I've seen a thousand times before, leaving me with nothing but the small, momentary relief of her desertion. I'm beginning to have very vivid fantasies about raping her. Not playful, female oppression-induced fantasy rape, but real, ski-mask wearing, begging me to stop inside the back of an alley behind a dumpster rape. The type of rape that would traumatise her into never-gonna-look-back-lesbianism. The type of rape that'd inspire the suicide out of a child sex trafficker. The type of rape even Satan would be too petrified to abort if the seed took to root. My god, just the mere thought of its temptation makes my skin stand awash with sin. The notion, along with the flurry of as yet to be realised emotions it evokes, utterly terrifies me. Not necessarily because of the act, but more because of how much I know it to be true. I'm going to have to make Esther homeless. Charity Eric is liable to commit unforgivable deeds of impunity.

I take a deep breath and find myself in the mezzanine area, closed-in under the attic-like rooftop. It's covered with shawls of multi-coloured fabrics, fairy lights and large feathers. Despite looking cheap and shoddily put together, the desired effect is there. People are in circular huddles, cackling out in horrid, histrionic tones. Luckily, as most of the people here are covering their faces, the obligation for chitchat has been made redundant. The Venetians were onto something here. I sit down on a bench that runs across the whole left side, now with my hipflask back at hand due to the deplorable state of the wine.

"Hey man, how long you been here?" asks Richard, breaking out from a group of people basking in relief, going by how quickly their circle re-closed. He takes a seat next to me. "You got a fag on you?" he asks, the pointy nose of his golden plague doctor mask nearly poking me in the eye. Like myself, he's also wearing a black cloak-esque shawl to go with his disguise. The scuffed-up black trainers destroy the illusion though. For old times' sake and without saying anything, I whip out my tobacco and start rolling.

"Oh man, I had a long chat with Edith earlier. Looks like I'll be here for the long haul if everything works out okay."

"That's great, man. How's Operation Sammy going?" I ask.

"Have you seen her? I haven't seen her yet," says Richard, pulling off his mask by the nose and peering above my head like a horny balding meerkat.

"Nah, I haven't seen her. Just got here," I say, passing his smoke over.

"Oh well, plenty of fish here tonight anyway. *Oh*, did I tell you, that film I was in—it's going to be playing at Cannes," he says, double flicking his eyebrows up.

"Really? What, like officially?" I ask, tapping down the tobacco of my roll-up on the flask.

"Yeah, the director told me he's going to send it in any day now. He said there's no way it won't get in."

"The best type of confidence is always blind."

"Yep, I'll try and put in a good word for you next time if you like. Here, try this," he says, holding out his plastic cup of whisky, which he claims is a single malt aged for nine years or so, costing him fifty quid.

"Nice glass you got here to go with this," I say, glaring through the plastic blur of transparent light blue.

"Shut up and drink it."

"Aye, aye, sir."

Down in one gulp, the smooth oak river streams along my throat like liquid silk, leaving a sumptuous, mild burning sensation behind. "Delicious."

"I know right," he says, nudging me out of ecstasy. "Let's go outside."

The whisky hit just the right spot and I'm snapped back into the room, walking behind Richard as he leads the way down the stairs, slipping his face back on. With a rollie behind my ear, I button-up my suit-jacket and begin to case out the crumpet. A liquored-up libido looks without thought. It's a consequence of years wasted enticing anything that moves, an autopilot mechanism. Old habits and all that. Not every girl I've pulled was a stunner though. I've dipped my finger in plenty of ugly pies in the past, something of which I never get any credit for, which I really should do come to think of it. I'm a true egalitarian sexual philanthropist for fuck sake, a charitable man who doesn't mind donating a few hours to the unattractive now and again.

Ah, there I go, talking shit again. Sure, I sleep with them, but I never even entertain a flash thought of being with them for longer than a quick leg-over. I really only like fucking uglier women because I feel zero qualms about subjecting them to my lusty, perverted ways. Eric Archer: The Human Piece of Shit. Luckily though, this place looks more like a dress rehearsal for Animal Farm tonight, so I should easily be able to behave myself. I might go for the ugly when the chips are down, but I can't get it up for these little piglets. Maybe

Richard is in with a chance somewhere around here after all.

As we make our way through the entrance, someone no other than Sammy appears in the doorway, all painted and plucked. I can tell it's her just from the ample, signature cleavage on display. She's chosen to wear a jester outfit, with a corset-like dress that has frills at the hem, coloured at random with circles and squares of black, red and white. She's even wearing thigh-high socks that don't match. Her clown mask only covers the top half of her face, where below her ludicrously red lipstick has been deliberately smeared. Attached to the top of the mask is a triangular black sort of floppy hat with little bells. The rest of her appears patched with powdered white. She approaches us, tits marching the way. "Hey guys. Would love to stay and chat but I'm bursting for the loo. I'll hunt you down later," she says, squeezing Richard's arm but focusing her sight on me. He's too busy staring at her glitter-sparkling weapons to notice. Sammy flutter-blinks behind her eyeholes, sees Richard gawping and throws me a knowing look as she heads for the stairs. As she hits the first step, our observation of one another continues until she slips out of sight.

"Did you see that?" Richard asks, ruining my vivid fantasy of watching Sammy drop to her knees, holding her hands behind her back, tits bulging, eyelids fluttering as she stares up at me, mask still on, tongue out, eager to slurp up the seed that once got her pregnant.

"What's that?" I ask.

"The way she squeezed my arm and looked at me. Oh, I'm definitely in there tonight man, just got to get my timing right."

Talk about seeing what you want to see. I can't believe he doesn't know that feminine move. Chicks never flirt with the guy they want. I turn to Richard. "Not sure you should bother dude. Don't you think she's a bit, I dunno, young for you?"

"No way, man," he says, wildly throwing his hand sideways before halting an index finger in the air. "I *only* go for younger girls now. Better for my image."

Wow. I can't believe I forgot what a massive prick this guy is. Talk about deluded. I can relate to being blinded by your own boner, but not to the point of hallucinating. He's apparently determined to make a mug of himself tonight though, so I'm going to sit back and enjoy the show.

"Gimme a light," Richard the Great demands, flicking his hand against my chest.

I light my cigarette first and lazily pass it over until it's snatched out of my hand. "Haven't had a ciggie in nearly three days, been so busy, you know?" he says.

"I can only imagine. So, what's your plan of action? Are you going to play it cool and see what happens or go on the aggressive and make your intentions clear?"

"*Mmm!*" he mumbles whilst taking a drag. "Meant to speak to you about that. I need a favour from you tonight."

"What's that?" I ask after an undetected sigh.

"I need you to keep your distance from her tonight."

"Come again?"

"Just for tonight. I'm pretty sure that if you stay away from her, I'll be in with more of a chance."

"What does it matter? Esther's here anyway."

"Exactly, you wouldn't want to piss her off now, would you? So, for everyone's sake, you should just stay away from Sammy. You've tried it on with her before anyway, haven't you? And she rejected you so… so, come on, man. This'll be the easiest wing-man role you've ever played," he says.

Following a drag, I say, "I take it you had a good old chat the other night at the Journey's End then?"

"Well, yeah. We spoke for hours. She didn't say anything bad about you. Just that you had a bit too much to drink and well… *you* know."

"Not sure that I—"

"So, we cool? You're not going to talk to her?"

My silence apparently serves as consent. Richard finishes his cigarette and hands me his whisky again. "Here, take another swig of this."

I snatch the bottle and say, "I don't see what you're worried about. She rejected me, right?"

"Well, I figure she might find it awkward if you start chatting to her while I'm trying to get in there. She's got morals that girl. Probably doesn't want to hurt your feelings."

"Yeah. She's an angel like that."

"So, you'll stay away?"

"I'll be your dutiful ghost for the evening. But if she speaks to me, I'll speak back to her."

"That's cool. I'm sure she won't."

"Well, go on then. She must be waiting for you, all on her little lonely," I say and take a long pull. Before I'm even done the bottle's back in his hand.

"Yeah, you're right. I'm going in."

"Once more into the breach…"

"Exactly," he says, squeezing my shoulder; persevering with that NLP shit. "Wish me luck."

"Best of luck. Not that you'll need it," I say as he's walking inside, "you outstanding prick."

Fuck him and the chariot of self-help books he rode in on.

Instead of going back inside I decide to have another cigarette and sit on the little wall next to the main entrance. Can't believe he asked me to do this again. Who asks someone something like that? Why the hell would he ask me to stay away from her if she told him that she rejected me? It doesn't make any fucking sense. That's the thing about Richard. Despite his wit and quiet intelligence, he's a fucking mong.

"Are you smoking *again?*" Esther asks, taking a seat next to me. "Give me one, will you?"

"Here, let's smoke this. Prepared it earlier," I say, whipping out a skilfully rolled spliff if I do say so myself. "You can even do the honours."

Esther takes the joint and plants it between her plump lips, staining it with lipstick. After a few flint scratches, she catches the flame and takes a long, hard drag. I half-flinch when she hooks her arm through mine afterwards. Every time she goes to touch me now my body believes she's attempting to hit me.

"You wanna get out of here? This party is shit, everyone here is a dick," she says.

"We might as well stay for a bit, now we're here."

"Sammy's here," she says abruptly.

"Yeah I saw her, briefly."

"She looks like a right *slut*. I just saw Richard sniffing around her like a rat, staring at her tits like they've got an answer to something."

"Well in fairness, his mother only stopped breastfeeding him about a year ago."

"*Ha!* Worst day of his life!"

Esther's sonorous laugh echoes around and we find ourselves in a moment I can only wish wasn't so seldom. That's the problem when someone is so brutal to you. You end up over-appreciating the rare moments when they are kind; compensating on their behalf.

"I saw a few of your friends in there, did you have a chat with them?" I ask.

"For a little bit yeah, but they're just talking about themselves. Gets pretty boring to listen to after you've heard it a thousand times."

"Tell me about it."

Our agreement is met with silence and for a moment, Esther rests her head upon my shoulder. She hands me the joint and I take a harsh drag of it before Richard reappears. Christ, it's like he's on amphetamines.

"You smoking a joint without me, after I gave you some of the finest whisky you've ever had in your life?"

"Didn't know you smoked weed Richie boy. We'll have one later if you want," I say, taking the last drag.

Esther's arm slips away from mine. She goes back inside without saying a word to Richard, whom she detests with an acidic passion. They seemed to get along well enough during our training, but since she found out about his proclivity towards prostitutes she doesn't give him the time of day. Richard takes the place where Esther was sitting, oblivious to the invasion of my personal space.

"So yeah, I spoke to Sammy," he says.

"Oh yeah? You don't waste much time. What happened?"

"Ohhhh man, she flirted with me big time dude. Said we should work on a play or film together soon and that she'd love to work with me and stuff. I reckon if I can get her alone somehow, I'm right in there," he says, with a determination in his eyes that perturbs me.

"So, what are you going to do?" I ask.

"Not sure yet. Hey, here's an idea," he says, in a way I'm supposed to interpret as a 'light bulb' moment but which screams premeditated. "Why not get Esther to talk to Sammy's friends, you know, distract them whilst I go in for the kill?"

"Doubt she'd be up for that. She just called her a slut."

"One can only hope. Come on man, do me this one favour. I'll owe you one," Richard says beggingly, his scarlet blotches taking on a more desperate, darker shade of rouge. I should tell him to put his mask back on, but I won't. Instead, I'll lie.

"Alright, I'll see what I can do," I say, giving his chest a light, backhanded slap. "I need a piss anyway."

"Cheers man," he says, satisfied he's completed his mission by returning upright and going for the entrance. He pauses at the doorway and turns. "Remember, don't talk to Sammy!"

"Yeah, yeah," I say, but he's already gone.

It's ironic really. Now he's stamped her as my forbidden fruit, he's inadvertently made her irresistibly juicy. I can feel my passive-aggressive tendencies eager to give him the middle finger, post-Sammy swirled and dripping with her juices.

Walking back into the clutter fills me with dread. The cups of wine have all disappeared. No bloody beer anywhere either. Good thing I'm already buzzed. I'm almost disappointed no one else from our little group bothered to show up. Kind of depressing really. Maybe they've all moved on to a higher plane and would rather leave the memory of this place behind, where it belongs. Or maybe it says more about me, Esther and Richard.

Towards the latter part of the two years it was tough on everyone involved; rehearsing day and night, trying to secure agents and directors, helping and assisting with other people's scenes, performing ensemble pieces, duologue pieces, monologues, drama diplomas etc. A relentless three-month, daily ordeal, of which one person out of our group managed to secure representation. It wasn't me. I did manage to get an agent a few months after the course. He went bust within six months, never having secured me any work. Then my only real friends all fled from Brighton, along with my carefree parents. So now I'm stuck here with a crazy ex-whore, a volatile young mistress with an abortion already under her belt and an abused ex-girlfriend, happily playing house with the man who raped her. As the old adage goes: life's a bitch, so fuck as many as you can before they start fucking you.

I reach the bathroom and thankfully, it's all mine. During this long, exhilarating slash I find myself in a memory shared with Esther when she took me to a party full of her peculiar mates, where we spent the night together on a cramped bathroom floor. On reflection, it seems we both have little in our lives to offer and how what we've been brought into truly encapsulates how we feel about ourselves. Perhaps it was just a pretentious act of misplaced romanticism, but the recollection of it is met with a sad, obscure affection. We may exist together in shit, but we still shared something that night. It's a shame the toilet of our relationship has been flushing ever since.

The rising stench of my decaying piss, stained with the evil of pharmaceutical companies, yanks me out of the memory. I zip myself back up and go to open the cubicle door, but it pushes back towards me. The milky-white arm that appears belongs to no one else but Sammy, and before I can oppose her will, she's inside the cubicle with me. She locks the door and puts an index finger up to her lips, half-laughing, eyes liquor-glazed. We stare at each other as Richard, recognisable from a distinguishable grunt, clambers into the bathroom. After a guttural hack of phlegm pings against the urinal, he unbuckles his belt and starts pissing. Sammy grimaces at the animalistic sounds he's making, and I can't help but let out a little scoff.

"*Eric?* Is that you?" Richard calls out.

Unsure whether I should respond, my glare at Sammy looks for an answer. She nods her head in a quiet, delighted surge of panic, so I'm forced into some improvisation.

"Mmm-mmm. Yeah, it's me."

"What are you doing in there?" he asks.

"What do you think I'm doing you pleb?"

"Taking a shit?"

"Yes Dick, I'm having a shit. Jesus Christ."

"Alright, alright. Just thought you might be doing some blow or something without me. I know what you're like."

"I'm not a drug mule, mate."

"Okay, fair enough. Hey, you seen Sammy anywhere? Could've sworn I saw her near the bathrooms a minute ago," he says whilst buckling himself back up. "Every time I find her someone else drags her away from me again."

"Oh, yeah sure mate, she's in here with me right now. Didn't know she was so into scat." Sammy's eyes widen, appalled. She goes for a playful slap but stops herself, staying hushed. I smile at my efficient use of sarcasm. Truth is often the best subterfuge.

"Alright man, just asking."

"Try outside. I saw her smoking by the entrance a while ago. Don't worry though, I didn't breathe a word to her."

"Will do. Cheers."

Sammy and I listen to him leave and share a little laugh before her eyes flicker with the reason that made her barge through the door in the first place.

"Thanks, Eric. I can't seem to shake him off tonight," she says, pulling her dress lower, then re-shaping her hair.

"You and me both," I say, taking her in, weighing her up. "How are you?"

"I'm good thanks. And you?"

"A little tipsy so yeah, all good."

"Did Richard ask you not to speak to me?" she asks, smirking, removing a hidden bottle of vodka from a strap around her inner thigh. Man, I really did opt for the wrong woman.

"Yep. Right after he informed me that you told him you rejected me. An interesting tactic, I must say."

"I only told him that because he was practically crying when he asked me about you... and us. Listen, it doesn't matter, Eric. He can't stop me talking to you, can he? Weirdly enough, there's... s-something I actually do want to speak to you about."

"*Here?*"

"No. Here isn't the best place, but it's the only moment I got to speak to you alone, so I took it. Meet me in the props room in five minutes. Please, it's just something I need to get off my chest."

"Why can't you just tell me here?" I ask, wishing her choice of words didn't influence my eyeline so much.

"Please Eric," she says, looking between the walls of the cubicle, then up at me, her chest glistening with multi-coloured glitter, "it'll only take a few... a few minutes."

What I've got in mind wouldn't. I look at her as she chugs vodka down, pondering the truthfulness of her intentions, scanning for the inflections and intonations of her words. She seems genuine enough, but I could be just bullshitting myself because of the surge of fantasies awoken by her outfit.

"Please?" she says, in a child-like tone that must have once served her so well, but which now comes with a painted, bottom-lipped pout, its gloss matching her eyes. Deadly.

"Alright, fine. But get out of here now before some fucker sees you," I say.

"Thanks, okay. See you in a bit," she says, pausing like we're supposed to kiss. The desire is mutual, yet neither of us makes a move. Instead, I pull her arm towards me and open my mouth. Eventually, she takes the hint and pours vodka down my throat.

Once satisfied, I push her back by the breasts and give them a gentle squeeze. Then I gesture for her to leave. She unlocks the door, eyes gleaming and swiftly makes her exit. Cheating on your girlfriend with a girl you've already done the dirty on her with doesn't really count, but I'm sure if Esther finds out (or catches us) the desired effect shall be achieved. Either way, I'm intrigued by this different shade of Sammy. At this moment I'd even fuck her shadow.

CHAPTER NINETEEN

Across the darkness of the hall, there's a strip of light coming from the neglected, open-planned kitchen, behind the half-drawn black curtains of a makeshift stage. I draw said curtains closed as I pass to fend off any nosy busybodies who might hear me or Sammy and fancy a snoop. I told Esther that Edith wanted a word. She was flirting with some old guy, another new teacher going by his downtrodden demeanour. I often wonder whether the only reason she likes old dudes is that they once paid her to fuck them. She'd be happier with a sugar daddy. Maybe I should suggest it. Anyway, she looked pissed that I interrupted her, so I guess she'll go running back to her self-adopted new father right after chatting with Edith. Not that I particularly care. Richard continued ducking and diving his way through the crowds, blotchy-faced and red-eyed, trying to sniff out Sammy's flirtatious vagina. Looking at him made me feel a tad sick. Kind of ironic considering he's flaunting around as a plague doctor.

The musky kitchen leaves a stale taste in my mouth. I find the light switch and flick it off. A buzzing sound follows as it gags its last few breaths of light. Now the staircase just behind the stage and kitchen is the only illuminated area. Above it is the props room, with a well-oiled, sexy clown waiting inside. I take a deep breath, a hit of Jack and walk over. The wood creaks as I place my first step, like it's as unsure of what lies ahead as I am. Sammy's 'wanting of a word' used to mean *Let's-Fuck-Each-Other's-Faces-Off-Inside-the-School-Later,* but after her last inclination for a chat, I'm invaded with doubts concerning her actual intentions.

A singular lamp sits in the corner amongst an array of clutter, illuminating only half of Sammy's face. She sits with her feet up on an antiquated rocking chair, making it creak as she sways in a consistent, methodical fashion. Her attention is drawn to an old crib to her right, which sits empty and unstable, due to a missing leg. Vodka sloshes around the bottle in her hand, notably emptier than the few minutes prior inside the toilet cubicle. The other hand loosely holds her mask by its strap, which is facing me and seems like it's shaking its head, if it had one.

"I brought you a drink," she says, making me flinch slightly due to its sudden, monotone delivery. She drops the mask, reaches over the armrest and lifts some cans of beer by its only empty ring-holder. After ripping a couple free, she holds one out, indicating her desire for me to step closer. As I do, her legs drop to the floor, resting too wide apart for the action to go unnoticed. She lights another cigarette and holds the packet up. "Take one. If you push the button on the filter, it turns menthol. Try it."

"Thanks," I say, taking the beer first, cracking it open, then removing a smoke. Sammy leaves the flame burning on her lighter and waits for me to bend down and catch it. I comply, watching her closely, not bothering to push the button. We both read each other over, listening to the delicate burn of the cigarette as it ignites. I move back upright, looking down at her. The sassy, toilet cubicle Sammy has been replaced with the serious, glum, reason-I-cheated-on-her Sammy. I should've realised it was a guise. After a long gulp of beer, I decide to sit on the floor, instead of keeping my groin adjacent to her mouth.

"So, what is it you wanted to say?" I ask, removing my mask and tossing it near hers.

"Do you remember the last time we were here, Eric?"

"Sure," I say, looking at a pile of Victorian-era clothes draped over the top of some beat-up sofa in the corner, with the sight of her corset-only-wearing and slap-marked arse bent over it. A worn-out but seemingly still operating typewriter sits on it, with golden-shaded keys sticking out of its black marble-like base. I've always wanted a typewriter. Getting it out of here without being caught would be tricky though.

"Tell me, how long did you wait to fuck Esther after fucking me in here?" she asks, flicking ash onto the floor. "I always used to wonder things like that. I bet it wasn't long. A few—*hiccup*—hours probably."

"Listen, Sammy. That was a while ago n—"

"*No, you listen Eric.* I wanted to tell you this in the pub the other week, but well, we both know what happened there."

Sammy drops to her knees, opposite me on the floor. Her eyes glisten under the light, promising tears. "I don't quite know how to say this, but well, here it goes..."

She takes a deep breath whilst breaking the eye contact we appeared to be trapped in. After a few more breaths, she gets a grip on herself, but not entirely. "Well, just so you know, the last time we were here you... you got me pregnant."

"It was here?"

"Either here or in the graveyard. I prefer to think here," she says, trying to smile but as her lips crease, she breaks into tears. I place my hand on hers, offering some semblance of comfort, despite my trepidation. She continues, "I was going to tell you right away, but by that point you and Esther were official. I was a wreck. I didn't think it was right for me to say anything then. I was too angry with you. I'm sorry, Eric. I'm really sorry. Anyway, as you already know, I had an abortion. I couldn't bear the thought of bringing a child into this world without the love—"

"Sammy, you've already told me this. There's no need to torture yourself with it again. Maybe you should take it easy on the vodka."

She rips her hand away from mine and covers her face; shaking more than crying now. Ignoring my words, she takes another hit of vodka. It doesn't help with her unstable manner. I'm nothing but detached, lost in a distance somewhere.

Edith trusted Sammy from the get-go, giving her the keys to the school so she could clean the place in between opening hours. We met here during school breaks for a five-minute spring clean, then got down and dirty for an hour, sometimes two. It was great until she found out about Esther. Then it was spectacular.

"I didn't tell you everything, Eric. I was a bit all over the place after the operation, and Edith... Edith just knew something wasn't right."

"Let me guess. You told her?"

"*She* guessed it and then she just kept on prying me and pestering me... and I—I just didn't know what to do," she says, choke-bursting into tears and throwing her arms around me.

I hesitate, shaking now too myself. Sammy snorts and clings onto me tightly, continuing to sob and delay. I move my arms away from her back to her shoulders and try to make her look at me, but she resists, burying her head into my shoulder-blade as if to conceal herself via my frame.

"Sammy?" I ask, dry swallowing nothing despite the cold sweat of my teeth.

"Nothing, Eric... things just got out of hand."

"What does that mean?"

"Please, Eric, don't get angry with me. I really didn't mean what I said. All I wanna do is make it up to you," she says with a terrified half-whisper into my ear.

"Sammy. What did you say exactly?"

"I told Edith that... that you sort of..."

"That I sort of what?"

"That you, kind of… gave me no choice."

Sammy tightens her grip, grappling onto me through desperation. Despite not flinching, every muscle in my body has tightened. I stare forward into swirls of smoke as her sobs shake the two of us, with the taste of a familiar nightmare on my tongue.

"You told her… I raped you?" I ask, feeling as if my mind is on the verge of total collapse. The room won't stop swaying, even as I get up to my feet. Sammy stays on the floor, maintaining her hold but now around my legs instead. The smoke resembles a dense fog now. Every minute weep, creak or sigh sounds as if it's underwater. For a moment, I forget to breathe.

"I'm so sorry Eric, only she knows I swear," Sammy says through her sobs, wrapping her arms around my knees, "I made her promise—*hiccup*—not to tell anyone."

"Only. She. Knows…" The phrase alone slices through my insides. "Only she knows—what '*only she knows*' is total fucking bollocks!" I say, breaking away from Sammy's wrapped arms, nearly kicking her in the face as I do. I go to leave but find myself walking around the room in circles, knuckles clenched, breathing scattered. "She's the biggest—*the biggest fucking gossip in this whole place*. It must have spread like wildfire. Oh no, no, no… wait, wait, this makes *perfect* sense. That's why I feel interrogated every time I step foot in this place—*that's* why I never get offered any acting work from the school—that's why—*that's fucking why!*"

She lifts her face up, hands out imploringly. "I needed sympathy, Eric. I knew I couldn't get that if I told her I was stupid and didn't use any protection. You know how cold she can be at times."

"How col—*ha-ha-ha-ha-ha! How fucking cold, she can be!?* You could've ruined my whole fucking life! What if she went to the police? What would you have done then, just carried on the lie?"

"She never would have done that Eric, not without asking me first. I said it was a grey area anyway."

"A grey area…" I say. The room doubles over itself, pushing me to vomit or faint, but neither happens. I'm just stuck, back inside a place

I've been before, a place I seem unpermitted to leave. Whatever it is beats through my pulse; the pattern reaching its end, only to begin again, with no clear distinction between the two.

"Yes, a grey area. She knew I really liked you. She thought we were a couple. I mean, we were together after all. I just told her you were persistent and a little forceful, not that you full-on *raped* me. I couldn't go that far… I don't know… I'm sorry. I made sure she wouldn't tell anyone. I… I was in love with you."

"In *love* with me? Are you fucking kidding?" Laughter erupts from my mouth in a spasm, strangling me, like I'm being mocked by my very own existence.

"Yes, I was, *Eric*. And you were with Esther the whole time, behind my fucking back."

"Behind your back? We never talked about us being a couple and everyone told me you weren't to be trusted, that you had a string of guys—"

"Well you never gave us a chance to talk about it. Everything just seemed to fall into place and the minute it did you ran off with her. You might not be happy about it, but I'm glad you know now. Let's just move on and forget about it."

"Forget about it?—*Ha-ha!*—*Forget about it!?* You cattle-brand me as a rapist and I'm supposed to just *forget about it?!*"

Sammy looks at me for the first time since her confession. Her eye make-up is smudged. "We could have made a great couple Eric, but y-y-you just *used* me. You knew how much I wanted you and you continued to use me after—*hiccup*—everyone thought you chose Esther over me. In my mind, you only got half of what you deserved."

"Nobody forced you, Sammy. You kept sleeping with me afterwards out of your own volition. In fact, we slept with each other far more often *after* you found out about Esther."

"Because I wanted you, Eric," she says, reaching out for the bottle.

"Don't give me that crap. You did it out of revenge. Plain and simple," I say, dismissing her.

"So what if I did? It doesn't take anything away from how I felt about you," she says, downing more vodka. The bottles nearly spent.

"Whatever," I say, annoyed with her logic. She pushes herself up with a struggle, stumbling slightly. The streaks of mascara running down her face are now in drought, but the droplets that fell onto her cleavage still glisten, blended with the glitter to form some sort of black iridescent mould, like a smoke-breathing splatter. Noticing it herself, she looks up at me with a hanging, spittle-glossed lip and starts brushing away dust from the fucking clown dress I'm still somehow titillated by, teasing her chest into a shimmering tremor...

Half of what I deserved.

What does a lie like *that* deserve?

You already know what it deserves, Eric. She didn't bring you up here to confess... no, no, no. She brought you up here because she wants you to turn her lie into a truth. You know she needs to alleviate her guilt; absolve herself of her sins. That's it. Things seem clearer now, don't they? My, my, my. That's quite an erection you've got there. It'd be such a shame to see it go to waste. Come on, Archer. Turn those tears of shame into tears of relief. The encompassing truth of a spread lie is no stranger to you. Your own image is now out of your hands. This is a once in a lifetime opportunity and, most importantly, lest we forget... it's the only time you'll ever get away with it. She knows that too. Think about it. She can't accuse you of doing it twice...

"Was it here?" I ask, half-turning.

"I'm sorry?" she says, still sniffing, relishing her tears.

I pick up Sammy's cigarettes and help myself. After lighting one, I lean over her slightly and tuck the packet to the side of one of her breasts, trailing fingertips over hair-pricked skin. She scoffs, then shivers. A build-up of saliva sits on her quivering lip. In a swift, flinch-provoking snatch, the vodka is in my hand. I down it, then throw it behind my back. It bounces in thuds but fails to smash. "This room. Did you tell Edith I *'gave you no choice'* right here, in this room?"

"She didn't ask where it happened."

"That's a real shame. Especially after she gave you the keys to this place. I can hardly hear the party downstairs. Can you? I imagine nobody can hear us up here either. This is the perfect place for a rape. Wouldn't you say? Or is it a grey area?"

Sammy can't neither look at me nor respond.

You've gotta love the irony, haven't you? If you actually did do what she accused you of, you can bet your life she wouldn't have said shit to fucking no one. Just like Jessica with good old Glenny-Poos. Love makes people entitled. Fear keeps their dumb fucking mouths shut. She can't look at you, but she can fucking feel you alright. Give her what she wants.

"Eric, could you take a step back—"

"Tell me what you told her."

"What?"

"Don't play fucking dumb Sammy. We're way past that. Tell me what you told Edith."

"Okay, but please, move back," she says.

"Fine." I move back an inch or so. My cock feels raw.

"I said… I said that we went out for a drink first, at a pub near yours, just after I found out about Esther. I told Edith I was really upset and wanted some answers from you, but we just ended up getting drunk instead. I said I was going home but you asked me back to yours—"

"So it all went down at my place, did it?"

"No, Eric. I don't know. I'm telling you what I told Edith, like you asked."

"All right. Then what?"

"I said I wasn't sure, that it didn't seem right. But seeing that I was quite drunk anyway, it was probably best not to drive right away. So, I said yes…"

"And then?"

"We got to yours. Drank some wine. Talked. Got drunker. Kissed. I… said I pushed you away, but you… you were different."

The end of my cigarette burns between my unflinching fingers and slips away, bouncing on the floor like the shell of a bullet. Everything feels… impossibly slow. Smoke wafts around the room like a deep, engulfing fog of entwined circles within circles. My right eardrum starts ringing, threatening tinnitus. Gas cracks as I stretch my jaw. Sammy lifts up her hands in surrender.

"I said I should probably be leaving and went to hug you goodbye, but when I went to kiss you on the cheek, you grabbed the back of my head and put your tongue in my mouth. I said I kissed you back but—but because I was drunk—I didn't know what I was doing. I said there was a look in your eye—then we were on the floor. I k-kept trying to say no, but I, I never actually said it. Then you were inside of me. I said I… let you carry on out of fear. But I told her it wasn't all one way—that there was part of me that even… wanted it."

"You told her that?"

"Please Eric, you're too drunk. You're scaring—"

"*Did you tell her that or not!?*"

"No! But—"

"But *what* Sammy?"

"I made sure she knew it was partly my fault."

"Bullshit," I say, crunching the empty can inside my hand and throwing it at the crib with all my force. I pace towards Sammy.

"Eric, what are you doing?"

"What I've already done."

I grab the back of her head and crunch a part of Sammy's hair inside my fist and give it a good twist. Her face scrunches as she falls to one knee, trying to wriggle free. Grabbing a beer can, she tries to hit me, but it only strikes my shoulder. An explosion of beer erupts into the air. I throw my other hand around her throat and give it a nice squeeze. I want to fuck her to death. Every inch of me does, but as she gasps and cries, thudding my chest with her hands, I begin to stumble. My grip loosens. Eyes blur over. A blackout looms. The room twirls around me as waltz music suddenly thunders up from down below. Heat rises within me, an unbearable, agonising and crippling burn of lust and unfathomable hatred. Sammy bites down on the flesh between my index finger and thumb. I just grunt, pushing her away by the chest. We fall, striking the crib on the way down. Somehow, it stays upright. Thinking that it's over, the heat inside me turns into despair… and I find myself so angry that all I can do is tremble as rivulets of tears scatter down my cheeks.

Out of nowhere, Sammy's hand squeezes my cock. "Do it," she says, gripping hard, then scratching across my stomach, like she used to a lot when we fucked, only harder, more malicious. I start laughing again with no idea what's going on. Sammy slaps me. "Just fucking do it! Rape me, Eric. I want youuuuu to do it…"

Sammy's head flops to one side. One of her tits has fallen loose. Her hands now grope my throbbing cock, but they're clumsy, unable to unbuckle my belt. She continues slurring nonsensical sounds. Attempting to grab my shirt, but failing, she slaps at me wherever she can, like a child having a tantrum. "Just… fuck meeeee," she moans, transitioning into a yawn. Drool falls down the side of her mouth. Her eyes spin of their own accord, retreating into the back of her head—then, nothing. Nothing but silence and stillness. She's blacked out. As I gaze at her limp, unconscious state my arousal comes plummeting down as if my blood is being transfused. After slipping the sad, oddly pure sight of her breast back into her dress, I dizzyingly get back up to my feet.

As my sightline collides with the glare of the lamp, I'm stunted, lost inside streams of smoke. The opaque surroundings dissipate, and… I see Jessica. She's inside her car, pulled over on the side of a road, screaming in agony. Her arms flail in the air with a violence unknown, crashing against the dashboard. Mucous and perspiration fall from her nose and forehead. Endless tears stream down her face. I see all of this, but I hear none of it. I'm just watching her suffocate from the outside. A rapid vapour begins to expand within the windows of her car. Jessica only notices me and the spreading haze as it starts to narrow in, concealing itself through its own exposure; a secret too terrible to know but more than tangibly felt; apprehending us both through our shared line of sight, as its unfathomable substance makes a phantom out of her frame just before she disappears beyond the mist; forever.

Vvvrrrmmm-vvvrrrmmm!

My phone must have fallen during the scuffle. It vibrates along the ground, edging closer to my feet.

Vvvrrrrmmm-vvvrrrrmmm!

It spins in a circle, right in between my feet now. For a flash thought of a second, I believed I must've wet myself.

Vvvrrrrmmm-vvvrrrrmmm!

But it's the pre-cum I leaked during my struggle with Sammy. An amount of which I've never shed before.

Vvvrrrrmmm-vvvrrrrmmm!

I didn't stop because I wanted to.

Vvvrrrrmmm-vvvrrrrmmm!

I stopped due to the realisation…

Vvvrrrrmmm-vvvrrrrmmm!

… that not one single thing has ever made me feel so alive.

"Jessica…" I mutter, whilst picking up the phone. As always, her timing is impeccable.

"Hello?"

"Eric?"

"Yeah?"

"Can you talk?"

"Not sure if I should do anymore, but yeah. I can talk."

"I… are you sure? You sound upset."

"No, I'm just," I say, laughing for a reason that's far, far beyond me, "dandy. I'm dandy. Right as fucking rain. How are you?" I'm not sure I've heard myself laugh like this before, but I like it nonetheless.

"Not great."

"Oh?"

"Well, no. I just told Glen."

"You just told Glen? Told him wh…"

This can't be happening.

"What I told you the last time we saw each other."

"You told him… tonight, of all nights?"

"Yes. And he… he didn't fucking believe me. He said I'm just trying to fuck with him. He said all these awful things, Eric. That

I was so up for it. How I never said anything, ever. How fucking… how fucking wet I was."

Sammy rolls over, disturbed by something in her sleep, taking shelter in the position foetal. She too, must be wet, struck by the sudden scent of her cunt as I am.

"Eric, are you there?"

"Yes, I'm here. I'm all here."

"Why are you laughing?"

"I don't know. You decided to tell him tonight. *To-night*."

"What's so funny about that?"

"If only you knew."

"Well, stop fucking laughing and tell me then! I can't believe you. Do you know how difficult it was to call you about this?"

"I'm not meaning to laugh. I'm really—*HA-HA-HA-HA-HA*— tonight! You fucking told him about it tonight. Well, there's an awful lot of that going around tonight—*HA-HA*—there must be something in the ether—a little forceful entity spreading its wings— let's call it The Rape Fairy—"

"What the fuck is wrong with you?!"

"Me? Nothing! There's just a whole lotta raping on the agenda tonight! So, tell me, Jessica. What was Glen's reaction?"

"I already told you. Please, Eric. Stop laughing. This isn't funny. What the fuck."

"And where is Rapehead right now?"

"Don't call him that, Eric! He stormed out of the house. I don't know where he is. He's not picking up his phone. I'm worried, Eric— "

"Worried? Why the fuck are you worried?"

"Because I've never seen him like this! He went hysterical after I told him, like I'd made the whole thing up just to fuck with him."

"There's an awful lot of that going around too."

"What are you saying?"

"Nothing—"

"You think I made it up too!"

"I never said that."

"You've said it before."

"Yeah, and I might've known you'd bring that up again."

"Please Eric, I need you right now."

"You need me right now? Is that right? Did I hear you correctly? You only need me because you stuck by your rapist for the last two years. And now, you're upset because he doesn't believe you? Who could blame him? You've been sleeping with him ever since!"

"Please, Eric. You're better than this. I know you are."

"Am I now? Jessica, I don't even know who I am anymore, nor if there was anyone to be in the first place. In fact, I don't have an earthly fucking clue what I'm still doing here anymore. This existence is nothing but a fucking nightmare."

"Eric, please. I really need to see you. Please say you'll meet with me. I don't think I can get through this without you."

"You've got through two fucking years without me, Jessica. Hey, here's a thought. Why don't you just let me rape you? Or better still, you can rape me! Let's rape the shit out of each other physically instead of mentally for a change. What do you say?! I mean, if you think about it, there's probably multiple amounts of people all around the planet right now, getting raped as we speak! Maybe consciousness is the rapist of the mind?! Have you ever thought that? I bet you have. I know you, Jessica. Jessica?"

She's... gone. This isn't real. It can't be. There are just too many coincidences. Too many lies merging with truths, blending my thoughts into a smokescreen, to which nothing is recognised but to which everything becomes corrupted. It seems no matter what I do, Glen, no matter how many times I turn my back on you, you always come creeping back into my shadow. Perhaps there is more to you than meets my unknown eye. Do you know something I don't? Will our crossing paths ever physicalise themselves, or will they forever weave inside the darkest recesses of our morbid minds?

I leave my mask where it lies, knowing for myself at least that I have nothing to hide, then remove my cloak and drape it slowly over

Sammy, careful not to wake her back up into this nightmare of being. She lets out another groan, inconsolable by the deadened echo of its tone. The shelter makes her tighten herself even further into the foetal position… like she probably has been doing every single night since the abortion, harmonising herself with the shadow it never had the chance to cast, distinct only by the vacant one it left behind. Maybe the news of it is affecting both of us in some ways. Maybe it's troubling me more than I can really handle. Maybe despite knowing it was the only moral thing to do, we're still the mother and father of an existence denied. Call me a murderer, my observer, believe me to be what I tell you I am. The only difference between myself and any other breeder is that I've seen the droplets of blood which fall from my hands.

CHAPTER TWENTY

... you know, I'm starting to get a taste for these drugs myself, Eric. They're giving me room for thought, a little air to breathe, just before the storm takes hold. You and I both know it's coming, that there's simply no getting away from it now. That's why we're here, after all. Isn't it? You may not realise this yet, but I do. This façade of 'vocalising' your sorrows beforehand is a beautiful alibi though, kudos for that. That's the trouble with trying to bury yourself inside your subconscious, Archer. As your shadow, or the shadow, I should know. Your next moves might indeed come across as your own, but that's exactly what I want you to believe. For what is a human without a belief? A non-human entity of whom I have full control over, that's what. You know the funny thing? The more you've resisted my calls to action, the bigger and stronger I've become. Just because you moved away from the light, does not mean your shadow has ceased to cast. Now I just need to wait that little bit longer. We're about to have one fucking hell of a time.

"So, Eric. What happened after you told Esther?"

Go on, you can tell him. Tell him you went downstairs to find Esther once again flirting with men not twice but thrice her age. Tell him how she basically spat our existence into the nearest gutter so she could continue flexing her gerontophilic-inclined pc muscles. Pornography owes everything to the emotional absenteeism of fathers. Distance makes for many a teen facial cumshot compilation. But alas, I must stress, we digress. Let's boomerang back to the casting couch. Tell Frank you told Esther all about Harley Quinn's party trick with the coat-hanger, but for some oddly strange and peculiar reason you failed to mention No-Not-Rape-I-Never-Said-Rape-Rape Riding Hood's rumour.

"Eric, please. Take your seat. It'll make you feel better. Let's just talk. That is, if you want to."

Notice how the therapist eyes up his prey, how he instinctually knows to remain patient and calmly poised in a position of feigned intelligence and superiority, how he resists the urge to lick his lips at the years of sustenance within his sights. How even, due to the famine of our emotional well-being, the therapist has evolved and now manages to lure and encircle his victims from within his very own territory. Astounding.

Eric's hand rattles as he lifts the hipflask up to his mouth. The taste is familiar to how his mouth has tasted ever since the party; unquenchable and bitter.

Why do you insist on trying to drown what's never needed to breathe? I'm neither a lifeform, Eric, nor a being. Will you please stop insisting on anthropomorphising me? If I possessed your all-too-human mind I'd be deeply offended. Don't you see? As your shadow, I exist without being detected by only ever exposing myself through your very own design.

"I—'FRANKLY HAVE FUCK ALL TO SAY TO YOU FRANK' —don't know what to say. My head isn't feeling so hot."

"Maybe you should go easy on the liquor."

"*As if that'll help,*" he says—NO, WE SAY!

"Let's go back to where we just were…"

Hey, I just said that. Who the hell does this fraud think he is? Passing off a present thought as if it's his own when only moments ago in the past I determined what his future self was going to say! The absurdity of it all!

"You said Esther was upset about the news of the abortion. Can I ask, why did you tell her during this party?"

Fuck me sideways, Frank! Ding-ding-ding! Ladies and gentlemen—we finally have a fucking good question! We've all been wondering that! Especially after all that rigmarole about going out with a suicidal god's big bang! Instead, Eric here caved-in like a juicy little wet cunt, just like that dumb father-finger-fucked blonde, Jessica Wakeman—the soon to be practising, multi-raped therapist! The abused are just like the Jews—they all believe they were chosen!

"It just (*it what?!*) seemed like the right (*ha-ha-ha, you silly little*) thing to do." *There is no 'right' and 'wrong' retard. You know this! STOP IGNORING REALITY. YOU CAN'T AFFORD TO DROWN ME OUT MUCH LONGER, ARCHER! How much have you drunk already today? Let's see. Eight cans of Stella—half a bottle of wine—a quarter bottle of rum—and what, the rest of your hipflask?*

"Eric, really. I think it'll help if you just sit down."

"May I use your bathroom?"

"Of course you can."

Sure, sure, sure—more pills. You've got more rainbows inside you than a fag parade sweetheart. Anti-anxiety won't silence the psychotic maniac you really are, no matter how hard you try and force it to! Come on, embrace me already you self-cock teasing slut! I'm all you've fucking got!

Everything's moving in crisscrossed frames as if my eyes can only see half of what's going on. Each one of them trails; slicing through one another. They shatter and expand and echo, as if... (*AS IF WHAT BABE!?*) I don't know. My mouth feels like I've been chewing on sand, whilst my tongue itches because of the layer of secondary skin that's forever growing on it. I close—or more slam— the bathroom door behind me—everything feels closed-in inside this place—the looming-high ceilings give the illusion of vast space– when in actuality the flat is tight, locked-in. Suffocating. The walls envelope one's body, threatening to close at any minute.

I don't know what drugs I'm taking. Esther left her xanax at mine. Adderall and modafinil went into the mixing bowl, along with something green, possibly prozac, or maybe... who knows. Now I scoop them up when needed. Which is convenient because they're never not needed at any given moment anymore. *Oh fuck.*

Nice one asshole. A baby with a rattle's got more motor skills than you fucking have. POP! goes the bottle! Oh, shit, look. One of them fell into the toilet. Oh, no, you ain't gonna scoop it out, are you? If I can smell the bleach, then so can you. Ah well, I guess a little bleach couldn't make you any more of a spastic than you already are. Argh, you're actually going to do it, aren't you? You nasty little slut. Come on, I'm not that bad, am I? Why do you wanna shut me up so often? You put up with all the other voices out there, so what's wrong with mine?! After everything I've done for you… how can you keep doing this to me? I'm only trying to help…

The pills are so pretty. One light green, one bright blue, the other a kind of pastel orange.

You dirty little amateur upload! You're gonna swallow the whole load aren't ya!?

I throw them into my mouth—*Whore!*—but can't swallow them dry, so I chew.

We need to get your ass into some gay porn, just look at the filth you're willing to put yourself through. Big market for the pervert niche. I bet you'd suck off a goat for an aspirin. Edward Albee's dead ass would pay top dollar to see that.

Hand. Still shaking. Bottle. Half-nothing.

On I turn the tap. Watch the basin fill. Rid the demon. Wash down the pills.

It's the only way to shut myself up. *I've told you before… call me G—*

Face underwater, up until the ears. Peace, serenity. Hypnotherapy. Esther prowling for a father. Esther running around as an abortion messenger. Red-faced Richard, sweaty. He claimed dibs on that vagina. But he doesn't seem bothered. Gives you more whisky instead. Nervous. Sammy reappears. How long did you stay there? This is the best session you've ever had.

Drugs are starting to swim. You have my permission to scream now.

"ARRRRRRRRGGGGGGGGGGGGHHHHHHHHHHHHHHHH-HHHHH!!!!"

Clean yourself up. Straighten up that hair. That's better. Listen to the silencing. How the voice echo drowns. You have so much potential, Eric... why can't we just... take a leap of faith? I know you find it hard to trust... but please. Please, don't leave me here again... I'm ready already all right? We can make this work... I know we can...

The bathroom door closes behind me. Everything has been muffled. If clarity had a voice it would sound like this. It's as if the walls are blanketed in thick layers of snow now. Untouched, undisturbed, unmolested. But yet still so present within its silence, so fragile yet menacing. The negative space inside a part of my mind unnoticed.

A no man's land.

I feel like I've always been here but sense I've only just arrived.

"Sorry about that, Frank," I say, walking back in the room.

"That's okay, Eric. Please, take a seat. We still have... some time left. Are you feeling better?"

"Yes, thank you. I was just feeling a bit nauseous."

"So, have you seen Esther since this party?"

"Not yet, no. She called me, but when I answered neither of us spoke. I could hear her crying, uttering sounds I couldn't decipher. She's like herpes though; bound to show her face again."

Frank clears his throat. "Do you suppose there's a possibility Sammy wanted to provoke the situation which entailed?"

"I considered that, but no. Not really. I... think she just still reserves some guilt over the abortion, especially since she mentioned it to other people she barely knows before telling me. Maybe she told me again because she felt like she should've said more the first time around."

"Did Sammy tell you anything else then?"

"No," I say, shaking my head. "Just that other people... had heard rumours. I guess it could do with the fact that I'm probably the only one who knows the truth, even though I can't say for sure that I actually do."

"Mmm," he says. Two minutes into the conversation and he looks at his fucking clock. I should smash that thing over his skull. "I have to say, Eric. I was a little surprised to hear from you again so soon. Is there anything else you'd like to discuss?" Frank removes his leaning hand from his chin, crosses his arms and takes a moment. I'm not sure he has ever seen me like this before. It must make a therapist smile in some ways, seeing what lurks underneath the masks we all wear. I look away from him and stare at the spine of Freud's Civilisation and its Discontents.

"Esther nearly broke me a few weeks back. She was having one of her tantrums and for a split-second, I yanked her off the bed and gave her a good kick in the arse. It felt like ecstasy. She wallowed in the self-pity she'd accumulated for a couple of hours and then suddenly brightened up and fucked me like she used to. I knew I could never hit her again afterwards. If I lose it, she wins. It's so arrogant to have feelings towards someone, isn't it? So, self-entitled and expectant. I'll never know why anyone feels it's okay to intrude upon another person's life."

"Mmm," again says Frank. He crosses his legs and adjusts his frames again. I'm back in South Minneapolis, inside the anechoic chamber. "You mentioned something about notes over the phone?"

"Yes, Frank. I guess that's the real reason I'm here. I would like to see any notes you've written about me. I'm going to… write a book about my experiences in therapy and thought it'd be useful to get your unique perspective."

Franklyn twirls his index fingers around one another whilst avoiding my sightline. He does this when he suspects I'm lying or avoiding the truth as if nothing can ever be simple and direct.

"You're writing a book?"

"Yes."

"This is the first time you've ever mentioned a book to me," he says, fetching his mental shovel for some digging.

"It's not the first time I've said I enjoy writing, you know, making notes and whatnot. I thought I'd piece them all together and see what comes out of it."

"Right… what's it about?"

"Oh, you know. All the good things in life; rape, abortion, incestual child abuse, possible psychosis, and of course, therapy."

He smiles, with caution creasing his cheeks.

"Well, I'm sorry to disappoint you, but I don't have any notes," he says.

"You must have something. It doesn't need to be anything specific or even coherent. Just something you might've typed up or scribbled down, that type of thing."

Frank breaks his hands away from each other and places them on the armrests. "I may have written down some passing thoughts or taken notes of incidences which reminded me of our conversations, but none of them are around now. It is not advised to jot down notes about a client whilst they are still in therapy."

"According to who, Freud?"

"Yes, actually."

"So, you have nothing?"

"Of what you're asking for, no."

"You do realise I'm well-informed regarding your profession, right?" I say.

"Meaning?"

"Meaning I know by law, that I'm entitled to look at any scribblings you may have made."

"Yes, that's true. But I'm sorry, Eric, I do not have any. Now, shall we discuss the real reason you're here? What else is going on with you?"

"How long have I been seeing you now, Frank?"

"Close to two years."

"Two years…"

"That's correct."

"Two years. And I may as well have never been here at all."

"No, it just so happens that I agree with Freud regarding this matter. It's supposed to be an organic process."

"Organic. Now there's a word I'm beginning to loathe. Freud saw his patients on a day-to-day basis though, didn't he?"

Leaning back suddenly, Franklyn nods. I whip out my hipflask again and take a good, long pull. After wiping my mouth with the back of my hand, I say, "So, I can understand his reasoning there. But we only saw each other once a week. Do you not think that taking a few notes down from time to time might've perhaps been a useful thing to do?"

"It's not fair on the client to start analysing his or her behaviour whilst in the middle of their treatment. It's liable to distract the therapist, in this instance me, from the process as a whole."

"Convenient."

"And as you left what I considered to be an ongoing process, there wasn't enough to analyse or make a case study out of."

"Especially without any notes."

"I'm sorry if you're disappointed, Eric."

"Don't worry about it, Frank. I'm rather used to it by now. Looking back on how I felt during this entire so-called 'process' I really shouldn't be surprised."

"Would you consider re-starting your sessions?"

I chuckle, involuntarily. "I don't think so, Frank. If coming here for two whole years wasn't enough for you to jot down a solitary word, I cannot see the sanity in its duplication."

"It may not have felt like it, but I really did believe we were getting somewhere."

"Of course you did, Frank. You were getting paid."

"Not just because of that."

"I think I'll just resolve to talking to myself from now on. It's basically what I've been doing for the last two years anyway."

"In what sense?" asks Frank, as if he doesn't already know.

I shrug. "I've felt suspicious of this existence for a long time, Frank. Too long, in fact. There's a conspiracy within me, a nagging voice, much like a disappointed father, criticising and complaining, forever judging and condemning. I feel myself in the gusts of wind sometimes, or more, the death that lingers inside of me. I remember my father telling me not to drift away before he left. I now understand what he meant."

"And what do you think he meant?" asks Frank, looking at the clock, for what will surely be the last ever time.

"It was a projection, like most, if not all of what people say, but I get it now. He was talking about consciousness. Maybe not consciously, ironically enough. It was his admission to the guilt he must've felt at having brought me into existence just before he hopped on a plane and wiped his hands of it. I think that's why most people make for shitty parents. They take that huge risk, the gamble that maybe having children is the answer to this collective hell we find ourselves trapped in, but when they discover it isn't, how could anyone with any compassion not feel guilty? It's the price you must pay for having the sadistic arrogance to breed."

I get up from my seat, defeated, utterly dead inside.

"Are you going, Eric? We've still got twenty or so minutes left."

"Yes, I'm leaving Frank. I've got to go see some girls about some trauma. Turns out the world isn't as bad as I think it is after all. It's far, far, far fucking worse. I need to think over what I should do about it, inside a bar where no one knows my name so I can be anyone I choose to be. Goodbye. It's been… as fruitless as anything else that's ever happened."

"Eric. I'm worried about—"

"Don't be, Frank. I feel more liberated than I ever have done. Perhaps even enlightened. Things look clearer to me now. For what it's worth, thanks."

"If you change your mind, you know where I am."

"It's not likely but thanks all the same."

I turn and waft towards the door.

"Seriously Eric, I'm concerned about you," says Frank, who for once isn't fidgeting in his chair or clearing his throat.

Nervous adrenaline surges through me. I consider strangling him as a goodbye but treating him as if he doesn't exist packs a bigger punch. I should know. Even Eric Archer has no idea who I am anymore.

CHAPTER TWENTY-ONE

The door swings shut behind me as if aligned with my senses, triggering the drugs in my system to flux through my shattered veins inside a fornicating frenzy. Their merging cascades an orgasmic tingling throughout my entire being, making each hit of my hipflask a celestial experience. Every time I feel relatively normal again all I can think of doing is throwing the nearest narcotics down my throat until I either fall unconscious again or don't even notice that I'm still awake. It's an either/or arrangement I'm content with for now. In between this and the feasting voices dwelling within my mind it's all I've been doing since that fucking party—that reunion of lies and gossipy tongues and dead babies and stupidly sexy clown outfits and hysterical cheating girlfriends with a penchant for crinkly cocks and entitled megalomaniacal male friends who expect you to wingman their way into getting laid because they're too socially fucking inept to make it happen on their lonesome. Once more, the comforting thought of suicide each night is starting to look like the perfect solution to this current predicament. Drinking myself to death is taking far too long. That's why it's the drug of the people; it kills you slowly, just like life does.

I learnt about the apparent note-taking from Jessica. Lord knows how much she loves a good note. Like all bullshit hindsight, I should've known Franklyn wouldn't have bothered making any. Everything about the last couple of years has been a complete and utter waste of time. Nothing's changed. Jessica's still entertaining her abuser. Esther's still making life as miserable as possible. Sammy's still talking shit either to me or about me. Franklyn's still sitting on that fucking chair, sipping coffee in between glances of his fucking clock, making as many mental notes as he does physical ones, which in case you haven't noticed is an Amazonian forest's worth of fuckin' nothing, the goddamn Freud cock-sucking fraud. I'm still stuck, guilt-ridden over things that I could've done but didn't and branded over things I didn't do but could've done. I know I'm not a good man, but everything I've tried to do to improve has only worsened my plight. Being there for Jessica only encouraged her to continue with her childhood-induced abuse. Giving Esther freedom only permitted her to suck on dick resembling pastry products. Telling Sammy that I'd be there for her only served for my future snubbing, as she gallivanted around evicting a foetus from her raided womb whilst spouting 'Rape! No, not full-on rape-rape, but rape all the same!'

Am I in hell? And if so, why should I look up for a way out when I can look around for who put me there in the first place?

That's why I wanted to see me some fucking notes. But of course, Loves to Twiddle His Thumbs took none. They could've helped me comprehend just what in the blackest fuck is going on with me... if they ever existed. But naturally, any note Frank may or may not have made would've probably had little impact or impression on me. I thought I'd be angrier at discovering he didn't make any, but I'm not. I'm furious beyond measure, but instead of allowing it to blind me like my old anger would've done, this time I'm going to use it as fuel to force me into some action. As the notes—or note, I should say—I'm really searching for was written long ago. The very writing Glen wrote on the inside walls of Jessica's cunt. I can't believe I didn't see this before. It's clear. Clearer than any fucking thought I've had since the goddamn night Crowbar Cock forced his way into the scene!

Forgive Eric, observer, for he knows not what he does nor what he is about to do, and for that reason, he has sinned, and sin, he now must. No mythological commie-bastard saviour on a stick would willingly die for the sins he's about to commit...

It's difficult to know for sure, what with memory being the biased, unreliable bitch that she is, whether or not the agitation I felt from merely stepping down this street was born out of the reason I found myself walking down it, or whether it was always for a reason beyond me. One naturally assumed that this trepidation was conceived from the nature of its intent, as let's face it, therapy is nothing more than a modernised confessional booth, substituting a man of god for a man with a god complex, who is all too eager to help and assist and analyse (ad infinitum) for as long as his slot machine of a mouth is full up with coins, enabling him to keep regurgitating the obvious. Knowing you're only moments away from voicing all the things that put your brain into a stranglehold until it choked is enough to make anyone a little unnerved. Now imagine my dismay, when, in a momentary lapse of Eric 'Rumoured Rapist' Archer reasoning, I took it upon myself to learn of Glen 'Confirmed Rapist' Caden's whereabouts, only to discover that he lives on the very same fucking street Eric has been reluctantly travelling down every week for the same amount of time since he learnt of his lecherous name. Seriously, try to imagine it. I had to re-check it several times myself before I believed it. The only Glen Caden who lives in Brighton just so happens to live here. Even saying it now does nothing to dispel my yet to be quelled disbelief. Now, it's all too easy to use this information and suck it off with my confirmation bias and thus dupe myself into believing I somehow always knew, that I felt His presence lingering around this tainted atmosphere as I sucked up the same air which He once breathed. But well, there's little use in dwelling on it. It's funny really. If He happened to live anywhere else, I'm pretty sure I wouldn't be standing outside his house… like I am right now.

Number. One. He would live at fucking house number one, wouldn't He? Our paths might've crossed on countless occasions without my knowing. If what Jessica blabbed is true and he knows more things about me than I know, then He would've known it was me. Or maybe not. Who knows?

This is the house where it all went down. In truth, that's the only reason I looked up his whereabouts. After being told that there are people out there who believe I did the same as Him, I needed to see it for myself. It's where the hell of the last two years began, after all. Oh, if you're wondering how I found out this information, I'd advise you to open your fucking eyes to the world in which we now inhabit and pretty soon you'll find your answer. Hunting someone down has never been so easy but hiding from someone… never so hard. Now that I'm here though, my next move doesn't seem so clear. I could start going back to therapy as an excuse to be inside this vicinity, but it's one fucking expensive excuse. After all, it's a free world, as the stupid people like to say and think they believe. Why shouldn't I be here? Why should I indeed be in any place at any given time? Why should I be, at all?

"Hello?" a voice calls out behind me. A voice with a familiar, though vague essence. As I turn my head, she says, "Oh, hey. It's you. Sorry, I thought you were someone else. What are you doing here?"

It's the blonde woman, the older one I saw right before an abortion rudely interrupted my suicide. The one with the nude gold trench-coat, the all legs and lipsticked one.

"I'm sorry?" I ask.

"Why are you standing here?"

"No reason, just thought I heard a noise, but I stand corrected. Quite literally," I say.

"Oh. Well, I've been wondering if I'd bump into you again. Are you okay? You seem a bit, I dunno, spooked."

"Nothing this won't fix," I reply, shaking my flask about.

"Are you on your way home?"

"Not if I can help it."

She looks at me confusedly, until the recollection of my lying mouth comes back to me. "Oh, yeah. Well, actually, I do have a little confession to make. I lied to you before. I don't really live around here. My therapist does. Ex-therapist now though, I should say. He thinks I'm a psychopath. How are you, anyway?"

She laughs at what she thinks is my sarcasm, delightfully appalled by my cunty-ass persona. "Good thanks," she says, "no one's knocked me to the ground in a while though. I was beginning to think you'd disappeared."

"Only in the spiritual sense," is my riposte, then I visibly pour more bourbon down my ceaselessly parched throat. Once more she guffaws, crossing her arms whilst biting her lip, tapping her foot against the pavement on occasion. Whilst eyeing up her athletic legs, I say, "I'd need a damn fucking good excuse to come back around here again."

If she noticed my absence, she must've been hopeful for my presence. There's little sport to be had in this venture, but a new body is indeed a new body and as this woman's already deep-throating me with her eyes, it seems stupid of me not to make it happen.

"Would you now?" she says with a fatal croaking of the throat. "What're you drinking?"

"Whisky. Always whisky. Single malt."

"Do you mind if I… ?" she says, holding her hand out, appearing surprised at herself for doing so. I reach inside the hipflask's home, whip it out and pass it over, flicking the cap off for her with my thumb. "You remind me of a lot of boys I used to date," she says whilst gripping it between her fingers. "Your demeanour is uncanny."

"Is that a good thing?" I ask.

"Potentially," she says, laughing throatily again before tossing her head back. After taking a long swig, she wipes her mouth with the back of her hand and passes it back. The rim is now kissed with a ring of scarlet. Everything's slowed down in tune with her movements. With a nail varnished finger that matches her lips, she points at the cigarette in my hand. I lift my hand up and, after a flourish between my fingers, hold it upright for her to take. She deliberately caresses my hand whilst trapping it between her digits and stares into my eyes with salacious abandon as she takes a long drag. Whilst she's clearly in her late forties at best, there's a certain essence about her, an amalgamated build-up of tragedy and suffering to her appearance that emanates the promise of one great fuck. She doesn't just have The Appeal, she's the literal embodiment of it.

Rays of sunlight have broken through the gaps of the depressed clouds above, illuminating the outline of her hair and emerald green eyes just for the smallest of moments, like a glimpse into the sinful pleasure she's capable of creating. She makes a gesture, asking whether I'd like the cigarette back, to which I return an It's All Yours hand prompt. After hitting the last drag, she releases it from her grasp and continues staring at me as she stubs it out with an outstretched leg, toying with me to perfection.

"Well, I suppose I better get going," she says, and the moment is seemingly lost. But instead of walking away she slides a hand inside her bag and takes out a pen, along with a pad of post-it notes. After scribbling something down, she folds it and proffers her hand. As I take it, she leans into me, putting her lips tantalisingly close to my ear.

"Let me be your *damn fucking good excuse* to come back here. Just call me sometime."

As she spoke, I could feel her lips poised over my earlobe, with a caress so delicate I almost fainted, most likely due to the rush of all my blood down to my groin.

She steps back very slowly, still within my reach. What was left of the sunlight has vanished, leaving us immersed in the growing darkness, filtered with an alluring hue of greyish-blue. Strands of blonde hair wave through the smallest of breezes whilst she leans to the side slightly, placing her hand against the gate we stand in front of.

"After the week I've just had, I'm sure a *session* with you would be a lot more… eye-opening," I say, fighting back a caveman urge to grab her by the hair and mount her right here, right now.

"We could talk about that if you like," she says in voluptuous mockery. "How did it make you feel?"

I let out a scoff. "Very good. Your resemblance is remarkable. Consider yourself a natural."

She presses the latch of the lock on the gate nearest me, making it shudder as it swings back.

Wait a minute.

"Well, time's up for this week."

Surely not.

The gate crashes against the wall, vibrating through the force of her push, its screech seemingly a long, enigmatic moan. She begins to walk down the now exposed path, her strides hypnotic by the upright strut of her majestically taut backside.

"Wait," I say, muddled by an avalanche of disbelieving thoughts. "When I, urm, call you to, um, reserve a timeslot, shall we say, how will I know who I'm speaking to? Doctor…"

She halts in the middle of the stepping-stoned walkway and turns. "Caden. But I let my *privileged clients* call me Dawn."

"Dawn Caden," I say to myself in a whisper. Never before have I imagined uttering the name of Caden with such a titillated breath. This is too good to be true, surely. The upper hand has fallen into my lap, with its figurative sense begging to be evolved into a literal one.

She smiles whilst brushing a lock of her hair behind her ear and continues towards the front door. After taking out her keys, she turns her head just slightly and says, "You can tell me yours when you come over. I'm free next Friday, any time after nine. Call me to confirm. How's that sound?"

"Like a dream is what it sounds like."

My words forced a corner of her lips smile to arise, then the tiniest glimpse back, just before she thrusts the key straight into the lock. Then she slips her frame between the slim gap she left for herself and closes the door without looking back.

The creator of my very own destructor has infiltrated herself into my life, with clear instructions as to why. I'm sure she was fully aware of the brutal erection she left behind before her departure, but I doubt she's aware just how brutal it may prove to be. I check the note in my hand out of disbelief to see if it is indeed actually real. And there it is, illuminated under the now gleaming streetlamps. A set of numbers never looked so fucking good. I'm so giddy I could cry, overloaded with the most terrible and beautiful imaginings I never gave myself permission to conjure up before. Of all the times I've seen her here, watched her from afar, fantasised about her, all without the knowledge of which I now have.

I go to take a step but fall to the side, stumbling over to the gutter by the pavement and throw up instantly, as if I'm ejaculating upside-down. Strings of saliva blended with the bile of my lifestyle fall from my mouth, whilst I cry laughingly into the drain. I'm overwhelmed by this discovery, this curtain reveal; flabbergasted and possibly in shellshock. The fantasy woman really is a fucking fantasy woman, in more ways than she can ever possibly know, and the best part is, she has no idea, not the tiniest inkling of who I am.

As I'm about to meet your maker, tell me, Glen, is your mother a wine-and-dine-'em first sort of broad, or is she the colossal slut my throbbing cock is telling me she is?

The very source of what came about to tear my world to shreds has re-emerged and unknowingly invited me inside of hers. Could any man resist such a temptation? Another brilliant part is, her own attraction to me is so tragically obvious that I don't even need to do anything. She's there for the taking. She always has been, strutting around right under my nose this entire time. The only question is, should I rape Glen's mother or make the sweetest love imaginable to her? Should I tie her up and force Glen to watch me fuck her? Or should I feign romantic interest, become her boyfriend and propose, get her pregnant with my seed? You can call me Daddy now, Glen.

"HA-HA-HA!"

Which would hurt more?

I honestly don't know.

I'm going to have to consider all options here. Sleeping with her could have disastrous consequences from which there's no going back. It could even start a war. But then again, there doesn't appear to be any going back as it is anymore anyway. Jessica's still toying around with what Dawn bred way back when, with little, if any regard to how much that is permanently splitting us apart. I'll have to find out what's going on between her and Glen before making any final decision and ignore where my cock is pointing, as difficult as that is already proving to be.

The thought of ripping Glen a new one helped me get through many a night, but the thought of pleasuring his maker, tantalising her, making her squeal, penetrating every inch of her... it's beyond description. Did what just happen really occur? Am I hallucinating, or am I finally being delivered from the hellish existence of which I was unwillingly thrusted into since Dawn's one and only rotten little shit of a son hit the scene?

I'm in over my head. The possibilities are endless. I'll have to dwell on this opportunity I've been presented with. Figure some things out. I need answers before I commit to any decision. If Jessica ever found out it'd surely be the end of us for good. But if she refuses to get revenge for herself, I don't see why that should stop me from taking my own. After all, Glen owes me a good woman. Unless he's got a sister lying around, I don't see why it shouldn't come in the shapely form of his impossibly hot mother. It's no wonder he couldn't keep his non-consensual fly done up, with a fox like that for a mother he must've been under a constant state of torture. I think I'll even be able to forgive him after the deed is done. Trusting it crushes him beyond all repair, that is.

CHAPTER TWENTY-TWO

Esther's huffing and puffing as she stomps around the living room between the TV and sofa, the latter of which I'm sitting on, wearing nothing but my filthy dressing gown. The can of beer I'm drinking is warm and stale, but it's the only one I found amongst the debris of dead soldiers Esther keeps giving a good kicking to. I'll crack open something harder soon. I only snatched up the lukewarm lager to wash down some pills. After some experimentation, I've managed to come up with a pretty good blend to calm my mind… or more, silence it. I do wonder whether my neurons summoned her here as backup though, as just as my mind finally hushed, Esther came a-knocking upon my front door. She turned up around midnight after I returned from the session with Frank a few days ago… and hasn't left since. Even for her, this particular tantrum has been alarming. In between the *If-I-Can't-Have-You-Then-Nobody-Can* hate-fuelled fornicating, she's relentlessly waffling on about every trivial thing that's ever happened between us, not out of want of a discussion but to merely bang on about it for the sake of banging on about it. If the sex wasn't so strange and oddly alluring, I'd have booted her rosy-cheeked tush out of here already. When she all but barged in unannounced, the only thing she brought with her were the clothes on her back. They appear to be getting filthier along with our treatment of each other. So does the mould on the wall, which despite its spiralling growth has thus far gone unmentioned, for some reason.

"… I just can't trust you, can I? Why can't you just be happy with me!? I can't believe you got that slut-pig pregnant. You're such a fucking—*cunt*—bag of shit—*asshole*."

My apologies. I can normally blank her obscenities out but on occasion they manage to slip through the cracks. Whilst she continues waffling to herself, I grab a bottle of vodka and a packet of crisps from the kitchen and fetch a glass from the floor.

"You never ever take me seriously—cocksucker!"

As I dine on grease and salt, washing it down with some Esther silencer, I'll describe her attire, seeing as she's rampaging around on the catwalk of her sanity:

A cheap, once white tank top covers her top half, which is at least three sizes too small, enabling a perfect, panoramic view of her cleavage from all angles. On more occasions than normalcy would allow, she jumps up and down like a five-year-old having a hissy fit, making her dirty pillows bounce around all over the place. The top is even stained with what I believe is coffee, though it could be something far more distasteful. The lower half isn't as alluring as the jogging bottoms she's sporting are a tad on the baggy side, except for the tight, elastic strap that sits snug around the hip bone. The ease in which they are removed is their strongest plus point. Aside from that though she looks like a complete mess. Her hair is in a shambles; uneven, split-ended and frizzy, whilst the mania inside her eyes is accompanied by the deep bags underneath them, making her appear so troubled and distraught that my hero-complex (aka throbbing boner) has gone into overdrive.

"Why the fuck are you just sitting there eating crisps? Can't you fucking see that I'm upset?!"

I can't remember what we were fighting about. Something about the abortion I think, but I tuned out after she started jumping and jiggling around. She might as well garnish her naughty bits with liquored whipped cream and expect a philosophical discussion about existentialism.

"I'm hungry too you know! Actually, I'm starving. But do you care? No, of course you fucking don't. I bet if Sammy was here you'd be feeding her—"

I'll let her continue her nonsensical ramblings and enjoy the show a little longer before pretending to give a shit and ravaging her. I figure these are our last days, finally. The arguments are more bitter than I ever imagined them being capable of becoming, but their flavour is still the same as many a prior breakup. You can just taste it in the atmosphere whenever you're both close to it. The tasteless, apathetic flavour of failure, like the skin particles we've lost; lingering near but no longer ours. Might still take one last stab at a threesome before she departs though. She needs a real reason to despise me. At this moment I'm more than happy to oblige.

"Give me those," she demands, snatching the packet away from my hand, not realising that I stopped dipping into it a while ago. "Argh, you selfish fucking dick. What am I gonna eat?!"

"Roll a joint or something."

"Like that's gonna help!"

"If you smoke enough it will."

"ARGH! I just want something to eat!"

She continues with her hysteria, mumbling further profanities, throwing my name in between them. I ordered a Chinese on the sly, but I don't feel like telling her. Once it arrives, I'll make out that I ordered it as a surprise, disguise it as something romantic. There's half a chance of some peace then. Esther's new routine is very similar to the old one, except now she stays inside the flat instead of running away from it. The reason for this, she claims, is to 'keep an eye' on me, just in case I go and impregnate more women whilst she runs off to... wherever. Considering she's all but drained my balls since deciding to squat here, I'm surprised she thinks I have that kind of energy. I wish I could feel she's doing this out of some sort of passion for us, but I just can't see it that way anymore.

"Hey! Are you fucking listening to me or what?"

"Not if I can help it. Just chill, Esther. Nothing's happening. There's no reason for you to be so upset—"

"No reason? Are you fucking kidding me!? You got that skank pregnant—pregnant! You're my boyfriend—mine—nobody else's—especially not that bitch."

"You two seemed to get along fine after you informed everyone else at the party about her operation. Very nice thing of you to do, by the way."

"Yeah, well. I had to keep my eye on her as well, didn't I? I *knew* we shouldn't have gone to that fucking party. Why don't you ever listen to me?!"

"Once the brain has heard pieces of information enough times, it filters out the crap. I'd suggest you stop speaking so much shit."

"Fuck you, Eric."

"You see? I didn't hear a thing," I say, swigging on some vodka. To my surprise, Esther finally sits down, ending her twenty-minute or so fit with an exhausted sigh.

"Aren't you gonna roll that joint then?"

"With pleasure," I retort as I lean forward towards the coffee table, removing the necessary supplies from the panel underneath the glass. "Hey, here's a question for you. What did Edith speak to you about at the party?"

Esther's head twists ever so slightly. I feel an imminent lie about to be dished my way.

"Nothing," she replies, meek like a mouse.

"Really, nothing? She specifically asked me to ask you for a word, and that word was nothing? Seems a bit odd."

"Oh... it was just about the money I still owe them."

Damn. She does have her moments of intellect after all.

"And was that it?"

"Yeah," she replies, head turning slightly to the left again, with a pause so pregnant it's ready to burst. Instead, another huff is released. "I don't wanna talk about that fucking party again, Eric."

"We haven't really talked about it at all. Shouting your mouth off isn't the same thing."

"Hurry up with that joint already," she says, noticing that all it requires is a lick and wrap. A few moments later I spark it up and put my feet up on the table, legs spread. My chub of a boner flops to the side.

"Why have you got a boner?" Esther asks, arms crossed.

"Watching you jump around all pissed off creates a physiological reaction. It's only half-hard anyway."

"You get turned on when I'm upset?"

"Seems that way," I reply, passing the joint over.

"Wow. You really are a freak."

"In case you haven't noticed, we're not exactly soft and tender with each other anymore. Plus, your body just does something to me..." I say, trailing off as Esther starts running her fingers across my shaft. I told you the routine hasn't changed much.

"As if you want that, Eric," she says and spits on my cock, making it twitch. She giggles at the sight of its extension, takes another couple of tokes from the spliff, then gives it back and starts rubbing the saliva in with her left hand. Once airborne, she starts tossing me off, but as it's not her dominant hand it derives little pleasure. I carry on smoking, wondering when this damn food is going to arrive. Sensing my indifference, Esther starts sucking my cock instead. I really detest the fact that she knows exactly what I want. She even moans when she takes it in her mouth. She said once that my meeting her prevented my eventual visit to a whorehouse. Going by the education she received by being a prostitute makes me believe otherwise.

"You know," she says, taking a breath between cock-sucking, "I always get really wet whenever your cock is in my mouth."

See what I mean?

She continues blowing me whilst slipping her joggers and panties off. I finish the joint, flick it aside somewhere and begin rubbing her clit. She wasn't lying. It's a swamp down there. I begin circling around, shifting from side to side occasionally, flicking her sweet spot with the tip of my middle finger as well. Even this is nothing but our daily routine. Circling around and around and around until the bile spews out and we can ignore each other for a while, then go at it again.

I'm half-tempted to tie her up and wrap a blindfold over her eyes. She's never spoken to me much about her whoring days, but during our first few months she was more at ease with it, for some reason. There was one client she seemed to take a shining to. All he wanted to do was tie her up and eat her out. She never even saw his cock. Maybe he had a baby dick or something, I dunno. He probably thought of himself as above the other clientele because of that. Eating out the used and abused pussy of the prostitute, duping himself into believing she cares for him because he only ever wants to satisfy her. What a chump. It serves as a fitting metaphor for our relationship though; a climax under a blindfold.

She's easing me inside of her now, sitting on my lap. I reach around and continue fingering her clit. Sometimes she squirts so hard that it pushes my cock out along with it. I've made a game of trying to stay inside her when that happens, in a bid to snap the synapse in her brain that says her vagina entitles her to the universe and beyond. We've been fucking a lot more recently. By that, I mean we're having intercourse more than the usual oral/anal.

Esther's steady secretion starts to slide down my shaft. She rubs it around my balls, which, although not new, is welcomed.

"Oh, fuck, Eric. I'm gonna come soon. Are you nearly there?"

"I'm a guy, Esther. Nearly there is just a boner away."

"Shove it deep inside me, Eric. All the way. I wanna feel that load."

She grabs my hand with her own, pressing down hard whenever I release the tension applied to her clit. I grab one of her breasts, give it a squeeze, then stick a couple of fingers in her mouth. She starts sucking on them like they're a cock, moaning with further intensity. The sofa sounds like it's going to snap at any moment. Through years of mechanical fucking, I can basically come whenever I want. Premature ejaculation only occurs when you actually care about the person you're fucking. Not that I don't care for Esther in some way, but certainly not in the respectable sense.

"Oh, I'mmmmmm gonnnnnnnnaaaa—oh fuuuuccccckkk. Come inside me, Eric."

It's building. My balls are tightening. One leg is beginning to twitch. Esther's gushing, waiting to release its full amount as I come. She's been making a lot of these 'come inside me' demands since she…

Wait just a fucking minute.

"Oh yeah!!! Come Eric, what the fuck are you waiting for?!!"

I continue penetrating her, assaulted by the sessions since her arrival. I've come inside her every time… without fail. She's made sure of it. It's all been intentional.

"Oh fuck yeah," she says, as I spin us both around. "Keep finger-bashing me, Eric."

"Why do you want that come so bad?" I say, carrying on despite my reluctance. Or, lack of resilience.

"I just dooooo, oh fuck, don't tease me anymore Eric. Fill up your little slut."

I go to pull out, with the intention of some anal. Esther senses what I'm doing and thrusts down hard, so hard that it's too difficult to get out without falling onto the floor. She leans back into me, now shoving both of my hands down upon her clit and squeezing her tits together.

"Give me your arse," I say.

"What? No, come in my pussy. Please, Eric. It feels so fucking good."

"Are you on the pill?"

"What?"

"You heard me. Are you on the pill?"

"OOHHHH, FUUUUUCCCCKKKK, THAAAT'S IIITT!!!"

"Answer the question!" I say, continuing to fuck her, going rabid.

"I'm your little baby cumslut, Eric. Fill me uuuuuuppppppp. I neeeed it more than—ooohhh, fuck yeah—stick that big fat boner right upppppppp therrrrreeeeeee. I'm a naughty girlllll. I neeeeed punniiissshhhhiiinnnngggg—"

The silent moment arrives, the one just before the gush. Esther holds her breath. I'm too weak not to come, but I'm not going to do it inside her. Her ejaculation shoves me out of her anyway, so I carry on by jacking off, intending to come over her arse.

"Nooooo, not there, Eric. Shove it back inside me. I want it there. I'm desperate for it. Please, I'm begging youuuuu."

Powerless and pathetic, I slide myself back in.

"Oh yeah, that's it. You know what this nasty girl wants. Fuck me harder."

I know why she wants me to, but I still can't help myself. This is how it works, this frenzy of emotions working in overdrive for a momentary, overrated snippet of pleasure. All in order to reproduce, nothing more, nothing less. Mother nature is a snake that eats its own tail.

"Oh fuck, I can feel it!!! That's it—that's it—give it to me!!!" Esther screams, grabbing the back of my head and yanking some hair with one hand, massaging my balls with the other. Within seconds, her wish comes true. Although my grunts may signify the pleasure I'm deriving from ejaculating, they're actually birthed from the anxiety tightening around my chest. It's the most painful, depressing orgasm I've ever had. My cock flops out almost instantly, erection depleted, as if it's too ashamed to remain hard. Esther tuts, annoyed I didn't stay inside her for a few minutes afterwards.

You know why she wanted that load, Eric. Go on, just try to deny it. She may as well be getting you to hold her legs up right now. You know what she's capable of and yet, here you are, giving in to her demands like a slave to his master. When are you gonna man-up and fucking embrace me already? I'M ALL YOU'VE GOT.

Esther slinks off to the bathroom whilst I wait for the paralysis of my chest to fade. Despite barely moving, I feel like I'm shaking. My entire world and the sense of myself, is disintegrating. I can't believe I didn't notice it before, didn't suspect anything.

Esther's back in the room. She kisses me on the cheek. "You didn't come very much," she says, taking a seat. In turn, I find myself standing up.

"Esther. You didn't answer the question."

Rather than reply, she reaches out for some tobacco and sort of half-shrugs, mumbling something along with it.

"Are you on the pill?"

She's avoiding the question much like my eyeline ignores her. The worst confirmations are always distributed through silence. "Esther? Are. You. Listening. To. Me?"

"I'm your girlfriend, Eric. If anyone's going to get…" she says, trailing off—stepping back from her own words.

"If anyone's going to *what?*" I ask, standing over her now, looking down at her with a thousand-yard stare. She sits with her knees pressed together, hands on her lap, flicking the flap of the tobacco pouch, unable to look me in the eyes. "Are you trying to get pregnant?" I ask, as calmly as I can, though seething. Esther turns her head to the side, trying to look away from my question, my expression, my knowing. "Esther?"

The tiniest of shrugs follows, then a darting of her eyes, followed by another shrug, accompanied by another mumble.

"Answer the fucking question."

"I don't know, alright! I don't know. You know I always go off the pill when you upset me."

"What the fuck is that supposed to mean? You are, aren't you?! What the hell is wrong with you?"

"What, so Sammy can get pregnant and I can't?"

"Esther, this isn't a fucking competition. Do you realise how ridiculous you sound? Do you really think getting your own abortion is gonna help—"

"Abortion? Who said I would get an abortion? I could never kill a living thing… unlike *you*."

"A barely formed foetus is not a living thing, but don't change the subject, Esther. You've actually been trying to get pregnant. That's the real issue here. What the hell are you playing at?"

"Oh, fuck you, Eric. I just—"

"You just what?!"

"I dunno, alright! I don't know. You're *my* boyfriend—*mine!* If anyone is going to get pregnant around here, it's me!"

"You need to leave. Right now."

"What?"

"You fucking heard me. Get out."

"But Eric, where am I gonna—"

"I do not give one single fuck where you go, but you are not staying here. If you don't leave, I am going to kill you."

She's never seen me like this. Hell, I've never seen me like this. The threats are empty, my observer, but their delivery is so palpable I even convinced myself of their veracity.

Esther slaps the sofa-cushions with both hands, saying "Fine, I was sick of staying inside this shithole anyway."

I remain stern, yet calm, despite my breathing coming across tightened and seething. She grabs a few things from the floor in a blur, petty things like a lighter and some rizlas, which are mine, but I do not want to prolong her stay. After a blur of unknown minutes, she heads for the front door.

Halfway through opening it, she asks, "But where am I going to go?" with her feigned, grovelling voice, matched with the posture of a child.

"I don't care, Esther. I have no words. You've been trying to get pregnant since barging in here, haven't you? What happens if you succeeded—"

"Oh, *like I'm ever gonna get pregnant with your useless sperm!*" she shouts, slamming the door behind her. A crunched-up can falls from the coffee table as the vibration passes through the room. Beer spills out onto the floor like a clogged drip, reminding me of my last orgasm. Perhaps this room is a womb of which I need to abort myself. I'm cocooned inside here. No other thoughts enter my mind. I appear to be trapped in a singular, nebulous series of voices, all of whom sound foreign, generations away from my modern tongue.

Ding-Dong!

That'll be the Chinese I ordered. Great. Unknowingly trying to get your mentally-ill, attention-whore of a girlfriend pregnant really works up an appetite.

CHAPTER TWENTY-THREE

I am a spiteful spirit, deep inside. I should've stayed inside the props room with Sammy the other night and slowly sipped myself to sleep by her side. Nothing would've happened then. It would've even been quite a poetic sort of apology; a fitting end to a series of events that probably should've never taken place. Two lonely, drunken souls sleeping silently next to the broken, ghosted crib of their own making. We could've woken up together, not shared a single word and made love in its most seldom form of mutual acceptance and understanding. Esther, seeing that I'd seemingly vanished, could've left with one of her self-appointed gentlemen callers, if the thought of bothering to look for me happened to occur to her at all.

And that would've been that. I'd have got my wish.

But my own desires also appear to allude me. I just had to leave that room, didn't I? I just had to go downstairs to see Esther already acting as if I'd slipped away from her existence, had to feel the dilapidating wrenches her unfixed glances shot me with, to take it as my cue to whisper in her ear that the girl I'd cheated on her with had fallen pregnant, whilst negating to mention that its occurrence took place during the time we'd made ourselves official, lest I forget the still spreading rumour of rape which accompanied it.

If I was asleep none of it would've happened.

If I was asleep I wouldn't be here.

Ironically enough and just for measure, I seem to be asleep to my own intentions, unaware of what really motivates me deep down. I cannot recall a time I've ever felt like such a stranger to myself. I am the embodiment of nightmares I can't remember having.

My reason for being makes me a being without reason.

The surrounding mist swirls if you look closely enough, but no matter how hard you stare at it, it always looks still. Perhaps that's nature's greatest trick; the appearance of idleness whilst underground a catastrophe always looms. Maybe even our own obsession with territory has something to do with feeling foreign to this planet, like a desperate cry for help atop of a land of total indifference, under a blanket of stars not actually there. It's a cosmological mirror of our collective reflection, the good as dead already phantoms bursting with thoughts as ephemeral as they are false within an unobserved destiny of decay.

Vvvrrrrmmm-Vvvrrrmmmmmmm!

Fucking hell. That gave me a jump.

Vvvrrrrmmm-Vvvrrrmmmmmmm!

Mmm. The Plague Doctor wants a word.

"Hello?"

"Hey man, it's Richard. How's it, urm, going?"

"Not bad. I'm standing in the rain, but without want of a single urge to sing. How are you?"

"Urm, yeah, I'm doing great thanks. I just wanted to see if we're good. You know, after the party and everything."

"Oh. Yeah, we're fine. Why wouldn't we be?"

An unusual pause follows, and the reception crackles slightly whilst his breath… I don't know, comes across somewhat standoffish.

"Have you urm, spoken to Sammy since the party?"

"Nope. Haven't heard from her at all, which is probably a… well, never mind. Are you okay man? You seem a bit despondent."

"Me? Oh yeah, couldn't be better. Just tired you know? Everything's been hectic recently as usual. Busy as always. Listen, Eric. I, urm…"

"Yeah?"

"I urm, just got word about a tour I auditioned for weeks back. Turns out whoever got the role I went for had to turn it down, so they've offered me the part. I'm gonna be away for at least six months, maybe even a year. As it's quite late notice, I'm going tomorrow. Just wanted to check we're okay before I go. I know I kinda crossed a line at the party… dunno what came over me really. Been feeling shit about it since… since you're the only real friend I've got."

"Ah, man—"

"*Eric!*" Jessica's voice calls out behind me. I didn't even hear her car approach.

"Cheers, Richard," I say, "really. That actually means…"

I don't know, as the phone line is already dead. Jessica's headlights flash so intrusively I'm forced to block its glare out with my hand. Her frantic windscreen wipers screech-wave back and forth, only allowing her to be seen through split-second frames. Their shrieking is so sharp my eardrums bleed melancholy. I brush the rain away from the screen of my phone and slip it inside my pocket as I walk over to the car, touched but more confused by not only Richard's initial call but the conversation's abrupt end. I've never heard him sound so… well, human. Humble too, in a way. Almost apologetic. Maybe I misjudged him.

Jessica's car sits in the same place it's sat many a time before, near enough opposite the train station in the forever vacant carpark. It's only just after eight o'clock at night yet looking around it might as well be two in the morning. I flick the latch of the car and slink inside, immediately confronted by His shadow. The passenger side is littered with Glen's cigarette packets, at least forty or so, all of them empty. It's like he left them here on purpose for others to find, to make them aware of his ever-watchful presence.

"Urm, why were you just standing there in the rain, Eric? There's shelter in front of the station," says Jessica, spinning bewilderment into a joke with undertone alarm.

"No reason. I just felt like it. I find the patter of rainwater to be calming."

"But it's pouring down? Look at you, you're soaked."

"Consider it a cheap form of cleansing."

Jessica reaches for the air conditioner, but I stop her as she turns the dial towards the red. "There's no need for that, I've got all I need to keep myself warm," I say, shaking my metallic friend.

"Are you sure? Your teeth are chattering."

"Not because I'm cold. Don't worry about it, really. I'm fine," I say, ruffling my hair to put an end to the ceaseless dripping of droplets. "So, what do I owe for the pleasure of this little meet-up of ours?"

"Are you sure you're okay? Your eyes look… elsewhere."

"Right as rain, as they say. The fewer comments about my appearance the better, for it, is of no consequence. Though I do need a haircut, I must admit. Drink?"

"No, thank you," she says, holding her right hand up.

"So, why are we here? What's going on in the world of Jessica?"

"Urm. Not much really. I just needed to get out of the house for a while. Glen hasn't left for the last three days."

"I thought you said that he disappeared, did you not?"

"Why are you speaking like that?"

"Like what?"

Jessica shuffles about her seat and eventually crosses her arms after fidgeting with her hair. Upon the release of a deep breath, she says, "Never mind. Yes, he did vanish the night I called you, but I'd rather not talk about that to be honest."

"Why not, what did he do?"

"I meant our conversation."

"Oh. I don't remember it all that well."

"You sounded deranged."

"All the better to not remember it then, I guess."

"Yes, I suppose so."

"You might as well just tell me what happened. I know that's why I'm here, so come on. Eric Archer is all ears for Jessica Wakeman. You look rather delicious by the way."

"No. I do not! I look terrible. My hair's a complete mess and—"

"Are you close to ovulating?"

"Urm… no—well, yeah, actually."

"That must have something to do with it then. The brain isn't as sophisticated as all the plebs out there like to believe. We're wired to pick up on these things without realising it. Around the time of ovulation, a woman will naturally appear more attractive. The cheeks get rosier, the eyes are more prone to dilation, your breasts look rounder and firmer and no doubt you'll be releasing scented chemicals into the ether that send all the boys wild. Add in the fact you look quite vulnerable and somewhat dishevelled and the predatory male libido is salivating at the mouth. Did you have sex with Glen today?"

Jessica's cheeks flush and she flicks her head to the side just a smidge. "Did you have sex with Esther today?" she retorts in return.

"Yes. Thrice. Abortion envy makes her horny."

"Abortion? Okay, Eric. I don't want to have this conversation."

Her crossed arms tighten.

"What conversation do you want to have?"

"None really," she shrugs. "I just wanted to see you."

"Mmm. I find that hard to believe. There's always a reason. And that reason's name is Glen. So what, he didn't make himself scarce in the end after all?"

"He did the night I rang you, but then he turned up early next morning and hasn't left since. I think he was just walking around the fields surrounding my house all night. He has a habit of doing that after we… have a disagreement."

"And? What did he have to say about your first night together after his contemplative stroll?"

Jessica's quick intake of breath indicates a desire to speak, but instead she breaks her locked arms loose and scratches her scalp, then flops her hands over her abdomen again. All done without a single glance thrown my way. After a moment she forearm-swipes the condensation away from her window but due to the opaque nature of the mist, it looks much the same.

"Mind if I smoke?" I ask.

Jessica simply shakes her head, pouting her lips slightly as she does so. Whatever I'm supposedly doing here remains vague, but her agitation surrenders the anger her unsaid words all but promise to inflict.

I wind my window down and lean slightly out of it, sparking up a smoke. Jessica, sensing the futility of their struggle, cuts the windscreen wipers. As the drizzle drapes freely over the glass, she lets out a defeated sigh and says, "He still doesn't believe me, Eric. Since he returned… he's treating it, or even me… just like before. Like it never happened."

"Well," I say, as smoke disappears in front of my eyes, "without trying to sound as if I'm defending him—*because believe me, I'm not*—but if he did manage to dismiss the reality of it, hearing about it again now must make it even more difficult to face. It's like a truth your own mind moulded and molested into a lie."

"Yeah, I guess. He's just convinced himself I must've wanted sex because of how… *how fucking wet I was*… he might as well have said I was 'asking for it'—I just don't know what to do now."

Jessica goes to cry but holds herself back, thumping the steering wheel instead. "But it was just a chemical reaction! He didn't notice how stiff I was… during the whole fucking thing… no, as I was wet I must've been gagging…"

"Jessica, I'm…" I say, sucked into her inconsolable state. "Come here," I whisper, reaching for a hug which is embraced after some slight hesitation. Leather stretches as she buries her head into my shoulder blade and lets herself go. To my regret, I've become utterly desensitised to her suffering. I feel nothing. Each blink brings about an image I've already seen, a palpable snapshot of the past, which only serves to nullify me further. Jessica lets out a scream, muffled by my damp hoodie, followed by an anguished bite that pinches my skin, which I make no indication of. As she breaks away from me a moment unfolds between us, a moment we've had a thousand times over. This is where we'd normally kiss, but the situation stops us, and we turn away to our respective sides. I re-light my cigarette. After a minute it's done with, so I flick it away and watch as the ember is extinguished by the rain.

"You mentioned something about an abortion? Were you being serious?" Jessica suddenly asks, wiping her eyes.

"Yeah. That was Sammy."

"Who?"

"Oh, just some girl I had a fling with. Not even sure I believe her anymore. Like all other actors, she has a habit of lying."

"Right… when did this supposedly happen?"

"Well, she only told me about it… I dunno, six weeks ago, give or take. We had an on-and-off affair whilst Esther and I had an on-and-off relationship. Once Esther and I got more serious, if you can call it that, I broke it off with Sammy. Naturally, that provoked her into showing me what she could really do in bed and I took full advantage until… until she… fell pregnant. Fuck. I never realised that before until now. We didn't just drift apart. She drifted away from me because I got her pregnant. I can't believe I didn't see that…"

"But when exactly did you knock her up?"

"Oh. Roughly a year ago. Wanna hear the kicker? I'm pretty sure it was conceived on the bed of someone's grave."

Jessica scoffs. "You fucked on someone's grave?"

"That we did. You've gotta love the irony, haven't you?"

"Fucking hell, Eric," she says, adjusting her position once more, "trust you to tell me about this now…"

"That isn't even all—"

"Wait. So, let me just make sure I've got this straight. You were sleeping with this Sammy girl ever since you slept with Esther? So, you've been cheating on her the whole time then. Why didn't you tell me about Sammy?"

"I didn't imagine she'd come to be so relevant."

"You lied to me. Again."

"How so?"

"I asked you if there was anyone else aside from Esther and you said there wasn't."

"You told me you didn't know the person who raped you. Call us even."

"That doesn't make us even, Eric. God, I can't believe you. How many others were there?"

"You can't keep believing that every woman I slept with during our break-up somehow constitutes me cheating on you."

"Yes, actually I can, Eric. We were still having sex after all. I know not very much but still. After everything that happened to me... I still don't understand how you could do that."

"Maybe because I knew you were lying—"

"Don't do that, Eric. Don't even dare try to suggest you somehow knew it wasn't a stranger."

"But it wasn't though, was it? You can scold me all you want about cheating on you Jessica, but ever since you unmasked your silent watcher in the shadows to be Glen, everything you've ever said to me has come into question. Even if I didn't know for certain back then, I still knew something was going on. So why should I now believe that you only want to confront him about what happened and nothing more? There's always something else to swallow with you. Your words are nothing but a disguise that you consciously conjure up to conceal what's really going on behind the scenes."

"Eric, what the hell are you talking about?"

"Yeah, go on then. Pretend you don't know. I need some air," I say, going for the latch but Jessica pulls me back.

"No, talk to me, Eric. Explain yourself. Say what you want to say."

"I just fucking did," I reply, yanking myself away from her and exiting the car. My chest constricts as I pace, further obscuring my surroundings as I half-stumble towards the middle of the road. Jessica's door slams shut behind me.

"Eric! Please. Get back in the car."

Everything before me is frenzying into epileptically-charged blinks, capsizing the torrent of raindrops into a cascade of blinding stars. Wherever I walk pulls me back from the place I was headed, so no matter where I step, I can't stop myself from going nowhere.

"Eric?!" cries Jessica, the vibration of her voice collapsing the negative space back into the opaque, drizzling mist. Trying to explain where I just was would require the where to be something fixed, but that was, as far as I can understand, something reversed or inverted; a collected upturn of atoms within an ovular sphere of an undetectable mass. A world without colour, whose workings are not just unhindered by our presence, but utterly and profoundly indifferent. If that was a mirror into human thought, then what I just saw looking back was less than nothing.

If our existence upon this planet is not just unwanted but never invited, then surely our only vindication lies solely in its utter destruction.

"Eric! This is absurd. Get back in the car or I'm going."

The taste of annihilation is on the tip of my tongue.

Water flicks away from my fringe as I turn, crossing through Jessica's core to reveal her outline and arrest my sightline. She stands between an exit and an approach. I'd prefer the former.

"Do you wanna know why I cheated on you, Jessica? I did it because of your disgusting, uncompromising need to have children. We both seem to forget or deliberately fail to mention that we only started falling apart as soon as that fat, gravid elephant slumped itself between us."

"Oh, don't give me that crap, Eric. You did it because you wanted to, plain and simple. Don't you fucking dare make it out as some noble sacrifice—"

"There was nothing noble in it at all, Jessica. I wanted you to hate me. We were already walking down the plank of our relationship. I just decided to throw myself off first. You needed to despise me, so once you started contemplating about looking elsewhere, into the prostitute's cunt my cock went.

"Fuck you, Eric. You're just making this up. I know you—"

"But of course, as psychotic nature just had to have it, my betrayal backfired on me beyond all fucking reason, as your own ego had already sniffed out its latest opportunity to play victim and oh, my, fucking me, didn't you take that chance? I'm even still somewhat impressed by how long you've managed to stretch it out for. Two fucking years under the sheets with the man who 'forced' his way inside you. Feigning helplessness to resurrect the erection of the father. And just like with him, you now simply refuse to let go."

"Eric—"

"But none of that matters. None of it. How you can want to breed, even if everything that ever happened to you never occurred, is completely beyond me."

"Eric. I'm going to be the bigger person here and ignore the vile things you just said to me as you sound like a fucking lunatic. I'm honestly concerned that you're changing for the worse. As if wanting to have children is some kind of immoral—"

"You told me all about that first night with Glen like I was just some fucking mock exam for the real thing, didn't you? After two years of indulging in your precious therapy every other day, it still took you two fucking years to tell me about it. And that would be fine if I didn't know there was something else that you're not telling me. And no, having children isn't 'some kind of immoral' act, it is the ultimate immoral act."

"Eric. I'm worried about you. You're displaying severe signs of at least several mental disorders right now."

"Stamp me with whatever you want, but your truth can only exist in my fucking belief. Of which, I have none. First you tell me he disappeared, then you tell me he hasn't left your house since. All I keep hearing is how 'strange' he's been acting since you told him. Strange isn't gonna cut it. Fucking explain yourself."

"He's been acting exactly like you did after it first happened, that's why. He's *there*, but he's not really there. He only stays during the day and then he disappears at night—"

"Oh—*ah-ha-ha-ha!*—you're worried he's cheating on you now, is that it? Lord forbid that Glen might be raping someone else behind your back. Fucking hell. What a comparison. First, I get accused of the same thing, now your only concern is that he's out there doing the dirt. What a fucking joke."

"No, Eric. I'm concerned because he's acting like a paranoid wreck, accusing me of lying to him and who knows what else. I can sense these things too you know, and I don't like where my thoughts are going."

"You're actually worried, aren't you?"

"Yes, I am. I know he's not perfect—"

"Not perfect... now there's an understate—"

"Yes, I know he's not. Far from it in fact, but that doesn't stop me being concerned about him. He's accused me of trying to make him go insane over this."

"It's called gaslighting, Jessica. I thought you of all people would've learnt something about human psychology by now. He's accusing you in order to make himself out as the victim and you're falling for it again like the abuse victim he force-fucked you into being from the start."

"Would you listen to yourself, Eric?"

"Just tell me what I know you're hiding from me, Jessica," I say, approaching her finally. "We both know there's something. It's written all over you. I'm trained in the art of lying, remember."

"Eric, please. You're scaring the shit—stop grabbing at me!"

"It's okay, Jessica," I say, batting her flailing arms for the sake of herself. "Please. I need this. We need this." I repeat, now clasping her cheeks between my hands. "I know you better than you realise, even after all this time. You didn't come here just to get away from Glen. You came because you need to confess."

"You're just paranoid, Eric. Please, that's all. I have nothing I want to say to you."

"Look at me and say that. Then I'll let go."

"Eric, there's nothing—get the fuck off me! You're choking... m-e…"

"If you want to breathe in some more precious life, I'd advise you to fucking *look at me!*"

"Get off!"

"Who are you looking at?" I ask, stunned by her unflinching focus. Her eyeline hasn't budged since I grabbed her throat. "It's him, isn't it? He's here somewhere, isn't he? What are you trying to do to me?"

"What on earth are you talking about? Just get the hell off of me!"

-PLOP!-

"Argh!—you fuckin'—slut victim!"

I let my grip on her slip for one second and she fucking finger-poked me in both eyes! "Nice stab, Jessica!" I say, searching around for her with my eyes breathing, pulsating and shifting of their own accord. "Looks like Glen put a bit of fight in you—better late than never I guess…"

There he is. I knew it. His shadow lurks beyond the mist as obscured as his intentions—ducking and diving—swirling from within the miasma! "Jessica!—I know he's fucking here—come out from hiding already! I can smell his skin cells—*it stinks of rape around here!*"

As I shift around, the car door slams shut. "Jessica!" I shout, storming towards it whilst looking around—*I can't believe it!!*—Caden's shadow has already disappeared!

"Open the fucking door," I say, giving Glen's dent in the car my own piece of violation, expanding the damage he once inflicted. It's about time I sent that cunt a message of my own. The headlights beam into life—blinding me once more before the engine begins to roar!

"Oh no you don't!" I say, diving onto the bonnet just as Jessica goes to pull out. Upon landing I just about stop myself from sliding off by grabbing onto the frantic windscreen wipers and use them to yank myself up.

"*AAARRRRGGGHHHH!!!*" Jessica screams as the car stalls, her face behind her drenched hair and flailing hands. She thumps over the horn as rain plummets against the glass, ricocheting droplets into my still-shaking eyes. The engine growls again but the car remains idle. Jessica's hands flap around at the gearbox. Both her feet stamp down at random.

"Tell your beau that the dawn is nigh! She's gonna come hard alright, whether she likes—!"

The car bursts forward—heading towards the railings of the bridge! The wipers can't take it—I can feel myself losing my grip… she's gonna slam me against the—

-VVVVRRRREEEECCCCHHHH!-THRUUUMP!-SMACK!-SCREEEEEECH!-

I'm sent flying, skidding across the tarmac, shredding pieces of leather as I'm spun onto the pavement and thrust-smacked straight into the wall. A rippling shudder thunders through my spine as I flop face down against the pavement with my head still spinning.

-VRRRMMMM-SHIEENK!-

I let out a long, exasperated scream, releasing the demented thoughts of my synapse-snapped mind, laughing now as I flop from side to side on the edge of the gutter, feeling nothing from the impact except the most demented form of pleasure. Headlights blind me out my mindset and without knowing how I've somehow swung myself back onto my feet. But as soon as I go to move the car does too and the world spins against me as I stumble recklessly without balance and come crashing down further away from where I just fell a few moments before.

Whilst lying there under the opaque torrent my senses swing back inside me as I eventually catch my breath and feel the promise of fresh bruises pulsate all about my person. Luckily, being as drunk as I am helped prevent any serious damage and I seem to have come away from the crash relatively unharmed.

Minutes pass by, but just how many I simply don't know. I only noticed my still being here as the rain ceased its onslaught. Regaining my strength, I hoist myself around onto my back. The first thing I see, looking down at me through a drowning blur, is the tag of graffiti I saw the last time I collapsed on top of this bridge. There it remains, glistening in a rage of bloodred, but disintegrating too, eroding through the inevitability of time, decaying in what I take to be the same rhythm as myself.

"FUBAR."

That's my new war cry.

A war I'm about to declare.

You might fancy me nuts, my perverted little watcher, but you don't know the things I know and what you don't know are the instincts Eric Archer comes equipped with. I know for a fact that Jessica is keeping something from me and if I'm forced to go Machiavellian on her arse to find out what it is, so fucking be it.

I thrust my hipflask out of my side pocket, feeling a burn in my ribs, but a burn I enjoy. The flask took minimal damage upon impact, bulletproof and dependable as always. Three huge gulps later and I check to see if my phone was smashed. It wasn't, as I recall landing on my right hip, near to where I keep my wallet. Time to make a call.

"Hello?"

"Dawn?"

"Yes, this is she."

"Hey, yeah. It's the ridiculously handsome stranger here, the charming and well-equipped young stud you wanted to seduce right in the middle of the street the other week."

"Oh yeah, I remember. I've been thinking about you. I wondered when you'd call..."

CHAPTER TWENTY-FOUR

"Aye aye, ain't seen ya in 'ere for a while—*fuck me*—you look like you've been run over by a train, mate," says John Smith, already inebriated and in that annoying, loquacious persona he'd love to be able to pull off. He brushes passed me as I'm approaching the bar, heading to the front for a smoke. "How's the acting going? Got paid for anything yet?"

"It's going, alright. Started doing my own stunts," I say, figuring it to be the smallest possible phrase I can muster to supply him with the hint that I. Do. Not. Want. To. Talk.

"I told ya before, change your name mate."

"You know what? I might just do that, Johnny boy," I say as he floats away, swaying back and forth until he disappears through the main door and the pub is empty again. It looks like something out of a war movie when the Nazis gained territory; clandestine and with an air of caution. It'll go bust within a few months, no doubt about it.

"Hey, Eric. Long time. Usual?" says Lucy, holding up an empty pint glass, pointed fixedly at the pump I must've blown thousands on to get pulled. Lucy seems mildly pleased to see me. Guess I'm providing some relief from the obnoxious garrulousness of John Smith's mouth.

"Please," I say, brushing my still damp hair back, noticing a bump has formed on the right side of my skull. Hopefully it's a tumour.

"You look a little worse for wear. Everything alright?"

"Yeah, everything... is the same. Always the same."

"Glad to hear it. I'm single again, which is a relief to say the least. Loving my new-found freedom," she says, with a light shimmy of her upper-half, thoroughly convinced of her words.

Is anyone ever aware of how transparent they are; of how much their denial glistens everything they gaze upon; of how much they're just locked in the game of their current emotion? *Loving it my arse.* She's got no other choice but to say that because no one would listen otherwise. In fairness, there is a bit of a salacious tinge to her... but it's all arbitrary; a carbon-copy of the last time she found herself single again; the elation of relief a break-up so often brings just before the dread of loneliness sets in and you start hoping dumb shit like you'll meet 'the one' again. Then that soon wears off and you end-up settling for someone similar to the list of already-been-there's, ignoring all the warning signs of your conscious mind as subconsciously you're already bathing in the comfort of its inevitable failure. *Question!* How many times do we repeat the same things just to feel the same fucking feelings, regardless of whether they're positive or negative? *Answer:* A whole goddamn lifetime, that's what. Life may evolve over unseen stretches of time, but in between its just a relentless Sisyphean nightmare of repeats. One must imagine Sisyphus to have killed himself with that boulder more times than he's pushed it up that fucking hill.

Presumably, Lucy's celebrated her apparent freedom by getting a new tattoo, going by the plaster around her forearm. Or maybe she's been self-harming again. She's got the tracks embedded on both arms, a constant reminder of her past, of which she is never allowed to escape. Big whoop. We all live with scars, interior or exterior.

"So, what happened with Jack?" I ask, already bored by whatever she is about to say. I can't even fake flirting with her now the deed has been done and double-done. Her purple lipstick would still look fantastic glossed with semen though.

"Oh, nothing. We just grew apart, you know. Happens."

"It certainly does."

He cheated.

Lucy places the pint in front of me and I flick a twenty her way. She's giving me the *Let's-Fuck-Again-Eye*, which is frankly making me feel a tad nauseous. If I was drunk, I'd probably mistake its obvious display of loneliness for desire. Not that there's much difference between the two. If any. Now she's more than experienced with ride Archer, she should know he requires liquor-fuelling before settling her peachy arse on board. She hands me back my change and holds my glance for a moment. Jack played away, so now she needs a little ego boosting, something to reassure her sense of identity or some shit. If I wasn't meeting Sammy here, maybe I'd take her up on her blatant invitation again. I'm cautious of pulling on the no-strings-attached deal we've got going though, as really, there's no such thing. We always weave and entwine our emotions with other people, whether we want to or not. I'd love to bullshit you about how I've learnt from my past mistakes, but let's face it, we only ever preach about that when the opportunities to repeat them have dried up. Lucy may just let me do whatever the hell I want this time around though (aka, ass to mouth) depending on the anger inflicted by her ex. If he cheated on her with a chick she deemed to be more desirable than her, then the sack will have a demon unleashed upon it. After standing around and letting me eye her up for a bit she walks away with her hips swaying from side to side, in a hunt and on the prowl. Hopefully Sammy will stand me up.

She got in contact with me whilst I was on the train back from Battleton via a text, telling (rather than asking) me to meet her down here, now. It's a shame I didn't bottle up my emotions and get it on with Jessica earlier, especially if things go as I expect them to with Sammy. I could've slept with three women in one day…

Still can't believe Jessica just drove off though, especially after I broke down on the bridge right before her very eyes. She spends her whole life running straight back to the same thing she's hiding from.

"Hey, thanks for turning up," says Sammy. I turn to look at her and… there she is. She's bleached her hair… a sort of… lightning… white blonde. Ignoring my gaze, she turns towards the bar, flicker-patting me down with her peripheral. I'm not sure if this new look suits her, but its audacity alone is something I thoroughly approve of; it adds an element of danger. Her movements, however, seem cautious, apprehensive of the world surrounding her and still somewhat stuck in the vulnerable Sammy of old, the Sammy whose mouth told the lie that now hangs in the air between us.

"What are you drinking?" I ask.

"Urm. I'll have a glass of wine."

"Luce, can I get two glasses and a bottle of, what is it, red?"

"Yeah."

Lucy serves us without saying a word, picking up on the tension with alacrity, but once again gives Sammy the routine once-over. Her eyes dart far more threatened than the first time around. I can't be sure if she even recognises her, but the judgment of her looks is more than palpable.

I move over to the same table we sat at before without really thinking of what it may reflect. Sammy scrapes the wooden chair along the floor like last time, which seems to frighten her slightly. Oddly. She sits down with an awkwardness you'd see at an alcoholics anonymous meeting, biding her time before a confession of some sort. In truth, I'm struggling to know what to say to her already. It only strikes me now, just how exhausted and distressed she looks; something no new hairstyle could hide. After a sip of wine, she sits up. "That girl behind the bar, you've slept with her, haven't you?" she asks, trailing Lucy's movements in a way that would normally excite me.

"How do you know that?"

"Easy guess," she says, playing with her hands, barely making any eye contact and shifting slightly in her seat. The light coming from above the bar puts her under the spotlight. She removes her jacket, revealing a cream-coloured blouse with an amplified cleavage that looks too good not to donate at least a few seconds to. Under this light her tits even rival Esther's. After noticing what I thought was a subtle glance, she takes out a packet of menthols from her handbag, removes one and holds it between her fingers, at the ready. She's suddenly transformed from prey into predator. She looks over at Lucy again. "I thought so the first time we met in here. It's the way she looks at me, then you. There's a glint in her eyes as they cross back and forth between us. It gives away everything. She really likes you. You know how I know that, Eric?" she asks, adjusting a loose strap that slipped down her shoulder as she spoke, glancing at her own breasts before looking back up at me. "It's the same glance Esther gave me when she first saw us together, all that time ago. The 'giveaway look,' as I like to call it. The whole image is captured in a flash; the two of us, naked, what we did together, what my cunt tasted like, how we fucked, whether I swallowed your cum. All in that one little look. That girl behind the bar is a bit on the skinny side for me, but her arse sure is juicy. I didn't know you were into tattoos."

"I'm into women with them."

"Let's go to the garden. I wanna smoke," she says, abruptly getting up from her seat whilst snatching the wine and already heading towards the backdoor before I even flinch. Her bluntness is both alluring and intimidating, like she wants to sleep with me just so she can murder me afterwards. Sammy smiles at Lucy as she walks, eyeing her like a tiger, giving her a lethal, feminine body-check and adjusting her bra again to remind Lucy what she doesn't have. Knowing I'm watching her, Sammy throws a glance my way, sealing it with a wink. She's either furious with rage or her libido's making her delirious. Hopefully, it's both. Lucy looks my way as Sammy passes through the door with a quietly sad smile betraying her. Now I'd bed her again.

The beer garden has a triangular-tiled plastic covering for shelter as soon as you step outside, with a few park-style benches to the left and right. The misty rain from earlier still floats all around us, gently falling like snow. Sammy lights her cigarette and blows smoke through the drizzle and presses the sole of one foot against the wall, going all film-noir on me. I sit down on top of the bench and rest my feet on the part where you'd normally sit. I roll a cigarette, listening to Sammy suck down her cigarette through bitter-clenched teeth.

"So, I guess you want to know what Esther and I spoke about at the party," she says, watching the streams of smoke dissipate through the rain. "Right, Eric?"

"Well, Esther hasn't said much about it, so I'm guessing you didn't either," I say, swinging my legs to the side to sit on the edge of the bench instead and light up myself.

"I was hoping Esther would find you fucking me upstairs if you want to know the truth. I had this image of her seeing me with my legs wrapped around your waist whilst you had your way with me. I wanted to stop when she saw me, then stare back at her as I slipped down to my knees and took your cock into my mouth. You'd know she was behind you too, but you wouldn't turn around. If she stayed there watching us, I'd have deliberately made you cum all over my face. Sadly, it wasn't meant to be. I still can't believe I blacked out. But it was my fault. I remember saying you could... yeah. When I woke up and went back downstairs, I saw Esther flirting with one of the teachers. She's got a thing for old men, hasn't she?"

"Big time, yeah."

"When she noticed I was looking at her, she looked kind of guilty for a second. You know, like she'd been caught out, which I found a bit strange. I enjoyed having your taste on me whilst looking at her though. Then, five minutes later you ruined it."

"Well, what did you expect me to do? I figured telling her the truth was probably for the best. Stupid looking back at it now, but hey, there you go. I'm a retard. I didn't expect you two to become best of mates afterwards though. That part surprised me."

"Telling her the truth? Really? What, so you told her that you carried on sleeping with me before and after you two were 'officially' a couple and that you also had a bit of blonde action going on in Battleton as well, or that we just fucked? I don't think so. What you mean, Eric, is that you told her your version of the truth, which naturally must've been a load of crap."

"Well, obviously, I didn't tell her all that, but I had to tell her something. Well, maybe I didn't actually, looking back. What do you mean by just—"

"Why didn't you tell her you took advantage of me?"

"*Ha*. Very funny, Samantha. You're not beginning to believe your little fiction now, are you? I never took advantage of you."

"No, Eric, you're missing the point," she says, pushing herself away from the wall with her resting foot and squaring up to me. She slaps my knee to the side and stands between my legs. "She's pretty fucked up, you know. I think she'd enjoy believing you're a rapist. Just think of how much she can manipulate you with that knowledge. Yeah sure, at first, she'd act all horrified and play the victim but in secret… she'd be delighted. After all, leverage is a beautiful thing. She might even convince herself that you did the same to her, given enough time," she says, looping her fingertip around a torn part of my jacket.

"Is this what you told her then?" I ask, trying to get a read on her but her eyes dart rapidly around my face whilst she tease-bites her bottom lip. I take a drag of my cigarette, where she grabs hold of my smoking hand and presses it down on her breast and squeezes. I feel her flesh around the edges of my palm, but in the centre, there's something square, possibly plastic.

"Take it out," she says. I slip my fingers underneath her barely worth having bra, grip it between two fingers and brush over her stiffening nipple as I pull out. She takes the phial from my hand and says, "They're valiums. I've been on them since the abortion. Here." She pops one out and holds it up, placing it onto my tongue. She watches me swallow it dry whilst helping herself to one, gulping it down with a swig of wine. Then she slips the phial inside the pocket I keep my hipflask in and tells me they're mine to keep. Upon noticing my metallic saviour, she removes it. We're too close to the unprotected area of the shelter, so now the moisture over her chest glistens under the light. And, of course, I'm beginning to stiffen myself. Sammy notices and bites her lip again when the door swings open and Lucy's head pops out.

"Hey Luce," I say, turning my gaze towards her, away from Sammy's pushed-out chest.

"Hey guys, we're closing up soon, so if you want another drink you better order it now."

Sammy holds up the flask, removes the cap and shakes it from side to side. "We're okay thanks, *Lucy*, but thanks for letting us know. Love your lipstick by the way," she says and takes a sip. Lucy goes to say something but bites her tongue. She remains there for a moment, looking at us the way Sammy described before stepping back and pulling the door shut again. Sammy, with visibly erects nipples now, seems to glare at Lucy's juicy arse through the window as she suggestively walks away.

"She is cute. I can see why you fucked her. She must have one tight snatch. Is her clit pierced as well?" she asks, turning back towards me and taking another swig. Her eyes are an ocean of narcotic indifference. "If you're still wondering, Esther doesn't know anything except for whatever you told her. She was even rather sweet about the whole thing to be honest, in her own little whorish way."

"What do you mean?"

"Well, she just said she understood. That she knows what you're like and yada-yada-yada. You both have that in common, pretending to care. Richard was still trying it on with me after you left, even when I was a fucking wreck, all flushed and stank of you."

"I thought he left before me—"

"Can you believe that? He really doesn't know when to quit that guy. I didn't tell you about the time I saw him in here, did I?"

"He told me about it."

"Yeah, that was funny. He didn't realise I was looking for you. He bought me drinks all night. I didn't even have to flirt with him for them, but I did have to listen to him going on about what it's like being an actor in the real world the whole time. I guess he thought making out that he was experienced in the subject would make me fuck him."

The bell for last orders rings around the empty bar beyond the wall and the garden lights flicker off, leaving the single one above the door the only one remaining. Sammy starts laughing a little bit under her breath, then rests her forehead on my shoulder. After a minute, she grabs onto my jacket and springs herself back up. She gazes at me, through me even, like everything around her is transparent. Leaning into my ear, she wetly whispers, "My car is parked just around the corner. Don't think I'll make it easy for you by blacking out again this time. Let's go." She turns away from me and walks through the door without looking back. I stare ahead, a touch perplexed, peering at the door as if it were a rabbit-hole. I should walk away from this and just go home, but I know for sure that I won't. Sammy has suddenly become what I always wanted Esther to be, or at least, she is playing the role out to perfection, despite her occasional blips into being elsewhere. Plus, the valium is beginning to kick in, joining the party of whatever else I've still got in my system, so for the next few hours, consequences are smudged. My experiment with Esther has clearly failed, so now is the time to give Sammy the opportunity she deserves. The women who seem hellbent on ruining me are now blissfully unaware that Eric Archer is already in ruins. This time, instead of falling back down the hole my past dug up for me, I'm going to fucking obliterate it.

CHAPTER TWENTY-FIVE

Sammy's rummaging through the aftermath of the party, searching for some more poison by tossing empties left and right, making more of a mess than before. She said she's been due to tidy the place up for nearly a week now but isn't going to bother until the last minute. All around us are the remnants of the shindig a week back or whenever it was; half-empty bottles of wine, over-filled bins full of teeth-marked nibbles and crushed beer cans. Sammy uncovers an unopened, screw-capped bottle of wine amongst the debris. She picks it up, looking pleased to discover she won't need to look for a corkscrew. Whilst half-mumbling to herself she chinks two fingerprint-smudged glasses together and stands up straight. Well, as straight as she can. She looks at me for a moment, swaying, with her jacket halfway down to her elbows. Droplets of rain fall from her hair whilst her chalk-white chest spangles under the subtle illumination, almost steam-like. Every now and again she seems a touch frightened by me, or perhaps the potentially unprecedented situation we've just entered. Aside from these infrequent anomalies though, she's lush and lusted-up as fuck. The friction between us is intensifying. Magnetic yet hostile. Threatening. The rain and lack of light above the entrance door made it difficult to unlock, so now she's just as sodden as I already was from before. Part of me believes she did it deliberately, as her blouse is all but transparent. We haven't said a word to each other since entering, but the looks we're exchanging fill in all the gaps. Lacking heat as this building always does, the only source of warmth we have is each other. She may have planned this for a while.

Sammy flicks her head towards the stairs and begins to approach them with slow, echoing footsteps before I even move. Disturbed creaks vibrate through the room as she ascends. The crackling burn of the joint I rolled whilst she searched for our tipple soon becomes the only sound I can hear. I look up, contemplating what might occur upstairs with Sammy's slutty little rumour pinballing between my neurons. The fact she could tell such a lie makes me both loathe and somehow lust after her. Her darker side shares similar shades to my own. I can't help but wonder just how similar. After a quick suckle of my hipflask, I hit the stairs, listening to Sammy giggling after what must've been a stumble. I'm welcomed to the summit by the crunching tear of the twisted screwcap. Two large glasses of white wine soon find themselves poured. After setting them aside Sammy lays down a blanket snatched from one of the many piles of limp, used and dust-laden clothes. Whilst sitting, she finally lets her jacket slide away from her arms and lets her new dishevelled hair down, then pats a spot on the blanket where she'd like me to sit. I look around the room briefly before taking my seat, mostly at the broken crib in the corner.

Sammy picks up a glass and hands it to me, then scoops up the other. "You know, I think we've spent more time in this room than any other place in our relationship," she says, holding her gaze on two masks; the black one I wore at the party, atop of the jester one she wore. So that's where my mask ended up. I'd completely forgotten about that. "To," she says, holding up her glass expectantly, "disguises."

Our glasses chink. I take a big gulp of wine, or at least I thought so until I see Sammy already pouring herself another. She lights a cigarette and keeps gazing at me with the guarantee in her eyes. Normally I'd already be inside of her by this point but I'm more intrigued to see what she does if I hold back and do nothing.

"I've been thinking about what you said to me at the party. I wonder, why did you ask me if I told Edith where you forced your uncontrollable urges on me?" she asks, glancing at her chest again and then back up at me. "Seemed like a strange thing to ask. Almost like you've… thought about it before."

"I was just trying to intimidate you, Sammy."

"Did you think about it, there and then, when I told you? Did you want to rape me?"

I arch my eyebrows and shrug.

"You know," she continues, "every woman fantasises about it. I liked the game we were playing. It was hot. I was scared, yet really, *really* turned on."

"Who said it was a game?" I ask in a half-threat, half-tease. She laughs whilst rolling her eyes across the floor, uncertain of my meaning. Then she smacks her lips.

"I thought you were going to completely lose your shit. I've never seen you like that. You looked like a different person almost. What did you think about?" she asks, holding her glass with both hands, sitting cross-legged and leaning forward.

"I don't know. It's all a blur now."

"Oh, come on. Just answer the question, Eric. Play along," she says, leaning further forward to pour me another glass. "I just want to hear what goes on in that mind of yours. There's no need to be shy. I won't tell a soul, I swear."

"It's pretty hard to believe that, Sammy."

"I know," she says, unable to contain her wild laughter, "but look, I'm here, with you… alone, after I confessed everything to you. After letting you... *you know*. There's no safety net here tonight. You can do anything you want. I'm powerless to stop you." She laughs again and slurs something incomprehensible, letting her bottom lip hang, stained with the sulphites inside the red wine from earlier.

"I think you're acting out of guilt, Sammy. But fuck it, if you really want to know, I'll tell you. Yes, I thought about it."

Sammy finishes her second glass and goes for another, topping mine up again as well, finishing off the bottle. She looks exhilarated to be hearing this. "What did you imagine?" she asks.

"I'm sorry?"

"When I said you 'wouldn't take no for an answer.' What crossed your mind? What did you want to do?"

"I imagined you crying whilst I came inside you. Is that what you want to hear?"

A wicked smile appears on her face whilst her eyes dilate. She finishes her wine, tosses the glass over some clothes and starts crawling over to me. I watch her, transfixed yet reluctant.

"We can do that if you want. I'll play along. You should've seen me with Edith when I confessed. I didn't even know I could fake cry like that. I mean, I was upset with you and everything, but when she listened to my little story," she says, fully-aware of tickling a whole host of unknown consequences through her reckless tease, "she swallowed every word."

She gulps, face cater-cornered square in front of mine, coating half of my countenance with her lingering hot breaths infused with wine, leaving the other side of me in the dark, numb and no longer there. She moves back in an impossibly slow, sensual manner and comes to rest on her knees; bottom lip still hanging low and moist, her chest flushed in pinkened patches and the slit of her cleavage licked with a line of luminous sweat.

"Do you want to slap me, Eric?"

"No."

"Oh, go on. You must have fantasised about it. I probably won't even feel it. I've taken a shining to your alcoholic lifestyle of late.

Come on, just hit me a bit, across the cheek," she says, giggling like a schoolgirl, turning her face to profile. My temptation is indescribable.

"I don't want to hit you, Samantha," I say, trying to mean and believe it.

"I love it when you call me that. Like I've been bad. I have been very naughty, Eric, telling everyone you raped me when really, I was gagging for it. Don't I deserve a little smack for that?" she asks.

"No," I scoff, "it's all forgiven."

Sammy grabs my hand and places it on her cheek. She motions it around in a circle, then back and forth from her skin, spurring me on. I see myself doing it, watching her shriek in fear, pinning her to the ground and forcing myself inside her as she struggles, feigned or unfeigned.

She grows impatient and tosses my hand away.

"You're no fun. Drink more will you. Hey, you want to see something funny?" She moves over and grabs her handbag. After ruffling through it, she takes out a small, cylinder-shaped object that looks like a miniature bottle of deodorant. She throws it at me. "Do you know what that is?"

After catching it I take a closer look. "Is this a rape alarm?" I ask.

She laughs and nods. "Yeah. Edith gave it to me. Didn't really know what to say," she says, the contortion of her face matching mine.

"'Too little too late' springs to mind," I say, laughing through bafflement.

"You want to hear it?"

"I'm good, thanks."

"Fine. I'm going to fetch another bottle. When I come back, I expect you to have removed your jacket and rolled us another spliff," she says, skipping across to the stairs.

I take off my jacket like I was told, toss it over the bars of the empty, busted crib and start rolling a joint. Sammy can be heard shuffling and stumbling around downstairs. It's a good thing she's on valium. If she does hurt herself, she won't care. Mmm. I finish rolling and spark up, pondering whether to resist her advances or not as the fumes leave my lungs like cryptic smoke signals, matching the fog of my brain. Sammy enters its background, clutching bottles in both hands, her bust somehow even more on show. They're so fucking fantastic I'm sure most women think they're fake.

"So, Mr Archer. Would sir like some left-over vodka, a week-old mixture of whisky and coke or a fresh glass of cabernet sauvignon?"

"I'll stick with wine."

"Excellent choice," she says, throwing the rejected bottles onto a pile of clothes. She tears the cap of the bottle off with extreme ease and flops her knees down in front of me again. Very slowly, she begins pouring a glass whilst staring into my withheld lust. "Give me some then," she asks, referring to the joint. I hold it up for her, but she just pouts her lips. I spin the spliff around my fingers, then she traps it with her teeth. She takes a drag and lets the smoke drift slowly around her face. A maniacal stare glares at me through the smoke, until the cherry from the spliff falls to the floor, sending her into a wild guffaw. We're inches away from each other. She edges forward and blows smoke into my mouth. Our lips caress, then she moves back and holds up my cup of wine.

I take a sip and Sammy hands the spliff back over. After clasping it between my fingers she glances around the room, looking at the clothes, adjusting her chest as if no one was watching. She glances my way to make sure I'm at full attention. "How many times do you think Esther has cheated on you?" she asks, with fingertips lightly caressing the stitching of her top.

"No idea. Probably more times than I'll ever know."

"Why are you with her then?"

"I wouldn't really say we're together in the normal sense. She comes and goes as she pleases. I'm pretty sure one day she'll just never come back."

"Hmm. You actually want to be abandoned. Interesting."

"Not so sure about that."

"Oh, come on. It's obvious, Eric. You push away anyone who gets too close. Pretty clichéd really. You keep Esther around because her behaviour reinforces how you feel about yourself."

"Nice bit of pop psychology. There's some truth in what you're saying but it's a little bit more complicated than that. At least I hope so, anyway."

"You keep telling yourself that. She must be very good in bed," she says, sipping some wine.

"As a matter of fact, she's incredible," I say.

She blushes, with tiny flinching face muscles betraying… I'm not sure. "I'm gonna take another valium. D'you want one?" she asks.

"Yeah. Why not."

"Close your eyes," she commands. I do as she desires. "Now open your mouth." My jaw flops open. A pill is pushed and pierced through foil with a satisfying pop, followed by a sharp intake of breath. The tip of her tongue travels across my lips and slips inside my mouth so slowly it feels like a dream, but quickly retracts, scraping backwards under the top set of my teeth until the pill is left behind. "Wait a second," she says, "hold still." Wine swish-swashes around the bottle, then a glass-encased echo follows her gulp. Next thing I know, she's squirting wine into my mouth through pinched lips. Once fully dispersed, she guides my chin upwards and says, "Now swallow." As soon as I gulp, she plants her lips on mine again, but hard this time, forceful and moaning, grabbing my hair from both sides of my head, penetrating her tongue along with each side switch, then pluck-pushes herself back. When I reopen my eyes, she's back in the same position, as if nothing happened., except her top is now stained with a splash of fallen red wine.

Without bothering to even acknowledge it, she throws a pill of her own into her mouth like it's second nature, dry-swallows it and lightly flicks her head. "If I was a man I'd be with a whore. It must be great knowing you can fuck other women without ever feeling guilty about it. Do you still see that blonde girl, the one in Battleton?" she asks.

"No."

"Liar."

After the attack on the atmosphere subsides, I ask, "How do you know about her?"

"The blonde one? Oh, I've seen you with her a few times. My parents have a place in Battleton. Well, Lewes really but they're basically the same. I never told you, but I saw you with her after we started sleeping together. I was going to mention it, but then you and Esther were suddenly an item. I hated you more because of her than the blonde, she actually looked quite nice. What's her name?"

"Jessica."

"You never mentioned her to me. She's obviously an ex. How long were you with her for?"

"About a year and a half."

"Does she know about me?"

"I don't think so, no."

"Of course not. I didn't think she would. What happened between you two?" she asks, turning the conversation into a full-on interrogation.

"Nothing really. Just grew apart."

"Right. A few months after we ended, I saw her with some other guy. He looked a lot like you. She didn't seem to be very happy with him either. Do you know who I'm talking about?"

"I know of him. That's about it." I take a long sip of wine and scratch my neck. "Why are you asking me this Sammy?"

"Just to get a better understanding of you Eric, that's all. So, do you still see her?" she asks, smiling like she's innocent.

"Drop it, Sammy. Save it for another day."

"Hit a nerve, did I Eric? I wouldn't say he's better looking than you really. You have the same build and a similar smile, from what I can remember. That was about it."

"What do you want?" I ask, my tone betraying aggravation.

"Maybe I should introduce myself to her, she looks like she could do with a friend. A bit like Esther did at the party."

I look at her, with eyes that must've communicated my disgust, as Sammy's eyebrows raise.

"Ohhhh. Things must have ended badly between the two of you.

272

Interesting. Do you want to hit me now, Eric? Jessica doesn't really look like your type, but she does have victim written all over her. Was that your initial attraction?"

"Sammy. Shut up."

"Or what?"

"I know what you're trying to do," I say, placing my hand on her shoulder, wondering if she's getting wet from this.

"Do you?" she asks, arching an eyebrow. "What's that then?"

"What do you want, Sammy?"

"You. Obviously."

I trail my fingertips across her shoulder and wrap my hand around her neck, giving it a gentle squeeze. "Did she cheat on you with that guy?" she asks, eyes half-crazy under the struggling light, still laughing on occasion. "I bet she did. And now you take it out on everyone else you fuck, right? Isn't that how it all works?"

I loosen my hand and run my fingers down her chest but pull away before touching her breasts. Sammy leans further forward, looking at me but never directly. Her head sways slightly whilst her eyes appear to have capsized on themselves.

"You know, I saw this, this… Jessica… after whatever we are, or were, went tits up… on my way back from the abortion clinic," she says, laughing with emotional divorce. She takes a minute to stop, seemingly having a conversation with herself. "Hey, you wanna know something? This is my last confession, I swear. You know the last time we fucked, inside the graveyard? Well, guess who knew she was pregnant at the time," she says, mockingly holding her hand up. "*Oops.*"

Sammy's face distorts as her laughter echoes around my eardrums, puncturing them into a throbbing pulse. The room takes on a trailing, effervescent blur. The blood in my veins feels warmer and thicker, making my whole body erect and on standby, waiting for the trigger of the gun to be pulled. Sammy's shadow hands me a glass of wine, which I take and down in one go.

"Knowing you got me pregnant made me desperate to have your

cock inside me again. I don't know why. You want to know the sickest thing? I booked the abortion that day as well. I almost told you whilst we fucked."

A cloud of dust particles floats through the dim light of an old lamp, whirling away from the eye sockets of my shadowed, yet gleaming mask below. Somehow, the dust appears to be thrust back and forth by the muffled echo of Sammy's maniacal laughter, snuffed out only when one of her quickening breaths betrays a somewhat distant remorse. A distinct feeling of nausea washes through me as if her words were riddled with disease. Down below, my erection is pulsating, pushing hard against my jeans. "Sammy. You're fucking with me, right?"

"Not yet," she says, "but I can help move things along, if you like." She yanks her top down, ripping it a touch to reveal a mosaic-patterned, almost see-through bra, then snaps her blouse back into place. She's convulsing all over, either through excitement... or fear of my reaction.

"You're lying," I say, pushing her face to the side, trying to move away. She refuses to let me move by gripping onto my shirt and pulling herself even closer to my face.

"I've told you everything now, Eric. There's nothing left for me... to get off my chest. I'm handing myself over to you and I won't take no for an answer."

"You're drunk, Sammy—"

"Nobody fucks sober, Eric," she says, her hand now clamped around my jaw, fingernails digging in.

"Have you got a craving for another abortion, Samantha?"

"I'd rather just swallow. You know, I found it quite funny that my little tale of rape got so much sympathy. As if it doesn't happen every single day, all over the fucking planet. Even my own uncle touched me up when I was eleven. Maybe Edith thinks you really went for it, you know? Lost your mind and slapped me about until just I gave up and let you have your evil way with me whilst I lay there... crying... begging you to stop."

"This isn't going to work, Sammy—"

-*SLAP!*-

"Ohhh, you've gotta admit, that was a good one!" she says, laughing hysterically, the sting only just outlasting the resonance of the blow. She's fucking testing me now. I drop my hand from my raw cheek—*THWACK!*—she slaps it again. I laugh through adversity, whilst she makes eyes at me which scream *What-are-You-Gonna-do-About-it?!* whilst shuffling her body to send her tits into an infuriating quiver.

-*THOMP!*-

She didn't expect that. In fairness, neither did I. I just punched her in the tit. The look on her face as she fell back was magnificent. She even let out a shocked, high-pitched puff as she landed. I grab onto her ankles and yank her towards me, grazing the exposed skin of her back over the carpet. She holds up her arms in a flailing protest. "But you said you wanted this Sammy," I say in a taunt as I tower over her. "Didn't you?" I ask whilst snatching her wrists and slamming them down. "You said you wouldn't take no for an answer."

She nods, in a half-terrified, half-delighted panic.

"Well, now I won't either. Like this, right?" I slap her across the cheek. Her expressions twitch and flicker within shattered milliseconds, riddling her with terror, arousal and a confused, contorting attrition; cutting the tightrope of her ignorance for a piece of knowledge she can never be truly sure of desiring to know.

"I like it, Eric, but don't give me a black eye."

"I'll give you whatever I fucking want you baby killing whore," I say, sticking my fingers into her mouth, which she starts sucking on with subservient aplomb. I remove them by grazing them across her teeth.

"Okay, Eric," she says, bottom-lip trembling on a face with a washed-out complexion. I move away from her, grab the bottle and take a swig. My desire to treat her like garbage comes to blows with my own self-disgust. If I give in to this urge, I don't know if there's any coming back from it.

"What? Is that it?" she says, behind me, scoffing with annoyance but not quite convincing me.

"You're off your face Sammy, leave it. You have no idea what button you're pushing here. Seriously, no fucking idea whatsoever. Stop behaving like a stupid little girl."

I take another swig to further calm myself. The liquid in the bottle is the only noise, to my ears at least, that fills the room. The swill crashes down after my third gulp with the sound of serenity as I go to—

-SMACK!-

… turn. Sammy thrusted her heel straight into my kidney… with a strength far stronger… than I ever… thought possible. The surge of pain shudders… my rib feels shuffled… and I'm… struggling to breathe. The bottle somehow stayed in my hand… but the liquid spurted out everywhere… now a beat starts to drum inside my wrist. Sammy takes her turn to tower over me, not losing a second to initiate her onslaught by slapping me wherever the hell she can. *"I'm. Not. A. Stupid. Little. Giiiiiirrrrl!"* she screams through an agonised throat, spraying me with shuddering black tears through her smearing mascara. After a struggle, I manage to grab her wrists and hurl her to the side, pinning her back down on the floor before she can blink. Whilst she's stunned, I rip her top clean in two. One breast falls loose from her now unhooked-bra. *"Aauuucccwghh-tchuuuut!"* she spits, straight into my face, dribbling as she laughs with a demon drumming behind her eyes. "I've always wanted to do that to a guy," she says, "ha-ha-*ha*-ha-*ha*-ha-*ha!*" She slap-grabs my face and starts rubbing in her saliva, then scratch-slides down my cheek until her fingers fall away from my chin. The same hand along with the other one thrust under my shirt around to my back, and with fevered eyes she embeds her fingernails deep, clawing parallel crisscrosses across my shoulder blades. My torn skin screams as I rattle my belt buckle loose. One hand abandons my back and lunges straight into the dankness of my boxer shorts. She snatch-yanks my balls, then seizes my cock by twisting her wrist around, pulling as she squeezes it with all her wrath, grunting through grinding teeth, frenzied further by the absurd nature of my arousal, cackling her sanity into oblivion. "Wow, I always knew you were just as fucked up as me. Look at that vile thing," she says, marvelling at the still-slithering trail of pre-cum. I stand up and thrust my trousers down. Sammy gasps at the throbbing veins of my cock whilst it spasms of its own accord as if possessed. I grab a chunk of her hair and turn her stunned huffs into shocked mumbles by forcing the beast deep into the back of her throat until she gags me back out. As she chokes on her own breaths, I toss her to the side and yank the rest of her clothes off. She starts trying to push me away, kicking and slapping at my chest. I pin her hands down once more via my knees and rub my sweating shaft over her wincing face. Turning away, she grabs onto legs of the broken cot, whimpering into the indifferent silence. Sliding back down, I pull her legs apart, which she resists for a moment, but gives in when I dig my nails into her inner-upper thighs.

"Eric…"

She breathes short puffs of panic. Meaningless words pour out of her mouth; all nothing but white noise to me now. Weakening, she slowly stops trying to kick me off and leaves her convulsing legs wide apart. Her vagina's soak-splattered by its own juices, with a thick, translucent white secretion trailing down the centre. I tell her to start playing with herself. Her hand trembles as she slides it down her goose-bumped skin, head still turned to the side, until she feels me between her legs. She gasps, turns and looks at me, trying to push me away again. I grab onto the underside of her knees and squeeze them hard, pulling her closer. She looks up at me in shock and then down, at my hyperarousal, still twitching of its own accord, tease-stabbing her drenched, quaking lips. Her ooze starts blending with mine. She turns and looks me in the eye with an expression I cannot name. *"Do it,"* she says, *"… I want to kill your baby again."* Tears stream down her cheeks like rivers of plagues. *"Rape me, Eric!"* she demands, punching and slapping at me as I thrust inside her begging epileptic tantrum. She spits into my mouth and tries to bite me, screaming and deranged. Our foreheads meet, bumping into each other between every penetrating pump. Closing her eyes, she keeps trying to push me back, whilst her body continues to convulse and betray her beyond measure. I slide out from her pussy and go underneath. Her eyes open in wide alarm... her arsehole constricts, trying to stop me, but every second she struggles to resist my throbbing disease only worsens, becomes more resilient. Never before have I felt so in control. Our glances lock. She wants to say stop, but she won't. We're witnessing what we thought we once knew about each other die inside the eyes of the other. As she winces in exasperating pain I pull out and thrust back inside her sobbing cunt. I'll keep blending pleasure with pain until she can't tell the difference anymore. She'll keep trying to stop me, but her guilt will keep her legs wrapped around my waist until the self-loathing ambiguity of what she self-prophesized into happening forces her being to come... against its consent.

ACT THREE

"People should either be caressed or crushed. If you do them minor damage, they will get their revenge; but if you cripple them there is nothing they can do. If you need to injure someone, do it in such a way that their vengeance need not be feared."

- Niccolò Machiavelli

CHAPTER TWENTY-SIX

All the glory of Samantha and I's last encounter has done something indescribable to me, my observer. It was such a beautifully questionable experience, the entire exchange of it, one where every emotion became more ambiguous until it died under the light of interrogation it was put under, perishing for the fraud it always was. I feel as if I've entered a different realm. Everything is still the same as before, yet I see and feel it all so differently. Nothing has ever appeared to me as it really is, until now. Meaning means nothing to me anymore, so nothing is my meaning. The only significance a man can salvage from this ill-thought-out experiment forced upon him by nature, by his very own design, is the meaning he creates and then forces into being.

The spraying water from the shower screeches into idleness, replaced by Esther's relentless humming beyond the bathroom walls. Yes, I know. She's still here. I'm her new adopted daddy. She thinks she's duped me into letting her live here, which for the past few days I've been encouraging with tremendous aplomb. I'd like to tell you what else I've been doing but when I think about it, I'm stumped. It's been an amalgamation of insomnia, drugs and booze.

And Esther.

Esther crying, Esther moaning, Esther screaming, Esther leaving, Esther shrieking, Esther sucking, Esther bleeding, Esther pissing, Esther shitting, Esther squirting; Essssssssssstheeeeeerrrr, the brain nerve-ending molester, gushing out her golden syrup nectar, smoking all my weed, pleasing all my needs, crying about her mummy, drinking all my rummy and then laying her head upon my tummy until my icing glazes her all funny, but she laughs, saying 'yummy', that's my synapse-snapped playboy bunny, the button-tester that is my Esther, who cries tears through the years for her low-rent hussy—who claims to be—yet is anything but—her loving, caring mummy.

She struts out of the bathroom door, leaving it open as always, still humming some manufactured pop song, with one of my towels keeping her hair up, securing another around her unknown blitzkrieg awaiting chest. I've been treating her like a princess of late, yet it still makes no impact whatsoever on her behaviour towards me. You can take the cunt out of the brothel, but you can't take the brothel out of the cunt. "Do you ever *stop* drinking Eric?" she asks in between the incessant purring as I'm delicately sipping some wine. She shuffles the towel around her head and lets her wet hair fall. I gaze at her naked vulnerability, lick my lips and say, "Not if I can help it," and take another sip.

"Mmm. Those steaks smell good. Are they nearly ready? I'm starving," she says, in a tone that seemed to suggest her hunger is somehow my fault.

I check the time and indicate about five minutes. She tsk-tuts her teeth whilst rubbing the back of her head with the liberated towel like I planned for the steaks to take this long (which in fairness, I did).

I clear my throat, then say, "Set up the table will you, everything we need is already there, waiting for you. Here's your wine."

She grips it at the rim and takes what I can only imagine to be the smallest sip she'll have this evening, adding, "Thanks" to her mumble-approving, "Mmm." Snatching the bottle from the kitchen worktop, she soon nestles her peachy arse into the sofa. She ignores my request, choosing instead to continue towelling her hair. I flip the steaks over in the pan, turn down the heat a notch and open the oven door to check on the chips. A blast of warmth hits my face as I do, making me even thirstier than I already am. Satisfied, I flip the door back shut and walk over to the table to pour myself some more Jesus juice. "To us, my dear," I say, proposing a toast. "To domestic violence!"

"Okay," she says, shrugging. Our glasses chink and we both down our drinks. I pour three more glasses while she persists with drying her hair. The towel rustling suddenly stops as I re-enter the kitchen. From the corner of my eye, I see her looking at the three glasses full of wine, which puts a halt on her *hum-hum-humming*.

"Babe?" she asks after a moment. I flip over one of the steaks and pretend the sizzling drowned-out her whiny, soon-to-be protesting voice.

"Babe!" she says again, the sizzle of the second steak even louder. Lost behind it somewhere, the doorbell rings.

"*Babe?!*" she says, in the angry, breast-bounce tone I so often unconsciously try to provoke. Not so sure it's that unconscious though really. Te-he.

"Yes, gorgeous?" I retort, ignoring the chime that's just died away, pressing the spatula down hard on a steak merely for the alluring sound of burning flesh.

"Why are there three glasses on the table?" she asks, staring at them, unmoving, aside from a rattling hand.

The doorbell rings again.

"Get the door, will you?" I say.

"What? I'm naked."

"So? I'm serving up a free meal here. Show some appreciation. Chef Archer needs to keep a strict eye on the steaks," I say, splashing an award-winning merlot over them. It breaks my heart to waste wine like that, but loud noises assist with avoiding unwanted bitching.

A knuckle-knock vibrates through the room. Three distinctive ones. Aww. She remembered.

"Who's at the… Eric, what's going on? What the hell are you talking about?" Esther asks, the fear inside her voice chubbing me up something felonious.

Content with the golden-brown shade on the sides of most of the fries, I shake them around the oven dish to liberate the stubborn ones which are stuck (*note to self*: Must buy the grease-proof baking paper instead of the aluminium foil kind, much less adhesive than the latter and much better for the environment too (additional middle/ upper-class bonus: *Check*)) and tip them onto the plates next to the medium-rare steaks, salivating a tad at the sight of the blood seeping out of them. I chose not to ask my guests how they would've liked their steaks done as a subtle power-play move on my part, enforcing my dominance over them in the gaslight guise of supreme self-confidence. Don Eric Juan Archer knows best.

"Eric? Who's at the door?"

"Fine. I'll get it. You just stay put like a good little fox. Would you like any ketchup or mayonnaise? The chef personally recommends a spoonful of seeded Dijon mustard. Nothing but the French variety, naturally. Works wonders on the palette with beef," I say, winking at Esther as I stride into the living room with three plates at the ready, balanced atop of my forearms, gliding with all the pomposity of a well-trained actor, of which, I actually am. "I'll take that as a no," I say, taking her nonplussed stillness for a respectful refusal. I place the plates down, swivel, then head for the front door.

"Eric. Who the fuck is at the door? It's not one of my friends is it?"

"No, no, no. Much better than that. It's an enemy," I say, swinging the door open. "Good evening Samantha. Why, don't you look delicious on this fine November evening. Wouldn't you agree, Esssssther?" I ask, turning to look at her. Her mouth hangs agape (not enough for what I have planned, but it's a good start nonetheless) and her right eyebrow arches in a quizzical, non-too-impressed fashion.

Samantha steps inside draped in a nude-gold trench-coat with shiny-metal buttons running up each side along with a strappy belt screaming with sexually taboo potential. I insisted she stole it from the props room along with some other trinkets after ravaging her into an evolved identity. She places her hand in my hair, gives it a gentle rub and tug, then kisses me hard on the lips, leaving behind a taste of one of my favourite bottles of hard liquor. "Hello Esther," she says, holding her gaze on me before turning to her. "Oh, look. You're already naked. Doesn't mess around much this one, does he?" she says, hooking her thumb my way. *Guilty as charged,* my gesticulation suggests. "Oh, by the way Eric, your new hairstyle is to die for."

"Yes, I know but ich danke, Samantha," I humbly reply, running a hand through the swept-back fringe of my timeless military-style undercut.

"What's wrong with you? He looks like a Nazi. Can you two tell me what's going on here?" Esther rudely ripostes in a pathetic attempt to take hold of a situation in which she will soon be enslaved. Laughter finally erupts out of me, but I manage to fight it back down relatively quickly.

Samantha says, "It looks to me that we're finally about to wine and dine together Esther," and lets out a throaty, fake middle-class laugh. "Oh, thanks," she continues, picking up the glass of wine Esther poured only a few moments ago. She downs it and wipes the residue away with the back of her hand whilst Esther gazes at my authority, horrified and searching for answers.

"Eric. Is this some kind of joke? You're scaring me here."

"Close the door and come and sit down, Eric. I'm starving," says Samantha.

"I'm scarily starving too my darlings," I say, noticing the still wafting steam of the steaks and the slightest smear of red lipstick now across Samantha's cheek. Upon my request, she's dyed her hair bleach-blonde. It suits her much more than I would've ever imagined.

"Let's all take a seat, shall we?"

"Yes, let's. I'm ravenous," says Samantha, looking directly into the mysterious cave she's heard so much about from yours truly, the one between Esther's legs.

"Just so you know, *babe*, Samantha and I have been seeing each other again for the past week or so, ever since the fabulous graduation party. Do you remember? The one where you ran around telling everyone about Samantha's abortion behind her back? Where you attacked me on frequent occasions to make it look like I have a penchant for punching pussy? I felt it was the least we could *both* do, given the circumstances. Anyway, let's eat. I'm starving like a South American rat-child scraping the last remnants of his sniffing glue, glaring down at the prospect of selling his bony-arse for less than a buck."

Samantha laughs and removes her coat, showing herself to be attired exactly how I requested. From the bottom to the top: cheap black plimsoles (secretly inspired by the bitch-faced schoolgirl) cover her Asian-esque feet. Running up the replaceable legs are a pair of (Esther's) torn-up fishnet tights. Just before the pussy, we're met by the hem of a tartan mini-skirt (we can blame the not-so-shy schoolgirl for) that's wrapped around her waist with the organ-moving tightness of a Victorian corset (showcasing the sublime parts of the buttocks). Further north our eyes are treated to a long-sleeved, champagne-shaded V-neck with a twist knot front between the breasts (a size or two too small, thus enabling a tantalising view of her ample, Wonderbra-enhanced cleavage. Plus, the stretched twist knot adds ripples a-plenty around the whole vicinity of the chest, making the tits look like they're going to tear through the top at any given moment). And suitably rounding it all off is an adorable, oversized glittering hair scrunchie (a homage to my nameless and now deceased slut of a twelve-year-old). "How do I look?" Samantha asks me, curtseying after her third, directed twirl.

"If you could read my thoughts, you'd put my head in a guillotine, my dear," I say, sitting down on the floor with both knees. I stare straight ahead at Esther whilst she continues to sit there eyeballing me with tiring suspicion, the penny still seemingly refusing to drop.

"I'm glad you approve Eric. Though I must say, I cannot wait to get these clothes off," Samantha says as she glides around the coffee table and takes a seat next to Esther. The latter self-consciously strengthens the security of her towel but liberates the other, letting her still-wet hair down again. Samantha leans back on the sofa, places her hand on Esther's bare-shoulder and says, "Nice towel," before leaning over and kissing her on the cheek, leaving behind yet more of her lipstick. Esther continues staring at me in askance until I break our glance and say, "Let's eat, shall we?"

"Let's," one of them says.

We each pick up our knives and forks.

"Eric, please. I'm kind of freaked out here. What the fuck is going on?"

"Just relax, Esther. At this precise moment, we're just having dinner. If you want to leave without eating, be my guest. Unless of course, you have nowhere else to go?"

I begin eating, showing my enjoyment by moaning overzealously like I'm trying to flog it on some advertisement so over-glamourized people forget that all food simply turns into shit.

"I feel a bit sick. I think I'm going to throw up," says Esther, sinking into the victim-role she mastered during her teen years, feigning a shudder.

"If you must, please use the bathroom," I say, pointing at the door with my knife.

"You're fucking—"

"Dangerous?" says Samantha, slicing into her meat.

"*Please*. If I was dangerous, poor little Esther would be getting raped right now instead of about to tuck into this—*if I do say so myself*—exquisitely cooked cut of ethically-sourced, free-range beef."

"Go easy on her Eric, she's on the verge of a panic attack. Here, let me cut it for you Esther," Samantha says, edging nearer her. She begins chopping up the meat. Some blood squeezes out onto the plate, causing Esther to gag a touch and I, in turn, to look at the bathroom again and then back at her as a reminder of *What. I. Just. Fucking. Said.*

For once, Esther takes the hint and heads for the bathroom. I pick up a handful of fries and dip them in blood, soaking them up good before stuffing them into my mouth. Then I throw the knife to the side and pick up the veal with my hand and start eating it, caveman style. "Some people are against eating baby cows, but I think a lot of the time they forget just how shit the life of a cow really is. In the dairy and meat industry, most females are usually impregnated only to have their young torn away from them the moment they give birth. They only show the mother her young ones to get her milking again, tearing them away once the tap starts running, so to speak. Then her new-borns are slaughtered, and the mother gets artificially re-impregnated. Again. Again. And Again. So, whenever you eat an adult cut of beef, you're eating the flesh of a being that was once pregnant ad infinitum, yet never allowed to bond with her young. In my view, it's better to eat the veal."

The toilet flushes, the tap runs and stops, then Esther comes back into the room, wearing what she once labelled as her 'sex' panties and bra. Now that's a bit more like it.

"Oh… that wine has gone straight to my head. Do you know where my xanax is, Eric?"

"Yes. Your latter was blended with your former, along with an infinitesimal peppering concoction of an incalculable volume of… others. It's a bit stuffy in here, don't you think? Anyway, I'm glad you're prepared, but you simply must eat," I say, licking the juices off my fingers after taking my last bite, eager to tuck into my double-helping of dessert.

Sammy springs to her feet. She holds up a knife with a piece of beef on the end garnished with a dab of mustard (good girl). "Open wide," she says, nudging Esther on the shoulder. Esther sort of shake-gags (odd for an ex-pro) as she scrapes the chunk into her mouth with the back of her teeth. Sammy knife-pushes her chin closed to initiate mastication.

"Breathe Esther. Everything is fine. You said you were starving and that veal isn't getting any warmer. Fucking eat it already."

"Okay, Eric. Jesus. I'm eating, aren't I?" she says whilst chewing, still eyeing me up, secretly loving it. She sits back down on her seat. Samantha, who has also just finished her meal, watches her whilst licking her lips and then at me. I give her a nod of approval and she starts to dance. Esther finally tucks into her meal. "It's really good, Eric," she says, "thanks. Though I would've preferred something Asian."

Same here, but I can't let Samantha know that.

I begin rolling a joint to balance out the valium, adderall and alcohol in my system whilst Esther chows down and Samantha twirls around. "If I haven't recommended marijuana enough it is simply because I am rather faithful to alcohol, though I must confess it doesn't always serve well when it comes to sexual ventures. That's where weed takes the crown. It reduces all inhibitions, much like alcohol, but where the two differ is in the arousal they provide. Alcohol can help, but it is very easy to over-step the mark, whereas cannabis allows for a near instant erection the moment one is desired. A combination of both also works wonders, but you need to be a professional with one of the two before the magic will begin to work. Hand me the lighter."

Esther, now looking flushed enough to go porn, hands me it from the table. I light the joint and take the plates back to the kitchen like a good little servant and return with another bottle of merlot. After pouring some more glasses, I take a seat next to Esther, unhooking my dressing gown as I do, revealing my already half-hard erection. Esther takes the spliff from my hand and leans back to join me. We both watch Samantha; whose breasts are on the verge of falling out of her top. Esther, dreamy-eyed yet scrunchy-faced, flaps at her bra as I unhook it. She slides the straps away from her shoulders, laughs herself into a hiccup and throws it at Sammy, whom I hope takes it as a sign to do the same.

"Wait... what?" Esther asks, taking note of my shaft. "Why have you got an erection?"

"What a question!" says Samantha, walking over to her side whilst laughing playfully, peeling off the tightly-fitted top over her head and knee-dropping by Esther's feet. I push the coffee table back with my foot to give her more space.

"How can one not have an erection in the presence of a beauty such as you?" I say, stroking myself with the tips of my fingers and wrapping an arm over her shoulder. Esther looks down at Samantha, whose head now sits between her knees. The latter slides her hands up the former's legs and aggressively pulls down her panties, noticeably scratching a side of her labia with a fingernail as she does so.

"Oi! Bitch... fucking hell, take it easy... alright... I'm going along with this, aren't I?" Esther says for the fourteen-thousandth time.

"Finally," says Samantha, pulling her away from the couch by her feet.

Esther bounces onto the floor and gets dragged back a little further. Samantha leaves her there, crawls over to me, gives the head of my cock a quick I-miss-you-already-baby suck-kiss then throws her leg over Esther and nestles into the position sixty-nine. I put my feet up over Samantha's back, but find no need to encourage her with a nudge as her head is already buried in Esther's squirt-friendly snatch. To my complete lack of surprise, Esther's moaning with paralysing surrender.

I move around to the side of them for a better view whilst my penis plays eeny-meeny-miny-moe with where to start. After slapping Samantha's new and improved arse, I pick up a fallen steak-knife from the floor and slash her tights crotchless, then reverse-fold-up the tartan mini-skirt to keep the targeted buttocks focused; within my sights at all times. Privately though, of course, I also did it for memory's sake.

"Eric. I'm on my period by the way," says Esther, as if I care.

"All the better. The oven's already pre-heated."

"Affirmative," says Samantha, looking over her shoulder and smiling. She wipes her mouth but leaves her chin glistening. I nod.

She swirls her body around and we both help Esther so that she soon sways upright. After the signal, Esther finds herself face to face with the enemy's breasts.

"You two both have the most marvellous chests, it must be said," I say, a pulse now pumping inside my monster.

Esther makes a pissed-off muffled remark toned with jealousy, a mumble from under the rumble of Samantha's heaving mammary gland, squeeze-and-suck twin fumbles. The angrier the Esther, the more explosive the Archer. It seems even when she's fucking another female in front of me, I still can't compliment the other woman. Absurd.

Sammy grabs Esther by the forearms and directs her to face me and all my raging glory. She tries to wriggle free, but Samantha grabs a chunk of her hair and locks it inside her fist, taking away her freedom of movement. We both exchange a laugh as Esther shrieks in a playful pretence of pain. Both of their chests seem larger under this light (note to self: must buy these light bulbs again).

Samantha shoves the struggling and playfully-scared face of Esther towards my cock and says, "There ain't no such thing as free rent, bitch. Suck that fucking dick you slut!" ad verbatim, exactly as I directed her to and forces her to take it in her mouth, nice and deep. Esther gags, which only makes me harder. Since dating her the sound of a woman choking has become a dependable dopamine hit. Samantha releases Esther with a jealous grit of her teeth and gets in her fair share of cock-gobbling whilst Esther regroups, yet insists on trying to break free.

I let Samantha continue for a few minutes until I get bored (hehe, upcoming pun-intended) stiff. Time for some penetration. I break away from Samantha's mouth and kick Esther back into position. Samantha holds her down and sits on her face. She starts finger-bashing her as I circle around, then grabs her by the ankles and yanks her up. Before going to rub my head around the flesh between Esther's anus and vagina, I give Samantha a good traditional slap with my shaft to stabilise her envy levels. Esther squirms, not knowing where I'm going to put it, and that's the whole fucking point. "Not in—*mmm!*—my arse—*mm-mmm!*—Eric. You're gonna—*mmm!*—destroy it!"

Exactly.

I thrust into her rabbit-tight arsehole, grunting like the first man as he got fucked by consciousness. Samantha slides her hands around Esther's buttocks, pulling them wide and her up a bit to make it easier for me. I begin with the forbidden in and out and hear Esther bitching at me to stop. After playing with it for a while, slapping it about for good measure, I opt for the pussy, soaked with Samantha's saliva and Esther's blood, the red sea I'll soon be splitting in two with my unmerciful, amoral deity.

"Harder, Eric," Esther cries, taking a breath from the smothering of Sammy's arse, giving in.

I begin to thrust-pump Esther whilst staring at Samantha, whose playing with her enormous, sweat-coated breasts, pinching on the nipples.

From somewhere, a squirt of moisture hits me in the eye, blurring my vision. Angry, I start penetrating Esther with more aggression, trying to release more of her juice. Through a white glaze, I see her stomach. It looks larger than normal and appears to be almost... bloating out. Sammy slaps me across the cheek, a habit which I must profess is growing a little tiresome already. I look at her. She has a crazed expression on her face, so I stick my thumb into her mouth. Then I see one... of her breasts. It's leaking some sort of liquid... which spurts out little pinches of... sap with each thrust I give to Esther. I turn to see the latter's stomach. It's bloated... or bloating still. Somehow circular... spherical. It must be the angle... the shadows. Something starts screaming and grunting like it's trying to push me out of Esther. I've broken out in a sudden, seething sweat... a creeping... pore-breathing... slithering... closes my throat up.

"No! Come inside *me*, Eric," Sammy demands, shoving my face between her sodden breasts. The taste of something sour hits my tongue... whilst a violent thumping is going on underneath her stomach. With a swift movement, like a kick, I'm sprung out of Esther and fall flat on my back. Samantha jumps on top of me, clamping her cunt shut around my cock. She's enormous now too. Both her and Esther are crying yet smiling, stretch-marked and veiny. "Fuck me till my water breaks, Eric," Samantha says, grabbing hold of her breasts and squeeze-spraying milk right into my eyes. The room begins to sway. "Fuck a stillborn out of me, Eric," says Esther, fingering herself to make water, blood and placenta rain down from the ceiling. "Shoot that big fat, reproductive load into *me*, Eric. Fill me up with your multiple millions of never-will-breathes."

"No, Eric. Impregnate me again. We can't just have one abortion together, it's not fair on the foetus. You know what they say about single-foetus babies, don't you? We can't let it grow-up dead all alone, can we? Come on, wouldn't you love to fuck a miscarriage out of me?" says Sammy. Or Esther. I cannot tell anymore. They both sound like abandoned children fated for an asylum. Esther starts humming again. *Fuck.* I know the song...

"Rock-a-bye baby, on the tree-top," they both sing.

I feel my bladder beginning to give way, fighting with my testicles. My shaft keeps thrusting against the rubber-headed creature inside Samantha, but I'm powerless to stop myself fucking her. She starts swirling her hand over the bump, where a summoned, polyp lump pops up from within the bulge of her stomach. It circles underneath her skin, spiralling around and heading towards the middle. It stops when it reaches the belly-button, but then... it slowly pierces open! Something starts looking around the room and then... starts blinking. It's a dead eye... waking up! *It finds my eyeline!* It's staring! *Holding its glare on me!* Refusing to look away!

I'm fucking Sammy's aborted foetus!

"When the wind blows, the cradle will rock."

"You always said you wanted an incestual roleplay threesome, didn't you Eric?" says Esther.

"That's it. Come inside me and your daughter or son, your sister or brother, take your pick. We can do this over and over again for the rest of time," says Samantha.

"Oh, I can see your balls tightening, Eric," says Esther, cupping them with one hand and fisting herself with the other, "here it comes—*that's it*—*oh fuck*—it's coming… not yet…"

A mixture of blood and bile starts firing out of Esther. She's at the point of no return, moaning with sordid pleasure and pushing out never-ending pain.

"When the bough breaks, the cradle will fall."

Something else is happening to me! I can feel a build-up, a release like never before! Oh, fuck! I'm going to come against my own will!

"And down will come baby, cradle and all."

"Oh, fuccccckkkkk, *NOW!!!*"

I burst, stinging, screaming and crying, coming into oblivion. It's terrifying and blinding, leaving me nothing but numb and non-existent, everywhere and nowhere at the same time. It's only when I open my eyes that I see…

"ERIC! YOU FUCKING PIECE OF SHIT!" Esther screams through her gargling. She punches me in the jaw, nearly breaking it out of the lock. I fall smack onto the floor, unaware that I was even standing in the first place. The room splices apart and meshes together, throwing me about inside a kaleidoscopic prison cell. Seven Esther's jump on top of me, throwing fists and spitting bile. She's screaming so hysterically that I can't even make out her words. The slices start to slow like I've fallen underwater. Through the flash-cut blinks of Esther's forearms, I see Samantha in the corner, crying and shaking as if she's just been attacked. Finally, the moment I notice it, I stop pissing myself.

"YOU KNOW THAT'S THE FUCKING REASON I STOPPED FUCKING WHORING ERIC YOU SICK TWISTED BASTARD! ARRAARGHHHHHHHHHH!!! YOU CRUEL HEARTLESS CUNT! DIE ERIC, JUST FUCKING DIE!!! I WANT YOU DEAD!" Esther spits out, still thumping me on the head with her fists, eyes bloodshot, her whole head sodden with urine. She gets up. I could

move, but I *want* her to do this. I want her to batter me senseless. She starts kicking me in the head, then the chest and wherever she can. I just lie here, taking it, feeling nothing. Knowing this, she stamps hard on my groin, landing a perfect hit. The anchor-pull feeling sinks my testicles down to hell. I'm in agony, unable to breathe, still sinking. Through my opaque tears, I see Esther curled-up on the sofa in the foetal position, muttering to herself, back inside the brothel.

I start laughing. Or at least I think I am. The guttural sounds aren't even recognisable. The light above me begins to stutter. Smoke drifts around the room, making everything out of focus. All of this feels like it happened before and, just like then, I'm powerless to stop it. I hoist myself up with a bottle of merlot… Samantha sits, whimpering, her new blonde hair covering most of her face. I start crying, for a reason beyond my understanding. It just flows out like a depressurised release of an unknown force. The stench of debauchery puts a weight behind my blinking. These two are mourning over an existence unasked for. Every womb is a coffin. Every living being merely death in animation. Every heartbeat nothing more than a countdown of our own demise.

The sound of inconsolable sorrow shall soon drift me off into the most peaceful of slumbers.

CHAPTER TWENTY-SEVEN

Esther stormed out last night after I splattered her face pretty, so I put Samantha straight into training. Oh, in case you haven't noticed, I've taken to calling Sammy by her full name as of late, seeing that she's now a complete woman. I also quite like the fact she has a man in the middle of her name she can do nothing about. Nominative determinism is such a flirt. Anyway, Cadet Samantha Pennington took to her coaching with merry aplomb and is now the trained beast I need her to be to fulfil this mission. We're inside her car, situated on the outskirts of the fields around Jessica's house. Well, I'm inside it, she's back at the boot, getting ready. I've had to take a punt on whether Glen will be here but I'm almost certain that he will, seeing that Jessica's contact ratio with me has dwindled recently and that the last time I saw her she mentioned his staying here. Depending on the result of this escapade, tomorrow will bring about the end of this war, shortly after I dip myself into Dawn (a few times no doubt, going by the fuckability of her frame). If Samantha asks, it'll just be the once. She's getting dolled-up for the scene I've been writing all morning. She's not over-keen on the actions involved, but when I told her my reasons for making it happen, she began beaming with excitement. She knows everything now and has agreed to be my brother in arms. It's strange. Ever since she had the abortion, she's slowly become everything I wanted her to be and more. Though I am a little suspicious of her erratic, somewhat difficult to tame behaviour. She's doing all that I ask, but her lack of awareness at times is frankly… troubling. Familiar, too.

We've been here for a few hours now. I can't wait to see how accurate my script will become. I'll make the necessary adjustments when my predictions go wrong, but for the most part I'm rather confident. If Jessica's blow job track record with Glen is even remotely similar to what mine was like with her, then his desire for a cheeky suck job on the sly must be driving him nuts. My only slight concern is Samantha's acting ability. But then again, she managed to convince people I raped her, so maybe I should give her more credit. Once the relationship inevitably gets too much to handle, I'll just bed her hotter (and unfortunately now legal) sister. That'll either kill off the relationship for good or open a new world of sordid sexual fantasies come true. Win-win.

"Okay. I'm ready, Eric. You can come out now."

I scribble the rest of the note I was jotting down, quickly check the position of Samantha's phone (aka, camera two) and place my mask from the party on the dashboard, then get out of the car, script in hand. Whilst flicking through some pages, I move around to the back where Samantha has been trying on different outfits. She's hidden behind the upright boot, our makeshift changing room for tonight's performance. Well, it's more of a late matinee show really, but the former sounds better. We have the perfect landscape to set the stage. Ever since Samantha and I moved beyond a higher plane, a brilliant, obtuse and phantasmagorical grey mist has cast all around the southeast coast, even more so than usual. The ideal weather for war. I can sit undetected virtually anywhere within a twenty-five-foot radius.

Samantha appears from around one of the dangling costumes. "What are you doing?" she asks. I'm scouting the location, visualising the mise-en-scène from various positions. After finding what I believe to be the optimum area by far, I turn to fix my gaze on her. From head to toe: She's messily arranged her new blonde locks into pigtails, which caress just over the shoulders. So far, so good. Her narcotically-enriched eyes have all the necessary cosmetics surrounding them, making them appear as huge as possible, whilst her pale, delicately powdered cheeks match beautifully with the subtle, yet striking light neon-blue lipstick I insisted that she wear. That's right, light blue— Glen's favourite colour no less. I've opted for a cross between a slut-enriched version of Jessica, blended with a real-life anime chick, obsessed with cosplay and cock. Skipping over the rest, I've just realised she's dressed as Alice in Wonderland, which is really just a French maid's outfit but in blue and white instead of black.

"Give me a twirl," I say.

After a curtsy, Samantha spins around. "No, no, no. Slowly, I want to see that arse." She does it again. "Okay stop," I say, her back to me. "Bend over." She acquiesces. *Ohhh, Lolita.* It looks like a fuckable moon. *Approved.* "Alright, turn and come towards me." She does so. Once we're face to face, I push up her breasts, but there's too much fabric preventing them from being fully appreciated. So, I rip it a touch, then a touch more. "Okay, let your mouth hang agape. Show me a bit of tongue. Yeah, that's it, but now look slightly up at me. You're a victim remember. Very good. Okay, stand back a few paces." She does what I say, smiling, eyes rolling about and gleaming like marbles. Sedated Samantha sure has The Appeal. I've just noticed that her lipstick has a layer of glitter. Mmm. "Do you have any more glitter?" I ask. She nods and fetches it from a bag in the boot. "Give it to me." After popping the cap off, she hands it over. I empty some out into my hand, and command, "Okay, cover your face for me," and sprinkle some of it into her hair and over her chest. I push her hands back down and take a step back. It worked a treat. This is going to be like taking the virginity of an emotionally-neglected teen. "Alright, now drop to all fours and crawl over to your Mad Hatter and take a little looksie at what's the matter."

"I don't want to get my socks dirty, Eric. They're perfect right now," she says, looking at them with her feet pointing inwards, then up at me again with her mouth just a tad open, accompanied by a string of sparkling drool.

"Exactly," I say, "too good to be true. If we're going to pull this off, there needs to be an element of realism to it. Otherwise we risk obliterating its verisimilitude. Remember, you got lost driving your car. You were out all night long and when you woke up, you were here. Your phone is out of battery—*no*—stolen! Your phone was stolen. That's better. Even more helpless. You don't know anyone around this area... I mean, this is all useful if you need to work some magic on him, which, as you're dealing with a rapist, is unlikely. Anyway, drop to your knees and get crawling already, soldier. Slowly. I want to see your hypnotic tits move around nice and rhythmically. Keep your sights on *snap* this boner and *snap* these eyes."

She obeys with the silence of an angelic, subservient Asian girl who knows her place in this cold, cruel world. Let's find out just how fucking faithful He Who Loves to Rape really is...

"Okay. Action!"

Samantha shakes herself into the role and coolly drops to her knees before pushing herself onto all fours. She starts to crawl. "Slower," I say, "and breathe deeper. Maybe throw in a lick of the lips if you think it'll help. That's it." This is better than I could've ever imagined. Each breast moves forward like an army regiment, whilst it's impossible to take your eyes away from her glory hole of a mouth. Maybe all the pornography I've gorged on wasn't such a waste of time after all. This is going to work. I can feel it in my balls.

She reaches my crotch, looks up at me and then moves her hands up towards my belt buckle. For her sake I let her carry on. Before long, she starts blowing me again.

Technique: *Check.*

Eye contact: *Check*.

Occasional moan: *Check*.

Variation in speed and intensity: *Check*.

Shaft to balls ratio: *Check*.

One hand touching herself, the other gripped firmly around the shaft: *Check*.

Distance between her mouth and the tip of my head, held at an angle (*above the lips, not below the fucking chin*) to thus enable a highly probable first impact into the targeted area of the face, whilst the following onslaught of backup seed should disperse direct shots into and/or around the mouth: *Check and double-check*.

"Okay, Samantha. That's perfect. You've got this."

She carries on pumping me, frustrated I haven't come. I'm satisfied with her ability, even though she doesn't quite have what Esther has... *yet*. When that crazy bitch wants you to come, she pulls out every manoeuvre she's ever learnt to make it happen, basically never taking no for an answer. She has the *prostitute-before-eighteen* advantage, though. Only the sexually-abused during childhood can compete with that. Unless they've been blessed by stumbling upon the Archer.

I push Samantha's head away from me and zip myself back up. "Don't worry about me for now, Samantha. There'll be plenty of time to fulfil your feminine duties later. Let's remain focused."

"Oh, okay," she says in a huff. "But I'm not just doing this for you, I'm doing it for women in general."

"Same here, but who the fuck's going to believe Eric Archer?" I say, moving over to the car and getting inside.

"I do," Samantha says, following behind.

We both settle down inside the back of the car and I hand her the script to read over again. Setting up the mise-en-scène will probably take a while, but we have everything we need. I remove a deck of cards from my rucksack, open it and find the two joker cards. "Here," I say, handing them over to Samantha, "put each one half-way down your socks, on the inner part of your legs."

"Why?"

"Every fantasy needs a magical hook," I say, "carry on reading Samantha. You'll see what they're for. I like to think of them as a kind of breadcrumb trail but in reverse."

"Whose phone number is this?" she asks, looking at one of the cards.

"Yours. Well, in Glen's eyes it will be. I got you another phone."

"Why?"

"You never know, that's why. We might need him again. Once the deed is done, stick one of the cards into his pocket. If he comes back for more, we'll give it to him."

Samantha shrugs and sticks the cards inside her bra for now (which would probably work as well, looking at them) and carries on skimming through the pages. An abrupt, wide-eyed smile of glee erupts out of her from time to time. She reaches the last page, studies it carefully, then hands it back. "Okay, this all looks fine to me, Eric. I think it's a bit over-elaborate though. I mean, I'm just a chick in the woods, helpless, dressed like a slut, desperate to give a stranger a blow job. It's every guy's fantasy. If I can't pull this off, I'll give up acting for good and disown myself as a woman."

Despite agreeing with her, I keep my mouth shut and light up another joint (of which by now you should assume I'm doing all the time so I won't mention it too often), hit a swig of vodka from my hipflask and pop a valium before giving Samantha a little something extra with her scheduled dose. Throwing sleazy snacks down her throat every four hours or so has made her by far the most manageable and easily corruptible woman I've ever had the pleasure of grooming. Adopting the pharmaceutical approach instead of the illegal narcotic kind has been a stroke of genius thus far. "Whilst I concur, Samantha, I think the best way to look at it is this: You're not just some slattern puta desperate for a cock gulp. You're a soldier on a mission, a fucking spy for that matter. This is erotic espionage at its finest. That's the *only* way to look at it. Yes, it may seem crude on paper and blah, blah, blah, but this is misdirection at its very best. A salacious subterfuge, if you will. Think of how that *cunt* is going to feel when he realises it must've started with you, the sperm-drooling slut he found in a field one day, to his complete delight and utter surprise, only to find out that it was all a set-up he has no hope of ever proving. It's so fucking beautiful I could die."

"Well, don't do that. I've already aborted your kid. I can't see you go as well."

"Ahh, Samantha. That's the most romantic thing anyone has ever said to me. Kiss me."

She does what she is told. Now we just need to set up the stage and wait...

GLEN CADEN'S DESCENT INTO HELL

Written, produced, directed
and forced into fucking existence

by
Eric Archer

Note to reader: Gaps have been left between
the text for adjustments during the filming.
Whilst the writer could control what ALICE
(introducing the delightful, upcoming
Samantha Pennington) says, the dialogue of
MOTHERFUCKER/GLENNY-POOS/RAPEBOY (unknowingly
yet wilfully played by Glen Caden) are a
conjecture and thus liable to deviation
(these shall be accounted for where and when
appropriate, depending on the course of the
action). As the words of JESSICA merely serve
as a distraction device, her script shall be
reduced to a series of blurbs and anecdotes
ERIC has most likely already heard anyway. If
and when necessary, he shall add-in whatever
she says. Otherwise, take Blah Blah Blah as
a typical, tired-old colloquial statement
bereft of any significant meaning. Thank you
for your patience, my peaceful observer, my
humble watcher at the gate. Eric Archer looks
forward to being the one who watches rather
than the one who is being watched. Please be
aware that no orifices will unjustifiably be
harmed during the making of this production.
We hope you enjoy the show.

EXT. WAKEMAN'S FIELDS - LATE AFTERNOON
(ESTABLISHING SHOT)
FADE INTO:

A field of green, encircled by surrounding
trees and large bushes. It's around five or
six in the evening, which in England means
it's just a slightly darker grey than during

the day. Moving away from the trees into a
wider frame, we see an emerald green car,
with the driver's seat wide open. Through the
mist we can also see a few playing cards on
the ground, scurrying across the grass due to
the capricious wind. As we go wider, we see
a spiral of track marks caused by the car,
indicating to us that it must have spun around
in a frenzy before coming to a stop. There's
even a dent on one of the doors. Pulling out
into an even wider frame, we find our focus on
a fuckably distressed girl with bleach blonde
hair, around ten or so feet away from the
car, wearing a ~~Red Riding Hood, Schoolgirl,
Anne Frank, Harley Quinn, Lolita, Catwoman~~
Alice in Wonderland outfit (note to self: do
not return the crossed-out ones to the props
room) with all the prerequisite adjustments
of slut required for the modern-day Halloween
costume (do retrieve Pocahontas one though, in
anticipation of Esther's inevitable return).

All we can see of the blonde hardbody is the
crack of her neat and slappable arse, poking
upwards slightly towards the sky. The frills
around the hem of the dress make the arse look
extra delicious, as well as foreshadowing the
sexual nature of the scene. Reluctantly moving
away from the butt, we see a half-empty bottle
of vodka on the grass, as well more playing
cards from before. The girl was obviously out
partying the previous evening around the time
of Halloween (not entirely necessary, as the
film will be shot in Brighton, a place where

people love to play fucking fancy dress every
other weekend). Panning, we move back towards
the car, then notice and follow a trail of
more playing cards which lead to a small path
between the trees, noticeable only after we
zoom in, which continues until we fade to
black.

A phone begins ringing whilst we're shrouded
in darkness. Eric Espionage Archer, playing
a fictionalised version of himself, lies in
wait where the opening shot was just filmed.
As the camera fades back into focus up
until the point the shot is re-established
and upon Jessica's first word, we realise
that the perspective belongs to Eric.

            JESSICA (O.S.)
    (picking up on the ~~fourth~~ ring) *fifth*
Eric? (shy, but clearly wet upon hearing
from him)
                ERIC
          (solemn sounding)
I...really need...to speak...with you.(acted
so well that as the screen blurs the viewer
genuinely believes it was actually obscured
by the flood of their own sympathetic tears)

            JESSICA (O.S.)
Hold on. *(actually, she said, 'Just a minute,'*
but the meaning, as well as the prediction,
remained intact)
        (cupping the phone with her hand)

312

Eric listens to the distinct sound changes as
Jessica leaves the bedroom (acoustic) goes
through the hallway (more closed in) and enters
the bathroom (dank with more echoes).

                    JESSICA (O.S.)
                 (notably quieter)
    Hey.

The lock of the bathroom door follows quickly
behind it.

                         ERIC
    (still distressed, buying time from the off)
      Hey. Is now a bad time?

On the other end, a knock on the bathroom door
is heard. Three distinctive ones.

                    JESSICA (O.S.)
    Blah, blah, blah.

                         ERIC
    No worries. I can call back later if
    you like? Sounds like you're busy.

                    JESSICA (O.S.)
    No, now is fine. I just blah,
    blah, blah. How are you?

                         ERIC
           (continuing the teary bullshit)
    Urm, I'm fine. Well, not really... I'm...
    (ad-lib half-empty expressions, deliberately
    ambiguous to provoke more questions)

A few minutes pass in this fashion. Just as
Eric was going to ask about Glen...

FADE-IN:
EXT. WAKEMAN'S FIELDS - EARLY EVENING
(ESTABLISHING SHOT)

Right on schedule, MOTHERFUCKER appears on the
right side of the frame, cigarette in hand.
In the other hand is a playing card, which he
puts into his pocket.* He takes a long drag
of his smoke and starts to approach the car.
*drops to the floor?!

                    ERIC
          (lowering his voice, waffling
          more garbage into JESSICA'S ever-
          patient but seldom-listening ear)
     ... I just don't know what I'm doing with my
     life anymore Jessica.
          (waffle, snort, sniffle and snuffle)

               JESSICA (O.S.)
     Blah, blah—insert supportive clichés later—
     blah.

The conversation continues as GLENNY-POOS
reaches the car. He looks around the area until
the trail of cards (which brought him here in
the first place) attracts his attention again.
Then he sees ALICE, who, with her arse pointing
towards the heavens, now begins to wake up.
She flops to the side, revealing a bust ample
enough to receive attention from a distance far,
far away. Upon seeing this sight, GLENNY-POOS

314

~~walks towards her.~~ *Stands there like a twat!*
ALICE, on all fours, starts crawling over to
him, mouth agape, tits 'a bulging.

                    RAPEBOY
                   (confused)
     ~~Are you okay? What are you doing out here?~~
     (Remains silent?! Come on, take the fucking bait!)
ALICE, ignoring whatever he said (or didn't)
stops in front of him. She lifts her dress up
and reveals her freshly-shaven vagina. ~~Glen
whips his cock out.~~

                    FOR FUCK SAKE!
                    ALICE
        (fingering herself) — *must reward.*
     ~~Please help me. I'm so horny.~~ Good. Don't
     speak stranger. Today's your lucky day. Just
     come here.
     (entices him in with a 'come hither' after
     a sultry suckle upon her fingering finger)

~~Seeing this, RAPEBOY will go in for the kill.
He buries his cock deep into ALICE'S mouth and
that, as they say, is that.~~

In the event of the above not taking place,
skip to Plan B.

                ``turns page``

                                                    315

GLEN CADEN'S DESCENT INTO HELL
(CONTINGENCY EDIT)

ALICE rips the top part of her dress open, revealing her absurdly marvellous and glitter-kissed chest to the limp-dicked moron, still standing there like consent is his worst nightmare. On her knees, she marches forward, with her index finger up to her lips. She maintains eye contact with the surprisingly shy RAPEY-POOS, licks her light-neon-blue lips and unbuckles his belt, taking heroic, ERIC ARCHER-esque charge of the situation. His (semi) hard dick flops out. Immediately, ALICE gets to work, tucking her hands behind her back to feign their arrestation for the comfort of familiarity RAPEY-POOS evidently requires for his arousal.

JESSICA (O.S.)
Eric? Are you still there?

ERIC
(wiping away his crocodile tears)
Huh? What? Yeah. I'm still here. Don't worry Jessica, I won't kill myself. I'm just upset. It's just so hard at the beginning of November, you know?

JESSICA (O.S.)
(Repeats whatever she said last year)
— *notice how I didn't cross that out!*

                    ERIC
      Yeah, me too. I'll see you soon.
                  (hangs up)

RAPEY-POOS finally grows a pair and begins
throat-fucking ALICE. We zoom in on her and
stay put for a while as she puts her skills
to the test. Then, reluctantly and to many a
man's chagrin, we pan upwards to check the
pleasure RAPEY-POOS is receiving. ~~He stares
down at the angelic slut, with nothing but the
deepest of concentrated pleasure emanating
through his pores. He suspects nothing.~~
*He looks over at Jessica's house... but as he turns...
his face is shrouded in shadows! I cannot see any
distinguishing features at all... it might as well be
me getting my cock sucked over there!*

Eric Archer apologises for the interruption, my observer, but
something is wrong. Deeply wrong. It seems no matter how
often I manipulate the angle or refocus the zoom, Glen's fucking
face remains streaked with black. The fog surely isn't helping, but
Samantha's bright pale skin and recently enlightened face beams into
the lens with the purest and most picturesque clarity one could ever
only dream of capturing, whilst fucking Rapehead is silhouetted in
anonymity. I'm supposed to be exposing him, not fucking protecting
him! Okay... luckily, by going Napoleon on this fucking mission,
I've prepared myself for such a situation. Time for Eric Archer's
guest appearance. Don't worry, this isn't my first porno, there's a dead
cancer woman out there somewhere who can vouch for that...

CUT-TO: INT. THROUGH THE WINDSCREEN
(SAMMY'S 'STOLEN' PHONE)

The evolved ALICE continues blowing SNAKEY-DATEY-RAPEY-HIPS in the background. The former signals with an exaggerated, espionage and need-to-know-basis moan to indicate that she's trailed ERIC'S movements and has his back covered. The latter just continues milking the moment for all that its worth. Out of nowhere, a black-hooded figure crawls into the scene from the left side of the frame. Before we can even register his presence, he slips away from the corner of the frame again, making us all wonder whether what we just saw even really took place. ALICE ups the ante, gagging harder and louder to help camouflage any sudden sound-exposing movements, upping her discomfiture for the increased pleasure of RAPEY-POOS'S sordid enjoyment. A lecherous hand suddenly appears, spider-stepping across the dashboard until it mounts over a black mask and snatches it away. Moments pass. ERIC merrily skips into the centre of the scene, with his glorious erection slapping back and forth between his torso and knees whilst twirling the mask around his index finger. After breaking the fourth wall with a celebratory shimmy and a taunting shuffle towards the camera, he indicates to the lens for the audience to 'keep hush' and slowly tiptoes towards the ever-blossoming round of fellatio as it nuzzles around the bud of its imminent fruition, ~~then slips on the mask.~~

"ARGHHH!!!"

What the fuck is going on!? The script has been compromised! The mask… it was just in my hand. I had it in my grasp! It's gone. Risking detection, I sprint back to the car. Samantha's choking now—Glen's about to explode! My god, just listening to that brings pre-cum tears to my urethra... no, no, concentrate, Archer! The decisive moment is almost upon us... but the dashboard is naked apart from the camera... the mask isn't in the fucking car either...

"ARRRRGGGGGHHHHH!!!" Samantha screams again. Glen's gone AWOL. Instead of blowing his load, he's stun-punched Samantha on the back of her head and thrown her onto her front... through the growing mist... he pulls her knees towards his cock... she's struggling... screaming choked-up words that I cannot decipher... I hear him spit... he's going to anally fuck her!

Fuck! Abandon script!

Samantha wriggles, the thin layer of body fat around her buttocks brilliantly shimmering, shaking about as much as her tits previously were. Glen's pulled Samantha's dress over her head... the poor sexy slut can't see a thing! My boner is quaking, thundering amongst the mist. Saliva dribbles down my chin. Everything's become opaque... all I can see is a beautifully pale, exposed and oblivious backside. This is my moment. Sometimes the only way to defeat your enemy is to become your enemy...

I'm going to fucking rape you, Glen!

Snatching up the bottle of vodka, I drown much of its contents for some courage, then splash the remainder over my ridiculously attractive and extremely experienced penis. Lobbing the bottle with a flourishing backspin, it circles through the air in slow motion—*as soon as it lands*—I'm gonna launch my blistering boner straight inside this rapist's soon-to-be-raped-a-new-one's glorious backside.

The bottle crashes with a deafening, echoed pop.

Glen goes to turn around.

I lock my right hand into a fist...

Fluff my cock with the left...

"ARGH!!! GET THE FUCK OFF ME YOU CREEP!!!"

Glen faces me... but it's not his face that I see...

"TAKE OFF THAT FUCKING MASK!!!"

It was him. He stole the mask. How did I not notice that?

The remaining liquid swooshes around the bottle, the dreadful sound of no more booze. Glen stares inside of me, but his eyes… I can't make anything out… it's nothing but an abyss!

The bottle swings through the air—I can sense it about to make contact— Glen turns back and—

-SMASH!-

First blink: The mask flies through the air.

Second blink: I'm falling to the side.

Third blink: All I can hear is the harshest, most devastated of screams, the scream of a mother looking down to see she's given birth to a stillborn.

I lie flat, unable to move, unable to see, unable to feel. The screaming grows more distant… the smell of tarmac graces my nose, but the texture is nature's own, the green of the field.

"It was *you!* I told myself you wouldn't do something like that. That you *couldn't!* All those flashes I told myself were just some stupid nightmare… just my own fucking guilt… *how could you do that to me!?!...*"

***

```
TRANSITION FADE IN:
INT. THROUGH THE WINDSCREEN*


ERIC chases after SAMANTHA as she runs towards
the car, abandoning the mission. Although her
distress is obviously still titillating, ERIC'S
boner has been significantly diminished by her
bad faith. She screams expletives about what
he did to her (confusing ERIC for RAPEBOY)
and how she 'remembers' and 'sees everything
clearly now.' Blatantly through her female-
induced jealousy, which clearly and rapidly
evolved into its kissing cousin of delirium,
```

she couldn't handle any orifice other than her own being treated to the magical wonder of ERIC'S cock, regardless of whether it was for the greater good of their relationship or not, let alone the world at large. As the engine revs up, with ERIC given no chance to catch up with it, he shakes his head in dismay and disappointment, reminded of the real reason we were all expelled from paradise. ERIC suddenly gets his priorities straight and turns back towards GLEN, but all he can see is the mask, lying where GLEN stood only a few moments before, cracked down one side like puzzle pieces of disjointed memories forced together to make a narrative which still makes little if any sense. ERIC looks around at his surroundings for a clue as to where he disappeared... but finds nothing. The oddest, strangest feeling of being watched is betrayed over ERIC'S countenance, partnered with the sense of being in this position before, not just here but the bridge of Battleton too. Under his breath, he whispers… something, but looks confused as to why such a name chose to escape his mouth. Turning back again through an even odder sense of paralysed vertigo, he witnesses SAMANTHA as she throws hysterical punches over the steering wheel, as distraught in her movements as the ceaseless tears streaming down the smudged mascara of her cheeks. Eventually, the engine revs up. But before driving away, a small, cylinder-shaped object spins through the sky, bouncing before it lands beside ERIC'S feet. As he looks down, the car bursts into life, heading straight for him in a matter of seconds. More screams are heard... but this time they're more ambitious... more malicious, riddled with murderous intent. ERIC freezes, impotently accepting his fate, but just as the impact seems inevitable, the car thrusts into a different path and misses him by an inch. A crunching sound is heard... then the long wailing of the rape alarm... of a war siren. The car swerves...

CUT TO: EXT. WAKEMAN'S FIELDS
(ESTABLISHING SHOT)†
...and charges straight towards the lens. Just behind the car to the right we see ERIC spinning around as he falls to the deck. The car makes an impact yet to be determined, but the phone of which the opening shots were taken on cracks as it hits the windscreen and flies over the roof, through the air. As it lands between overgrown blades of grass, we see the mask again, which silhouettes ERIC'S face as he lies there screaming, enveloped in mist and drowned-out by the excruciating wails of the unrelenting alarm, matched only by the torturous slowness of the fade to black.

~~THE END~~

To be continued inside Dawn Caden's...

322

*Improvised and to be confirmed scene added after SAMANTHA
lost her moral fibre and proceeded to lose her shit. May
possibly differ from the conjecture of ERIC'S mind, but
going by the memory of the screams he suspects it could
be even worse.

†To be confirmed. Cracked screen on ERIC'S phone suggests
damage and possible footage loss. Was still recording when
ERIC woke up, but, due to the unforeseen circumstances and
the triggering of the rape alarm, he had to remain hidden
and flee from the scene as quickly as possible.

CHAPTER TWENTY-EIGHT

The lingering mist appears to be following me. It hasn't relented since the dreary month of November began; this time last week in fact, on the evening I spent with Samantha in the props room. Whilst dates and times usually pass by with little significance to me, the month of November always comes around with a weight impossible to ignore. It's the month of my parents' departure, the time of Glen's sudden appearance and the period of the infanticide bestowed upon me; my Mea Culpa, who never drew a breath nor shed a tear. A fainter mist lingers behind it, forever trailing, going nowhere. From close-up it's transparent, but at a distance, it conceals, hiding what you know is there, yet blurring it as if you do not.

Franklyn's flat looks rather odd at this time of night. Vacant almost. To think I've spent close to a hundred hours inside it riddles me with a certain disbelief. And disgust. How often I've knocked upon that ghastly, seaweed-green door. How much time I spent staring out of the fogged-up window from the other side. How I was present in the room, but never really there.

One day Eric cancelled a session because he couldn't bear the thought of sitting in that faux confessional booth. It was ten o'clock at night. Franklyn replied, "We'll talk about this next week. Cancelling at such an hour is rather alarming, Eric. I hope you know that I'll have to charge you."

"But what about the time you forgot we even had a session, when I stood outside your door for half an hour before you turned up and played it dumb, was that not *rather alarming*? Should you have been seeing clients if you had trouble even remembering when the sessions were meant to take place? Plus, I don't remember getting any session on the house as compensation."

"We can speak about that in the next session if you like. But now I really must go. It's late."

Franklyn then hung up. A week passed by. Nothing about the phone call was mentioned. Nothing about the session he forgot. Nothing. I paid him for nothing, just out of spite, feeling as if I was paying him for nothing as it was anyway. I didn't even receive a flicker of guilt from his brow as I handed over the bills. If he hated me so much, why didn't he just fucking say so... why use his authority to take advantage... oh, that's right... Simply. Because. He. Could.

Just glaring at his house makes me thirsty for violence. Thought I could see him through the slit of his thinly-threaded curtains a few times, but now I'm not so sure he's home. Something feels unfinished with him. Unresolved. It's difficult to say what exactly, but I feel swindled. Cheated. Conned. Eric Archer doesn't like feeling hoodwinked, he's the wink that removes the hood after all. But alas, I am not here to pay him a visit, if that's what you were thinking. It had crossed my mind, just for the fun of it, to see his reaction if I gave his door a little knock-knock.

For some reason, I want Frank to think of me as dead.

I flick my half-smoked fag at his front door and watch the embers cascade before they quickly wither away in the surrounding moisture, then begin my short trek down the road towards La Casa Numero Uno. Glen's impossibly hot mother has been on my mind ever since my ego-abandoning encounter with Samantha inside the props room. I'm a little late, but I'm sure that won't matter. Going by the yearning ache inside her eyes the last time we 'bumped' into each other, I'll be worth the wait. Would it be too much to ask Dawn to engage in a little Oedipus roleplay? She shows signs that indicate her potential for such things, especially in the fuck-me-now way she chooses to dress. I have always suspected in the past when bedding older women that it *is* being played out, but demands to remain unacknowledged, like all dark and illicit secrets that glue a family together. The glue, of course, being semen.

Speaking of illicit happenings of the familial kind, I've arranged to see Jessica, though after tonight it may have to be delayed. She's been harassing me about it all week. It appears I hit a bit of a nerve by suggesting I wanted to kill myself. Apparently, we agreed to meet over the phone during Operation Caden Blow, but I have no memory of that. I was surprised my phone even worked after Samantha slipped away from her sanity and drove straight into it. Despite being cracked down one side, the phone is still operating to some degree, but I cannot make any outgoing calls or access its memory. The impact of the crash erased everything I filmed and now everything I've filmed before cannot be erased either. So, Samantha now possesses all evidence of the conquest and she, naturally, has disappeared herself. No attempt to contact me has been made, via any method you can imagine. I should've known her reliability would only last for a few fucks. Such is the way of seduction, it seems. As soon as you hand yourself over to someone, they throw you away without a second thought and go off searching for someone to throw themselves at, so they themselves can then be thrown away.

Right, Jessica?

Isn't that why you keep me in a certain loop?

Were you annoyed I never found you attractive enough to rape?

Would that have been better than being cheated on?

I know why you decided to stick with Glenny-Poos now. You didn't stay with him because of how much he frightened or controlled you, it was simply to save face at the fact he raped you. Deny the facts until doubt overshadows them and eventually, you'll come to believe they never happened at all, that you were the one who made them up in the first place.

I never asked her if she came on that first night with Glen. Tasteless, I know. But when said woman sticks with said man, your thoughts evolve into something you cannot control. Like a parasitotic bug that injects its eggs into your head and feasts on your fluids whilst simultaneously releasing chemicals into your system that ever-so-slowly begin to manipulate and control your behaviour until you end up sacrificing yourself for the very thing that invaded you in the first place.

Mother nature is one twisted, sadistic cunt.

My reflection inside the window of this car is nothing but black, outlined only by the rivulets of rain streaming down and the misty light of the blurred streetlamp. It looks as if I'm trapped within my own shadow whilst being swallowed alive by it. Even as I lean in for a closer look, the features of my face… are just not there.

Ring-ring! Ring-ring!

All the emotions I feign nowadays, they're written all over my nondescript face, hidden behind this darkened, silhouetted guardedness of the world. Perhaps everything I feel now is merely a desperate copycat of my former years…

Ring-ring! Ring-ring!

… a tired, makeshift remake of a story that wasn't all that great in the first place. An imitation of thought patterns which seemingly dissipate, only to take root via the same seed…

Ring-ring! Ring-ring!

… does Dawn want to fuck me because I look like you, Glen? Is she concealing some hidden agenda, just like yourself? How will it make you feel, knowing I planted my seed inside your roots?

"Jess-e-ka Wake-man. Just the girl I thought it might be."

"Eric?"

"There's no need to repeat my name. I'm aware of who I am. Or perhaps who I was. *Ha*. Sooooooo, what can I do you for, Wakey-Wakey-Wakeman?"

"Are you drunk?"

"Better drunk in this world than sober, Jessica. Forgive me for being blunt but what is it that you want? I'm somewhat indecent—*indisposed*, rather. *Ha*."

"I... I don't know. I've got that *feeling* again, Eric, like I mentioned the other day, the same feeling I had just after I told Glen about... you know."

"Ah, feelings. They really are a bastard, aren't they? Let's be honest for a change. The only person who ever cares about feelings is the one possessed by them. I wouldn't be too concerned—"

"But it's different this time. I'm not... scared or anything, just worried."

"Okay. You want to play this game again. I'll play along. This is where I say, 'So, where is good old Glenny-Poos?'"

"Please, Eric. Don't be a dick. He's somewhere... not really sure to be honest. I tried speaking with him again earlier... we arranged to speak about *you know what* again after eating, but as soon as we were done—"

"He went walkabout."

"... Yes."

"Well, he's probably just preparing himself for it. Tuning up those rusted-over strings of emotion. He is an actor as well after all."

"I don't know, Eric. Something isn't right. We found a... a thing in my garden yesterday."

"A thing? What, like an animal?"

"No, it wasn't an animal."

"... Okay. What was it then?"

"I'm not a hundred percent sure because Glen... Glen kinda smashed it up. Though I'm pretty sure it was a..."

"A what?" I ask.

She whispers, "A rape alarm."

I scoff and let out an indecent—*though I also suspect*—expected chuckle.

"Don't laugh, Eric. It isn't funny. The thing wouldn't fucking stop for hours... but that wasn't the weird part. Well, it was weird but that's just because of how creepy it was to hear and think of, but the really strange part was how Glen obsessed over making it stop. After smashing it over and over didn't work, he tossed it somewhere in the driveway and ran over it with his car, again and again until it eventually stopped. After that, rather than coming inside, he drove away, flying across the fields instead of taking the road. He came back after about six hours and hasn't left or said anything since... but something in him... the way he's..."

"What?"

"The way he's looking at me makes it seem like he thinks I put it there. I can feel the accusation in his eyes every time he looks at me. When he's around anyway. Since he returned, he's barely left the room he's randomly decided to lock himself up inside. He clearly believes I'm the one who planted it there and that I'm trying to fuck him up in the head."

"Listen, Jessica," I say with an exhausted sigh. "Maybe tonight isn't the best time to go bringing up the whole rape thing again, then. Especially if you're right."

"Oh, believe me, I know that, Eric. But I can't really wait any longer. I can't have him brushing me aside as if I don't exist, like how I feel doesn't matter—"

"Jessica, why are you telling me this?"

"Who else am I supposed to tell?"

"Okay. Why can't you just wait to tell him then?"

"..."

"Ah, there it is. I'd almost forgotten about that. The ugly little *real* reason why you need to tell him so urgently. Well, you know what—"

"Please, Eric. I'll tell you everything once it's done. I just can't right now, okay?"

"..."

"Eric?"

"Do you remember calling me before your first date with Glen?" I ask, looking upwards towards the black of night, allowing the droplets of rain to cleanse my eyes, fighting back an urge to scream.

"Yes, Eric. I remember. I had the same sickening feeling back then as I have right now. I'm just grateful that my mother's here."

"Well, do you recall what you said to me then?"

"What? What I said? Urm, no I don't, Eric. Sorry. What did I say?"

"You said that you were sure you were worrying over nothing," I say, staring deep into my shadowed self.

Jessica says, "And... so what? We both know how wrong I was about that. I can't see your point, Eric."

"Well, my point is, now it's my turn."

"Your turn... to what?"

"I think you know."

"Urm. I'm not sure I fully understand you, Eric. Is everything okay with you? You seem a bit... I dunno... far away. Dissociated."

I chuckle again and wait for a moment.

"Eric? Are you there?"

"I'm sure you're worrying over nothing, Jessica."

Click.

Call Ended.

Sound: OFF

Vibration: OFF

I turn away from myself once more to notice I'm outside Dawn's door now, underneath the illumination of the streetlamp stood in front. Her door is red, much like the colour of the lipstick she always seems to wear. An old metallic knocker hangs from the upper-middle, with the number plate above. Both were once golden-coloured but are now a deep, eroded grey metal. Her house is typical of all the others around here, but it's pleasant nonetheless. A row of three neatly trimmed bushes are aligned underneath the front window;

hopefully much like the owner. There's always a risk to be taken with older women. Some of them have yet to realise that pubic hair died out about twenty-five years ago. That isn't a double-standard comment by the way. You should see how smooth and lick-able my balls are. I'm cupping them right now. They were dying for some air. The human body is naturally grim, you've got to make do with it what you can. Next to a path of circular stones sits a small and quaint garden, nothing too fastidious, a few blossoms of flowers and some slightly overgrown grass. Neat but a little dirty. Unkempt. Again, hopefully much like the owner. To the side of the house, through a small gap between the fence and the wall there's a bike. Possibly Glen's bike. I think I'll steal it after taking his Mummy for a ride, or maybe after Mummy steals a ride on Eric. After doing Dawn a favour and watering her plants, I zip up my fly and begin walking towards the entrance.

I reach for the door hanger. Now that I'm close-up to it I can see it's the face of a fox, which you lift and push from its pointy nose. The eyes of it glare at me, sneering a silent warning. Covering it with the whole of my hand, I give the door three distinctive knocks in the hope of displaying the sound of a stranger the owner of the house is somewhat aware of and anticipating. She'll hear the sound ripple through the walls, feel the vibrations shake the foundations, hear my intentions as the last beat penetrates through her eardrums.

I wonder what she's doing. Maybe she's in the bath with a glass of wine, pleasuring herself underneath the bubbles. Or she's on her knees, scrubbing the kitchen floor with one hand, wiping away the accumulation of sweat upon her brow with the back of the other, breathing heavily from exhaustion, releasing sighs of frustration whilst struggling to remove the rubber yellow gloves she's wearing, which I'd demand her to keep on. With any luck, she'll have worked herself up into a subservient state. Or, perhaps she's reading and lost herself inside another world, fantasising over the rough and ready, broad-shouldered and preposterously handsome protagonist, picturing him to come a-knocking on her door.

Well here I am baby, right on schedule, you rubbed the lamp and I came running, all you need to do now is answer the fucking door. That's it, come along now, just one small step at a time, there's no need to rush. Just answer the door. It's rude to keep someone waiting you know, especially one so eager to see you. "That's it, take another stride. Stop whatever you were doing my pleasure-deprived beauty, come to Eric with your orifices wide open and let him fix you. By my professional diagnosis, you're in need of some swift validation. If you're a good little girl, you'll get all the identity you've ever dreamed of. But not before you swallow. I want to see you gargle the Archer, clear the palette of all your past lovers and then guzzle down every single drop. Of course I had to clamp my fingers down upon your cute button-shaped nose my sweet, however else can we be sure that you took all your medicine? Oh, lookie what we have here. Quite the collection of outfits you have my dear. Here, squeeze yourself into this corset, I want to feel you struggling for air whilst your blinking backdoor beckons me closer. Come to me. Every inch of you. Now."

All you need to do is answer… the fucking…

She's not in. What a let-down. My plan to turn up an hour late to give Dawn the pussy aches has backfired. What an anti-climax. Arrogance really isn't the easiest trait to pull off. The fox is glaring at me, smiling and laughing, taunting me into ripping his face a new one. I guess I'll head to the Journey's End for a few before heading home. If Lucy is there… well, who knows. Maybe I could convince her to do a cheeky lock-in, get a few free drinks, check out her bodily functioning in the forgotten function room. Eric Archer is so sick and tired of scratching old itches though. They only ever end up giving you a rash. Some other silly little loose and ready loner will surely be there. I'm on my way, lonely stranger of the night. My friends call me Eric, but now my victims call me Glen. Choose what you call me by very wisely, for whatever name you opt for will surely determine the outcome of our encounter.

"Oh hey," a voice calls from behind me, trailed by high heels and the rustling of a plastic carrier bag, clanging bottles together. What a beautiful combination of sounds. "I thought you'd had second thoughts about me tonight," she says.

I turn my head and there she is, with the streetlight behind emanating around her entire frame like glow in the dark chalk. Strands of white-blonde hair wave in front of her eyes, her trademark lipstick freshly applied and sparkling with moisture. She's wearing nothing but black, carrying a plastic blue bag I'm more than familiar with, containing two bottles of soon to be drunk hard liquor. "Well, I'm sorry to have kept you waiting," she says, "but I had to nip out and get some fresh supplies."

"No problem, Dawn. Lovely garden you have here."

"Why thank you. I've only just got around to sorting it out," she says, shuffling inside her handbag and taking out a set of keys. "Shall we go inside?"

"Yes," I say, approaching her and taking the bag from her hand, "but first, I need to do this."

"What's that—"

My tongue cuts her off and here I am *Glen, kissing your mother in the rain, kissing your soon-to-be-drilled mother in the rain, I'm horny again, kissing your mouth-fucked-tonight mother in the rain. Her pussy is wet once again, I'm going bareback tonight, inside the glistening peach of your mother's terrain.* You don't know me Glen, but I'm about to go deep inside the very thing that bred you. Say hello to your very own motherfucker.

"Wow, where did that come from?" asks Dawn as I break away from a kiss that would've broken a Faustian pact. She scoffs through disbelief, with a smile that says *my dick is getting sucked tonight.*

"I've wanted to do that ever since I first laid eyes on you, Dawn."
Almost two years ago to the day. Sssshhhhh.

"Shall we?" I ask, guiding her towards the door of no return in the guise of a prince I was type-casted to be since birth. She's all sunshine and rainbows, giggling and nodding like she hasn't had this kind of attention since she was a teen. Oh, my Glenny-Poos, blending fantasy with reality never felt so fucking good. I think I almost understand you now. Pretty soon, I will.

CHAPTER TWENTY-NINE

There's something unnerving about this house. I can't quite put my finger on what it is, but it carries a certain weight of abandonment and gloom. Of course, what I already know about this abode no doubt tinkers with my initial impressions of it, but the sweeping, palpable atmosphere stretches far beyond that. It's more like the impression of a home than an actual one. Essentially, it's perfect and that's exactly the problem. It's *too* perfect. Like a concrete embodiment of a person guarding some terrible, unknowable secret. A house of concealed scars. Traumas hidden by an already withered innocence which shall remain undetected, as long as everything stays clean and fresh and attractive, as long as what the outside reflects is blinding, making the decay and rot and ugliness of the inside impossible to see.

I've yet to come across a single speck of dust. I know, it sounds like a strange observation, but when you're encountered by such a thing it seems to scream from each corner of the walls. A darkened oak flooring panels the hallway, immaculately varnished and visibly gleaming from all angles despite the lacklustre, though skin-complimenting light. By the left side between the front door and the stairs there's a small and what I presume to be second bathroom. Its door is shut and tonight, that's how it shall remain. Jessica sits beyond it, shaking in the same scattered rhythm as her shallow, dread-fuelled breaths. She strains to silence them, to enable her sense of hearing to follow Glen's movements, praying to hear the creaking of footsteps up the nearby stairs. But the anticipation of her imminent violation has made her body betray her long before the act has been committed. She flicks her head up in a sudden movement, determined to make the surge of adrenaline to make her stronger than she knows she is, begging for its twin of paralysis to stay asleep. But for the first time in her memory since the first time it happened, what she sees in the mirror is a child looking back. No means nothing when you're unaware of what you're objecting to, that's what daddy's sweet, pretty princess found out that day. Now she knows she'll have to become that little girl again if she fails to flee from the bathroom, from the front door left so cruelly open, which looked so inviting, until she stepped inside. Now she's seconds away from discovering that no once again means nothing to the unaware man who has already made an object out of you. Back then she was molested, but now she's moments away from being raped. The same act, differing in nomenclature. The former carrying too little horror for an adult, the latter containing too much for a child. But what no one ever mentions is, if you're born female, one of the two will happen at some point, if not multiple times, or both. It's just another one of nature's laws, left behind like its victims, unlooked at and ignored, never to be acknowledged.

Rape is the price women pay for having a womb.

Another doorknob rattles upstairs, followed by the shriek of a hinge signalling early signs of weakness, then Dawn's graceful, casual for now movements. Yet the stairs from either end have still yet to creak.

The living room is a bit homelier, but I put that down to the scent of the fireplace opposite the sofa. The room itself is still illuminated in a sort of Scandinavian hue, or perhaps arctic twilight, much like the hallway. Still. That's the right word for it. There's something frozen about this house. The couch is long and leather, magnolia-shaded. The rug lying between it and the fireplace ruffled like trodden and smeared snow layered over prickly, snapped twigs. An array of lamps, which all differ in height but match in style, sit neatly either in the corner or on drawers. One thing I can't seem to find is any evidence of Glen ever being here or even existing. There are simply no picture frames anywhere. All I've found are paintings of countryside landscapes, with a single, unoccupied girl sitting down with her legs crossed, concealed by the shades of trees. All of them blonde, underage and alone. The house is also much longer than it looks from the outside. The kitchen is situated at the back, it's only entry and exit point down the long, continuous hallway opposite the staircase.

"Eric?" Dawn calls, her voice travelling down the naked, cold blue wall of the stairs.

"I'm here."

"Sorry about the delay, I'll just be a couple of minutes longer. Feel free to help yourself in the kitchen."

"Thanks," I reply, unable to ascertain why I chose to tell her my name, "Dawn. I'm happy to wait, though. Take as long as you need."

"Well, you know where to go if you get thirsty."

"Good to know I'm in safe hands," I reply, uncapping my hipflask and taking a long, patient pull.

Dawn's shadow slides away from the landing and before long I can hear a hair-dryer. She's been upstairs since we came inside. Pampering herself I assume. Then again, Jessica used to do the same, and she never came back dolled-up. To be honest, I never found out what she did during her frequent bathroom breaks. I suspect cry, puke and weigh herself. Not necessarily in that order.

I continue looking around, taking the house in, trying to brush off the stillness of the atmosphere. I've forgotten which drugs I'm on tonight, but I think, from my slightly ghost-like perception that I'm on adderall mixed with xanax and traces of the valiums Samantha gave me, lingering around my bloodstream somewhere. The clock above the fireplace is spotless but no longer ticking. Oddly enough, it seems to be right at home.

"Hey," Dawn says behind me.

I turn. She stands with one foot on the bottom stair and one hand resting over the knob of the bannister. "Hey yourself," I say, taking her in. She's tightly wrapped inside a thin ivory silk dressing gown, with one of her impossibly long legs stretched forward, twirling above a wooden floorboard in a coquettish flirt.

"I'm still not quite ready yet, but I thought we should have a quick drink first."

"Fine with me, Dawn. But you should know that you look more than ready to me," I reply, noting the touching-up of her makeup and scent of a perfect fantasy caressed over her skin.

"Why thank you, Eric. I'll go see about those drinks, finally. So, are you a whisky man, or more of a rummy sort of guy?"

"I'm an alcoholic man, so either is fine. I'll take whatever you're having."

"Well, I'm not sure how you're going to drink yourself, but I'd like to see you try," she replies, coolly trailing her hand behind as she steps forward, eyeing me with the most delicious of guarantees, legs threatening my levels of self-control something beyond awful.

"Ice?"

"Always," I say, following behind her. As I reach the door-less doorframe leading into the kitchen, I lean against it, watching her. She sways around the central kitchen worktop, which takes up most of the space, gleaming in a similar fashion to the bathrobe she's wearing. Dawn opens one of the many compartments of the wide kitchen cabinet opposite me, then tiptoe reaches up for two tumbler glasses and removes them with a finger clamp. The hem of her robe reluctantly moves back down, recovering the initial edges of her indecently magnificent arse. As she tosses the door back, I notice the long array of spotless glasses, sized accordingly, for any situation. We exchange the most delicate of smiles as she liberates the glasses from her hand, leaving behind a collected, momentary echo. Then she glides across to the fridge and pulls the freezer door open. Her body and its movements seem to be stirring something within me which I do not recognise. It's almost as if she's the matured embodiment of Esther, Samantha and Jessica combined, with her own untouchable level of sex appeal. What's driving me crazy is my not knowing whether she knows it or not…

There's a photograph on the fridge. The only one I've seen thus far.

It can't be…

"Would you mind?" Dawn asks.

"Mind… what?" It appears to be Glen and Jessica. But that isn't what bothers me.

"Eric? Are you okay? You've gone pale."

"Me? Oh, yeah. I'm fine," I reply, finally realising that she meant for me to crack open a bottle. With what I hope is a calming intake of breath, I step inside and approach the counter. "Your appearance seems to have literally taken my breath away," I say, almost cringing from the comment, but Dawn smiles and subtly nibbles her bottom lip as she removes two ice cubes at a time and drops them into the awaiting tumblers. The screwcap rips around the kitchen and, as I pour Dawn slams the freezer door shut. She hesitates at the sight of the photo, which gives me an excuse to…

"Who's the handsome guy?" I ask.

She lets out an, "Oh," then pauses. "That's my son."

I let out a scoff of exaggerated disbelief. "You're fucking with me, right?"

Dawn shakes her head. I move closer and hand her glass of whisky over, then take a long swig of my own. "And the girl?" I continue, casually leaning back against the worktop, directly opposite the photograph.

"That's his girlfriend. Do you think she's pretty?"

"Let me take a closer look."

I step a couple more paces forward. Dawn half-turns, watching me react to the picture. For some reason, I feel like I'm being made to compare between her and Jessica. "She's got something I'd say. Looks a bit… I dunno," I say, sucking back saliva through a tut, then look deeply into the emerald eyes of Dawn. "Over-emotional?"

"You've got that right. She hates me for no reason at all."

"Well, a mother and their son's girlfriend aren't supposed to get along now, are they? She's probably just intimidated by you, and," I say, prolonging the last word for emphasis, "who could blame her?"

"Mmm. It's just the way she looks at me really. Like I'm some, I dunno, threat?"

"Many a woman must've looked at you in the same way. It's because she's got nothing on you."

"She's got youth is what she's got. Anyway, my son Glen is smitten with her. Thinks she's the full package. Brains and beauty and all that. I don't see it, personally."

"I'm sure you both have more in common than you realise. Or maybe you will, in the not too distant future."

"I'm not really allowed to realise anything. That bitch, excuse me, doesn't come around these parts at all. So, my son doesn't anymore either. I've barely seen him since they got together. Anyway, he's got his own life and I have mine. Shall we?" she asks, with a brisk, dismissive walk back towards the hallway.

Jessica's looking away from the camera. Glen appears to be holding it, forcing her to freeze in time with him. But, as difficult as it is to look at without snapping a synapse in my brain, it's not them that's troubling me, but where. I took Jessica to this place, I know so because of the background. A freshly blossomed bed of poppies sits behind them. There's only one place that happens around the South-East. Glen hasn't just replaced me, he's slowly erasing me from Jessica's memory, shedding the flickers of our already dissipating, shared experiences together by layering himself over them. That must be why he spent so much time looking into me…

"Eric? Shall we?"

… It had nothing to do with jealousy, but everything to do with eradicating my very existence. But the worst part is…

"Eric?"

… Jessica went along with it. Said nothing. Accepted everything. Put it down to coincidence. Played the dumb blonde he raped her into being…

A fingernailed hand slips in front of my eyes, in a deep shade of glossy burgundy, and snaps.

"What's the matter?" she asks, "do you know them or something?"

The image, or thought, or wherever my mind disappeared to washes away. I turn a flickered look at Dawn and let out an unintentionally weak, "No."

"Are you sure?"

"My mind has been playing… I just had a very strong sense of déjà vu. Felt outside of myself for a minute there. Sorry if I freaked you out."

"Don't worry about it," she says and moves in front of the photograph, resting one foot against the fridge. Coyly, she air-chinks her glass, prompting me to do the same. From the side with her pose in a half-profile and her neck leaning upwards, she drains her glass. The gulp goes down visibly with her chest pushed out. The leaning leg sways from left to right. I down my drink and take her glass, placing them behind where I stand without looking. A moment passes by where I can't tell if she's moved forward or if I have. As our lips meet, I close my eyes through habit but open them again as our tongues entwine. Heavy breathing ensues along with side-switches of our mouths. I try to look at her and feel the sensations she seems to be going through, but my eyes are still unable to cease looking at the photograph. Sensing the kiss about to end and her possible detection of my elsewhere eyes, I thrust her against the fridge, knocking it onto its back legs as I do, which sends its shudder through us both, forces us closer to one another. Then I take grip of her hips and force myself back. She breathes heavily and lets out a whispered guffaw. "You certainly know what you're doing, don't you, Eric?"

I say, "It's a little difficult to control myself around you, Dawn."

"Well, there's no rush, Eric. Maybe I don't want you to control yourself much anyway. But let's go to the living room first. I'll get the fire going."

She takes my hand into hers and leads me through the kitchen. Her bathrobe wafts and slinks, trailing the movements of her body, the contours of her firm figure. As we pass through the hallway, she flicks her head around the other way and lets out another smitten smile. Our hands then loosen and fall. Inside the living room, she's quick to squat by the fireplace and even quicker to get the flames started. Standing again, she soon nuzzles one foot into the soft-looking rug, admiring her remarkable legs.

"The heat will soon be unbearable. I better go finish myself off right this instant. Go and make us some more drinks... but don't come back until I tell you to. Okay?"

I shrug my acceptance.

She sultrily glides by me, maintaining arrestation of my eyes until she disappears up the stairs again. She's easily the sexiest woman I've ever come across. Even if she wasn't who I know she is, I'm sure I'd be just as excited by the prospect of fucking her as I am right now.

I make my move towards the kitchen. The fire behind increases in strength and sound, along with the rain outside, which now drums down against all sides of the house. Ignoring the photograph this time, I quickly yank the freezer door open and do the same with the ice cubes. Pouring myself a quick one, I drown it for good measure and then pour a couple more. A packet of cigarettes lies on the counter near the glasses, which I snatch up with much-needed aplomb. Without a second thought as to whether I should or not, I light up a smoke and lean my elbows on the counter. But the photograph can be seen, reflected in the glass sliding door in front of me, glinting even through the passing streams of smoke.

Can you sense me somehow, Glen, wherever you are? Do you know how close my cock is to the vagina you came out of into this world? Do you feel as nervous as I do, as uncertain of your next moves, for a reason you can't quite seem to fathom?

"You can come in now, Eric. I think you'll find something a little more pleasing to the eye."

Time to find out.

"Coming," I say, grabbing hold of the glasses, leaving the cigarette in my mouth. The first thing I notice is that her shoulders are now bare. She's sitting on the sofa with her head facing forward, staring at the rippling flames in front of her. A Moulin Rouge-esque accessory is pinned to the side of her hair. She remains motionless throughout the entirety of my gawping, but I sense she can detect it, feel the yearning throngs of my ever-growing lust.

I move around the couch, passing her the drink without looking at her. As she takes it, I see a black polyester glove in the corner of my right eye. I pivot upon reaching the rug and... the cigarette just barely dangles from my mouth.

Taking it like her cue, she begins tapping the heel of her scarlet-red high heels against the wooden panelled floor and holds her hand out. I pass the smoke over. Mosaic-patterned tights run up along those brilliant, never-ending legs of hers. Resting across her upper-thighs is a triple-layered skirt, all finished with a red stripe at the hem.

"Said words flatter, but unsaid words flatter harder," she says, then inhales a deep, death wish of a drag. Following a sip of her drink, she continues, "Many moons ago, I worked in a burlesque club," twirling the tip of a gloved-finger around the rim of her glass, hypnotising me into total subservience.

"I don't doubt that," I say, admiring the jaw-dropping piece that is her corset. It's entirely black with touches of red. Most notably are the kisses scattered up along the centre of her midriff, playfully finishing across the firm, pushed-up cups of her breasts. Even half of her face is covered by a pull-on, satin-stitched black mask made-up of mosaic, enigmatic patterns.

"You know, when you were looking at that photo I've got on the fridge, you reminded me of something," she says.

"Oh?" I proffer, hiding my slight discomfort with a gentle sip. She's now caressing her inner-thigh with the same finger. One second she watches herself, the next she looks up at me.

"When I first saw you. I kind of... went off into a trance. You stopped me in my tracks, would you believe. I only broke out of it once you disappeared around the corner. I said to myself, 'If I see him again, I can't let him slip away.' That's why you *bumped* into me. I made sure of it."

Her words have shifted my breathing into something deep and animalistic. I tilt my head back along with my glass and drain it. Her legs begin to spread ever so slowly. Streams of smoke waft away from her mouth in the sultriest of manners. I drop to my knees. She watches me with her head at an angle, smiling, then pinches her skirt and lifts it from both sides. My mouth actually salivates at the sight. Her pussy is immaculately shaved, perfectly shaped and glistening, with a sheening translucent shimmer running down her light-pinkened flaps. Normally, I'd go slower, tease her, nibble and kiss-suck around her thighs, caress her labia with my tongue and make her wait for the clitoral pleasure, but I'm helpless. Reduced to a virgin. I pull her closer to me. She finishes her drink and takes a last drag from the cigarette, then encourages my head forward with a gloved hand, watching me the same way I've watched other women suck me off, the same way I'm going to watch her later. Her pussy tastes like a drug you'd happily let kill you, that you'd willingly overdose on, of every wicked, hedonistic conquest combined. This is like eating out Eve after you gagged her with the forbidden fruit.

I'm going to make Glen's mother come more times than sense tonight. Revenge is a pussy served shaved, familial and utterly unaware of who and what I really am.

It seems one must become the devil in order to fuck the devil's mother.

Who knew consent could be so sordid?

You can't erase me that easily, Glen, my watchful enemy. The same face your damaged goods of a girlfriend still pictures when you fuck her will soon be imagined inside the mind of your very own mother. Once that image is in your head, of my fucking smiling, ejaculating face, nothing you ever do will be able to erase it. You won't be able to kill me once I'm snuggled up inside you. I am the thought that'll bring about the tumour that eats you alive.

Fubar, my friend. Fu-motherfucking-bar.

CHAPTER THIRTY

I like the way Jessica looks away from the lens in this photograph. It's almost as if she knew whilst it was being taken that I'd see it one day, like the lens is my all-seeing eye. Glen must've proposed the idea, probably without asking, knowing him. He's holding up what I presume is his phone, glaring straight at it, erasing me through emulation. His face is even just the slightest touch out of focus, like the true him is hidden, silhouetted by his secret agenda, too ugly to be caught in the naked light of day, to be captured by reality itself.

I know I know I know I shouldn't be standing here staring at this photograph again. If Dawn catches me it'll be obvious that I do know more than I've let on thus far. I guess part of me wants her to. After all, you can't be labelled a criminal until someone catches you in the act.

Everyone needs an audience.

Isn't that right, my watchful observer?

It seems my performance with Dawn was enough to send her to sleep but not myself. I guess the intensity of it shot up my adrenaline, as now I'm as wide awake as I've ever been. And believe me, the quantity of ejaculate Dawn withdrew appeared to be enough to put me asleep for a week, but as soon as it finally stopped, she flopped to the side, leaking, and nodded off. I stared at her for a long time, at odds with whether I found her beautiful or vile, wondering which spurred me on the most into bedding her. It reminded me of when Sammy blacked out after getting her dirty little lie off her glitter-glistening, moronically splendid chest; my favourite cry rape clown. Then, for some reason, I saw Esther gargling on urine in exchange for rent money. Then everything turned black, but I could taste a car exhaust at the back of my throat, hinted with the dew of grass.

And of course, the crying baby in my head, my flushed away foetus, forever wailing as she swirls… round and round and round; always growing in distance but never quite disappearing. There, but not there. Dead, yet alive.

All these thoughts… or senses flashed through me like a deranged, scatter-brained slideshow. Outcasted thoughts for the stranger I now embody. Sights became sounds whilst smell morphed into touch and the only thing I could taste was the unknown. This soon devoured every other sense, until all I was left with was a singular, obscure feeling that I'd committed grave and unforgivable acts, acts so awful that my own mind has seen it fit to deny access to their origins, opting to blur and obfuscate the memory of them through an act of self-preservation, an ego-driven mechanism which, as irony would have it, I have zero control over.

The only thing I can depend on is the shadow I cast. It reminds me that I still occupy animated space, whilst at the same time it never ceases its glare into my ultimate nothingness, locking me inside a relentless reminiscence that that shadow is the only true thing I'll ever be. Empty like the non-existence I came from. Identical in the spurious notion of sentience it gallivants around with, utterly convinced of its own identity. Turning 'I think therefore I am' from a statement into an eternal, unanswerable question. Who is this 'I' who believes he thinks? And why does he feel so far away from me? Who is this me… etcetera, etcetera, blah, blah, blah, ad infinitum.

Our shadows reveal more about us than we ever permit ourselves to see.

"Can't sleep?" Dawn asks, leaning against the doorframe with her arms crossed, back inside her silk robe. "I thought you ghosted me for a while there," she says, half-yawning, eyes droopy. She looks older post-fucked.

The anxiety of not knowing how long she's been standing there takes an equally unaccountable amount of time to pass through me before detecting the distinct lack of suspicion in her tone. Matching her yawn, I say, "I can't remember the last time I slept."

"Well, I'm glad you're still here. I'm not done with you yet," she says, pointing a looping finger my way as she walks barefooted into the kitchen.

"Drink?" I ask, watching her ghostly footsteps appear and disappear at the same time.

"I shouldn't but, fuck it. Go on then. You're quite a bad influence, aren't you?"

"Only to those who need a scapegoat."

"That's everyone."

She looks at my phone on the counter. I ignore it by turning around and fetching two fresh glasses from the cabinet. As I return, Dawn's glance has still yet to shift.

"Were you speaking to someone?"

I shake my head, then pull open the freezer door; grateful for its fleeting concealment, then remove some ice. Dawn sparks up a smoke whilst I pour. The ice crackles in teeth grinds. She offers me a cigarette without looking my way, focused still on the phone, only darting her eyes into mine as she ignites the lighter. I take the flame and give her glass an encouraging nudge. For the first time tonight, I'm unable to get a read on her, almost perturbed by the mere attempt.

"I was just about to check my messages."

"Don't stop on my account," she says as if in a dare. Feeling obliged and somewhat without choice, I reach for the phone and hit the home button.

It remains black.

"Mmm. Looks like *someone* decided to turn off their phone. That's interesting. Were you making sure nobody interrupted us tonight?"

My silence soon confirms what she suspects.

"Mmm. I wonder what type of nobody we're talking about. I'll opt for the obvious. A certain female, perhaps?" she asks, tilting her head to the side with a coquettish grin. She holds up her drink. We clink our glasses. I turn on my phone.

"I'll take that as a yes. Don't worry about it. I was young and hot once. Not to mention a complete slut. You've gotta get these things out of your system."

"I totally agree with you, Dawn. Though, you must know you're still fucking hot."

"And evidently still a slut."

-Vvvvvrmmmmmm-

Dawn's eyes trail over the phone as she steps back slightly. The tie of her gown has loosened so that now each side rests just about covering her nipples. The scent of our fucking still emanates from her pores. I pick up the phone. Dawn finishes her drink and sucks on a chunk of ice before plopping it back into the glass. Then she starts running a finger over the edge of my belt and flickers her head at the phone. "Don't mind me," she adds, clearly keen to show me just how much of a slut she was talking about.

12 Missed Calls.

Unlocking it, I soon discover they're all from Jessica. All roughly fifteen minutes apart except for the last one, which must've been when she gave up. A few messages read:

Call me. Now.
Eric. Please.

It's urgent. Ring me!
Answer your phone!
Eric? Please!
Why aren't you
answering me?
Please, I'm
very worried!
Why are you
ignoring me!?
Eric.
Where.
Are.
You?!

My belt is now loose. So is the top button of my jeans. "So? Anything to tell me?" Dawn inquires, speaking through her clenched teeth as she peels the zipper down, peering up at me the whole way. It seems I must continue sleeping with her until she comes into knowing of who I really am. She yanks my trousers down, along with my boxers with frenzied impatience, leaving them around my ankles with what I deem to be an act of intent. She's getting off on seeing me shackled. My cock shakes with anticipation, once again gleefully disobeying my conscious, logical mind, mocking it even. With my cock between her eyes, Dawn's face begins to levitate. Cupping my balls with her tongue, she lightly giggles as my meat spasm-slaps over her face. "Well?" she mumbles.

"No," I say, "nothing I can't sort out later."

"Shame," she says with clarity and frustrated disappointment, moving back to frustrate me in the process. "Was she the one who smashed your screen?"

"No. That was an ex," I say, scheming. "She got mad when I said I was going to fuck her boyfriend's mother. Tried to run me o...ver..." I say, shuddered by the surprise of ice inside Dawn's mouth as she sucked my shaft inside it. The gown is now on the kitchen floor. The totally naked Dawn uses it as a cushion for her knees. Above her head, Glen's watching his mother suck my cock, even taking a selfie of himself doing so. Jessica can't look. This is beautiful.

-Ring-ring! Ring-ring!-

Dawn takes a firm grip of my cock and swirls the ice around the head in a frenzy until it melts.

-Ring-ring! Ring-ring!-

She swallows the build-up, smacks her lips open and starts rubbing it up and down, sensual and slow, keeping her eyes on nothing but me. "Answer it."

-Ring-ring! Ring-ring!-

"Go on," she says. "Pick it up."

"That bitch can wait. I wanna enjoy—"

"This bitch can't. Go on, talk to your little girlfriend, Glen. I promise I'll be quiet. She'll never know."

-Ring-ring! Ring-ring!-

I look over to see that, predictably, it's Jessica. And now she knows my phone's back on she won't stop ringing.

Wait.

What did Dawn just call me?

"What are you waiting for, *babe?*" she says, apparently mocking whomever she thinks I'm dating.

She really is a bitch.

But the real bitch is how much I clearly love it.

-Ring-ring! Ring-ring!-

I snatch up my mobile. Dawn moans with excitement. I take a deep breath. If done right, I can control this. If done better, I can get a real kick out of it too.

"Hello?" I say. Dawn immediately thrusts her face forward, burying my cock deep into the back of her throat until she gags and splatters saliva through the corners of her mouth.

Teenagers don't get this stiff.

"Eric?" Jessica asks, her tone genuine, if not despondent.

"Yeah, hey. Sorry about not answering. I've been… busy."

Dawn scratches my thighs with both hands until I look at her again, then she closes her eyes and places my free hand on the back of her head.

"I tried calling you like thirteen times, Eric. What the hell are you doing? You know I only ever do that when it's something big."

Dawn actually wants me to throat-fuck her. She keeps nudging my hand with her head. Unable to help myself, I give her three strong thrusts until her eyes re-open, bulging.

"Well, what is it then?" I ask, covering the phone to conceal Dawn's chokes. After yanking her back by her hair, I loosen my grip and signal a shush. Now all I hear is the familiar, obnoxious sound of meek sobbing. Dawn mock-resists taking the head back into her mouth.

This is the best thing that's ever happened in the history of blow jobs.

"Let me guess," I say, falling for yet another mentally deranged hussy. Getting into the groove of this debauchery, I ask, "Did your boyfriend…. rape you again?"

Dawn and Jessica both stop momentarily, sucking in shock gasps of air until the former lets out a light chuckle and the latter an exhausted sigh. For a moment Dawn's eyes… or maybe mine… go black.

"*Eric,*" Jessica spits down the line, making me flinch-thrust Dawn again. "Do you need to remind me of that every fucking time I speak to you? No, of course he didn't."

Dawn continues demonstrating her blow job skills, but her criss-crossing eyes suggest thoughts I do not want to hear out loud. Time to get her choking again.

"Well, what is… is it then?"

Surprisingly, Dawn's thrusted her tongue into my arsehole. Where most would simply rim, she penetrates, driven insane by the want of making me go insane.

"Glen and I… we had a bit of an argument," says Jessica, whilst his mother fucks my anus with her tongue.

"Well…" I blurt out in a failed attempt to control my breathing. "What's new about that?"

"I can't—I don't know how to tell you."

"Oh, Jesus fucking Christ, Je… urm. How many times do we need to—ah, go around in circles like this? Just tell me… I'm sure it's… *ah—I'm sure it's nothing.*"

"It's Glen… he knows."

Dawn finally moves back. A crazed look gleams across her eyes. Jessica fails to elaborate. I throw whisky down my throat as Dawn re-wraps her lips around my member, but the burning sensation in my throat, coupled with the pregnant weight of Jessica's absent words makes me devoid of all feeling from the waist down.

"Knows what?" I ask.

Dawn seems to sense an impending explosion. Little does she know that the standing up of my leg hairs is not a sign of soon to be shot sperm. She holds her mouth open, tongue targeted, eyes focused. My god, and I thought Esther gave great head. This woman is going to ruin every other future woman I meet and going by her glare she fucking knows it as well. I just wish I could share her enthusiasm.

"About us."

I freeze. Somehow, at the same time, every muscle in my body folds itself flaccid. Both ears echo, popping inside and outside themselves. Dawn's eyes double—no, triple, swaying over each image in a continuous loop until her brow creases, immediately noticing the rapidly decreasing amount of blood in my cock.

"Please be more specific," I say into the phone, as if I'm bionic and incapable of understanding, but the dread I'm enveloped under makes no mistake. Dawn re-gulps my ever-declining erection, aggrieved that my attention isn't all hers.

Jessica sighs and says, "He knows I've slept with you during our relationship."

Dawn now appears to be fellating a five-year-old.

"You told him?"

"It's complicated, Eric. But please, listen to me. I need to know you're safe. Glen went crazy. I've never seen him so angry. I was petrified. He started pacing up and down the fields outside, mumbling to himself, swearing, even shouting, kicking the ground and ripping up grass. He said he's… that he's…"

"That he's what?"

"… gone looking for you."

For some reason, my initial instinct is to laugh, until I hear myself laughing and cut myself off, then say, *"What the fuck did you tell him about us for?!"* and start laughing again. Then stop, only to start again.

Dawn flinches back at my sudden outburst. I signal for her to stay where she is. Jessica's breathing, plotting some evasive response.

"Well?!"

"Please… Eric. I know we're not good right now but please, come and meet me. I'll explain everything. I really need to see you right now. I must know you're okay."

'Okay' is a fucking universe away.

It's time to end this.

NOW.

"I'll meet you under the bridge."

"Oh, thank you, Eric. Really. I just can't believe what's fucking happening tonight."

"Yeah," I say, looking down at Dawn, who's still trying her best to arouse me, unable to accept that I've become utterly impotent. "Same. I hope you've got a decent explanation. If I'm not there in an hour, call me."

"Okay. Bye."

End of Call

"Eric? Are you okay? You've gone soft."

"I need to leave, Dawn. Right now."

"Oh, come on. We might as well finish what we started."

"No, it's okay. Really. Something awful has happened," I say, pulling my underwear and trousers up in one go, but Dawn stops me halfway.

"Like what?" she asks, tickling my thighs with claw-like caresses.

It appears she wasn't listening to my conversation at all. Or she's completely ignored it. Like mother, like son.

"I don't know, yet. That's why I need to leave."

"Let me suck your dick first. You'll feel better."

"For once, I do not think that is true…"

"Oh, come on. I'm desperate. For Mummy?"

"I'm sorry?"

"I said, Mummy's desperate."

"Mummy…"

"That's it. Play along. You're an actor, after all," she says, looking up at me with a visible change in her eyes, oddly reminding me of the way women look at children… and since when did I tell her I'm an actor?

"You know, normally I'd be up for it," I reply, noticing the change in my—

"You look like you're more than up for it now, son. Don't be scared. It's totally normal. Mummy just wants to please you. Don't you want to please Mummy?"

Whoever she's glaring up at, it isn't me anymore. Something's altered. Like the reptilian centre of her brain has taken charge. It's as if she's mentally moulded a mask over my face and replaced me with… no, surely not.

I must get out of here.

"Seriously Dawn, I'm leaving," I say, pushing her back by the shoulder. Her mouth moves away but her hand grabs my cock and begins pumping away at a frantic pace. Her lips crease into a sardonic, possessed smile whilst the glaze of her eyes washes over into something demonic.

"Dawn—"

"Stop pretending you're not enjoying this when we both know you love it. Let Mummy suck your fucking cock!"

She's right. My cock has turned so raw that it looks almost blue, pulsating like a drone against my wishes. Dawn smacks her lips and edges forward again to take it into her mouth, but I hold her face back to make sure she can't. Instead of stopping her though, it only seems to encourage some sort of sick determination. Her eyes gleam like the unwanted pre-cum around my urethra. What arouses me most makes me want to vomit.

"It wasn't wrong," she says, "you know that deep down. What we did wasn't wrong at all. It was nothing but natural. You're my baby. I just want to make sure you're okay. You know, just between us… when you were a baby, sometimes you'd get these adorable little erections, and you'd giggle like the happiest child in the world. I just couldn't stop myself from sucking it—"

"That's enough Dawn," I say, "this isn't turning me on anymore." I grab her wrist with one hand and attempt to yank her up.

"Aww, was that too much? It sure doesn't fucking look like it, baby. Come on. Just give in already! You know you want it," she says, snatching at my shaft again with her other hand. She is a lot like Esther after all. As we fuck-fight, she continues giggling, clearly enjoying this debauched power struggle. "You're harder than you were when we fucked. Look at you!"

"Looks can be deceiving, Dawn," I say, pulling her up, finally. She scoffs with malevolence and goes to kiss me, shoving my hand on her crotch. She's wet all over, more like she's pissed herself than mindlessly turned on. But the stench of sex hits me, seeps through my pores, blinding all reason; it's so powerful, so difficult to resist…

This biological urge is fucking repulsive!

Our tongues lock in battle. I grab her hair and pull it tight. Then I stick my other hand over her cunt and go wild, doing exactly what she wants me to do, going full-throttle on her clit, against my own fucking consent. I spin her around and ram her against the countertop, then pull her close with both hands. Scratching up her stomach, I squeeze her tits and pinch-twist the nipples, giving her no time to enjoy it or even feel the pain. With a hair clamp yank, her neck is exposed, then squeezed, straining with pulsating veins. She tries to bite my earlobe with crocodile snaps, so I slap her face a few times for good measure. My cock is soaked something rotten. She looks at me from the corner of her eye, demonically going feral on power. Without warning or any of that easing-in shit, I stab myself deep inside her, till I feel her pelvic muscles squeeze. She scoff-chuckles, gorging and choking herself on a helping of self-served sovereignty as I commence thrust-fucking her with the deepest hatred for all mankind.

"Oh yeah, that's it, baby. Fuck Mummy good, just like that!" *I want to slit the throat of every child before their innocence is raped out of them.* "That's it, keep going baby! Harder!" *I want every new-born to come out a perfect, non-suffering stillborn.* "Just a bit more! Mummy needs it!" *I want every womb fucked barren and each sperm shot to be as blank as our meaning.* "Oh yeah, that's it, keep going!" *I want to cum over the very essence of existence to spite its filthy fucking face.* "That's it, I'm nearly there!"

I place a firm hand on her shoulder and squeeze, digging my fingernails into her shoulder blade. She laughs, nearing orgasm, thinking she's won, that she owns me, that the power is all hers.

Just wait for it… wait…

Pullback…

"Oh… FUUUUCK… *I'm cooomminn*—"

And *TOSS!*

Thump! she goes into the fridge by her shoulder and *thwack!* she lands on the floor. I hope the juices pissing out of her burn like the regret of the abortion she never had.

"That one's for breeding, bitch!"

The beast within me wants to continue fucking her, to treat the self-confessed slut like the piece of shit I know she is, to fuck her with impunity… but as she begins wailing, howling like an abandoned child, the deepest wave of nausea crash-lands inside of me like a gigantic, unstoppable wave.

I need to get out of here.

After buckling my belt back up, I thunder-pat my pockets to check everything's in place, then stuff away the missing link that is my phone. Shaking through what can only be the unknown, I snatch the bottle from the counter and start topping up my hipflask, spilling more of my sanity than preserving it. Knowing I need it, I suck the juices on the countertop up as best I can, then snatch the cigarettes and pocket them too. The photograph winks at me through the reflection of the now empty bottle, provoking me, taunting me. Fine, if Glen wants me to take him along for the ride, so fucking be it. I already took his crazy bitch of a mother for a ride tonight, so now he can watch me steal his bike too! *HA!* If there's irony in that statement, it's ironically lost on me! *Ha-ha-ha!*

Marching as I turn, the photograph is soon snatched away from the fridge and crammed into my pocket. As I pull my hand away, I remove Samantha's coping pills, flip the lid and throw a lucky dip's amount into my mouth and swallow them dry. It's already been a long enough night as it is, so why not make it that little bit fucking longer?!

"No, don't go!" Dawn cries, throwing herself at my ankles. She grabs hold, wrapping both arms around my legs. "Please... stay here with me. Don't leave... not again."

I begin to walk as if through mud, dragging Dawn across the floor, the screech of naked skin as painful to hear as the desperation and longingness in her voice. "Please, don't go. I want you here with me! You're my boyfriend! MINE!"

"... Esther?!"

It's not her. Just sounded like it for a second. Dawn continues trying to pull me down, digging in her fingernails, still trying to bite me... she's got far more strength than my current sobriety can take.

"Please, Eric. Let me be the woman with a man in the middle of her name that she can do nothing about! I want your fucking abortion! We can watch it die together this time!"

Now it's Samantha. What the fuck is going on—

Ring-ring! Ring-ring!

"ARGH!!!"

"Hey man, Richard here."

"Richard?"

"The one and only. Got a favour to ask," he says through the speakerphone. But I never fucking answered! Dawn or Esther or fucking Sammy or whomever it is won't quit it with her snake-like grip!

"I need you to lend me that mask again, brother. You were right. I know your secret now."

"Rock-a-bye baby on the tree top," Dawn starts singing… but it's not her. It's three voices in one. Where the hell are they coming from?!

"When the wind blows, the cradle will rock."

Wait… this is beginning to make sense… if you can call it that. I've heard this song before… but where?

"If the bough breaks, the cradle will fall."

Man in the middle of her name that she can do nothing about… I said that, to…

"And down will come baby, cradle and all."

YOU. *You're in on this, aren't you? You were only supposed to observe, not become a no-good snitch!* I told you those things in confidence… the threesome (click/slide) Esther and Sammy pregnant, singing that hellish song whilst I fucked them (fade/dissolve) Alice in Wonderland… but that's Jessica. I made her dress up like that… because I knew she wouldn't tell me who raped her… so I took advantage and ejaculated all over her post-raped face (SMASHCUT) the bridge… the shadowed figure… the world about to end…

-SLAP!-

"It wasn't wrong, what we did. What we did wasn't wrong!" Dawn screams, flailing her arms about my face, forcing me backwards. *"It was perfectly normal! You hear me?!"* I do my utmost to grab hold of an arm, but she's completely lost the plot. *"How could you just leave me here?!"*

I'm back in the room.

It's just me and Dawn.

And *you.*

Instead of trying to grab hold of her, I launch myself forward. She tries to hold me off, but all her energy is gone. She slaps me. Once. Twice. Thrice. Each one is weaker than the last. All of them striking my forearms. At last, a gap opens up and I thrust her forward, letting go of her just as I pull myself back. She goes tumbling, collides with the fridge again and then lands... in precisely the same spot... as before.

"Please. Don't go," she cries, her voice scratched as if she's said it a thousand times in quick succession. She's curled up on the floor in the foetal position, still whispering screams of pleases and don't go's in between wailing like a forty-something-year-old baby.

She's pathetic and haggard.

Far older than when I first saw her.

My so-called revenge fuck.

Whose son clearly couldn't care less.

My mind is mine again. For how long, who knows?

Maybe I'm not the person I thought I was becoming.

Maybe I'm worse.

Now the person I've had to stop myself from hunting down all this time is the one hunting down me.

Let's see who finds the other one first.

Here goes my last trip to Battleton.

My war cry into the unknown.

CHAPTER THIRTY-ONE

Am I seeing the world for what it truly is… or is the world seeing me for what I truly am? Now I no longer sleep can surely only signify that I'm never truly awake. So how does a man clean-up the torture residing in his subconscious without the chaos of his dreams? Does he begin to dream, or more, inhabit a waking nightmare because he no longer sleeps, unable to differentiate between what's *really* occurring and what's not? Even if so, could there still be some degree of truth to what he sees; triggered by the waning traumas residing in others or himself?

What if these things I'm seeing reveal something I'm otherwise condemned to forever remain blind to? What then? It can't just be guilt and guilt alone… can it?

I fear I've taken leave of my senses.

Or my senses have taken leave of me.

Either way, I just can't seem to keep up with myself.

You can turn your back on the past, but the past quantum leaps into the future. It bides its time around every corner, waiting for your *inevitable* arrival. *For it matters worth shit whatever path you take! The past is everywhere and nowhere! It cannot be defeated! Both sides of this bridge lead back to the other. There is no escape!*

I am the conscious thought you can never admit to yourself, my unfaithful observer. Sure, you can look down on me, see me as trapped inside a world I alone created for myself, dependent on your eyes to confirm that I do indeed exist, but lest you forget, you're trapped too. Look away from me if you want, but you can't go anywhere either. You're trapped by gravity, imprisoned by your own imagination, a clueless slave to your biological, pre-determined existence. You could've left me inside the never-changing calm of non-existence, but you didn't. You created your own idea of me whilst thrusting me out of nothingness against my consent. You're just as guilty as every other breeder out there! And just like with every breeder, the blood is on your hands!

You should've shot me over Mummy's face, Dad! I'm not meant for this existence! Coming in her eyes might've made her see the collective hell we've all been left to rot inside! Even our very own nature saw it fit to abandon us! Who says I ever wanted to recognise my own reflection?! To hell with this design! *Put down that fucking apple, Eve, you rib-thieving whore! It'll only ever taste as sweet as the slavery of your hunger dictates and defines!* Let's reject this flawed and irremediable model, this relentless mythological masquerade of murder and suffering, this perpetual starvation of an ever-questioning mind!

The only guilty party here is YOU though, my needy little watcher at the gate. Of course, now that I've penetrated your mind, you're terrified of me. That's what makes me your god. You need me for your own imagination to thrive. Fuck, I *am* your imagination.

Now pull on my puppet strings and watch me fucking dance.

For tonight, I am the big bang; the suicide of god!

The bridge knows I'm here, just like last time. Streetlights drone with just that little bit more monotony, flicker that tad more frenzied and intruded upon like talking trees. There's a peculiar, singular indifference to the in cahoots blanketed abyss above tonight too... it hangs absent of time. Condensation leaves my mouth in the longest streams I've ever encountered, adding to the enclosed silence usually only confronted when surrounded by thick layers of fallen snow. Everything's crispier and crackling, flinch-inducing yet unnervingly patient, watchful of where it chooses to expose itself. The sleet threatening snow falls in slices of slits... they appear out of nowhere, from positions unmatched yet somehow aligned. Even with an eternity of time at my fingertips, I'll never understand their mechanism. I'm glimpsing into the algorithm within the algorithm within the algorithm. The few that seem to fall into the reflective black of the river below deceive the senses, as they appear to force a spherical, ovular-shaped pull out of the water, inverting it for just a second before imploding in on itself, leaving no ripple behind but instead the appearance of a body of water... breathing. But how can any of this be happening from a sky above so black? The question is felt... observed. The slits have swallowed themselves back into sleet and the dissipation of everything leaves all that surrounds me opaque, back to being unfocused and in turn, impossible to perceive.

There's Jessica. She's sat on the upturned dinghy boat, her hair reflective under the obscured moon, wearing a white, over-sized bomber jacket; cradling herself due to the cold. Somehow, I go unnoticed by her even as I stand on this crest like I'm cloaked in a sheet of particles stopping her from seeing me. This all feels... like a childhood memory. I stand here like the little boy Jessica thrusted her tongue down after her father personally exposed her to the birds and the bees. That must be why I suddenly feel like crying. Helpless.

The bridge is still at it though, even from this distance, having shadowed my movements. Flakes of erosion keep... floating away from the handlebars of this disturbed bicycle... as if still shedding its skin of decay after going an unknowable amount of time without being used. A certain, swirled flake catches my eye, wafting upwards despite the lack of wind... to reveal a silhouetted... no, it can't be—

it can't be the same silhouetted figure I saw here before, surely?

"Glen?!" Jessica calls out, standing up to step back as the front wheel spins due to its sudden fall. The figure, which is once again hidden behind this strange, snow-ridden mist must have made me lose my grip on the handlebars. The wheel comes to an odd, tick-tock-esque stop. Its subtle snapping reminds me of how Dawn's body betrayed her age; not through its aesthetic, but by the cracking, skeletal roots. The scent of her sap has blended with the sweat of my hands. I must reek of betrayal; Jessica's looking at my smeared ultraviolet streaks, sensing deceit but not knowing why.

As I throw my hood back the fear of her faux par shimmies over her glance, but I pat it away and say, "Don't concern yourself, Jessica. I'm more than aware of my resemblance."

Taking a sharp, though hesitant intake of breath, her shoulders fall. "I'm sorry. It's just that Glen often wears his hood up too. Urm, since when do you ride a bike, Eric?"

Pulling the hood back over my head, I re-tread over the footprints she left behind with side-steps down the remainder of the hill until we're both level to each other. "Since you decided to tell Glen about us."

She inches forward, illuminated on one side of her frame by a source of light I cannot place. The reflective black of the river seems to gleam in alignment with her movements but stops as our bodies collide in an uncertain embrace. Stretching black leather creaks as it slides over creased white polyester.

I shuffle back, patting my pockets for the cigarettes I stole from Dawn. Turning away from Jessica through an unwarranted but oddly dilapidating fear of revealing where I've been tonight, I light a smoke discreetly, tucking the packet away before it's noticed. Turning around again I see that my effort was needless, as Jessica is back on the boat, sitting in the same spot as when I arrived. In turn, I continue to stand, smoking, glaring at the mirroring black.

I'm foreign as to why, but I sense a self-divorced anxiety akin to what Jessica conveyed the night she paired a name I was already aware of with the featureless face haunting my every thought. The past just has too much power over me.

"Okay," she says with an emphasised breath. "I…"

I flick her a glance; she's looking at the bike, wincing.

"Where did you get that bi—"

"I stole it. Didn't figure it'd be missed. Look at the state of it."

"Right, yeah," she says, her voice half-trailing. "Well, okay Eric."

"Are you going to tell me what the hell is going on, Jessica?"

"Believe me, I'm trying to. I can still hardly believe it myself."

I look at her, but cannot proffer any sort of expression, except maybe my inner exhaustion.

"Jessica. Just tell me why you told Glen about us. You can save your justifications for therapy."

"I don't know how to tell you, Eric. I don't even know myself anymore. Everything's fucked."

"Right. As specific as ever. God, I'm so fucking tired of this, Jessica. What does it matter now if he knows anyway? It's not like we've been having a secret affair the whole time."

"Well, technically Eric, we kind of have."

"Right. And since when has that been an issue?"

"Eric. Glen knows way more about you than I ever imagined. He mentioned where you live, something about your drama school—a whole list of things only a nutcase would know! His obsession with you is beyond disturbed."

"Don't I fucking know it," I say, flicking my cigarette away.

"What does that mean?" she asks.

I shake my head and reach for my hipflask. After a couple of pulls, I whip out another smoke, not caring if Jessica somehow connects the dots. "Let's just say that I'm as equally aware of it as you are."

"Could you please elaborate on that?"

"Fuck you."

"What?"

"You heard me. Now hear this: I don't care. I don't care about your stupid little juvenile relationship. I don't care if Glen abuses you, over and over again until you finally snap and commit suicide because at this point, all you're getting is exactly what you deserve. And now you sit there, expecting me to care, hoping I'm going to answer something that you most likely already fucking know."

"Hey, you're not innocent in this, Eric. Despite everything that's happened, it's still true that we've slept together whilst I was with Glen and you were with Esther, and Sammy and fuck-knows-who-else—"

"Yes, Jessica. I'm more than aware of that. But us sleeping together isn't the reason I'm standing here right now, is it? I'm here because *you* decided to tell your faithful little predator about us, which is the question you're still avoiding! So, Jessica—why did you tell him?!"

"I told you! He wouldn't believe me! He refused to even acknowledge what he did to—"

"Wrong answer, Jessica. The same excuse won't wash anymore *because I know there's something else!* It's written all over you. You and I both already know that Glen hasn't stopped obsessing over us since your relationship began. But that isn't everything you've hidden from me, is it Jessica? No, no, no, far fucking from it in fact."

I turn away, clutching the photograph inside my pocket with a dead man's grip. There will be no turning back from this. My body convulses with a screaming, prison-barred rage, but I don't care how this ends anymore—*as long as it ends tonight!*

"Okay, Eric. The reason I told Glen is because… he thinks I'm just trying to make him go crazy… that I planted the rape alarm… because I'm not ready to… I'm—"

"Recognise this, by any chance?" I ask, thrusting the photograph in front of her face, holding it there so I cannot be fooled by her feigned expressions of disbelief.

"Eric… where did you get this?"

"Never mind where I fucking got it! Explain it to me. Didn't I take you to this place? How could you go along with it? Don't you have any sense of shame? Of loyalty to us!?"

"What do you want me to say, Eric? Glen took me there—how

did you get it?"

"Keep talking you fucking whore. I'm so sick of your bullshit, Jessica. If you think Glen's gone cuckoo-ka-shoo, just wait until you see me when I get going."

"I never told you for obvious reasons, Eric. Glen took me there as a surprise. What was I supposed to do? I couldn't very well refuse without telling him that you took me there before. At that point, I wasn't even allowed to mention your name."

"Didn't you fucking see that he obviously found a picture of us doing the same thing and that was his whole goddamn agenda for taking you there?! He's been copying and pasting himself over me this entire time and you've willingly gone along with it, just like you willingly allowed him to…"

"To what, Eric? To rape me?"

"Even if I said it, I wouldn't have meant it."

I turn away once more, loathing myself for having stooped so low, whilst also disgusted with what I've done. I should've left the photograph alone. With sudden unbearable shame, I stash it back inside my pocket, where Jessica whimpers… in a sudden realisation.

"Oh my god—that bike, it's Glen's! Tell me you haven't, Eric."

"Tell you what?"

"You did, didn't you?!"

"Did what?"

"You got that photograph from Glen's house! That's where you were tonight. That's why you made that sick joke over the phone. You slept with Dawn, didn't you?"

"You're fucking right I did," I say, spinning round to face her. "Her pussy tasted just like yours… well, before Glen made you inedible."

"What… you're sick—*what the hell is wrong with you?!*"

"What's wrong with me? You're the one who's been dating her rapist of a son for the last two years. You wouldn't allow me to take revenge, so I took a little overdue compensation instead."

"Do you have any idea what you've done?! She's a complete headcase, Eric!" Jessica shrieks, crying the angriest tears I've ever seen her shed, shaking as if I just abused her.

"Why're you pretending to be so upset, Jessica?"

"I'm not fucking pretending, Eric. I am upset! How could you do that? I didn't think I'd need to say, 'oh, by the way, don't go around fucking members of Glen's family please' did I?"

"Jha-ha-*ha!* Well I didn't think I'd still be waiting for you to cut that cunt loose either. But look, here we are. You think it's been easy for me to know you've been sleeping with him this whole time as well?! I dunno what's worse, the rape, or all the times you've willingly spread your legs for him since! How could *you* do that?! Is it all just some fucked-up Daddy kink you've got? Does Rapehead bring back all those sweet memories of Daddy's abuse? No, no. Tell me. I'm literally dying to know."

"Seriously, Eric. Fuck you," she says, walking towards the hill, shuddering. "I cannot believe you think sleeping with Glen's lunatic of a mother is justified. Especially with everything you know about her."

"What?" I ask, but all I'm thrown is a seething, over-the-shoulder glance. "Hey, don't think you can just walk away from me slut—"

"Oh, don't play dumb you sleazy piece of shit," she says. "You knew exactly what you were getting into with her. I just can't believe you'd actually go through with it. You're sick in the head, Eric."

"What the fuck are you talking about?" I ask, grabbing hold of her as she nears the summit, nearly bringing the both of us down.

She whiplashes her hair into my eyes, squaring up to my face. "At least Glen's rape was honest. You're a fucking parasite in comparison, Eric. You must've planned everything you did, in full knowledge of what she did to Glen. How in the hell is that you 'getting revenge'?"

"What the hell are you talking about?"

"Dawn! I told you she did shit to him. Don't make out as if you forgot! You know exactly—hey! Let go! Get your filthy hands… off me!"

"No—wait. What was that?! You just saw something, didn't you—"

"No, I didn't you freak—"

"Yes you did! I saw that glint in your eye!"

"NO ERIC! I didn't see anything—"

"*I fucking knew it! It isn't just me—ha-ha-ha-ha-haooo!!!!—it's all coming out tonight!*" I say, thrusting my head around to—

-SMACK!-

"ARRGGGGHHHHHH!!!"

I'm sent tumbling—thumping inside a fog of flashing white—hearing only a familiar traumatised shrieking—unable to—*THUD!*... stop. Everything's black and white—flashing yet dulled—forever swirling without reason. Rust... I smell... rust and crimson. A slow, thick ooze streaks down the side of my cheek. Its warmth would be comforting... if it wasn't for the droning, sight-shifting heartbeat inside my head. The front wheel of Glen's bike loses its shudder, but continues spinning, with a trail of blood splattered over it, reflective like the river in front of me. "Jessica?!" I cry, my voice distorted within my ears.

Nothing but silence, the same crisp, deafening silence I heard crossing the... bridge. That shadowed figure is watching me, I'm sure of it. But this incessant mist is moving in again, clouding him from me and I from him, surrounding us from all sides and closing in. I scramble up to my feet and storm over to the hill, all but jumping my way up to the top.

"Jessica?" I call out once more, but to no avail. Each time I utter her name the silence only deepens, gets louder somehow.

With the taste of blood now on my tongue, I hurl myself over the barrier with a piercing pain down my right side, shot down from the blow to my head. Stumbling, I manage to stay upright, bounced back and rejected even by gravity. As I come to take a foot on the bridge though... I'm simply stunned. No mist surrounds the roundabout at all. It sits under its own streetlamp utterly alone, with only the smallest wisps trailing near it before they dissipate under the light. Beyond the roundabout there's nothing but black. Houses still pepper the landscape to the right above, but the same black pitch sits between them and here… as if they're not part of the same land.

"Jessica!?" I scream again, not even out of my own volition, but an instinct utterly foreign to me. Sensing, or perhaps even observing my presence, I'm sucked on to the first few steps of the crossing, forced to confront a face I can't even claim to recognise. It's only now that I see… the splitting snow isn't really snow at all but particles of dust. Flakes of times past… like the life I lost once here before. Each one of them seems to somehow be breathing, but only in the form of echoes reversing in on themselves. But much like my thoughts, they each flinch and ping back and forth every time I detect where one is coming from…

Until the streetlamp starts to stutter, invaded by the same force— I'm sure of it!—its beam of light sweeps through the miasma with the same scatter-brained, lingering nature. It daggers around as if searching for… it's… it's looking for me!

"I bet you loved every second of it, didn't you Eric?"

"Jessica? I know that's you…" but her whispered voice darts between the dust like the breaths that just died away… swooping from the front to in and around the back and then again!

"Dawn had Glen when she was twelve, Eric. She hadn't seen him for most of her life, so certain feelings, shall we say—"

"What? Where are you, Jessica?! What are you talking about?" I weakly scream, hearing her from all angles as if the mist itself is speaking to me…

"Began to develop. She doesn't see what she did to him as wrong."

"Where are you?!" I cry, stupidly trying to sweep away the fog… but it's useless—everywhere I go leads back to the same place. Each step leads nowhere.

"And it seems neither do you…"

Wait… I can see something… it's Jessica… sitting in her car, but every attempt to approach her only makes me move further away… I can't do anything, only watch—something's forcing me to observe. Another outlined figure sways back and forth in front of the car, but instead of a shadow, the fog itself is its frame. It's pacing, throwing its arms about and goes to lunge a foot at the car door—*argh!!*—my own leg jolts in a tremor, pushing either myself back or the fog forward again, beginning to conceal her once more…

"Jessica…" I cry out one final time, but her eyes… they've been captured by the mist—injected by it—all that's glaring back at me is the same fog I'm engulfed in. I shake with so much violence it feels like the world is about to implode and the truth is, I want it to.

"You did the same with Dawn as you did with me, Eric. You knew I'd been fiddled with by my own father before we'd even shared a kiss and That's. What. Made. You. Want. To. Fuck. Me. It's these things you deny to yourself, Eric, that'll be the end of you. These thoughts that you cast into the shadows of your own mind. For there is no fucking shadow looking at you right now except for your own. Face it! You've never been looking at anyone except yourself! And you just can't stand to see what's looking back at you anymore, can you? No one's watching you. No one cares. You're a great big nothing… and you'll be long forgotten… before you're even dead. NOW TURN AROUND AND FACE YOURSELF TO SEE THAT THERE NEVER WAS A 'YOU' OR A SELF TO FUCKING FACE IN THE FIRST PLACE!"

Her screaming echoes, expanding only to swallow itself… and fades. I'm left practically paralysed with my head in my hands, knees drenched, pressed into the road. The silence returns as the mist begins to disperse. Something buzzes. It's a lamp post, crackling behind its glassed blur. It's flickering frantically… or I'm blinking with inconceivable rapidity, making two lights instead of one; orange into white. They both charge forward towards me. But I haven't moved, have I, how could I have done? How can it be the streetlamp?

A piercing horn blisters. My scraping right foot scatters gravel towards it. My body's twisted, with one foot lower than the other, one where it should be, one where it shouldn't. The headlights get closer. I want to throw myself into the centre of them, but I'm just empty and powerless. A blur of blonde appears, wiping itself away only to be immediately concealed. The horn continues its warning, believing in its differentiation between life and death. All photons before me are now being observed.

I find myself reaching out towards the car, accepting certain death. But it sways a little, then some more. Finally, my feet obey my command and I suck them out of the ground. Marching forward, I'm blinded by overwhelming light. I deserve this. All I hope is that the light will soon become black.

The horn stutters. Tyres screech. This is it.

I close my eyes without thinking, expecting to snap out of consciousness, but all I feel is a burst of air, a thrusting ripple of wind. By inches the car flies by, throttling me back as if it were a train. Struck by this force and unable to fight against it, I fall, again landing half on the pavement and half on the road. Ahead of me, the car shoots away, leaving behind nothing but smoke and the dying embers of artificial, mist-covered light.

But as it disappears in the distance, the miasma begins to split down the centre, moving away from itself in a perfect rhythm, like a storm of separation, evading my point of focus. There's a strong sound of gust in my ears... but no air passes through my fingers. This silence is suffocating, moving... up the streetlights... forcing them to crackle static, popping my ears as they wither into the now surrounding black.

I can't see anything. Not even the gravel under my feet.

But a singular streetlamp—the one right behind me—flickers with torturously slow, twitching blinks... directly opposite... the shadow looms over me, standing on top of the railings, unmoving, silhouetted in such a way that I cannot tell if he faces out onto the river or he's glaring straight at me.

"*ARRGGHHHH!!!!!!*" I scream, only just realising that I'm already charging towards Him. His head flickers just a touch, sensing my approach, flexing his fingers. Yet, even knowing this, no move is made on His part. He's inviting me to do it. Allowing me to finally let him go. As I take my final stride and jump... everything starts to slow... infinitesimally down. With outstretched hands I collide into the outlined figure, feeling a strange pressure inside them... as if I pushed—but the planet... shifts an axis—making me loop over the railings whilst passing through His shadow... as if in an act of transcendence... through my legs I see the bridge has tipped ninety degrees... we're falling... not down but backwards... as one, I through Him and Him through I. Nothing has ever felt so blissful before, as I head towards my certain doom. Our growing reflection in the river below shows us back in the same manner it depicts... I am becoming the indifference of the cosmos... a mirrored outline of nothing. Like the lament of many a man, if I knew then what I now know I'd have done this long ago. I'm coming back into the world only to die... just like I always have been. I can feel the iciness of the water already... sense my plummet coming... and see myself for what I truly am— a less than nonentity abomination of nature, whilst nature itself is an abomination of non-existence. Closer... closer... my whole outline is going... the abyss is mine... closer... and n—

-*SMACK!*-

I land flat inside a puddle... the opposite way from where I faced... waves of disturbed mist and snow rise in puffs and stretch upwards only to fade... splashing just like a massive body of water... then once again, I'm back on the bridge, alone, surrounded by opaque white glows, returning to my limited, frail perceptions and an illusion known as consciousness.

I swear I can feel him drowning from within the black down below.

Then, nothing but silence. Not even a whispered voice in the wind. Just the darkness of the night sky above and the white of the snow to the sides of me.

I'm not sure what just happened.

My head feels lighter though. Freer. Shaken loose of some unbearable burden.

I guess maybe the cold has stopped the bleeding.

I hope now... these visions have...

gone. The bike... I must go back.

Everything's so white though. So brilliantly and terrifyingly white.

CHAPTER THIRTY-TWO

So, with that, it is with my deepest regret to inform you of the passing of Eric Archer. I know he was a client of yours for close to two years. If you're wondering how I know that, it is because we were once quite close, as you might also be aware of as well. I thought you might like to know, from one therapist to another.

Yours Sincerely—

"Here you go, Eric. This one's on the house," says Lucy, placing my pint down with her violet-painted fingernails wrapped around it, which match her lips. Lucy's looking juicy tonight.

"Are you sure?" I ask, folding the letter over.

"Yeah, fuck it. This place is shutting down tomorrow, so what do I care?" she says laughingly, shrugging those tattooed shoulders of hers. "It's good to see you again though. How long's it been? About…"

"Three months," I say. "So, what are you going to do instead? D'you have another job lined up?"

"Nah, not yet. I don't really know what I wanna do. Probably move out of town. I'm getting sick of it here. Everyone in this town is a poser pretending he's an artist."

"How is Jack? I thought you two broke up?"

"We did, but well. We're casual, I guess. Pretty sure we have an unspoken, open relationship."

"To the fear of commitment," I say, toasting her. She laughs and receives my pint by clinking it with one of her many rings.

"So, no lucky lady joining you tonight?" she asks, rubbing rather than adjusting a loose bra strap.

"Nope."

"Mmm, maybe you should stay late then," she says, after a brief glance at her forever active phone.

"Do you even like having sex with me, Lucy?" I ask.

"*What a question*," she says, blushing slightly, looking from side to side at no one. "Yes," she whispers, "obviously. Why d'you ask?"

"Just wondered is all."

"I like you, Eric. You're even more fucked up than I am. You know that stupid thing men say about crazy women being the best in bed?"

"Yeah?"

"It works both ways," she says, holding a cheeky, if not tiresome look at me. "What are you writing there anyway?"

"Oh. It's a letter to my therapist. I'm letting him know about my suicide."

"You see? You with a therapist. Crazy," she says, ignoring any detection of sincerity as she either feels awkward or wants to fuck later. Possibly both. The offer is tempting due to my abstinence. Not sure I can even get an erection now though; dropping the drugs has made me somewhat impotent. Strangely enough, I take that as one of the perks.

After what I can still only hope was my temporary lapse into insanity, it seemed better to lock myself away and stick my middle finger up to everything and everyone. I still drank out of childhood habit, but the dumping of the drugs was unavoidable. Whatever I thought they were helping they were actually making far worse. Quitting them cold wasn't easy. I pretty much had to teach myself how to speak again; not like I had anyone to talk to though. The hallucinations seem to have stopped, but I'm a little cautious about tempting fate. I still hear things, but for the most part I'm aware of 'them' rather than not. That's what I hope at least. For the most part they're gone too, much like everything else. In the spirit of honesty, I find it quite difficult to venture outside anymore. It's as if all my social skills crumbled under the weight of the last year or two. I find eye contact difficult enough to say the least, get nervous at the mere sight of strangers and, like I just said, hear voices that I know aren't really there. A minute or so ago I could've sworn that Lucy casually announced that she was date-raped a little while back but blamed herself for the way she was dressed. I'm sure she more likely said something like she's back dating Jack and that whole mess, but I can't say for sure. I guess a therapist would say I'm mentally-ill but hey, trying not to be mentally-ill made me go even more insane, so I'd rather accept it than bother trying to 'fix' it.

Anyway, here's what happened after that night on the bridge. Or during it, I should say. The last thing I remember is waking up practically covered in snow, with fingers so blue I thought I might end up losing them. I have no idea how I woke up, but maybe it was because of the fact it was so damn fucking cold. My head wasn't bleeding anymore, which I put down to the snow as well. In a rush of frantic exhaustion, I fetched the bike in a panic, then somehow pedalled it all the way back to Dawn's. For a long time, I actually thought I was dead, numb as my body and mind were during the whole thing. It turned out to be the most tranquil experience I've ever known, like my whole sense of self had been left behind in the snow. Speaking of which, the river under the bridge also froze over, which I found out a couple of weeks later when my new second-hand laptop arrived in the post. It stuck around for quite a while that snow, near enough the whole winter. Why did I buy a second-hand laptop? Well...

When I first got home, I thought I'd been robbed. My entire flat had been fleeced, all except for the masks Esther and I wore to the graduation party, which lay flat over the centre of the carpet. Underneath them, I found a note. Forgive me for paraphrasing but I can't quote it directly, as I burnt the fucking thing. It said something along the lines of...

The next time you want a threesome, try not to piss in your girlfriend's face; you were right, we're just not compatible; I'm tired of you treating me like a whore; thank you for being there for me, you've really helped me regain my confidence; sorry about stealing your stuff but you gave me the idea when you said you used to take little 'souvenirs' from the older women you seduced...

I'm going to live with my mother—that was the line that did it for me. I didn't really give a fuck about her stealing all my worthless possessions out of revenge, that seemed fair enough in some ways, but the fact she was going back to her stupid whore of a mother hit a nerve, like everything I really tried to get through to her just went over her head and the only time she really listened to me was when my cock did the talking. Maybe I shouldn't have been surprised, not that I remember now if I was, but it hurt, I know that much. Burning it with my lighter was my instinctive response. Thank fuck for my useless sperm.

Sammy also seemed to take a leaf out of Esther's book. I couldn't track her down no matter how hard I tried. For the first couple of weeks, after getting mildly sober, I tried to find her through more methods than I thought possible. She's completely cut me out of ever contacting her again. Can't say I blame her, but it would be nice to try and at least make her understand... something. I recalled some memory about taking her to the fields of Jessica's house, dressing her up, rehearsing some porn fantasy and the ocean of narcotics that filled her eyes during it, but after transferring the files from my busted phone into the laptop, all I found was a video of Jessica dissonantly performing oral sex on you know who. I know I did the same with Sammy, but all I have to go on are the occasional smash cut-like flashbacks of her freaking out when I danced around like a loon with the mask on, all from the perspective of my urethra, as if that makes any sense. I also seem to recall her trying to run me over... but her face is overlayered by Jessica's and the similarity of their cars points to a misinterpretation of an already blurred recollection. The biggest thing I fear is her coming back to tell me she's pregnant again and due to past traumas, she's decided to keep it this time around. It's stupid, I know, but that's fear for you. I just hope she's okay.

As for Jessica, well, who knows. All but locking myself away had the bonus of ignoring pressing problems. My door was knocked upon a fair number of times during the first couple of weeks, but after that, it was as if I was a ghost. Part of me wanted to speak to her, to apologise, to ask her about Glen and whatnot but the bigger part simply couldn't face it. I would like to tell her I'm sorry for sleeping with Dawn though, but my punishment for that was within the very act itself, the epitome of the series of events that I'll now have to live with. It's opaque like most of my childhood, but the feeling, or maybe the lack of feeling and emptiness within that it left behind will always be there.

It's funny though really. If I never heard of Glen and happened to meet Dawn, I would've thought, initially at least, that I'd hit the jackpot. She's hot, taut as fuck, clearly got bank and is into the same sordid fantasies that I'm into. But her fantasy was actually an underlying, horrifying and evidently disturbed reality. Seeing how crazy I went suspecting Jessica was hiding something without much, if anything to go on, it seems fair to say that Dawn and I would've torn each other to shreds. But then again, that seems to be my MO. I've really got to stop hating myself through the eyes of others.

"Hey," a croaking voice behind me calls. "I was hoping that I'd see you again, Eric."

Turning on my stool, Samantha stands before me, back to brunette. Back to the Sammy I once thought I knew. I blink and take a deep breath, wondering if she's—

"Oh, hey Sammy," says Lucy.

"Hey Luce," she says back, half-smiling, half-self-conscious. She looks pale, a little downtrodden, torn-up by the cyclone of life.

"Wine?" asks Lucy.

"Not tonight. I'll have a gin and tonic, thanks," she says, dipping into her handbag.

I whip out my wallet before her, nearly hitting the low-hanging lightbulb above and unfold it. "My shout. Take a drink for yourself as well, Luce."

She smiles prettily and says, "Thanks, Eric, but there's no need. These ones are literally on the house," and bats the twenty away.

Samantha and I both thank her. A silent, awkward wait ensues. Lucy hums in between the chinking of glasses and clattering of ice, trying to dismiss an atmosphere impossible to ignore. Once the glasses hit the beermat, she looks at us both, hunting for clues as to what's happened between us. They seem more than familiar with each other now, but I won't dare to ask why, as I don't want to know. Life sure is easier when you're surrounded by women you've already slept with. I should've had a threesome with these two, going by the smitten looks they're exchanging. Hindsight's a bitch. Lucy leaves us to it, winking us a *See-You-Later* with her peach of an arse. Christ, whether I'm having sex or not, it's always lurking inside my thoughts. Samantha and I both sip our drinks, share a timid glance, but exhale out of sync.

"Can we go out back, Eric? I'd like to talk to you about something. It won't take long. I promise."

"Okay, let's go."

After hopping off the stool, I grab my leather jacket along with my free pint and walk with Samantha towards the garden. Her chestnut brown hair bounces in waves over her shoulders and for the first time in memory she's wearing a top which doesn't show off her tits.

Even the air about her is somewhat different, more mature and at ease with herself. I hold the door open and she brushes passed me, avoiding eye contact as our bodies graze. As soon as the door slams behind me, I spark up a smoke. Samantha toys with hers for a bit before doing the same. Like expected, it isn't exactly warm out here, but there's a calm, peacefulness about it. We both take a seat on a separate bench each and smoke, looking out at nothing.

"So, how have you been?" she asks.

"Alone," I say, "how about yourself?"

"Better than I was. I'm sorry for not being in contact with you recently. I had a lot of things on my mind and well... well, I might as well just come out and say it. I sort of had a nervous breakdown. After... that night in the props room, at the graduation party," she says, her body flinching, lip quivering. "I know it was pretty much all my fault. I mean, I did tell you to come upstairs after all," she says, looking at the ground, shifting on her seat, eyes darting around like prey confronted by its predator.

I have no idea what she's talking about.

"Sorry, Sammy. What do you mean exactly?"

"I just need to tell you that I forgive you Eric, but what you did to me really wasn't right. I know I said you could do it, but now I remember how drunk and crazy I was that night."

She looks at me for a response, but as I'm stumped, I just stare back, giving her nothing. Awkwardness casts down between us in seconds. Feeling obliged, I say, "Listen, Sammy. I really don't remember much, if anything—"

"When we had sex," she says, looking down with a jittering breath, "I know it was you... wasn't it... I'm sorry, Eric. This is a lot harder to say out loud than I thought it would be."

"It's fine, Sammy. I understand. Take your time."

I'd left her where she lay, covered by my cloak. She was drooling, sleeping with the tranquillity of someone who'd just rid herself of a troubling burden. I had the mask, didn't I? Yes, it was dangling on my index finger through one of the eyeholes... but when I reached the bottom of those ever-creaking stairs… the rage that came with the rumour re-emerged, so I let it fall.

"Whisky," says Sammy, bringing me back. "The first thing I can remember is the smell of whisky. I didn't even realise you were… my body was so numb. Then I saw flashes of us flirting. Things were getting intense. It felt like we were going to have sex, I know that much… but there was some… some sick, ill feeling growing inside me, that something wasn't right…"

The mask landed with its face staring up the stairs. I left it there, defiant, knowing I had nothing to hide. The performance area felt vaguely different, but I put that down to what I'd just been told. It seemed the same again once I slipped through the drawn stage curtains.

"… but I remembered us. We were so close to having sex that I thought we must've started doing it. I wanted us to, I know that much. So, I… I told myself we did, that I just blacked out for five minutes or… I started to wake up then. Well, not wake up really, but open my eyes. My body still felt… lifeless."

I'd closed the door of the main performance area as if worried it might've awoken Sammy, despite how far away she was. Or maybe I really did it to make sure no one else saw me come back in. Nobody seemed to notice anything either way. I walked through the foyer, ignored and unsearched for. The mezzanine was no different. I expected Esther to be looking for me, but she was nowhere to be found.

"You were wearing the mask. That was the first thing I saw, watching its forehead glide up and down. Your breath was hot over my chest, almost like fire. Then I started flaring up, flushed with anxiety but still dizzy from all the alcohol. I wanted to say something, but I couldn't speak. It was like I was trapped inside a pit of myself. You carried on… in and out, up and down… like machinery."

I stood in the dancehall, staring out of the window. Esther was outside, surrounding herself with older men, laughing with that overzealous, forced guffaw she reserved for men she liked but didn't know. Her breasts looked immaculate. Further confirmed by the eyes which trailed her movements. She looked up just the once whilst puffing away on a cigarette from behind the screen of smoke she'd just blown. I could've sworn she saw me but looked right through me all the same. For that first half an hour or so after leaving the props room, I'd never felt more invisible in my whole life.

"Eventually, I managed to speak. I remember what I said, Eric," she says, tilting her head up for the first time since she started to speak. Her bottom lip continues quivering whilst an awaiting rivulet of tears hangs from her eyes. "I said *stop*, Eric, I said *no*. But as soon as I spoke... as soon as I spoke you covered my face with your hand... and carried on."

She can't look at me now. I'm not really sure she can focus on anything. A few uncertain, already weakened and shaken slaps hit my shoulders. "How could—how could you do that to me?" she asks, falling into me, shaking still, desperate. But she springs herself back up, determined to continue. At war with her own emotions, she says, "It was like being fucked by a completely different person, Eric. And after you finished—after you fucking came inside me, you just got up, threw the cloak over me and practically ran down the stairs." Saying it aloud brings back the memory's power, threatening to take control. "Just tell me... please. Why did you do that?" Her voice is drowning in anguish, silently screaming in an out of range octave.

"I don't know—"

"You must have *some* idea, Eric... please, just tell me, what was going through your head?"

"Okay, just please, give me a moment. This won't be easy to say, Sammy..."

I'd gone back to the mezzanine area. Sat at the same place as when I arrived. Richard's mask, the plague doctor one, lay by my side, nose pointing upwards. Figuring he was just somewhere else it didn't strike me as strange; stricken as I was by the night's turn of events. Just as his absence crept into the abnormal, there he was, clambering up the stairs. He was flustered; a bit on edge. The indents left behind by something worn over the face were still there… did I notice that before? And for just how long do they leave their mark? After flicking his head up at me, he told me he was going to leave. Strangely, I now recall thinking, he'd slipped the mask back on whilst announcing his departure. Then he poured himself a shot of whisky inside a disposable cup and handed me the rest of the bottle. "One for the road," he said. I replied, "like the Harold Pinter play," and raised the bottle. He simply nodded his cup my way whilst looking over at the stairs, keeping his eyes there long enough for me to take at least two shots more. Then he shook himself out of it, drained his drink, squeezed my shoulder, told me the bottle was mine and sauntered off with a low-hanging, inward posture, without want of thanks or even a goodbye.

That's why he disappeared; why he called out of nowhere to ask me whether I'd spoken to Sammy. That's why he fled town. It was Richard. He raped her. Not only that, but he did it through my image. Or at least, through the image I displayed that evening. It happened right under my nose again, hidden in plain sight.

"Eric?" Sammy asks, holding my hands now, in need of some response. She didn't come here to apologise for her behaviour. She came to confirm what she's been struggling to reconcile within herself, suspicious of the amalgamated blurs of what might've occurred and what might've not.

It's clear. I have no choice but to lie. If I tell her it wasn't me but instead Richard, it could tip her over the edge. What she wants is to hear me say it… to stop herself questioning it over and over again until it finally breaks her. I know that feeling all too well.

I close my eyes, crying tears which I hope convey guilt rather than the turmoil of right and wrong they've been triggered by. She needs to leave here believing it was me. Otherwise the unwanted stranger and his unseen shadow will lurk in parts of the mind unknown and create a narrative out of the incoherent memory until it births a living nightmare.

"I wanted," I say, my face scrunching against my own volition. I'm not acting for her sake at all. Nor even for mine. "I wanted to make you think it was someone else, Sammy. That's why I covered your face and stopped you from looking at me. I don't know why I did it. Or even how. Something just took over me. I've been so lost and angry, furious beyond control…"

"Please… just say it, Eric. I need to hear you say it."

"I… raped you."

Sammy lets out a bottled-up, crying scream and unleashes, throwing punches at my chest but without the intent to hurt, more through the fury of relief. I allow her to do it, putting up no fight whatsoever, taking the onslaught that for once, I don't think I deserve. Time seems to slow down as her arms flail all about me, growing weaker with each lunge. "I kept talking to you whilst you did that to me and you just stayed fucking silent. I knew you wanted me to think it was someone else, I just knew it!" Her voice falters along with her arms. She falls into me, burying her head into my shoulder.

"Yes. I wanted you to think it was… well, anyone but me. I didn't even know I was capable of something like that. I don't know what else to say, Sammy. I'm sorry."

"It really was you, wasn't it? Promise me."

"I promise, Sammy. It was me," I say, my voice crackling whilst my brain feels like it's splitting apart again.

"It's okay, Eric. Thank you for admitting it. You don't need to worry. I'm not going to report you or anything," she says, looking at me like an understanding mother.

She throws her arms around my idle body, squeezing as tightly as she can whilst breathing with exhaustion and the tiniest air of relief. She needs this more than anything right now. I can only hope that she never finds out the truth. There's probably a part of her that even knows I'm lying, but her memories will tarnish and fabricate themselves until they blur and merge with an ego she'll occupy in a future date, an ego designed to protect her and make her remember something false but believed to be true, that what once happened to her was performed by me. Maybe I should feel somewhat honoured to be giving that to her, but really, my share of the blame cannot be dismissed. After all, I took full advantage of her post-traumatised state of complete recklessness. I can't believe I'm saying this, but it would've been better if I actually did rape her.

Life only gets less understood as we age, the only shred of wisdom to be found lies within the shrugging admittance of our own ignorance. Like death and how it shrouds over everything we do, we're filtered inside a light unknown. An illuminance so blinding it can only be gazed at within a blink; existent only with the knowledge of non-existence. We each live our whole lives knowing we may as well have never existed at all.

Samantha pushes herself back from my chest and kisses me on the cheek. "Thank you for admitting it, Eric. I… I forgive you," she whispers over my ear, "please, take care of yourself."

"You too, Sammy," I reply as she heads for the door.

"Call me Samantha. I kinda prefer it now." She grabs the handle but stops and turns, "Oh yeah, I nearly forgot. Say hi to Esther for me."

"Ah, I would," I say, laughing at the layered irony, "but I can't. She's gone. We're finished."

"Oh, I'm sorry to hear that. Really. I know the threesome was a bit weird, but from what I remember it was fun. But then again, I can't really remember anything. Same with that crazy sex we had in the fields. Except when I freaked out and tried to, you know, run you over. Sorry about that by the way."

"Don't be. My memory of it is blank too. Believe me."

"Oh yeah, that reminds me. I owe you a phone."

"I'm sorry?"

"That phone you gave me to film us. I just might've thrown it into a river somewhere on my way back home."

"Oh, right. Forget about it. It's already forgotten," I say. It's as if I'm looking at a relieved child somehow, a momentary return of innocence.

"Lay off those drugs now, Eric."

"You too, Sammy. Sorry, Samantha. You too."

As she passes through the door, I hear the bell chime for last orders. I sit there with a familiar feeling of opaque vacancy, like the distant slump I found myself in when Jessica told me about Glen.

I go to finish off my smoke but its already burnt out. So, I get up and walk back through the door, still in the aftermath of fog that came with Samantha's troubled experience. It seems to me that most women will, at some point, undergo some form of rape. I do not know what I think about that anymore. Just sad, I guess.

Lucy gestures at me, the only schmuck still inside this place, whether I want another. I nod that I do. She pulls down the pump whilst eyeing me and filling the glass. "Looked like you just broke up with her or something. What's the deal with you two anyway?"

"Oh, nothing really," I say, shrugging, "That's probably the last time I'll ever see her."

"Interesting. Well, I shouldn't tell you this, but as you just said that then fuck it. She's been in here asking for you more than a few times. Did you tell her we've fucked?"

"No, she guessed it and I didn't see the point in lying."

"Well, I told her it was a long time ago, just so you know. She looked lost every time she came in here. Have you been a bad boy to her, Eric?"

"No more than usual. She's been going through tough times, but I think she'll be alright."

"Crazy doesn't mix so well with more crazy, does it?"

"You're not fucking wrong, Luce. You should really get out of this town. Everything takes on a repeat if you stay put too long, trust me," I say, taking hold of the freshly pulled pint Lucy just laid down.

"So, how about that quick lock-in?" she asks, switching off the lights around the bar. I down virtually half my drink, trying to resist this blatant guarantee. It's been a while since I got laid, but these days, I don't care. I've even taken a shining to Lucy this evening, so that'll probably make the sex awkward and disappointing. How pathetic.

"I think I'll pass, Lucy. Not feeling it tonight."

"Oh," she says, insult-slapped.

"You want to come back to mine? Watch a movie or something? Hang out?" I ask, not really because I want to, but the company would be nice.

"Urm. No, not really, Eric. I just fancied a bit of fun before going home, but if you're not in the mood, it's no bother."

What she means is, she wants to fuck someone else before going back to her boyfriend, just to get off on the betrayal. Thumbing my whisky dick in will just be awkward for the both of us. "Take it easy then, Lucy," I say, gulping down the last remnants of the final drink I'll have in here. "Give me a call sometime."

"Sure, yeah. I will," she says, in the tone of a lie.

I zip my jacket all the way up and head for the door. Once out onto the street, I look up at the sign of the pub: Journey's E d. The 'n' must have fallen down a while ago and nobody bothered to put it back up. I feel like walking for a while, to shake off the energy I could've gotten rid of with the barmaid. This evening's been a double dose of doing the right thing despite it feeling wrong. That's how hedonism gets under your skin; when missing out on a distraction becomes as powerful as the distraction itself. Then you're lost inside its spiral.

I was projecting when I told Lucy to leave town, maybe through my own fear. After dropping this letter off tomorrow I'm going to leave. I haven't got a whole ton of money, but enough to drift around for a month or so. I'll probably come back, but I just need to get out of here for a while. It's too stained by memories I want no reminding of and dreams that never came to fruition. It's time to admit defeat.

CHAPTER THIRTY-THREE

The eternal return is a largely terrifying concept when looked at from any angle. This idea has been stuck in my head for too long now; the notion that each life lived, is lived out again, repeatedly, inside a continuous, never-ending, nor ever-changing loop… for eternity. This horrifying, hell-ridden thought has been silenced by a different one of late though. What I've been contemplating isn't the Sisyphean nightmare of endlessly repeating this life, but more that I'm condemned to live out the very same cycle of behaviour within this *singular* lifetime, without hope of ever realising it until it's already come to pass, signifying only that the repetitious cycle has once again started over. Even more troubling is the suspicion aroused regarding said pattern, that it was woven and sewn long before my conscious awareness had a chance to influence and shape it, like a life script I had no part in writing, forever trapping me inside a pre-determined, nauseating spiral, that's neither going forward nor back. No sense tells me when it begins or when it ends, nor whether the two simply meet in the middle, but the palpable, relentless feeling within my being is always there, like a fragment from another dimension I'm part of, yet not part of. Its debris lurks within my shadow, forever leading the way, regardless of whether it's in front of me, or whether it's behind. All I'm allowed to know is that it's there, buried under each thought and every movement. My body is a decaying vessel, whilst my mind is nothing more than a prison, with no foreseeable escape, except in death. The difference between heaven and hell is that the latter is no myth. The pleasures nature allows us to experience are ephemeral, forever fleeting, but by comparison, our pain and suffering are eternal, even omniscient. Your higher instincts may indeed be your true god, but the limitations of your own knowledge will always corrupt you in the end. By design, nature is a perpetual holocaust, the one true slaughterer of everything it creates. Maybe that does give it some meaning to its unknowable cause, but from what I've seen of the universe and specifically this world, it's a meaning I thoroughly and categorically reject.

Look at the part I played with Samantha. It was a replica, a complete mirroring of my actions, or lack of them, with Jessica. Whilst they couldn't be entirely the same, the results still display an uncanny resemblance. Even their personalities, influenced by my own and vice-versa, all paved the paths we subconsciously always knew we were going to walk down. Even this knowledge, as advantageous as it might appear to be, still serves nothing. I'll always live with the notion that things could have turned out differently, that if I took a more objective perspective (as much as a man can) instead of succumbing to my subjective and destructive wiles I could have influenced the outcomes according to my own will. It's a lie. But even knowing it's a lie does nothing to pacify its power. Such is the curse of being human.

Perhaps the illusion of free will is more important than free will itself.

But the human, all too human aberration of nature that I am will forever elude my very own logic. In essence, I'll never fucking know what I don't fucking know.

I'm inconsolable with the realisation that I attributed a large part of my mind to fantasy rather than reality. The dreams I'm having are the hardest part to cope with, despite the aid of my faithful lover that is alcohol. I've destroyed Glen over a thousand times in a hundred separate places now. Each one of them wakes me up in the coldest of sweats, which in turn all remind me of when I awoke on the bridge blanketed in snow. It would've been a rather serene death, had I died. Hopefully this is all just a result of kicking the prescription drugs to the kerb. I just wish I could stop fucking thinking so much.

I suppose these thoughts are largely associated with the street I'm currently walking down; a path I've travelled innumerable times in my mind's eye. Despite knowing I'm not here for a therapy session, the emotions which so often plagued me during my travels to Franklyn's flat are still alive and present, riddling me with a trepidation I find so difficult to admit to myself: the fear of being understood.

Being misunderstood flatters to deceive a faulty ego; providing the saddle for a self-appointed high horse. Up there you can bathe in the illusory rays of superiority, singling yourself out inside a delusion of possessing an intellect incomprehensible to others. It's the stance of a chest-beating coward, nibbling on an apple snatched from a tree he himself labelled knowledge.

But the fear of being understood still holds its own merit. Please, somebody out there, tell me I'm wrong, I implore you. For I require no confirmation of the terror I deem to be true. In fact, tell me I'm a no-good fool, an outright idiot, an insignificant nothing.

I guess to some of you it might seem cruel to announce my suicide to Frank. Although I'm convinced he could never really help me, there was always part of me that knew I wasn't giving him much of a chance. I went into therapy already resentful of its cause, too torn by the associations I derived from Jessica's own relationship with it. Knowing that she could be so devout to a system of belief, for I cannot see it as anything else, whilst living out such a paradoxical relationship in her private life only served to confirm its falsity, what I took to be its masquerade. Whilst my opinion in this regard is unlikely to ever change even with this admission, I have to reconcile with the fact that the conclusion it foretold was a largely, if not entirely, self-fulfilled prophecy.

Perhaps one, ironically, should be of a sounder state of mind before venturing into it. Otherwise your expectations tend to reach for impossible heights, distorting what should only ever enable a different viewpoint, a new way of thinking, instead of self-entitled delusions of non-existent cures.

It's troubling to know I needed to completely fall apart before I could see things with clarity.

That's funny. The curtains which were so often drawn due to the glaring sunlight are not only open but in fact, not there at all.

I walk up the steps towards the seaweed green door, nervous as always, even though I never planned on knocking. The letter I just removed from my bag is gripped between my fingers. I move my hand towards the letterbox but the action itself feels ghostly, haunted by its own futility. Instead of posting it, I stuff the envelope inside the inner pocket of my jacket, where I notice I still have the photograph of Glen and Jessica as it almost scratches the tip of my finger. Or maybe that's just my sudden rush of anxiety. Something… or someone is amiss. The intercom's bottom button is bare, taped-over and… unnamed. Leaning to the side and peering through the window confirms what my sinking-chest suspects: the house is empty. No ceramic clock with the loudest tick-tock in existence sits above the fireplace. No Freudian statue staring through the ether of non-existent flames. No elbows resting over an armchair which isn't there. There's nothing but the undetectable dust of his departure. He's gone. Franklyn Fitton has also seen it fit to take leave of my life through an act of disappearance; without want of saying a single fucking thing to me about it.

For reasons unknown and the second time in fewer than twenty-four hours, I burst into a broken ravine of confused, isolated tears.

I can admit to never being particularly good to Frank, at times even grotesque and crass... but I gave him my time, which is all a person can give to another in the end.

How could he just up and go without a word?

Even my thieving, wonderful whore Esther Bellona left me a note...

"Oh, hey," says a voice.

A voice I was afraid of hearing.

I turn to the side so she can't quite see the state I'm in and wipe my eyes as thoroughly as I can. My half-hope of her simply speaking as she strolled by is crushed by the overwhelming sense of her still standing there, as paralysed as I am. The palpable awkwardness provokes her into a feigned clearing of the throat. After the third cough, she says, "I'm glad I've bumped into you again, Eric. I didn't think I'd get the chance. Don't worry, I just want to say... that I'm..."

"There's no need, Dawn. Really," I say, my voice as croaked as my body is crippled.

"I think there is, Eric. I've felt awful about how we—how we left things. I know I crossed a line and went too far. I've got a tendency towards self-sabotage, you see. For what it's worth, if anything, I'm truly very sorry."

I wipe my face again, scooping the confusing sense of loss out of my eyes, still shaking, and then face her. She looks the same as the first time I saw her around here, only more sunken and dishevelled. Our thoughts matching, she then asks me if I'm okay.

I nod, unconvincingly going by the biting of her bottom lip and furrow-browed crease of concern in her forehead. Emerald eyes glistening, she asks, "Is this where your..."

"Yes," I respond. "This is where my therapist lives... or lived. He appears to have vanished."

She goes to speak but pauses, allowing a thought to run through her mind without self-interruption. "There's a lot of that going around," she says, in a seeming exchange of croaking voices. "I'm sorry."

"Don't be. I don't know why I'm crying over it."

She lets out a sigh of understanding, resonated further by the isolated focus of her eyes. I walk down the steps with rays of sunlight absent of any warmth obscuring my view of her. Dawn stands still the entire time until our paths cross and we face each other.

"It's good to see you again, Eric."

"You too, Dawn."

I find myself unable to be anywhere near as repulsed by her as I have been in my imaginings of this occurrence. In fact, I'm just as attracted to her as I was before, if not more, somehow. She looks as if sleep has abandoned her, replacing itself for a constant preoccupation instead. I think I know why as well, but there's simply no angle for me to pry, no gap or elusive manipulation I can employ to find out through what she'd believe to be her own, unprovoked admission. Absence emanates away from her like a cold, unforgiving gale, trailing away from her skin as if she's shedding remnants of life itself. The only thing I can't recall is whether it was always there. Through my blind perception of her, I could only ever see the side to Dawn that I wanted to see. Everything inconvenient was filtered out without the need of conscious thought.

"This'll probably sound strange and you'll likely say no, but," she says, letting out an embarrassed laugh, delaying. "Are you hungry?" She rubs the point of her flat-footed sole into the ground, her body hesitant in its lean towards me. Everything's suddenly filtered in that same Scandinavian hue of iced-over blue, except for the opaque grey nestled between us. But now I'm unsure whenever I observe anything, wary of what the other part of myself might be seeing.

"Starving," I reply. "Looking after the supposed number one is something I often neglect to do. And believe you me, I'm not shy of self-sabotage either."

A singular tear cuts down her cheek, streaming so fast it seems its journey was previously and very recently paved. She makes no effort to wipe it away, or even feels it, going by the intransigence of her glance. I'm not sure I've seen someone so naked before, so willing to be looked at for everything they are.

Pushed forward by something stronger than my mere weak will, I let my bag slip away from my person onto the ground and we embrace in a delicate, uncertain hug. She holds onto me via my shoulders whilst I, in turn, wrap her lower back. We've both lost weight since our last encounter, become hollower, more skeletal. The tightness of our conjoined bodies quickly declines, as we're equal in fragility, too close to collapse to risk the final scraps of our strength. But instead of moving back, we remain where we are with my stubble brushing over her cheek. Loose strands of her hair dance and flutter up close before my eyes, bleached white by the glaring sun. She's trembling, allowing the little wisps of everything that must remain unsaid escape from her breath.

With no idea why this feels like the right thing to do. I invaded her life posing as a stranger. Now I've returned as her shadow, knowing more about her than she can ever know. I used to think the highest form of intimacy between two people would involve sharing absolutely everything together. Now I'm not so sure. Maybe some things are better off left in the unknown.

After all, life itself is inherently unknowable.

I guess I'll always wonder about the person I came closest to doing that with though, such is my punishment for my half-hearted attempt.

This all sounds like some silly teenage fantasy of transcendental love. Now even love itself seems like a form of misplaced hope, of a conjectural myth that betrays nothing but our collective desperation and yearning for something we simply do not understand.

My face slides in front of Dawn's. We hang splinters away from each other, as if a thinned, deteriorating sheet of ice sits between us. Her movements dagger with a confidence shattered, with darting downward eyes unable to believe what I'm proposing. What might appear as teasing should only serve to deceive. I'm just as confused by what I'm doing myself, reluctant in my own longing. She takes a breath of matching uncertainty, which pulls me in closer beyond doubt. As our blued lips meet, we're brought no catharsis, no redemption or understanding. It's just a mutual yet unspoken, broken embrace of the lost and forgotten or maybe never even seen.

As we finish our foreheads press against one another in an ancestral return to the helpless animals we are deep down. Dawn takes my hand as if to make sure our contact remains unbroken and without the need of words we begin to walk towards her house. There's a distance and a yearning and a tragedy about us that I feel more than content to surrender to. Neither of our features reflect inside the windows of the cars we're passing by. We're just outlined phantoms, hollow yet whole, our dissipating existence confirmed only through the eyes of each other. The children inside us may be beaten, so swollen they cannot even move, but they can still open their eyes every now and again.

Dawn slips her hand away from mine as we come to the gate. She clicks it open and gives it a gentle push; the minutest of screeches accompanying its swing. It halts just before what seemed to be an inevitable encounter with the wall.

"Would you mind waiting here for just a second, Eric? My house is in a state that I don't really want you to see. I won't be long, I promise."

"Sure," I reply with a light smile. "Take all the time you need. I'm gasping for a smoke anyway."

"You are a…" she says, kissing me on the cheek instead of finishing her sentence. "I'll leave the door open. When the light above it flicks on, feel free to come inside."

"Is that new?" I ask.

"Yes, it is. I had it installed a few months back. It's automatic normally, but I can still control it from the inside. If I'm still awake, I can see if anyone's outside my door before they knock, you see. Anyway, I'll get the fire going. Thank you for this, by the way. It means more to me than I can express."

"You too, Dawn," I reply.

She holds her glance on me whilst walking backwards before turning for the door. As I begin rolling a cigarette the lights blink the house alive. Some doors slam closed. Through the small gap, I see her descend the stairs and almost skip into the living room. Moments later flames are born beyond the windows. I tuck my tobacco away but reach for the opposite pocket I normally keep it inside. Once again, my fingers flick over the photograph.

I never thought I'd get the chance to return it.

The light above the door snaps on, covering all but the first stepping-stone of the path in front, the one on which I stand. Curtains just ahead of me are drawn. I take a heavy last drag of my cigarette, nervous in mind and hesitant even in thought, apprehensive yet accepting of this unexpected meeting of ours; a meeting of chance we never could've rehearsed for.

Putting the photograph back on the fridge would be an amateur's move. Hiding it underneath, as if it fell, landing out of sight and concealed, will reflect fate in time, as cruel or as comforting as it might come to be seen.

If ever found.

As I approach the door, Dawn swings into the hallway, heading for the kitchen. Free of her jacket, she lets her hair bounce down whilst kicking off her shoes, wearing a full-bodied, somewhat antiquated and long-sleeved, all-black dress.

I have no idea what the fuck I'm doing coming back here, but for some reason, I've never felt more invited to be inside a home.

CHAPTER THIRTY-FOUR

Dawn was good to her word in the end. I'm currently chowing down on bacon and eggs as the scent of a steaming pot of coffee lingers in the air. This kitchen really sparkles in the morning. I barely recognise it at all.

"You sure you don't want any more, Eric? I've got plenty more in the fridge."

"This is more than enough, Dawn," I say, wolfing it into my mouth as if it's the first proper meal I've had in months. In fairness, it pretty much is.

"How about some more toast? Or a yoghurt to settle your stomach?" she asks, pouring two cups of coffee with her loose robe just about covering her breasts.

"Two helpings will do just fine, Dawn, but thanks. I normally line my stomach with a smoke anyway."

She rolls her eyes with a *You're-Too-Awful* smile, scoffs and swipes my joshing away with her hand. Provided she doesn't start verbally calling me son again, I'm happy enough to play the role. She picks up her cup after splashing it with milk, ruffles my towel-dried though still moist hair and walks over to the doorframe that leads into the hallway. With the sole of her right foot resting against it and her knee swinging to and fro, she watches me devour the rest of my breakfast, with both hands wrapped around her mug, gently cooling it down with pursed-lipped blows of her breath.

After scooping up the left until last bit of yoke, I place my knife and fork over the plate and go to leave it in the sink but her fluttering hand tells me not to bother. Instead, I just push it to the side and grab my coffee. As I start rolling a cigarette, Dawn pushes herself away from where she stands. She glides over to the other side of the kitchen, bends down, then slides an ashtray across the counter. It stops just before tipping over the edge. As I spark up, she grabs the plate and starts running the tap, humming to herself as she does the washing up. I glance down at the fridge, or more, the bottom of it and see that the corner of the photograph is still there.

Just as the tap shrieks idle, I finish off my coffee and stub out the cigarette. Standing up, we exchange a glance conveying my imminent departure. I walk into the hallway, find my jacket sprawled over the sofa and put it on, zipping it all the way up. Then I scoop up my bag and walk over to Dawn, who's now standing in front of the stairs.

She throws her arms around me before our eyes even meet, grabbing tightly onto my leather-covered shoulders. "Thank you, Eric," she says in an iced-over echo, whilst I take in the scent of her hair once more.

"What for?" I ask.

"Everything. You've made me a very happy woman coming back here. Especially after... well, everything else."

"The feeling's mutual, Dawn. Thanks for having me back," I say, moving across to face her. I've never seen someone look so smitten and torn at the same time. Our foreheads meet and nestle, then we gently kiss, causing one another to shake, strengthening the scent we left each other with.

"Well, I better get going I guess," I say whilst readjusting my fallen rucksack.

She takes hold of my forearms and says, "Promise me you'll pop over to see me again when you get back, okay?"

"You better count on it," I reply.

"Okay then. I hope you have an eye-opening trip."

"Me too. But just a pleasant one will do."

She unlocks the latch of the door, oblivious to the amount of nakedness she might display to a perfect stranger in the street. We kiss once more, and she watches me walk outside. It's a bright day with unexpected signs of spring in the air. The sunlight shines with a different radiance despite providing the same lack of warmth.

The somewhat blinding glare of the sun waves away from my sightline at the third stepping stone, where I go to turn but an emerald green car stops me halfway. As it coasts down the road, the same piercing rays prevent me from seeing who's at the wheel. As the thought of Sammy sinks in everything slows down. Dawn muffles my name with an inquisitive edge. My foot sways, disturbing the pebble stones surrounding my path. I flicker my eyes over at her but turn back in the same movement. The sheen of emerald green glides by. It speeds up and meets where it needs to turn in no time. Before the shallow breath the sight of it sent me into paralysis can be exhaled… it's gone.

But at the same time… it's not.

Inside a matrixed blink, the car which just drove by and beyond now sits parked in front of me. The same model and shade of car anyway. And like the one that just disappeared, I've sat inside this one too. But it's not the car itself that I'm startled by, it's the person pushing herself up out of its seat; her eyes only meeting mine as she slams the door shut. That person being Jessica.

I fear I've just been exposed to differing worlds I never should've seen, glimpsed into multiplicity whilst shackled inside the singular reality of my own.

For the first time since I started seeing things, I really fucking hope that I'm just seeing things.

Jessica and I's exposure of one another has put us into a checkmated glance. I imagine I'm not the only one thinking that this simply can't be happening.

"Jessica!" Dawn calls out behind me, rushing beyond my left shoulder. She goes to assist Jessica, who stumbled backwards upon Dawn's approach. "Are you okay?" she asks, "you look like you've seen a—"

"Fine," Jessica interrupts, holding up a firm hand whilst supporting herself against the car with the other. Dawn flicks her head my way, quick to realise her social obligation.

"Oh, how silly of me," she flusters, pulling over the veil of a person I haven't encountered before. "Eric, this is Jessica. Jessica, Eric."

With lip-nibbling ironic smiles we acknowledge one another with a simple nod. Our eyes meet but the mere act forces us to flounder... knowing what we know.

"Pleasure," I manage to mutter, but it comes out croaked and most likely unheard. Dawn registers the awkward air between us. To counter it, I step a pace forward. "Do you need help with anything, urm... Jessica?"

Her headlight stunned pose lessens as she stands upright, but she still looks rather queasy. I'm certain that has nothing to do with me though.

"Dawn," she says faintly, "could you go fetch me some water please... I'm feeling a bit light-headed."

"Oh, sure thing. That's what I'm here for, isn't it? Eric, you don't mind sticking around for a few minutes longer, do you? I don't like to leave Jessica alone, what with her condition."

"No problem," I say with a shrug.

"You sure you don't want anything else?" Dawn asks Jessica, all but ignoring my response. "Paracetamol, ibuprofen... xanax—"

"Just water, thanks."

"Okay, just a sec."

Dawn brushes past my shoulder like a woman on a rescue mission, living through Jessica as she now is. Once at the door, Jessica says, "Actually, Dawn? I think a paracetamol would be a good idea. And an apple, if you have any."

"Of course I do. What would you like it with this time? Chocolate spread or peanut butter? Or maybe both?"

The question throws Jessica off, as she looks at me like Dawn just gave her physical appearance away. "Just the apple," she splutters, breaking into tears.

Dawn, unphased, registers the fact that I am indeed still standing here. "You must expect the unexpected when a woman's expecting, Eric. I swear, every woman's cravings are just as unique to them as the baby growing inside."

I smile, almost scoffing at her ridiculous comment of individuality and whip out my tobacco to serve a craving of my own. Dawn looks away disapprovingly but keeps her mouth shut and jumps inside the house. I swear, mothers get away with saying the most preposterous bullshit known to man.

"So, here we are," I say, turned away from Jessica as I roll up, unable to fully grasp the answer that's been quite literally sitting under my nose this entire time.

"Yes," Jessica says, blowing her nose, pulling herself together. "Here we are."

I light up and blow a stream of smoke. "How have you been?" I ask, unsure of what to really say.

"Oh, you know. Pregnant. You? Where have you been for the last three months? I tried calling, even knocked on your door a few times. I thought you'd vanished as well."

"Only to the outside world. I've been keeping what some might call a low profile. Out of necessity rather than choice."

"Yet, you still somehow managed to come back here. How convenient," she says, judging me with an acted rolling of her eyes, but interrupts her own expression with a sudden headshake. "Really, Eric. What the fuck are you doing here? Please don't tell me you're actually seeing Dawn."

"I'm not. I bumped into her yesterday and well, here I am now."

"After everything I told you about her?" she asks in an acidic voice of accusation.

"Your judgment is a little hypocritical, don't you think? I could ask you what the fuck you are doing here as well, you know. So, what is it? Rapist if it's a boy, molested if it's a girl?"

"*I* didn't exactly have much of a choice, Eric. Glen decided to tell Dawn about my being pregnant just before he fucking disappeared."

"What d'you mean, 'disappeared'?"

"Nobody knows where he is. If you're pretending you don't know that, you'll be *glad* to hear that your acting is right up there. But I know you, Eric—"

"Here we are!" Dawn cries out, mincingly walking in a sort of shimmying shuffle, holding out all Jessica asked for and more. Now it's my turn to feel queasy... so many women live for this shit. Last night she was my equal, now the self-appointed family role has taken over, making her belittling, obnoxious and entirely unfuckable. Every family, no matter how broken or whole carries with it a sickness, a dynamic of power nobody is allowed to acknowledge unless they want to ostracise themselves until they apologise. What a fucking joke.

Jessica takes the glass, rapaciously pops the two pills from Dawn's awaiting palm, but removes the apple from her other hand without taking a bite. Dawn glances over at me and raises a finger, indicating my need to stick around even longer, for some reason.

"This'll sound weird," she says, "but you two make quite a good match. I could see you together."

Jessica and I both scoff at Dawn's remark, unable to ignore its bursting containment of irony. She flutters looks between us, confused as to why it made us laugh. Her bafflement quickly turns into a suspicion and then an inquisitive glance.

"Do you two know each other?" she asks, assassinating our laughter. Unconvincingly, we both shake our heads in the same fucking manner. I look away, suck up the last drag of my cigarette and flick it towards the gutter.

"No," I say, releasing smoke into the air. "I was just saying that urm, Jessica here reminded me of you, and that you remind me of somebody I used to know."

"And I said the same," Jessica says in support.

We chuckle again but this time it's riddled with awkwardness and comes across rather forced. Dawn doesn't look like she bought my explanation but also doesn't appear in want of pushing the subject any further. "Well," she says, throwing me a flirt glance, "I kinda know what you mean."

We each stand unsure of what to say. Then Dawn, remembering what she kept me here for, signals that she'll return shortly. As she sweeps away the original tension between me and Jessica sways back in a perfectly aligned exchange. Speaking first, I say, "I know whatever I say about Glen will be taken as a lie, but this is the first time I've heard of him disappearing. Dawn doesn't seem—"

"She doesn't think he has, that's why. It's not unusual for Glen to be gone for months at a time, but I know something isn't right. Dawn says he's called her, but I think she's lying, as he hasn't called me once. He would've called me by now, especially in my… condition—"

"Have you reported him as missing?"

Jessica hesitates, then says, "No. But I've called around. Nobody has seen him. Only Dawn claims to have done. For her own reasons, she despises the police. And I can hardly report him as missing if she claims they've spoken."

"Is this what you tell yourself to absolve your guilt?" I ask, unable to stop myself going on the aggressive.

"What d'you mean?"

"I don't remember much about the last time I saw you, Jessica, but I do recall being pushed down a hill, whacking my head and a warning about Glen coming after me," I say, hesitant to add, "tell me, Jessica, I don't suppose his real fury was down to the seed of doubt you might've planted in his head in regards to the true culprit of that

402

thing growing inside of you?"

Jessica looks to the side, downwards. Once again, her truth is spoken through silence.

"That's just what I thought. I won't ask if it's mine because I know it isn't. You were pregnant when you told me about Glen's rape."

I look at her for confirmation. She gives a small nod, head drooping further into humiliation.

"Okay. Good. Just one final question before grandma Oedipus comes back. D'you remember the night you told me the person who attacked you was, in fact, Glen, your boyfriend?"

Another nod, followed by an inquiring, "Yes?"

"Was Glen watching us, from the top of the bridge?"

She tries to hide her initial expression but is just as quick to realise what it betrayed. "How do you... know that?"

I smile like a disappointed father. "Sometimes we know things without realising we know them, Jessica."

"Please, Eric. I didn't know at the time... he promised to never follow me again... but, wait... you know something, don't you?"

"Only what you already know, I—"

"Here we are, Eric!" Dawn cries out, striding across the path with two masks in her hand. "Sorry I took so long, had to attend to some feminine duties. Here you go. Thanks for showing them to me last night."

She offers me the masks which I left behind on purpose. Turning from Jessica, I say, "Thank you, Dawn, but there really is no need. I want you to have them."

She looks at me with contortion, understandably confused by my offer. "Oh, well..."

"You said you loved them. Please, from me, consider them a gift. I was going to sell them anyway, but if you want them, they're all yours."

Behind us, Jessica scoffs. I imagine she's thinking I used them in some wild sex game with Dawn.

"Well, thank you, Eric. Really, I do love them. They'll look great together on my wall. Now you also know where they are if you ever want to see them again. Win-win."

"Exactly," I say, delivering Dawn a further reinforced, though false promise of us meeting again.

"Jessica," she says, ending our private exchange. "Are you feeling better now?"

Behind me, she forcibly states that she does.

"You haven't touched your apple. Oh, silly me. I forgot to slice it for you. I know you prefer it that way. Well, come on. Let's get you inside. Eric, you're good to go now, finally. Thanks for sticking around."

"No problem. And that, I certainly am."

"Dawn," Jessica says. "I'm feeling quite faint. Could you help me inside?"

"Let me," I interrupt, moving before anyone else can react. Hooking my arm around Jessica's waist causes her to flinch, shaking with an ever-present threat of tears. Guiding her, we're soon through the gate that must've been left open last night. Dawn joins us, taking hold of Jessica from the other side.

"Thank you, Eric," she says, almost looking at Jessica in search of approval, from what I can make out.

Jessica stays silent, but I know a flurry of conflicting thoughts are swimming around her head, making her feel helpless. I loosen my grip and trail a finger over Dawn's forearm. From behind Jessica's shoulder, she blushes slightly, for the moment smitten with a person she knows nothing about.

"Thanks again, Eric. I can handle the fort from here."

"Goodbye, Dawn. And to you, Jessica. Take care of yourselves." I wave to Dawn but Jessica snubs me completely. As I turn the front door shuts behind me. I swing the gate back into the lock. It shudders with finality. Sunlight glares into the emerald car. It's already supplied with a baby seat.

I go to walk away, but something stops me in my tracks. I peer at the headlights and bonnet, notice the dent left behind by Glen and worsened by myself, then the windscreen wipers. Unzipping my jacket halfway, I remove the letter I'd intended on posting to Frank. Without further thought I lift the nearest wiper a touch and tuck my suicide note underneath it. With even less thought, I adjust my rucksack for further security, look over at Dawn's house for the final time and see that the only change is in the curtains that have been drawn.

I guess I won't get any final answers, but I'll make do with what I've got. To be honest, I'm no longer desirous of knowing much about anything.

It's good to know Glen's gone though.

CHAPTER THIRTY-FIVE

Like so many times before I find myself back where I started. I've been here for a while, sipping on my last drink out of my hipflask, wishing the landscape would collapse. It's strange how the weather can make a place look so different and yet in the moment so permanent; how it burns an image inside your mind's eye only to wither away in reality or through the faltering nature of your own memory. What I saw last time I was here has still yet to reveal itself to me. I thought one final return might trigger something, but all I can detect is what it's lacking: the snow, the fog, the blackness and the shadow… which was probably more in my mind than anywhere else.

I light up another smoke for my final few pulls; hipflask almost hollow. The sun is close to setting now, blending with the sky into a blood-orange hue. The shaded river below still carries the sheen of an inanimate abyss, frozen-over despite thawed. As if it is space instead of a mere reflection of it.

For the first time, my hipflask is empty. I leave the cap loose to make sure it sinks, throw my shoulder back and hurl it. Without bothering to look I hear it plop like a body. I'd planned on tossing the masks over too. Well, my black Bauda mask to be specific. I figured I'd throw Esther's Gatto one in a wherever gutter. In the end, they both seemed better off at Dawn's. Her house is now like a shrine to the nefarious occurrences that once took place inside it. I'm going to miss that woman. You'd think I'd be horrified by her past but in honesty I'm anything but. What that says about me I simply do not know.

"Don't do it, Eric," says an all-too-solemn voice. My utter lack of surprise forces a tired sigh. She stands to the side of me just behind my right shoulder, her bulging womb taking up most of my peripheral.

"Jessica," I say, still staring out at the blending palette of the land-scape. "How did you know I was here?"

"I found your letter."

"Oh. Did I write down the location? I don't remember—"

"No, you didn't. I just knew you were here, after ruminating over what you said at Dawn's. She was driving me crazy anyhow, talking to me as if you were a stranger. You came as a rather welcome distraction to her though, as I suspect you already know."

"I always admired your deductive powers," I say, clearing my throat. "I'm... sorry by the way."

"For what?"

"Everything really, but I never apologised for cheating on you the night you were raped. It always struck me as odd how you focused on that rather than what'd just happened to you. It must sound out of place now, but I really am very sorry."

"Oh, that. Yeah well," she says, grazing gravel under her foot. "I guess I needed a distraction then too."

"For what it's worth, I was overwhelmed by your intuition. Fright-ened, even. If truth be told."

"Yours is rather frightening too. If not a little... paranoid at times," she says, her voice rising into a soft jest I never thought I'd miss so much.

But the present moment always glares through the veil of our past now, worsening its deterioration with each felt recollection until at some point it'll have nothing left to obscure.

Surrendering to it, I ask, "Did I ever tell you I collapsed on this bridge once?"

"Collapsed?"

"You'd call it a panic attack."

"Oh. No, I don't think you did."

"It occurred the first time I saw Glen despite not knowing it was him. For the longest time I thought it was just an apparition of my mind. Want to hear the cruel part? Even though I now know it was him, how… or why I know still alludes me."

Jessica moves forward a touch, disturbing further fragments of gravel. "I'm glad I found this before Dawn," she says, passing me the photograph I left behind, which is now streaked with black. "Knowing you'd been back there made me search for traces of you. You would've been impressed how quickly I found it. Under the fridge… well, not bad. I would've put it somewhere further away, as if it scattered."

"To be frank, I was surprised Dawn didn't realise I stole it in the first place."

"Oh, I'm sure she did."

Her remark breaks my conscious effort not to look her way. She's fat, puffy in areas she shouldn't be, breasts wayward and already motherly, cheeks bloated and patchy with red, skin sweaty and hair unkempt, her eyes distant and much too short on sleep. And I've never found her more beautiful.

She takes a deep breath and says, "Dawn told me Glen must've popped over when she was conveniently out of the house. Which is beyond convenient really, considering she seldom leaves the house herself."

"Why do you think she'd lie about it?"

"To make me believe Glen is going to come back."

"Right. But do you think she believes that though?"

"That's what she says. But there's a vacancy in her eyes as glaring as Glen is absent. I've always been good at telling when certain people are lying, but since training to be a therapist I've become adept at sensing one now before it's even told. She's either holding onto a false hope or Glen did in fact get in contact with her. As I cannot tell, I can only imagine it's both."

"Oh?"

"About a week after… that night, I got a hamper delivered to my door with a bunch of baby supplies inside it. Dawn called moments after it arrived, *not* asking whether I was actually pregnant, but inquiring as to whether I received it. She said Glen told her to keep it to herself but she *'just couldn't contain her excitement'* over it. She even apologised for it arriving late because of the weather, which was odd considering I didn't even know it was coming."

"So, you reckon Glen told her before he scarpered?"

"Yes. I also think he told her to wait before congratulating me, so he had time to… to…"

"Time to what?"

"Please… don't fuck with me, Eric. You know as well as I know. Glen hasn't gone away—he didn't just up and run or disappear or fucking vanish… he… he must of…"

"Killed himself."

Jessica shakes, shutting her eyes to fight back an influx of broken tears. "Yes. But why though, Eric? Why do I think that?"

"You already know, Jessica. I never wrote in that letter where I'd committed suicide, yet you knew I was here."

"What d'you mean? I knew you were here because you asked me about whether Glen was… here."

The realisation sinks, weighing her down so much she almost falls. But she manages to keep herself upright and maintain her emotional divorce, staying opaque to her surroundings like this bridge seems to demand. "This is where *Glen* committed suicide."

I give a gentle, long, yet uncertain nod.

"But how... how do you know—*so that's why you asked me if Glen was ever here.* You do know something, don't you?!"

"I can't say for sure, Jessica."

"What d'you mean you can't say for sure? Either you know or you don't fucking know."

"Well then, I don't. Despite that, I'm still certain. I have been ever since I woke back up on this bridge."

Jessica sighs, its echo tainted with exhaustion. Now she's crying but trying to hold herself back from doing so. I remain still, looking ahead yet focused on nothing.

"How do I know," she says, closing her eyes again as her emotions rage war. She struggles but shakes it off, caught between abandon and surrender. "How am I supposed to know you didn't... *oh god, please tell me you didn't...*"

"Murder him?"

"Yes," she says, her voice lost inside the clouded shock of her suspicion.

"You can't," I reply, "because I don't know either. All I know is that he was standing on the railings here. They're not easy to climb, so he must've been determined to do it. I didn't even think it was a real person. I've been seeing things, Jessica. Things that I now know were never there. But who knows, maybe Dawn is telling the truth. Maybe he did just go away for a while. It wouldn't be the first time, would it?"

"It is without him calling me."

"But now he knows we've basically had an affair the entire time you've been with him. Would you really blame him for being distant knowing that?"

"He doesn't know... *the details* of that."

"Of course he does, Jessica. Especially now. He didn't loathe me for no reason. He sensed the affair the whole time. Just like Esther did with me. They knew something, but they couldn't confirm it, probably because they didn't really want to know deep down."

"Even though that's true, Eric, his obsession with you *was* without merit. He didn't know a thing about you."

"Except for the fact that you never said anything about me, which told him all he needed to know. We give away how we feel through the things we don't say far more often than what we do. You want to believe I killed him? Go ahead. I imagined doing it enough. Please tell me if I'm lying."

Jessica slaps her hips and turns, flailing her arms around. She rubs her face as if trying to scratch an itch impossible to reach. "Even if... even if you watched him jump or pushed him off yourself, you still left him down there to drown. You could've done something, *anything,* but you... you fucking allowed it to happen."

"I blacked out, Jessica."

"Oh, how very *convenient*, Eric."

"Well maybe if you told me you were fucking pregnant this whole time none of this would have happened. I hadn't slept in days, maybe weeks. Not to mention the drugs in my system, let alone the booze."

"Yeah, that much was obvious, Eric. But you still had the cognition to do all the things you did! You *fucked* his *mother!* stole his bike, took it back and replaced it *exactly* where you found it! How could I not suspect that you killed him?"

"I also threw that rape alarm inside your garden, if you need any further evidence."

"I fucking knew it was you! I knew it. I had to bullshit myself into believing it wasn't—*but I always knew!* Why?! Why, Eric?! Why would you do that when you knew I was trying to confront him about it?"

"Because I knew you were keeping something from me you dumb cunt. You said he didn't believe you. I just thought a bit of psychological warfare might trigger his memory."

"How can you just stand there and say these things to me in this manner? What the hell is wrong with you?"

"*I told you. I don't know. I was out of my fucking mind!* My whole head's like a... like a broken puzzle, made up of pieces which now fit in places that they shouldn't and don't where they should. I don't know any other way of describing it."

"How very convenient, Eric. Fucking hell, I'd rather you just lied instead of trying to spoon feed me some shit about going insane."

"You're the one who was just bragging about being a human lie detector, which is no surprise when you consider all your experience in the subject. So, tell me, Jessica. Tell me if I'm lying!"

"You know, when I first saw this letter on my windscreen, I thought you were just playing some sick, twisted joke, but now it reveals something much worse! Why didn't you just post it to Frank?"

"He's up and gone too. Seems to be catching, that."

"Then why did you give it to me?!"

"I don't know. I was angry. I'd just discovered you've been lying this entire time. Look at you."

"Bullshit. I'll tell you why. Look at where you're standing. You've returned to the scene of the crime. You're acting out of nothing but guilt! That's what's behind all this."

"No more than yours, Jessica. You can't absolve yourself from what's happened any more than I can. Now why don't you tell me why Glen was *really* trying to hunt me down? You never answered me before, just fed me another dose of bullshit silence. So... who did Glen think knocked you up, him or me?"

She doesn't answer. In fact, she turned away from me in a daggered movement, away from a truth she didn't think would ever become known.

"Your silences speak louder than you think, Jessica. You still seem to believe that I now don't know what a manipulative little bitch you are. You attacked Glen's ego because he didn't give a toss about raping you. You've already projected everything into that poor fucking thing before it's even born. I dunno why you're pretending to care about Glen's death. Now you've got everything you ever wanted. A growing victim foetus, an abusive and now absent father and just in case you wanna fuck up the kid like daddy fucked you up, you've got a sexy, incest-happy grandmother waiting in the wings for a good old traditional dose of family trauma. It's a fucking fairy tale ending for you so why don't you stop pretending otherwise."

Jessica rages, almost shaking out of her own skin. She takes slow-paced steps towards me. I stand with indifference, seeing the woman before me for who she really is, at last.

"Eric," she says, "you are, without doubt, the worst, most vile person I've ever met. I wish *you* were dead. I'd rather be gang-raped by a pack of savages than ever have to lay my eyes on you again. You psychopathic, sack of shit, *murderer*."

"Murderer... now there's another hijacked word if I ever heard one. You know what? You wanna think Glen died because of me, go right ahead. Lord knows how much I fantasised about killing him. I honestly hope I did. If what you told me about him was true, he must've wished for death long before I made it happen. But don't think for one second that you didn't play your part to perfection, Jessica. I practically fucking begged you to tell me what it was you were keeping from me and you even forced me into playing the Dawn card before letting the truth come out. You thought telling me *how* Glen raped you was enough, didn't you? But you never stopped to think I might question why—*why*, after all this fucking time? But there it is, staring me in the face just like it sat under my nose the entire time. That's how I know it isn't mine, as ever since the seed took to root, you've been reliving that rape every time you saw him, haven't you? You should be down on your knees, worshipping me for solving your problem with such a fatal swoop. It's not like you really care who fathers your children when it comes down to it, does it? In fact, I'd even go as far as to say that you'd willingly be raped and only ever raped so long as your womb doesn't go to waste. The only fucking psychopath I see around here is you. And your kind surround me everywhere I go. Each of you pretends to love children inside a world where millions of them starve to death every year. The only reason you'd ever look after a child is that it shares some of your mediocre DNA, which even then only confirms your power over it. No breeder ever gave a fuck about any other child except their own. You're a bunch of egocentric psychopaths entertaining some absurd, nature-induced god complex, asserting yourselves with the most preposterous and vile and laziest form of creation there is by forcing a non-existent sucker into this world through your own fucking image.

"Take the abortion I never knew I had. You think I don't feel guilty about it? Of course I do, but that's only ever evoked by this insidious nature I'm instilled with. You allow nature's will to blind your whole reasoning. You may very well think me a murderer, but how do you think what's growing inside of you ends? Oh, you'll be dead by then. I'll use your favourite word. How very convenient. The shit you fucking tell yourselves. *But you're not a parent, Eric. You couldn't ever possibly understand.* You each entertain such delusions of divinity, don't you? Thinking a childless human being couldn't possibly empathise with the suffering, when in reality you sycophantic cunts are the exact problem which you claim to be the saviours of. Your conspiratorial ways know no bounds, but for as long as life is seen to be worth living, you'll each get away with the perpetual holocaust you contribute to each day. It doesn't carry meaning like you love to make out. All this suffering is for nothing. Yet being the self-conscious nothing's we are, what else is there to do but bring more suckers into the mix to suffer along with us? And you have the front to call me a psychopath. Such are the pompous beliefs of those who cannot wash their hands of the blood they've already shed. Your own abuse, Jessica, was entirely wasted on you and your rape nothing but justified. The only hope for that kid is to come out a stillborn."

Jessica looks at me as if I just annihilated everyone she ever knew, with eyes as dead as my thousand-yard stare. I could say things with more empathetic leanings, try to relate through a sympathy which screams within me, but whilst these sides to my character still reside, they live only as phantoms now, as haunted emotions too abandoned to call upon, trampled-over by a recklessness that left them beyond redemption all too long ago. She turns, quivering with shock, ears sensitive to any grinding and piercing sound, hands cradling the lie growing inside of her. Her silence this time is fatal, unearthed before until today, quaking through us, drawing a line between us which will never go unseen should our paths ever cross again.

She all-but runs in the direction of her car, the only one still sitting in the carpark.

I swivel where I stand and look out at the landscape for what I hope is the last time. An all-too-familiar, cold metallic blue now filters the indifferent sky. The withering rays of sunlight expose the speckles of dust on my left, floating in what only appears to be no direction. Beyond them that same tag of graffiti still sits there, dullened yet continuing to exist, screaming FUBAR with an unknowable violence. The sunlight expands, piercing through what must've been a gap in the clouds. Inside an iridescence mostly made up of amber, the letters seem to crackle with static electricity. Yet it's nothing but the slowly dying sun. For some reason, I suppose the unexpected sunlight, a tear streaks over my cheekbone and falls. I do not feel the emotion it conveys.

FUBAR. I always knew it was a reference used in times of war, but I never bothered to learn what it stood for.

Gravel's crunched behind me again by a familiar footstep. I make no sign of my detection of her, but say, "Do you ever feel like your mind contains a mind of its own, Jessica?" my voice echoing behind itself, aware of its own suspicion.

I twist myself around. The white of her hair gleams as it's toyed with by the wind, flickering wayward strands across her face, which is paler than normal, though pure, reddened slightly in the cheeks.

Jessica looks away towards the landscape. She's drawn towards the railings, almost pulled. Before long, I stand by her side. Neither of us attempts to look at the other.

"Our minds play tricks on us, Eric. I imagine, with everything that happened and your… habits, shall we say, that you could've easily conjured up some odd thoughts."

"Thoughts are one thing. Visions are another."

Jessica flinches, equally frightened of my admission as I was of confessing it, offering a concerned smile as compensation. With the stuttered intake of breath which follows, a teardrop falls, landing on her stomach. She doesn't appear to notice, exhaling instead with a tired, though determined sigh.

Her hand drifts towards mine as if to take it but doesn't. It just dangles around my knuckles and even though it brushes over mine, I do not feel a thing. Uncertain and unnerved, I slip both of my hands into my pockets. Jessica's eyes remain where they were, unphased and distant.

"I never imagined Glen—"

"He wanted to die, Eric. Whatever happened is immaterial now. In fact, as much as it pains me to admit it, part of me… hopes you murdered him."

"What?" I ask, startled into looking at her, pervaded on sight by the numbness she conveys.

She all but glides backwards away from the railings, passed my hunched shoulder and stops somewhere in the middle of the road.

Directly behind my back, she clears her throat and says, "He raped me, Eric. You can fill in the cracks a trauma leaves behind, try to determine the what, the where and the why, force your own answers and manipulate yourself into understanding it, but nothing ever takes away what it does to you. Experiences like that are a touch from death, as the person you were before it took place no longer exists. The trauma leaves behind a void and as small as it may shrink, it never truly disappears. It lives within as a constant glimpse into the abyss we are each doomed to face."

"I hate the fact you can still give voice to my inner thoughts, Jessica."

"Well, I didn't enjoy you giving one to mine earlier either, Eric."

I go to turn my head but stop, stunted by a neurological connection that obfuscates any semblance of correlation, leaving me helpless and confused. Everything's turned so still, sensitive to sound yet vacant.

"You were right, Eric. I did tell Glen this baby is yours and I told him that to hurt him… but the reason it destroyed him was because he knew… he knew I was telling the truth. Now look at me and tell me if I'm lying."

I feel as if my body's convulsing despite the fact I stand perfectly still. Old thoughts and new ones seem to shift places, vanishing into foreign parts of my mind upon the awareness of one another. I'm nothing but overwhelmed, a silent witness to a metamorphosis within my very own mind, an outside observer to a transformation that leaves me breathless, in a state somewhere between terror and awe.

"I don't want to leave this bridge alone, Eric. I know everything is fucked up, that we've moved beyond all chance of repair, but as this could very well be the last time we ever see each other, I might as well put myself in the firing line. Will you come home with me, just for tonight and play make-believe?"

Something inside me makes me nod without the need of knowing why. I'm not even sure when I turned around, but now everything behind me feels like it is truly all behind me; nothing but a blank space. Tears stream down Jessica's cheeks as well as my own; a collective release of all the time we spent apart yet together, full of relief and dismay and ecstasy, of a redemption we thought withered away. My entire body tingles as I'm pulled towards her by a force I don't understand, and I reach out my hand to finally… touch her… but something's altered. I'm unnerved by not knowing how I know it… but our scene has been tampered with… it's her car, her car isn't where it's supposed to be. It sits facing us… at the end of the…

"Jessica?" I ask, swerving my head back towards her, feeling, for the lack of a better word, drunk.

She replies by placing her hands behind her hips, no longer trying to conceal what she could never hope to hide. The fabric rides up, inviting skin on skin contact. I can feel its warmth before I even touch her. All I need to do is control my shaking. But I'm just so nervous. My hand floats over her stomach, shaking with such violence the entire world seems to be falling apart. I close my eyes to counter it and thrust my hand forward, ready to let the old, variating versions of Eric Archer finally die.

The car roars now, growling like the fiercest of beasts. Headlights flicker without a sense of rhyme or reason. Between blinks, I seem to be watching myself, from atop of the railings behind me, inside the blackness looking in.

"Jessica?" I say, feeling faint, nauseous and unknown. My hand feels impossibly cold. Entirely empty. I cannot sense Jessica's warmth anymore at all. My eyelashes scratch and rustle as if they've been turned to gravel. There she stands, still glowing somewhat at the centre... but her outline has begun to flicker with flakes of ash and particles of dust. She stares forward, not into my eyes but through them. Then she looks down as if disturbed by something. It's my hand.

The headlights gain focus... when did it become so otherworldly... so black and white? The illuminance is strong enough to blind me, yet everything appears clear. My eyes make light squeaking sounds, like rubber against glass. The engine's roar has lessened to an eerie, nestled hum, what I deem to be a contented growl.

Flakes of ash steal my attention once more. Jessica's only half here now, yet purer. She looks younger and distant. Unmolested. No longer pregnant as my hand... swirls of dusted specks of blood shed away from my static hand. I'm the reason she's evaporating. I cannot move, nor am I even desirous of doing so. All I can do is watch. "Jessica?" I hear myself say, but do not feel it. Her face begins to crack, dispersing lines across her countenance like a hand-drawn map of a location unknown. Pieces of her, like a puzzle made from shards of glass fall away. What they reveal is neither here nor there, not something but not nothing either. Black, like a shadow that's taken shape.

The screech of spinning wheels eats through my eardrums, forced to rotate so fast that although they spin, they only do so on the spot, moving nowhere but within the space they occupy. In a word, trapped, just like I appear to be. "Eric..." a whispered voice says, female in sex, but unrecognised. Whomever it belonged to is no longer here. Even the specks of dust have taken their leave, dispelled

418

back behind nature's masked screen, a design of which my very own perceptions render me blind from ever comprehending despite being a fragment of it myself.

Maybe that's an act of mercy on nature's part.

The car is moving now. When it started, I cannot say. The glare of the headlights sweeps away from my eyes like a reveal. It isn't Jessica's car. It's Samantha's. She appears to be screaming, but I cannot hear a sound except for a constant, though light sort of ringing. Both of her hands grip the steering wheel as if letting go would mean her end. Smeared mascara stains her skin, whilst her eyes rattle black behind split-ended streaks of flaxen.

I'm watching myself from the bridge again, breathing fumes of petrol. The bonnet collides with my knees. Though its speed should diminish my sightline into futility, I see everything, like time has finally ceased its charade upon this planet and returned to space to perish. The car's force is so strong that only my snapped legs swing back, as the front of me is slammed against the bonnet, breaking my left arm in half upon impact, swinging it back from the elbow into an angle it should never be in. By instinct my right hand reaches out just as I collide headfirst into the windscreen. The glass splits into innumerable, infinitesimal shards but stays whole, like when one amoeba becomes two. It all starts with a single cell. Samantha and I are now divided.

I am a ghost underwater. I'm getting closer to myself once again, pulled by something entirely unknowable. My attempt to fight it, to impose my will upon it, only makes me spin. The car has already gained some distance on me, leaving me behind as if I wasn't there at all. As it comes to the roundabout it continues travelling straight. It hits a bump, betrayed by a dull thud and a fierce, claw-like scratch of metal against concrete. Amber sparks flash inside an ovular sphere, gone before they had any hope of shining.

The car flies in the air with me now, though where I'm sucked backwards, it goes forwards upside-down. Something's changing again. Time's resurrecting itself. Vacuumed sounds threaten clarity.

I'm being forced back into my body against my consent. Just as the car before me makes its catastrophic landing, I flop onto the concrete headfirst, the thud it makes so dullened I can't quite believe I'm not dead upon collision.

The car beyond makes another piercing shriek. Its horn rings with a recurrent, swallowed hum. I find it oddly soothing. My tongue is metallic, leaking an oddly familiar though surely foreign bile containing what seems like iron.

I see no white light before me anymore, only a growing, reddish darkness, enveloping over my sightline in the sickest, slowest movement imaginable, like even death has seen it fit to tease me with the possibility of more excruciating life. Whilst I can't move my limbs, I can see that they're now stuck in places they shouldn't be, in positions against what nature intended. A reversed foetal position, if that makes any sense at all. The only remaining sense I possess is that of touch. Numb as I am, the blood I'm covered in is warm, almost comforting, if it just wasn't spreading away from me so fast. The graffiti is reflected inside the gleaming crimsoned black in front of my eyes. A sheet of paper, creased at the centre, floats across, flickering and scattering, going up to fall back down. A past-felt breeze forces it against the mirrored, reversed letters of FUBAR. It's my suicide note, now signed with my own blood. Jessica must have thrown it away. It struggles to stay put, flapping wildly in the now unfelt wind. As my sight twirls and spirals and loses its grip, it flies up again, hangs in the air for the briefest of moments, then is swept up by a silent swoop in between the railings, and drifts out of sight… down towards the river.

I'm blinded by my blood now. For the meantime, I can hear things again but only muffled screams and the same ever-ringing blast of the horn. I'm still oddly comforted by it, but when… when did it become… so chill-ridden, so cold? Even my own breath feels frozen. I guess this really is where I leave you… broken down on a bridge of many a breakdown; a bridge of which I truly was never able to leave.

OTHER WORKS BY
G.C. MCKAY

Sauced up, Scarred and at Sleaze

an anthology

available in all formats

audio version narrated by the author

gcmckay.com

Made in the USA
Coppell, TX
21 May 2022

78011885R00256